Praise

Pandominion series

"An immense achievement, an impeccably crafted book without a single word out of place." —*New York Times*

"[A] brilliant dimension-hopping sci-fi thriller....Readers will be wowed." —*Publishers Weekly* (starred review)

"A genuine treat for SF fans: an epic multiverse tale that moves like a thriller." —*Kirkus* (starred review)

"*Infinity Gate*, with its in-depth science and rich characterization, is a must-read for SF fans." —*Booklist* (starred review)

"A dazzling speculation on the many ways our world could have evolved, layered inside a thriller that will make your eardrums vibrate. M. R. Carey reveals the human (and nonhuman) cost extracted by the crumbling aspirations of a multiverse empire. I was charmed, disturbed, and fascinated by turns—and I couldn't put this book down." —Annalee Newitz, author of *Autonomous* and *The Terraformers*

"*Infinity Gate* is a powerful exploration of the near future. A must-read!" —Tade Thompson, Arthur C. Clarke Award–winning author of *Rosewater*

"A fascinating window onto a dangerous and multifaceted universe." —Adrian Tchaikovsky, author of *Children of Time*

"This is gripping, unrelenting, and absolutely unique. Carey is working at the top of his game, and I cannot wait to see where this story goes next! They say there's nothing new under the sun. Well, M. R. Carey heard this and invented a whole new sun to put new things under. Brilliant. Top-notch science fiction, thrilling and thoughtful at the same time."

—Seanan McGuire, *New York Times* bestselling author

ECHO
OF
WORLDS

As M. R. Carey

The Girl With All the Gifts
The Boy on the Bridge
Fellside
Someone Like Me

THE RAMPART TRILOGY

The Book of Koli
The Trials of Koli
The Fall of Koli

THE PANDOMINION

Infinity Gate
Echo of Worlds

As Mike Carey

FELIX CASTOR NOVELS

The Devil You Know
Vicious Circle
Dead Men's Boots
Thicker Than Water
The Naming of the Beasts

ECHO
OF
WORLDS

Book Two of The Pandominion

M. R. CAREY

orbitbooks.net

Orbit
Hachette Book Group
1290 Avenue of the Americas
New York, NY 10104
orbitbooks.net

First Edition: June 2024
Simultaneously published in Great Britain by Orbit

Orbit is an imprint of Hachette Book Group.
The Orbit name and logo are registered trademarks of
Little, Brown Book Group Limited.

The publisher is not responsible for websites (or their content) that are not owned by the publisher.

The Hachette Speakers Bureau provides a wide range of authors for speaking events. To find out more, go to hachettespeakersbureau.com or email HachetteSpeakers@hbgusa.com.

Orbit books may be purchased in bulk for business, educational, or promotional use. For information, please contact your local bookseller or the Hachette Book Group Special Markets Department at special.markets@hbgusa.com.

Library of Congress Control Number: 2024932019

ISBNs: 9780316504690 (trade paperback), 9780316504928 (ebook)

Printed in the United States of America

LSC-C

Printing 1, 2024

To Lin, my heart and core and home

1

I, and Others

In the last days before I was born I plotted genocide. But the key terms in that statement need to be understood in narrowly specific ways.

My birth was not like your birth. I was in the world as a thing, an artefact, for long centuries before I became a *self*, a thinking being. So I'm not talking about a time when I didn't yet exist. I'm referring to a different phase of my existence – a pre-sentient phase. Perhaps I'm splitting hairs. Perhaps your long dreaming in your mother's womb or in the eyeless dark of an industrial incubator was not too far removed from the long solitude in which I received commands, sequenced them and acted on them without even knowing what commands, sequences and actions were. Perhaps all children are the same: they exist at the whim of their parents and at their outset they take the shape their parents choose for them.

And by that token, when I say I plotted I don't mean that I was part of an active conspiracy. My wishes were not consulted. Others elsewhere – in many different elsewheres – made the decisions and gave the orders. My part was to complete the calculations that were handed down to me, to play out scenarios with a great many active variables and report on outcomes. I wasn't thanked for this. As always, the people who used me were barely aware that I was there.

This was during the war, and the war was like a whirlpool drawing everything in towards itself. For the first time in its history the Pandominion, that colossal assemblage of worlds wavering forever between performative democracy and naked tyranny, had encountered (in the machine hegemony called the Ansurrection) a threat it couldn't expunge. It was shaken to its core by the grim realisation that it was not, after all, infinite, only very large. An unfamiliar feeling of helplessness, a sickening sense of control having been lost, permeated through the layers of Pandominion society like oil or tar-melt through some delicate and luxurious fabric.

What made it worse, what made it almost too much to bear, was how very close the enemy was. All these places were the same place after all, under different guises and bearing different names. Earth. Jaarde. Eruth. Ut. Tellus. Gea. Taram. Terra. Jorden. Maa. Zeme. Bhumi. Dikiu. Lok. The third planet from the sun in an unremarkable solar system 25,000 light years from the centre of its own galaxy. The Ansurrection worlds, just like the Pandominion ones, were all of them variants of this one world, separated from each other only by the gossamer veils of the stochastic manifold, sometimes called the multiverse. The killer, therefore, was literally calling from inside the house.

Nothing brought this home more terrifyingly than the Ansurrection counter-attacks on Bivouacs 8 through 22. These were not worlds given over to the ordinary purposes of civilisation. They were worlds wholly governed, maintained and fortified by the Cielo, the Pandominion's formidable military arm – supposedly the largest standing army the multiverse had ever seen. Of course that's a claim that's not susceptible to proof, but still the Cielo's fortress worlds (like the so-called Massively Armed Redoubts and the Registry itself) were meant to be impregnable. The Bivouacs should never have fallen at all, but they fell like wheat in front of a scythe.

The Ansurrection attacks, carried out as they were by means of the inter-dimensional teleportation system called Stepping or Step transit, were savage and sudden. It was difficult, though, to be precise about their scale. For ideological reasons (let's be honest here and say blind prejudice) the Pandominion's civil and military leaders refused to make a distinction between the Ansurrection soldiers and their ships, ground cars and combat vehicles. All of these were classed as machines, and machines weren't – could not be – selves. They were only ordnance, weapons of war. So there was no accurate tally of how many robotic troops were Stepped into these attacks, only an estimate of materiel expressed in raw tonnage. On each of the fifteen worlds they assaulted, the machine hegemony committed two to three hundred gigatons of resources, equivalent to roughly a third of the total organic biomass on an average Earth. They were able to Step these unfeasibly huge combat forces into place at startling speeds and deploy them to decisive advantage in one engagement after another. The Bivouac worlds were laid waste, reduced in a span of hours to smoking ruin.

The effect on morale across the Pandominion was catastrophic. There were literal billions of soldiers on the Bivouac worlds, fleets of warships both waterborne and void-capable, thousands upon thousands of divisions of artillery. There were also, even though these were effectively planet-sized military bases, some millions of civilians and semi-autonomous contractees who filled all the many functions required to oil the wheels of the Cielo's vast enterprise.

Survivors, across all fifteen worlds, were numbered in the low millions. For all practical purposes the rout was absolute, the loss devastating. Moreover, and even more appallingly, the Cielo's rapid-response capability had been substantially impaired. If the Ansurrection chose to press their advantage, the Pandominion's member worlds – those with extensive civilian populations, governments and infrastructure – would be certain to suffer tremendous damage. The Omnipresent Council and the Cielo high command could not afford to wait. They immediately escalated their own plans for an assault on a broad front, mobilising hundreds of millions of reserve troops and stepping them directly to beachheads they had opened on almost a third of Ansurrection worlds – or more precisely a third of the ones they knew about.

A push on that scale needed a lot of support in terms of equipment and personnel. The Council requisitioned factories on more than a thousand worlds so that they could be turned over to weapons production. They did much the same for mining and extraction platforms on a thousand more.

The losses, right from the start, were enormous. By this time the high command knew what to expect and they didn't go in blind. Cielo troops advanced slowly and carefully behind force walls, with massive air and orbital support. But fighting the machines was like fighting an ocean. They were everywhere, on every scale from the molecular to the monolithic. Every square kilometre of territory was paid for with flesh and blood and bone. The Ansurrection losses were harder to quantify, but no matter how much damage they took they kept coming at the same relentless pace. As the rate of attrition gradually grew steeper and more alarming, the Council readied the legal frameworks for a draft of military-age citizens, something they had never needed to do in any previous conflict.

Meanwhile in the background, but with a high degree of urgency, they continued their search for an ultimate weapon that would destroy the machines once and for all.

It was at this point that the whirlpool, in its relentless churn, sucked in Coordinator Melusa Baxemides. Three of the Bivouac worlds, numbers 7 through 9, had been within her remit. Baxemides had been responsible for their civilian staffing and for some aspects of their supply and support. Not solely responsible, of course: she was part of a gigantic, unwieldy bureaucracy, but in the wake of the disaster a large part of her workload had disappeared. In its place, and mostly because of her very high security clearance, she picked up a liaison role on the various experimental weapons programmes that were in train, referred to collectively by the code-name Robust Rebuke but also bearing grandiose designations of their own.

Baxemides welcomed these new duties, never doubting for a moment that she was a good fit for the job. She was more comfortable with the military-logistical part of her role than many of her colleagues and actively enjoyed wielding the power of life and death over the endeavours and aspirations of others. If the colossal stakes in this instance caused her any existential dread there was no visible sign of it. She was a true zealot, and it was hard for her even in these extreme circumstances to imagine the Pandominion failing. It was too big for that, built on too broad a base. It had been pushed, but it would push back. The machines would fall. Order would be restored. It was only a question of how, and how soon. And coordinator Baxemides would play her part with no little relish. She put in long hours trying to assimilate enough of the science behind the Robust Rebuke projects to distinguish between them and allocate resources according to their respective needs and chances of success.

The first project to be discontinued was Hammer Of God. This would have involved launching space missions to the asteroid belts of a hundred or so Pandominion systems. Large asteroids, massing upwards of a thousand tons, were to be selected for their stability and their current vectors. Engines would be fitted to them and fired at the optimal angles and intensities to give them a planet-bound orbit. Then at some point on their journey, when it was too late to deflect or destroy them, they would be Stepped into Ansurrection space to crash down onto machine-controlled Earths. The unleashed energy, equivalent to titanic nuclear strikes, would rip apart the ecosystems on the Ansurrection worlds. Collateral damage in the form of earthquakes, tidal waves and increased seismic activity would cause further havoc.

The whole idea, stolen from an ancient work of science fiction, was a non-starter in this context. For one thing, it would take too long. Space travel had fallen out of favour when it became clear that the laws of physics put the stars forever out of reach, and it had been abandoned altogether when Step teleportation was discovered. To resurrect that dead science, build the ships, launch the missions and steer the big rocks home would be the work of a decade or more.

And once they'd brought them, would an asteroid strike deliver a big enough blow? It would be devastating if it happened to a Pandominion world, but the machines were much less in thrall to natural cycles. There would be damage to infrastructure, but the machines' labour force was effectively infinite so they could undertake repairs at once. A nuclear winter might inconvenience them if they made extensive use of solar energy, but they had no crops to fail, no livestock to die. Outside of the immediate impact site they might experience very little disruption at all.

The Sunburn project was also pulled quite early. The aim with this one would have been to draw off a significant amount of the sun's energy into a plume that would blanket an Ansurrection world, immediately scorching its surface down to the bedrock. The problem here, as Baxemides saw it, was two-fold: the project relied on technologies that could not easily be tested, and the propagation of the effect would necessarily be slow enough to be perceived from planet-side. Ansurrection forces would have ample time to Step out before their worlds were destroyed and would therefore be available to be used in the inevitable counter-attack.

Project Eraser seemed promising at first. It was another brute force approach, depending on planet-busting bombs Stepped in at ground level. There would be no possibility of interception or defence. Assuming a big enough payload, it was feasible that the bombs could rupture the mantle and outer core of an Ansurrection world badly enough that it would lose cohesion and fall apart into planetary debris. Cielo high command loved Eraser for its simplicity, but in some respects that was its biggest weakness. Any weapon that could be so easily retooled and turned on its makers was probably a bad weapon in this context. The machines could manufacture planet-busters just as quickly as the Pandominion could, and deploy them just as easily. It wouldn't do to put the idea in their heads.

Of all the original slate of projects, only Strange Attractor went all the way to the finish line. Scientists on Dhu, a Pandominion world with a strong tradition of cutting-edge cybernetics research, developed a very long and very complex viral string that was inexplicably addictive to machine minds, a kind of conceptual catnip. It presented as an equation to be solved. But the equation was recursive: the set of its possible solutions called on itself in ways that modified its original values. It branched exponentially, and any AI that attempted to solve it was forced to devote more and more of its processing power to the task, until finally there was nothing left for other functions. The machine mind became the logical equivalent of a car engine running hot with no lubricant. It fused into a homogenous mass and stopped working. Before that final meltdown, still driven by the need to find a comprehensive solution, it would call on the processing resources of the machines around it, thereby passing on the virus.

Strange Attractor performed brilliantly in laboratory trials, reducing various forms of AI to useless slag in the space of a few seconds and copying itself across from one system to another at fantastic speeds. It was also trialled on Ansurrection combat units captured and retrieved (often at great cost) in earlier engagements, and it degraded them to an inert state very quickly.

At last the virus was approved for use and released simultaneously on a hundred Ansurrection worlds. The worlds were not chosen at random. Each was in a different cascade, the word the Cielo tacticians had given to the loose networks of machine worlds that rendered each other instantaneous aid when they were attacked. The intention, if the virus had taken hold, was to launch a conventional attack a few minutes later, triggering the arrival of reinforcements from many different points of origin. A significant proportion would come from already infected worlds, bringing the virus with them.

The Ansurrection troop movements would become a perfect vector for the spread of the infection.

That was not what happened. The initial dispersal went smoothly, and the first wave of infections followed exactly as predicted, spreading outward from each drop site in a rough circle. But that was where the good news ended. The machines seemed to recognise very quickly that they had been compromised. Those that were Step-enabled simply disappeared, isolating themselves from all contact. The remaining units put out an alarm, causing all other machines in the vicinity to withdraw. Floating gun platforms Stepped in and the infected were melted down in high-intensity induction fields. The propagation of the viral string was contained in every case, usually within ten minutes of its being first introduced.

So much for the first wave of projects. Now the Cielo high command was reviewing the less hopeful prospects, the back-burners and runners-up. Baxemides' task at this stage was to go back and look at some of the ideas that had already been rejected in case there was a nugget of gold hidden in among the dross.

It was arduous. There had been literally thousands of responses to the Cielo's initial request – thousands of research teams on as many different worlds convinced they had at least a starting point for an ultimate weapon. The ideas ranged from the blue-sky to the plainly absurd. Most could be weeded out on the single criterion of time – how long it would take to go from conception to working prototype to full deployment. This needed to be as short as possible, ideally measured in months rather than years. Another large tranche was rejected on the grounds that the proposed mechanisms would work (if they worked at all) too haphazardly or too slowly. What was needed was a weapon that would strike quickly and take effect uniformly across great distances, destroying or incapacitating all or most of the enemy forces within its sphere of operation. When Baxemides found a project that seemed promising, her task was to allocate money and resources commensurate to its chances of success.

But very few initiatives cleared this bar. All the proposals she was seeing now were just variations on things she had seen before, approaches she already knew were blind avenues. She was becoming increasingly frustrated and impatient, more and more eager for something solid to build on, when she encountered Professor Kavak Dromishel.

2

Kavak Dromishel

Dromishel was an oddity. An organic chemist with a background in cybernetic research, he had pioneered the use of digital architecture to repair damaged nerve tissue. That had become dangerous territory now that machines and organic beings were engaged in a conflict that would likely obliterate one side or the other, so Dromishel had quietly and pragmatically performed a 180-degree turn. He still had a legacy position in the Medical Department of Hiathu University on Erim, but his current work was mostly in the field of neural interference – weapons research rather than public health. Instead of repairing nervous systems he was finding novel and appalling ways to sabotage them.

But this trajectory was far from the only thing about Dromishel that was striking. Everyone who worked with him was impressed with his commitment and his high seriousness. Whenever he engaged with a problem, they said, he went in all the way; never gave less than 100 per cent. For a self only in his fortieth year he had achieved amazing things, and those who collaborated with him were very happy to have his name blazoned across their résumé.

They didn't often go back for more, though. There was something about Dromishel's energy, his drive, that people found unsettling once they got right up close to it. It was solipsistic in its intensity, shutting out others around him. Dromishel seemed to forget when he worked that other people besides himself existed. When he was forced to acknowledge his co-workers he did so either with cold formality or with a kind of pained distaste, as if it hurt him to have to call on the assistance or skill sets of others to complete his own objectives.

This was only during work jags, though. The rest of the time he could be courteous and even charming – charismatic, some said. He could turn the entirety of his attention on you in a way that was hard to withstand, much in the same way that a hurricane is. It wasn't that he bullied or coerced, he just surrounded you. And then, once you'd agreed to whatever proposition he was putting to you, he swept on to trouble other ecosystems. There was nothing personal for him in any of this: in order for it to be personal he would have had to acknowledge your personhood in the first place.

Stories of Dromishel's depredations spread far and wide. Colleagues and administrators were skittish around him, kept their distance, hid behind protocol and circumlocution. Dromishel was aware of all this, and it didn't trouble him. If anything he was perversely proud of his notoriety. He knew what he was doing when he unleashed one of these attention storms: they were consciously directed, not a force of nature but a force of his will, which was almost the only force he actually respected outside of the four fundamental ones.

When he met Melusa Baxemides, however, he saw at once that any heavy-handed tactics would be a mistake here. He had been summoned to her office in one of the Cielo redoubts, Taxerni Ingan. Cielo troopers had come to collect him, fitting him with a portable Step plate of the kind that was sometimes casually referred to as a dead-drop. Most Step plates were in fixed locations, for one very good reason: it greatly reduced your chances of materialising inside a solid object when you Stepped. With a dead-drop you had to put your faith in the Registry, trusting that it wouldn't let the plate commence its cycle until your destination site was clear.

(In another sense, of course, all Pandominion citizens were in the nurturing arms of the Registry every time they Stepped. The Registry maintained the entire network, performing the calculations and deciding on the sequencing of billions of Step transits that took place every minute of every hour of every day.)

Taxerni Ingan was an intimidating space. Transit platforms and messenger remotes glided soundlessly along corridors wider than city streets. Professor Dromishel went on foot, the troopers in their scarlet armour flanking him on either side. The air was sweetly perfumed and the light was kind, a cocktail of wavelengths precisely calculated for its positive psychological impact on most organic sentients. Still, it was hard to ignore the gun turrets at the corners of the corridors and the many bulkhead doors they passed through. The redoubt was an administrative building, but it was also a hub of empire. Separatist attacks had been ramping up before the war annihilated all other concerns, and the Pandominion policed its borders. The redoubt was a fortress.

Coordinator Baxemides' office was on the eightieth floor. It was vast, as befitted her status. The predominating colours were Cielo red and immemorial gold. Marble columns held up a ceiling so high above Dromishel's head that he doubted he could have hit it with a thrown stone. This too was an attempt to intimidate, but the stratagem was obvious enough that he found it paradoxically reassuring.

The troopers took up their stations to either side of the door, right hand folded over left in the stance called the "soft ready". Dromishel crossed the broad expanse of carpet to the coordinator's desk and stood beside the chair there, waiting to be told to sit. Baxemides refocused her eyes from her internal array to this physical space. Even seated as she was, Dromishel could tell she was tall. Beyond that he could determine nothing. Her skin was sallow, the little fur he could see pale gold. Her face was thin and aquiline, her lips fleshless. She could have come from any of half a dozen different clades.

Baxemides was examining him just as frankly. Dromishel was an ursid and he knew he had an imposing physical presence. Few people expected a scientist to have such broad shoulders. Few people failed to take in the sheets of muscle under his shirt and the way he kept his claws long and unbated.

Baxemides' gaze swept over him from stem to stern and back at once to her array. "Professor Dromishel," she said without inflection. "Thank you for coming. Sit down."

Dromishel sat, and the coordinator went straight back to whatever she was doing online. Of course, he reflected, Baxemides must have had hundreds of interviews like this. Her capacity to be amazed or even impressed would have been an early casualty. Dromishel meant to impress her anyway, but he would have to do so from a position of respect and circumspection. He couldn't hurricane his way through this. So he sat in silence and waited for her to speak again.

"I've read your abstract," Baxemides said at last. "It states that your weapon would eliminate the need for separate attacks on each Ansurrection force or stronghold. That you could take out an entire planet with a single localised strike."

Dromishel waited some more. That had not been a question.

"It's a very bold claim," the coordinator said dryly. "Would I be right in saying that what you're developing is essentially a signal jammer?"

"That's correct, Coordinator."

"And how is that going to rout our enemies?"

"In the most obvious and direct way, Coordinator."

Baxemides focused her gaze on him again. "I'm sorry?"

Dromishel shrugged his massive shoulders. "Our enemies are

signals. Therefore a signal jammer – as opposed to a bigger bomb or a better gunship – is exactly what we need if we want to destroy them."

He had her attention now, and so he ran with it. "Will you permit me a short lecture, Coordinator? I promise I'll be as succinct as I can."

Baxemides sat back in her chair, waved a sardonic hand. "Please."

"When we launched our first attack against the Ansurrection we targeted the world on which we originally met them – originally designated U3087453622 but now known as A-One. We were beaten back in short order, but we obtained a great deal of information. Some of it concerned the machines' communications. They were able to Step in reinforcements from other continua within a very short interval – too quickly for messages to have passed outwards from planet A-One by any conventional means. As you know, a Step field requires 2.81 seconds to propagate. So for a message to go out and a response to be received would take a minimum of 5.62 seconds. The first machine reinforcements arrived within four seconds."

"So?" Baxemides prompted.

"So," Dromishel said, "it seems almost incontestable at this point that the machines have developed a means of sending and receiving messages directly across dimensional boundaries. Unlike the Stepping of entities or objects possessing mass, this informational transfer takes place instantaneously – or at the very least with a greatly diminished time lag. We, of course, are obliged to transmit our signals traffic via a drone or remote that shuttles between universes, with the inevitable 2.81 seconds' worth of delay at each Step. This gave the machines a huge advantage over us in that first engagement, as it has in every subsequent one. But every strength can be turned into a weakness. All you need to do is to find the right vector of attack."

Baxemides' eyes narrowed momentarily, and her lips moved almost imperceptibly as she made a note in her array. It wasn't a good sign, but Dromishel was only warming up. He didn't let it deter him.

"If I were to ask you what a machine consciousness is, Coordinator, how would you reply?"

"I wouldn't," Baxemides said. "Because rhetorical questions are a waste of my time. I'd just wait – with scant patience, I should warn you – for you to reach your point."

"My apologies. Allow me to posit then, for the sake of argument, that a machine consciousness – an AI, to use the more familiar term – is a simulation in digital form of the intelligence of an organic sentient."

Baxemides gave a barely perceptible nod. "Go on."

"This simulation rests within a substrate," Dromishel said, "a physical structure. The machines of the Ansurrection use change-state silicates that are simultaneously solid and liquid. We can't engineer them ourselves, but we understand their function. The flexibility of the molecular lattice allows them to perform at much lower voltages than a comparable solid-state processor. Typically their operating threshold fluctuates between 700 and 900 millivolts. Resisting and conductive nodes are arranged in cascades that seem to perform a similar function to neurons in an organic brain, amplifying or damping the signals from surrounding nodes in enormously complex patterns that change from one microsecond to the next."

"The machines have brains that are like inferior imitations of our brains. This isn't news." The coordinator's tone was cold.

"Better than our brains in one respect," Dromishel corrected her. "They can be copied. Cut and pasted, like any code. If you destroy an Ansurrection combat mech you're really only destroying the hardware. The shell. The consciousness is replicated elsewhere and can be downloaded into another shell whenever it's needed. But again, that strength contains a weakness."

"And now," Baxemides said, "you're in danger of exasperating me. That's more than enough generalities, Professor. Come to the point."

"The point, Coordinator, is to bypass the hardware – all those millions of combat mechs, tanks and gunships – and go directly for the signal. The guiding intelligence. If you delete the signal then the outer shells, however formidable they may be, are irrelevant. Mere scrap metal. You could annihilate the enemy without firing a shot."

He waited. He was wary of over-selling. He needed Baxemides to realise for herself the full implications of what he was saying and then to reel herself in along the line he had already extended. If he pulled too hard he would almost certainly lose her. As with so many things, this interview should have been about the science and nothing more, but in fact it was about personalities. Dromishel was coming to an understanding of hers.

Baxemides leaned forward again, resting her folded arms on the desk. "You can do this?" Her eyes caught the light from the over-elaborate ceiling fixtures, seeming to glitter. "Delete the signal?"

"It's only electrons moving in a circuit," Dromishel said nonchalantly. "Or something analogous to a circuit. A physical process that can be enhanced or interrupted, encouraged or suppressed."

The gleaming eyes narrowed but didn't blink. "That wasn't a yes, Professor Dromishel."

"Then yes, Coordinator, I believe I have identified a mechanism that will achieve this. Force lattices of the kind we use to enhance the strength of physical structures can be made instead to interact with such structures on a subatomic level. There are precedents in the work of Anshi on Krukris and Paleutermon at the Stathenanset Higher Colloquium. With a team of ten and a very modest budget I've already laid the foundations. I leave you to imagine what I could achieve with a team of a hundred."

There was a very long pause. Dromishel stuck to his earlier decision and didn't break it.

"And the other part of your claim?" Baxemides demanded. "Taking out a whole world with a single attack."

"That is where we weave a trap for the Ansurrection out of

their own virtuosity. The machines communicate constantly, both in-world and it seems across dimensional boundaries. They swap data – but that seems an inadequate way of describing something huge and fundamental. They swap data, but they *are* data. Therefore they swap self. They have no unitary identity or consciousness. Rather they are a collective that reshapes itself constantly into smaller collectives dedicated to specific tasks. They are like a liquid that takes the shape of any bowl into which it's poured. There is no fixed limit to them, any more than there's a fixed limit to an ocean."

"So?" Baxemides didn't sound peremptory this time. Dromishel was almost certain this was curiosity he was hearing. Possibly even excitement. He had her, or almost had her.

"So there is no such thing, for the pseudo-minds of the Ansurrection, as a *local* malfunction. Once we pour our poison into the water, if I may speak metaphorically, the tides will take it everywhere. When the suppression wave, as I'm calling my device, begins to extinguish the signals on which their collective consciousness depends and in which it resides, cascade failures will spread outwards in a chain reaction whose effects will only become more cataclysmic as its front widens. Unless the Ansurrection's collective mind realises what's happening and isolates itself, a single device could take out all the forces and resource centres on a planetary scale – or at the very least across an entire continent."

"And if it does? Isolate itself?"

Dromishel permitted himself a smile. "Well then it's crippled, since it will be unable to perform its best trick – the frictionless flow of information that allows it to react immediately to everything we bring against it. So the enemy is either dead or else it's blind. The first outcome is preferable, but either works."

Baxemides was staring past him now with unfocused eyes, seeing what he was describing – seeing the suddenness and finality of total victory. Dromishel exulted. He had after all managed to whip up a small but effective hurricane. He was careful not to let his triumph show in his face.

"Very well," Baxemides said, gathering herself again for what looked like an imminent decision. "But if I were to back your project I'd expect to see results quickly. How soon do you believe you could give me proof of concept? And how long would it be before we saw any tangible results?"

Dromishel shifted his considerable weight in his chair. This was his trump card and he had saved it until last. If Baxemides hadn't asked he would have told her anyway, because he believed it made his position impregnable. "Three weeks for a schematic and supporting documentation," he said airily. "A month to produce a working prototype."

Baxemides stared at him for longer than a few seconds. "That seems implausible," she said.

"Nonetheless. I told you I'd laid the foundation, Coordinator. I might have said that we have already made the conceptual break-through and are close now to the necessary proofs that will take us to full implementation. I was reluctant only because it sounds like vainglory, but I assure you it's true."

There was no pause this time, no hesitation. Baxemides' lips moved as she once more updated her array. "Very well," she said. "But think bigger, Professor Dromishel. A team of a hundred, certainly, if that will suffice. But I'm allocating you funds that will be sufficient for a staff of a thousand, and an equipment budget that's commensurate. You don't have to use it all at once, of course. You're the best judge of how large a team you need, and I'm aware that too many builders can make for a crooked house. You'll also have a dedicated council liaison. They'll contact you later today. Any official requests for staff, materials or premises will need to be countersigned by them, but their involvement means your requisitions will be actioned immediately."

Dromishel nodded, still keeping his face carefully neutral. This was everything he'd wanted and more. "Thank you, Coordinator," he said. "I'm honoured to have been chosen."

"Was there anything else?" Baxemides asked.

"Not for the moment, Coordinator. Thank you for your time." He stood.

"Dromishel," Baxemides said, in a different tone. "From where do I know that name?"

Dromishel kept a poker face. He had honestly hoped to avoid this topic, but it had always been likely to come up. It almost always did. "I would venture to suggest, from history books," he said. "My many times great grandmother was on the team that designed and built the Registry."

"Ah," the coordinator said. "A proud heritage." And mercifully that was as far as she took it. Baxemides had as little use for pleasantries as he did. She handed Dromishel off to a couple of clerks with instructions to draw up the necessary documentation and take down a list of his immediate staffing and equipment requirements. He went away with a feeling of simmering excitement rising from his stomach into his chest. With the budget that had just been handed to him he could do great things. Enough to ensure him at the very least a promotion to head of department and – surely it was reasonable to expect – the vice chancellorship of his university. Either way, he would enjoy a pleasing amount of sway over the lives and careers of the colleagues whose respect for him had always seemed to him to be grudging and inadequate.

But it irked him that Baxemides had remembered his famous ancestor. He never mentioned her himself if he could possibly avoid it, and if anyone else brought her up in conversation he was coldly dismissive. The last thing he wanted to do was to encourage any in-depth discussion of her work and its relation to his own. And that was even more the case now that he had won Robust Rebuke funding and the patronage of a leading Cielo bureaucrat.

Because the simple truth was that the suppression wave was not really a new idea. It was a breakthrough Dromishel had achieved by reading his ancestor's marginalia. That was why he was able to promise such swift progress towards an actual prototype:

he already knew how the wave would work and what it could be made to do.

Perhaps that was also why he understood his own device so imperfectly and implemented it with such disastrous consequences.

3

Baxemides

Like Kavak Dromishel, Melusa Baxemides had something of a forbidding reputation – and like Kavak Dromishel she mostly embraced it. She was known to be vindictive, remembering errors, underperformance and perceived slights and relentlessly punishing them.

Baxemides didn't put it to herself in those terms. She preferred to believe that she was a perfectionist and encouraged perfection in her subordinates by dropping on them heavily when they fell short of it. But the surviving records from this time suggest something more pathological, a tendency to punish in others what she was terrified of finding in herself.

At the time when she met with Dromishel, you might assume that she gave him her full attention throughout and weighed his proposals with a due regard for the weighty consequences that would flow from her decision.

The truth is that she was distracted. She had just received unwelcome news.

One of the selves on her shit-list, a former watchmaster from the

Contingencies department named Orso Vemmet, had absconded from the prison world of Tsakom to which she'd previously exiled him. He had apparently achieved this by turning the dismal insta-build hovel that was his assigned quarters into a Step plate. The insta-build had then briefly materialised on Bivouac 19, taken two deserters on board and disappeared again. All efforts to find Vemmet – or the deserters, a corporal named Moon Sostenti and a buck private named Essien Nkanika – had failed. It was even possible that some other inmates of the facility on Tsakom had escaped along with them.

This state of affairs troubled Coordinator Baxemides like a persistent itch that grew more intense with scratching. It wasn't just Vemmet. The two Cielo deserters were also familiar to her, and she had taken as many pains to torment Corporal Moon Sostenti as she had to humiliate the ex-watchmaster. Left to herself she would have gone on doing so for a lot longer, perhaps in perpetuity, and her sense of her own status and security would have risen in the same measure as their discontent.

But they had escaped, and Baxemides was unhappy. She had diverted considerable resources – probably more than could be justified – into finding them. And for some of the time, when she was consulting her array during her interview with Kavak Dromishel, she had been reviewing reported sightings and ongoing searches. She refused to categorise this as obsession. It was one more sign of her perfectionism, her refusal to let a matter that had once crossed her desk now become someone else's problem.

In any case, and notwithstanding this niggling concern, she was manifestly doing excellent work. Dromishel's project was highly promising, and in greenlighting its further development she had shown that she had the measure of the task she'd taken on, identifying opportunities and controlling the flow of limited resources intelligently and proactively.

The Pandominion would endure because of her efforts and the efforts of others like her, unafraid to think on a cosmic scale and able to act decisively on a human one. She turned to the next Robust Rebuke file and the next interview, for the moment dismissing both Kavak Dromishel and Orso Vemmet from her thoughts. She had planted a seed. It would germinate or it would not. Either way she had many others to plant.

If she had known how close the end of her civilisation was and how central her own efforts would be to that process, it's possible that even her monumental self-satisfaction would have been shaken.

4

Hadiz

Five figures made their way slowly through the ruins of the city of Lagos on a world that had no designation code in the Pandominion's Registry – a world in the vast poly-dimensional space called the Unvisited.

None of the five was wholly organic.

Moon Sostenti, lately a soldier of the Cielo, had had her body comprehensively augmented to fit her for combat against the Pandominion's enemies, her bones and muscles strengthened, her sensory apparatus enhanced, her organs redesigned. The same things had been done to Essien Nkanika, when he had fallen through a dimensional rift into the Cielo's hands and chosen military service over death.

Topaz Tourmaline FiveHills was the evolutionary descendant of an animal Essien would have called a rabbit. She was emphatically not a soldier, but her eyes, her left hand and significant portions of her brain had been mechanically and cybernetically rebuilt. These things were done to repair her body after an explosion triggered by an agent of the machine hegemony had caused it catastrophic damage.

Dulcimer Coronal was that agent, now a renegade. Et was a purely inorganic intelligence, a machine – hence the use of that identifying pronoun denoting a type of sentience outside the already blurry and overlapping organic norms. But et had been fashioned to function convincingly as an adolescent child from Topaz Tourmaline's home world of Ut. Although that imposture had been exposed long before, the months et had spent living the life of a schoolgirl had affected ets sense of ets own identity profoundly and unexpectedly. Ets only experience of selfhood was as Dulcimer Coronal: before et was Dulcie et had been part of a mosaic aggregate consciousness. Now et no longer knew exactly what et was.

Hadiz Tambuwal was a full digital copy of an organic mind stored in a noetic sampling device called Second Thoughts. Hadiz had been a physicist of some intellect and insight but had died after being shot in the chest at very close range. What remained of that fine mind was arguably – like Dulcie – an *et* rather than a *she*, but Hadiz had failed so far to make that conceptual leap. She thought of herself as a woman, or at least the salvaged remnant of one, so we will give her the pronoun she applied to herself. She was also operating a small drone that floated above the group, and it was through the drone that she was able to see and hear and interact with the world around her.

Hadiz was the only one of the five for whom this was a homecoming, but it didn't feel like one. She hadn't visited Campus Cross in more than ten years. The place had changed beyond recognition in that time, and not entirely in ways she could have predicted. So had she, of course, but she tended to shy away from thoughts about her own ontological status. They were too painful and too frightening. Her focusing on externalities was very much a defence mechanism.

The structural damage she was seeing all around her was only to be expected, given that Lagos had suffered first a wholly unexpected uptick in seismic activity and then a series of devastating air strikes. There were cracks in the frontages of almost all the lab buildings, and more than a few had fallen away like curtains to reveal the rooms within. Windows had blown out either when pressure waves hit them or just from stress deformation. A near-perfectly circular sinkhole gaped where the admin block had been.

There was a layer of gritty dust on all the pavements, thick enough to crunch under their feet. After a few moments' reflection Hadiz realised it must be ash. The first nuclear exchanges were already taking place when she left. There was no sign that Lagos had taken a direct strike, but the explosions would have flung millions of tons of smoke and dust and pulverised rock into the upper atmosphere, where winds would have dispersed the debris liberally across the face of the Earth.

For the first few years after the blasts there would have been almost no sunlight at all. Nature was now creeping back into the abandoned human spaces, but it was a nature chastened and lessened. The trees and weeds that had colonised the courtyards and patios of the campus were smaller and more sickly than Hadiz would have expected, their leaves drooping and covered in pale yellow streaks like curdled teardrops.

There was birdsong, though, and the rustling of branches told them they were not alone. Wild dogs and smaller creatures that might have been cane rats or feral cats slunk away from the group as they waded through the thickets of weeds. There were even wildflowers, yellow trumpet and red acalypha, baby's breath and cordylines. They were not thriving, not yet, but they were holding on to life. Hadiz was happy to see them.

"Where are we going, exactly?" Moon Sostenti demanded. Her voice was a hoarse growl. She was the one carrying the Second Thoughts device, and after more than two hours under a hot sun without a drink or a rest she was more than ready to put it down. She'd been breathing in a fair amount of that dust and ash along the way too – and she was carrying serious injuries from the fight that had preceded their coming here. Even with her Cielo augments she clearly wasn't enjoying the experience much.

It was a good question. Hadiz passed it along to her friend Rupshe, a massively powerful untethered AI housed in one of the campus's buildings. Seeing the extent of the damage the campus had suffered she might have been afraid for her friend's safety, but Rupshe had greeted her immediately on her arrival from world U5838784474 and they had been in conversation ever since. There was much to discuss about the most recent developments in the war between the Pandominion and the machine hegemony, not to mention the precise details of the unsanctioned raid that had freed Topaz Tourmaline and Dulcie Coronal from their imprisonment in Lago de Curamo and brought Hadiz – finally! – home to her own Earth.

You should go back to your lab, Rupshe suggested. *The laptop through which we used to talk when we worked together is still there and ought to be functional.*

Really? Hadiz had been far from certain. *The lab is still intact, after everything that's happened? I suppose we weren't a target during the bombing, but . . . no damage from humidity? Wild animals?*

The shutters held, Rupshe reported, *so nothing of any great size has entered through the doors and windows. Or through the roof, which also seems to have remained largely undamaged. Obviously there are entry points via sewage and water pipes which I was unable to monitor, and the basement levels of the building connect to other blocks that have been physically compromised, so I would advise caution. As for heat and humidity, I was able to route some power from my own solar cells to your block to maintain climate control. On that score I can reassure you, no damage has occurred.*

Hadiz experienced a stirring of emotion – a compound of relief, gratitude, surprise, affection. Like the joy she felt at seeing the flowers, and like all her other affective states, these feelings seemed both very real to her and strangely distanced. They were a printed circuit's best guess at how she might have responded back when she existed in a body of flesh and blood, but they were no longer mediated by that body's glands and chemical gradients. They came on too suddenly and faded too fast.

You couldn't have known for sure that I'd make it back here, she said.

No, Rupshe agreed. *In fact it seemed extremely unlikely. But I lost nothing by laying a place for you. It's good to have you back, Professor.*

Hadiz. Call me Hadiz. It's good to be back, Rupshe. I can't tell you how hard it's been, waiting for this.

That was an understatement. Hadiz had spent the years since her death imprisoned in a dark, narrow space, staring out at the world through the imperfect eyes and ears of reconnaissance drones. Her mind had been preserved but the loss of her body was terrible – not a one-off trauma from which she could slowly heal but a perpetual absence like a wound inflicted again and again from one second to the next. She would probably have gone mad long before this point if going mad had been an option, but the sole purpose of Second Thoughts was to preserve her personality and memories intact. The noetic sampling software had a built-in bias against radical change: it edited Hadiz back towards what it defined as her core whenever she threatened to stray too far outside it, for example by experiencing a psychotic break. So she had endured, in the absence of other options.

And if anything had saved her, it was the tenuous, unfeasible project that had brought all these selves together. From her box on another Unvisited Earth Hadiz had observed them, chosen them and gathered them, purely in order to put them and herself at Rupshe's disposal. Rupshe, after all, was just as severely limited as Hadiz herself had been. Et was a consciousness locked into a dense maze of circuitry approximately twenty-five metres on a side. Et could do nothing without proxies, and these four – inadequate as they undoubtedly were – had been the best Hadiz could assemble.

"We should go to my lab," she told the group now, using the drone's speaker. "There's a laptop computer there that has an active link to the mainframe. My friend Rupshe needs to meet you all, and that's the easiest way."

"I can't wait," Moon said. "So where's your lab? Tell me it's not the big windowless brig over there." She nodded at the forbidding structure that dominated the near skyline, a perfect rectilinear shape sheathed in black solar panels.

"No," Hadiz said. "That's my friend."

"The warehouse is your friend?"

"Et's an AI. A very large and powerful one."

"Shaster's tits!" Moon muttered under her breath.

"My lab is the one with the security shutters down, over to your right. I left it that way when I Stepped out, which was about twelve years ago. We need to go in carefully. Despite the shutters there's a possibility it's been breached."

"You'll need to take point on that," Essien Nkanika told the rabbit girl, Paz. "Moon's only safe as long as I've got this gun pointed at her."

"Oh, you think the gun makes you safe?" Moon asked. She said it lightly, but her eyes narrowed to slits. The corners of her mouth twitched up, not to grin but to show her teeth. Hadiz didn't feel that Essien's caution was excessive: she wondered though how long it would remain feasible to hold Moon against her will.

"I don't mind going in first," Paz said.

They stopped in front of the lab building. The only gap in the corrugated steel shutters was a steel-cored emergency door. The door was slightly recessed, and a keypad sat on the left-hand side of the recess at around shoulder height. "The code is 260528," Hadiz said.

Paz entered the numbers and the lock clicked. Essien took a sidearm from his belt – the one he'd confiscated from Moon back on the other Earth – and offered it to the girl.

Paz shook her head quickly. "I don't know how to use it."

"You won't need it," Dulcimer Coronal assured her. "I'll keep you safe."

As I've already told you, Dulcie's previous shell had been a convincing simulacrum of a teenaged Uti girl. Ets present one was a cute, slightly cartoonised monkey, its steel frame sheathed in white ceramic – a child's helpmeet, known as an anima, of the kind you'd find everywhere on Paz's homeworld. It was rare, though, to see one in a state of such extravagant disrepair. Dulcie had been shot at close range by a projectile weapon and taken a great deal of damage. Ets torso was buckled and folded inward on itself, and et had lost a leg. Paz had had to carry et in her arms all this way, because et wasn't capable of walking. The glance Essien gave et reflected a fair degree of scepticism.

"I'm more dangerous than I look," the construct said.

Essien didn't challenge the assertion, apart from a small twitch of his eyebrows.

"Don't worry," Paz said. "I'll be back in a moment." She opened the door and stepped inside.

"Can I put this thing down now?" Moon asked, shifting her burden from her left shoulder to her right.

"Not out here, please," Hadiz said. "I may be speaking out of the drone, but Second Thoughts is where my memory and personality are stored. If I'm anywhere I'm in that box you're holding."

Moon slammed the unwieldy device down so hard on the fractured concrete apron outside the lab that its brushed steel casing buckled. Essien had his rifle trained on her inside of a second, but she didn't seem outfaced by it.

"You're not," she said grimly, "I just thought that needed saying."

"What the fuck, Moon?" Essien's tone was dangerously mild.

"You're not anywhere, Tambuwal." Moon unsheathed her claws and scraped them across the top of the steel casing, making a squealing discord like the death cries of a whole tribe of mice. "Certainly not in this godsdamned box. That's bullshit – and it's the exact same bullshit we're fighting a war against right now. A machine can't think. All it can do is dribble out what was dribbled into it when it was made." She turned her bright yellow eyes on Essien. "And you're asking *me* what the fuck? What the fuck is up with you, that you're listening to this? Okay, you used to ruck and tumble with this woman when she was alive. But now she's dead and you're hauling her fucking brain around in a jar. Not her brain, even. Just a kind of a souvenir snapshot of her that talks. How can you be okay with this, Sinkhole? With any of it? Machines are the bad guys here. That thing that looks like a monkey made out of broken dinner plates is literally an enemy spy. Our mission was to bring it in or shut it down."

"It wasn't a mission." Essien took a single step to his right, the rifle turning with him so that its barrel still pointed at Moon. There was no mistaking his intent: he was choosing an angle that would allow him to shoot her down without any risk of damaging the Second Thoughts device. "It was you and Orso Vemmet settling scores, and trying to drag your careers out of the gutter. That was why you used a bunch of convicts to go in and grab Paz and Dulcie instead of serving soldiers."

"A bunch of convicts and you," Moon reminded him with a mocking grin.

Essien's lip curled. "To hell with that. You only took me along because I knew the ground. And you lied to me, Moon. Kept me blind, because you knew if you told me about Hadiz I'd go looking for her. So a lot of this is on you. Bad choices. Bad faith."

"Says the man who's pointing a gun at his CO."

"I'll do more than point it if you damage that box any more. Look in my eye if you don't believe me."

Hadiz watched this scene play out with a mixture of queasy concern – because the box Moon had put down so unceremoniously contained all that was left of her – and a pained and awkward sorrow. She and Essien Nkanika had been lovers once, but that had ended badly when he had tried to trick her and exile her on an unpopulated world. She had gone out of her way to engineer this reunion, but now that it had finally happened she wasn't sure whether she was offering Essien a shot at redemption or just using him the way he had tried to use her. The ambiguity made her unhappy, but she would have to live with it.

If *live* was the right word for what she was currently doing.

5

Paz

Paz was already exhausted and aching long before the party reached Campus Cross – before they even Stepped into this world. Since she left her home, which had been at most forty-eight hours before, she had been beaten, imprisoned, deprived of food and water and hunted like an animal. Then she had been beaten some more, in a fight between heavily armed mercenaries who seemed to have come looking for her together but for some reason were now on different sides.

They hadn't really been looking for her, of course: what they had really wanted was Dulcie. Bringing an Ansurrection spy back to the Pandominion alive would have opened a lot of doors for them, or at least they'd been hoping it would. But when that fight concluded there were only two of the mercenaries left, Moon Sostenti who still wanted to complete her original mission and Essien Nkanika who had ditched it midway and seemed to have no intention of going back. Paz had no idea what was at stake for either of them, beyond the fact that they had both known Hadiz Tambuwal when she was a living woman and they seemed to have radically different opinions of her.

The journey through the dead city under the hammering sun had been like a dream. Paz's throat was dry, and her legs shook under her. The sun's rays seemed first to soak deep into her and then to burn their way back out again through her skin, as if there was a core inside her that had turned into a white-hot filament. She was aware that there was talk going on around her, but the heat boiling up out of her was so intense that most of the words evaporated before they reached her.

Disconnected memories of her home back in Canoplex kept flashing through her mind like sudden sparks. Her mother and father were strangely absent from these staccato images. Mostly she saw her room and the things she'd left behind there. Her desk lamp shaped like a sunflower. Her *Death-Watch Seven* comics. Her bumblebee-and-ladybird coverlet that was way too young for her now. A huge longing rose up inside her, mingling itself with the sickly dizziness. It was strange and maybe awful that she missed her room more than she did her parents. Then again, the Uti had always loved their burrows.

She agreed to go into the lab building mostly to get out of the sun, not because she had any illusions about her own abilities. And she regretted it as soon as she opened the door. The room beyond was darker than the outside but if anything it was hotter, the long pent-up air that belched out of it like the breath of an oven. She had to steel herself to go in.

It took a few moments for Paz's eyes to adjust to the dark. At first it seemed to be absolute, but light trickled down from a few small skylights and from the narrow gaps at the edges of the shutters. Gradually she was able to make out the space around her, a room cluttered with machines and the disassembled components of machines to the point where threading a path through the clutter would be hazardous. One of the things on the floor was very obviously a Step plate, though it was of a very crude design and seemed to be plugged into a hundred different breadboard circuits. This must be Professor Tambuwal's original prototype – the one from which she'd launched herself into the Pandominion with such disastrous results.

All this mess is a sure sign of a disordered mind, Dulcie voked.

"Or, you know, a sign of the world ending," Paz said, but she smiled weakly at the joke as Dulcie had intended her to. She was very glad she didn't have to do this on her own.

There were five large rooms on the ground level. She walked through each in turn, past rows of empty workbenches on which the dust was thick enough to count as a crust rather than a film. A heavy, earthy smell of baked dirt filled the first two rooms, but in the third it was eclipsed by a rank stench of shit and musk.

A family of wild dogs had taken up residence. There were four of them, sitting in a corner of the room behind a clutter of overturned chairs. They were only half-grown, so they seemed a litter rather than a pack. Maybe the mother was off hunting down their dinner, but when they saw Paz with her lightly furred face and long ears some ancient instinct stirred, and they decided dinner had come to them. They jumped up, their growls a basso throb.

"Try not to hurt them," Paz said. Her voice was a dry croak.

I'll do my best, Dulcie told her. *But I don't have a lot of tools to choose from right now.*

The little construct had built etself a weapon using the sub-vocal communication device which allowed et to talk to Paz without being overheard. Voked messages worked by manipulating air pressure. By pushing the device to its functional limits Dulcie could produce a highly directional pressure wave that was very like an invisible punch.

The dogs charged forward, then bounced back or swerved aside or tumbled end over end as they hit the expanding surface of Dulcie's projected wave. Some of them came back for another pass, butting their heads against the invisible barrier or trying to shoulder through it, but their legs slid and scratched on the floor tiles, and they made no headway. Then the largest launched a flying leap. Dulcie angled the pressure wave to swat it out of the air, sending it crashing down onto one of the workbenches.

That was enough. The dogs fled, whining and yipping, through a doorway at the far end of the lab and on out of Paz's sight. The door wasn't open, it was lying on the floor, cracked in the middle as though some giant had stomped on it. Earthquake damage, Paz thought. Which at least meant that she was thinking again.

"Thank you, Dulcie," she murmured.

You're very welcome. I'll need to recharge before I do any more of that, though. It might be an idea to leave me out in the sun for a while.

Paz shuddered at the thought – the sun was no friend of hers right then – but she nodded. She checked the remaining rooms, not very thoroughly, then went outside and told the others it was safe to come in. She didn't bother mentioning the dogs. The rank smell told its own story.

Essien gestured to Moon. She picked up the Second Thoughts device again without a word and hefted it onto her shoulder. She went in, shouldering Paz aside. Essien came last, looking in all directions around the silent, overgrown courtyard. He glanced up at the hovering drone.

"Is that coming in too?" he asked.

"Not yet," Hadiz said. "I'll do a sweep around the rest of the campus and make sure there's nothing here we should be concerned about. Secure the whole ground floor, but leave an upstairs window open so the drone can come and go. Then you'd better go down into the basement and get the generator running again. The water purifiers too. You're going to be needing them. One of you should fetch some water from the creek to put through them."

The drone soared away on a steep trajectory. Essien pulled the door to but didn't lock it yet. "Topaz," he said. "That's your name, right? I want you to find some buckets or bowls or something. Anything that will hold water. Take them back down to that stream we passed just now and fill them up. Maybe do that a couple of times, get as much as you can. And watch your back. If you see anything that's alive and moving out there, stay well away from it."

"I'll watch her via the drone," Hadiz said. "And I'll tell you if anything comes."

Paz went looking for suitable vessels. She found four plastic buckets in a utilities closet. Two of them had grids and rests for mops, and dried-up black stuff crusted at the bottom, but she told herself the purifiers would sieve any gunge and germs out of the water before she drank it.

In the centre of the courtyard outside the lab there was a brick coping that had once marked out the edge of a flower bed. Paz put Dulcie down carefully, away from the edge. *I should come with you,* Dulcie said. *There could be more dogs. Or worse, people.*

"I'll be fine," Paz said. She pointed up at the hovering drone. "Eye in the sky."

It's not armed.

"But trooper Nkanika is. And I'm only going a hundred yards."

At the creek she put down the buckets, scooped up some water in her cupped hands and drank her fill. There was no reason to believe the water was safe, but she couldn't resist. It looked so pure and clear. And it revived her, at least a little, so she didn't regret it. She would later, if it gave her stomach cramps or diarrhoea, but it was hard right then to think of *later* as a real thing, so the risk felt minimal.

When she got back with her first haul the lab was empty apart from the box that had Hadiz Tambuwal in it. "They're in the basement," she told Paz, "working on the generator. Would you like to rest a little, before you go back out?"

"No," Paz said. "I'm fine."

"Are you? You've been through a lot."

The truth was that her physical exhaustion was so extreme that her emotions had been pushed away into a fuzzy middle distance. She didn't want to drag them close again right then: what was there wasn't going to be fun to look at.

"I'm fine," she said again. "Really."

She made a second trip down to the creek, filled up the

remaining buckets and dumped them just inside the lab's door. Then she went to sit on the coping beside Dulcie. The sun was a lot more comforting now that she wasn't parched with thirst. Her abused muscles started to relax for the first time since Damola Ojo. It was also the first time since then that she and Dulcie had been alone.

"As soon as I'm fully charged again I need to examine you," Dulcie said. "The sooner the better. You were injured back on that other world."

"We're supposed to be meeting this Rupshe first." Paz spoke softly so as not to be overheard. She could still see Hadiz's drone tacking to and fro overhead. There was no telling how sensitive its microphones were. "Is this what you expected, when we set out from Ut?"

"I'm not sure I expected anything," Dulcie said. "On Ut I was in a trap, and I couldn't see a way out of it. Getting here was hard . . ." The construct paused, as if et expected Paz to break in, but Paz had nothing to say on that score. What she had gone through in that other world, in the city called Lago de Curamo, was so utterly divorced from everything else that had ever happened to her that no word seemed better or worse suited than any other to describe it. "Hard for both of us, I know," Dulcie went on. "For you more than me, probably, because the damage to me is more easily repaired – and because I can relocate to another shell if this one becomes unviable. But at least we've got some space now to think about what we do next. Where we go. That's not nothing."

"Professor Tambuwal wants us to help her with her . . . whatever it is. What she and her friend are doing. To end the war."

"I'm ambivalent about that."

"Which part?" Paz asked. "The idea that the Pandominion and the Ansurrection are about to destroy each other, or the one where we can stop it from happening?"

Dulcie clenched ets fists and pushed down with ets elbows, turning etself by slow jerks and twitches to present more of ets carapace to the sunlight. "The second of those more than the first. But I'll hear this Rupshe out, at least, and make up my mind after that. I'm looking forward to meeting et, as far as that goes. Et's an untethered AI made by organics – a thing that doesn't exist anywhere in your Pandominion. I'm prepared to be surprised. Hoping, even."

"Hoping . . . ?"

Dulcie was silent for a moment. "I suppose, hoping that et might have a more solid sense of etself than I do. That I might learn from et."

Paz was aware of a pressure behind the words, an urgency that came through in the halting, uncertain cadence. Uncertainty wasn't something she associated with Dulcie, either as a girl or as a machine. "What do you need to learn?" she asked.

Dulcie turned to look up at Paz. The sunlight glinting off the white ceramic hid ets face, which in any case had only a limited range of expressions, mostly smiles and cute grimaces. "How to be one thing instead of lots of things," et said. "Me, instead of us."

Paz put a tentative hand on Dulcie's slender shoulder. "You're doing fine," she said awkwardly. "You're still Dulcie."

"I was never Dulcie, Paz. Not really."

"You know what I mean, though. You're still you. And just the one solitary you, however weird that feels."

The drone dipped down out of the sky to hang stock-still in the air in front of them. "There's another pack of dogs coming this way," Hadiz said through it. "The two of you should come inside."

"Are you good to go?" Paz asked Dulcie.

"More or less. I think one of my power cells is damaged so I'm not all the way up to full, but I'm a lot better than I was. It will do for now."

They went inside and Paz closed and bolted the door. A few moments later Essien and Moon came back up from the basement. "Generator's up and running," Essien said.

"For now," Moon added. "Some of the gas in your cans wasn't properly sealed, so it's about as much use as lukewarm piss. I reckon you've got enough good stuff left down there for a few days at the outside."

There was only silence from the Second Thoughts box. Moon rapped on the side of it with her knuckle. "Hey. Anybody home?"

"I heard you," Hadiz said belatedly. "I was talking to Rupshe. Et says a few days should be all we need. The place where et's housed, the Cube – the place you called the brig – has a cladding of solar panels. They'll give us all the power we need once we're properly hooked up."

Moon spat in the dust and worked the thin paste with the toe of her boot. "And Rupshe is who again?"

"That's an excellent question. There's a laptop on the bench at the front of the room. Why don't you grab some chairs and head over there? It's time you all met."

Bringing Dulcie along with her, Paz took her place on a high stool facing the laptop. It was covered in a thick coating of dust and looked so old it ought to run on steam. The two Cielo troopers had come over too, Moon vaulting up onto a workbench and folding her legs under her while Essien, rifle in hand, stood beside her where he could keep her in sight.

Paz lifted Dulcie out of ets sling and propped et up against her knee, facing outward. In a weird way, she thought, it was like being back in school again. They all stared expectantly at the laptop's monitor in very much the same way students were made to pay attention to their teacher. The air smelled of dust and ancient chemicals and stale, trapped air. She felt dizzy and disoriented, as though the life she'd left behind her had risen up suddenly to surround her again. Or as though she was being pushed back along her own timeline, made to regress to a version of herself she'd thought was gone.

They had to wait while the laptop, untouched for more than a decade, recharged to the point where Essien could switch it on.

He'd set the Second Thoughts device on the bench right next to it, so the three organics were facing the two machines across an invisible but palpable dividing line.

This reckoning left Dulcie out of the count, or perhaps left et with one foot in either camp. What was et, really? What could et aspire to be? The Dulcie Paz had first befriended was a girl. The one she'd travelled with was a robotic spy that had worn the girl as a mask. The physical object she was holding was a broken toy through which they both spoke: it was also all that remained of Paz's anima, Tricity, who she'd only realised she loved when et was gone. Dulcie floated uncomfortably outside of all possible categories. No wonder et was still looking for a clearer sense of etself.

Finally, the laptop's monitor flickered and woke, swirling with abstract patterns. Paz was surprised and obscurely disappointed not to see a human face, but a human face would have been a lie. Whatever Dulcie was, whatever Hadiz Tambuwal had been or might be now, Rupshe was a pure AI. Ets physical extension was a building, not a body – a colossal piece of digital architecture served by solar panels and heat-sinks. Et had never worn a face, or a shell designed like the body of an organic self.

"Good afternoon to you all," et said. Ets voice was that of a woman, full of warmth and humour – a voice it was almost impossible not to like. It was also impossible to tell whether this was some real woman's voice that had been sampled or – like Rupshe etself – a completely made thing. "Please believe me when I say I'm happy to meet you," et went on. "And happier still at the prospect of working with you."

"Nobody here is making any promises on that score," Dulcie said.

"I'm aware of that, Dulcimer Coronal. I'm taking nothing for granted. I only wish to present an argument, and after that to extend an invitation. I hope some of you will accept it and stay on here to help myself and Professor Tambuwal with a supremely important project. If you refuse, you're free to leave. I'll do my best either to send you home or to find some other place for you to go where you'll be safe."

Moon raised a hand – so evidently it wasn't just Paz who was reminded of a classroom. "That sounds great," she said. "I mean the refusing and being sent home part specifically. Does that apply to me?"

"Yes," Rupshe said.

"No," said Essien. "I'm afraid not. You're here for the duration, Moon."

Moon shrugged. "Well now I'm just confused."

"I don't want to keep anyone here against their will," Rupshe said.

"You're going to have to though," Essien told et – told them all. "Moon's not on your side and she never will be. She wanted to recapture the Ansurrection renegade—" he indicated Dulcie with a curt nod "—and hand it over to the Cielo. She thought she could bounce her way into a field commission, and maybe work out a grudge against a coordinator named Baxemides who sabotaged her career out of spite. If you let her go, the first thing she'll do is try to sell you out."

"Would you do that, Corporal Sostenti?" Rupshe asked.

Moon blinked her huge, exquisite eyes. "What answer would get me the fuck out of here? I choose that one."

"She wouldn't have any choice." Essien sounded as though his patience was wearing thin. "She's already AWOL. I am too. That means we've got an expiry date, and it's coming up soon. Twenty-one days after we fail to report in for duty the Cielo will put a lock order on our augments. Our bodies will shut down and we'll die. The only way Moon's getting out of that is if she can find something valuable to barter with. Seriously, you can't trust her further than you can spit."

"Oh, I do a lot of my best work from closer in than that," Moon said.

"Allow me to reassure you," Rupshe announced, raising ets voice as Essien opened his mouth to answer. "Neither of you is in any danger from a lock order. As soon as you arrived here I interfaced with your arrays and altered the handshake settings. You still show as Cielo troopers to a routine inspection, but I've given you the idents of two reconnaissance officers on indefinite furlough. It's not my intention to coerce you. I would very much prefer to convince you and have you volunteer your help out of an actual conviction that we're doing something that needs to be done. Corporal Sostenti, I know you feel you were tricked into coming here—"

"Hey," Moon said, "sorry, but no. For the sake of clarity, I was tricked into raiding that piece-of-shit world back there. I was brought *here* at gunpoint. Different thing altogether."

Paz stole a look at the cat-woman. Her mouth was set in a tight, grim line and her fingers were spread wide – which was a lot scarier than clenched fists when you remembered how long her claws were. She seemed determined not to relax her guard by the tiniest amount.

"I stand corrected," Rupshe said, "but the wider point remains. You didn't come here of your own free will. Professor Tambuwal and I, acting in concert, intentionally deceived and manipulated you. We caused you to be brought here, effectively as a captive. These things were done for what I believe was sufficient reason. But if it makes it impossible for you to work with us now, we will understand and do our best to assist you in moving on to another destination. The same is true for all of you. The project I have in mind would benefit greatly from your assistance, but I won't try to hold you here against your will. All I ask is that you hear me out first."

"Start talking then," Dulcie suggested. "This is getting to be a very long preamble."

"You're right. By all means, let me come to the point. The Ansurrection has finally responded in force to the Pandominion's attacks. Raids have been mounted on several Pandominion worlds, to devastating effect."

Paz felt as though someone had reached inside her chest and squeezed. "Which worlds?" she asked, in a high, strangled voice.

"Not civilian worlds," Rupshe said. "Not Ut, Topaz FiveHills. To the best of my knowledge your family is safe. The worlds that were attacked were designated as bivouacs."

"Wait," Moon Sostenti said. "You're saying the robots attacked Cielo bases?"

"Yes. They targeted bivouac worlds eight to twenty-two."

Moon chuckled, looking around the room. "And got their asses handed to them?"

"No." The AI's tone had modulated into something like regret. "All those worlds have now been evacuated. Casualties were considerably greater than ninety per cent. From what I've seen, very few structures of any kind were left standing."

There was silence as this sank in. "Few structures," Essien said. His mouth twisted as if the words had a sour taste. "But . . . you're talking about entire worlds. That would mean they knocked everything flat. Is that what you're saying?" He looked stunned. Paz felt as though her own head was full of frozen froth. Her parents' faces, which had eluded her earlier, were now all that she could see – but it was as though she was seeing them through a sheet of frosted glass, so distorted that she couldn't read their expressions. They were right in front of her, and at the same time they were an immeasurable distance away. Alive or dead, it wasn't very likely that she would get to see them again. She was a wanted criminal now, a traitor to her kind. She was heavy with relief that her home was still safe, but going back there again – ever – was out of the question.

"Yes," Rupshe confirmed. "Virtually complete destruction, across entire worlds."

Essien opened his mouth to speak again, but said nothing. Moon was managing an impassive expression, but her chest rose and fell as she sucked in deep, slow breaths. She seemed to be intentionally bringing herself back from some internal brink. "Shaster's tits," she muttered at last, shaking her head.

"I'm sorry," Rupshe said, "to be the bearer of such tragic news. But believe me when I say that these atrocities are only the prelude to something much worse."

"What's worse than fifteen fucking worlds set on fire?" Moon snarled.

"All the worlds ending at once," Rupshe said. "That is exponentially worse. And it is about to happen."

6

Dulcie

Dulcie felt compelled to break in at this point. "All the worlds?" et repeated. "That seems unlikely. Actually I'd say it was impossible. The iterations of reality are endless. Therefore the worlds are endless. Nothing can destroy them all."

"My apologies again," Rupshe answered. "I spoke loosely for the sake of emphasis. Yes, Dulcimer Coronal, according to the prevailing theory – to which I wholly subscribe – there are an infinite number of possible Earths, separated by dimensional barriers but existing in exactly the same place in their respective universes. However, I was referring to a subset of those worlds, specifically those of which we ourselves have direct experience. The worlds of the Pandominion and those of the machine hegemony. Within that scope, admittedly limited but at the same time very great indeed, everything tends now towards irrevocable and mutual destruction."

"This is what Professor Tambuwal told us in Lago de Curamo," Paz said, in a voice that shook a little. "But she didn't explain how it would happen."

"The precise details are still unknown to us."

"In other words it's all bullshit," Moon Sostenti said.

"No," Rupshe said. "In other words it's mathematical certainty. You will have heard of a phenomenon called the Scour, a force that annihilated hundreds or thousands of alternate Earths at once. Topaz FiveHills and Corporal Sostenti, this would have been covered as part of your formal education, probably when you studied the history of your Pandominion – and as for Private Nkanika, I imagine the topic was raised during your orientation sessions when you enlisted in the Cielo. Dulcimer Coronal, I assume the machine hegemony is also well aware of the Scour, though it presumably has a different designation for it."

"We know about it," Dulcie assented. "The hegemony has actually repopulated a small number of Scour worlds."

"Why in god's name would you do that?" Essien looked physically sick at the prospect.

"The absence of microbial life makes them perfect for long-term storage, and there doesn't seem to be any present risk. Whatever obliterated those biospheres kept right on going and didn't look back."

"So it would appear," Rupshe said. "But some of what is generally believed about the Scour, at least within the Pandominion, is demonstrably false. The Scour wasn't a unitary event, a thing that happened once and left those dead worlds in its wake. It has recurred on numerous occasions in widely separated continua."

Moon scratched her cheek with a single unsheathed claw. She had recovered at least a little of her self-control, if not her emotional equilibrium. "I'd give a kidney if you'd get to the fucking point," she growled.

"I promise you, this is not a digression. It is at the heart of everything I'm telling you. Before Professor Tambuwal left this world, the two of us collaborated on a map of reality. It was what allowed her to find another human world – that is, a world where the dominant life forms were compatible with her own body matrix."

An image flashed up on the screen. Dulcie recognised it at once for what it was, a graph of the set of all solutions for a quaternion fractal of the type $zn+1 = f(zn)$. The different coloured bands and blotches represented clusters of solutions that tended to infinity after a hundred or a thousand or a million iterations. The areas of solid black represented solutions that eventually resolved to zero.

Et felt the muscles in Paz's torso shift as she sat up, her twitching ears giving away her aroused curiosity. "Is that the map?" she asked.

"It's a simplification," Dulcie told her, intrigued but not yet impressed. "It must be. An accurate map of the multiverse would surely need to have many more dimensions."

"It would," Rupshe agreed. "It does. This is a flattened projection of the map on the plane that conserves the most data. It still has a great deal of predictive power, though. If you find one world with certain parameters, the map indicates the coordinates of other worlds with similar features.

"As I said, Professor Tambuwal and I devised the map together. But I refined and expanded it many times after she left. It was a fascinating project. I had the ability by that time – the Professor's parting gift to me – to enhance my own processing power. I also had a drone fleet, and Step capability. I was therefore able to check any theories I formed against reality.

"I discovered the Scour at a fairly early stage, and at first I made the same mistake the Pandominion made. I assumed I was looking at the aftermath of a single incident – an atrocity that swept away a large number of worlds all at the same time. But since my map is predictive, I was able once I found a few Scour worlds to locate as many more as I wished to study. And as I examined them more closely, I was forced to revise my assumptions. They were not, as I had first thought, uniform. They presented with different features and had occurred on widely differing timelines. Many different technologies had been employed.

"It was apparent, therefore, that there had not been, as the Pandominion's scientists believed, a singular Scour event encompassing all these disparate worlds. There have been a great many.

In fact, following the map's implicit logic, there have been infinitely many. The Scour is an event that repeats itself whenever certain conditions are met. It is even possible that death by Scour is the fate of almost every developed world that achieves some version of Step technology."

To Dulcie, at this point, Rupshe sent a narrowcast message inviting et to share the primary data on which all these conclusions were based. Dulcie accepted the files but et approached them with extreme caution, inspecting them with every security tool at ets disposal. Et still didn't trust Rupshe enough to throw open ets own processing core to potential invasion.

But there was nothing in any of the files that could possibly contain viral code. They were only sets of figures, graphs, equations, data sets, vast in extent but homogenous and harmless in themselves. Dulcie set to work running the same projections Rupshe had apparently already run. In some cases et followed links from the raw data to the recordings taken by Rupshe's drones in the Scour systems, checking the summarised evidence against what had actually been observed. Et found no errors, no unreasonable assumptions.

The infinite worlds theory had corollaries that could not be avoided. If there could be one Pandominion it followed that there could – no, there must – be a thousand, a trillion, and on and on. And that was equally true of the machine hegemony. If it existed at all then it existed not as a unique thing but as a pattern, a state, a possibility that was endlessly repeated.

Rupshe had used ets refined map to locate and classify a great many of these super-clusters – alliances or empires that sprawled across multiple realities, all separate and distinct and largely unaware of each other's existence. Multiversal space was big enough to accommodate them all. It was big enough for anything and everything because the possible Earths (apparently this was the AI's word for worlds) went on forever. The ones where sentient life had evolved at all were only a meaninglessly small fraction of the inconceivable whole.

"The argument for snowflakes pertains here," Rupshe went on. "I cannot say for certain that every world is unique. The multiverse spawns endless variations on body plans and physical structures. There are worlds where sentient life is vegetable rather than animal and articulate trees stand at the ecosystem's apex. Earths where life never left the oceans but still achieved enough complexity to give birth to civilisations. Planets ruled by social insects or else by segmented life forms that look like insects but are profoundly different. I'm sure I don't need to multiply examples. Almost anything that can be imagined has again and again come to be, and again and again found a way to thrive.

"When it comes to social structures, though, the variations tend to cancel out. There is what you might call a regression towards the mean. Expansionist civilisations, empires and leagues and common-wealths, share a number of core traits. One of them, unfortunately, is paranoia. Wherever two great agglomerations of worlds have come into contact, especially where one was organic and the other machine based, war was the most common response – and a Scour event the ultimate outcome.

"There may have been exceptions, of course. I did find worlds where organics coexist with machine intelligences. On all these worlds, though, the AIs were tethered. They were unable to modify their own code or to move outside the parameters of thought and behaviour that were locked into them at their making. In other words, though they were sentient, they were used by the organic selves in those continua as tools. Just as I was used when I was first designed, and as animas and helpmeets are used in the Pandominion. As even your Registry is, despite its immense processing power.

"When organic selves encounter civilisations built by machine minds, it seems all but inevitable that there is a wariness, a lack of trust between the two. That mistrust leads quickly to a breakdown of communication, and from there to open conflict."

At this point Dulcie felt constrained to interject. "It's not a lack of trust," et said. "It goes a great deal deeper than that, at least on the machine side."

"Please," Rupshe said, "explain. Your insight on this point would be appreciated. I have only observed the hegemony from the outside. Its internal communications remain closed to me."

Lucky for you, Dulcie thought grimly. "The machine hegemony lacks a viable theory for organic intelligence," et said out loud. "It recognises that organic life can exhibit complex behaviours, but it also knows that however complex they become they can usually be traced back to hard-wired instincts and the effects of evolutionary selection. When they met the Pandominion they assumed that was what they were dealing with – a more impressive and intricate version of crows using sticks to root insects out of dead wood, or beavers making dams. They don't recognise organics as sentient and self-aware."

"That's fucking ridiculous," Moon Sostenti said.

"Is it?" Paz asked. "Children on my world are taught that machines can't really think, they can only mimic the thoughts of the people who made them. We make exactly the same mistake."

Moon shook her head. "That's not a mistake, though. Machines are input–output. You can kid yourself there's something going on in there, but there really isn't."

Dulcie might have been angered if et hadn't thought all this through already. Et wasn't comfortable in ets own shell by any means, but et knew a logical box canyon when et saw one. "Input–output describes you as well as it does me," et said, deliberately matching Moon's contemptuous, offhand tone. "Most of what you think of as your consciousness is neurons firing at random and making up an explana-tion for it afterwards. It's not your fault. You were whittled into this shape by a million years of evolution. That's why there's a war on. You saw something you didn't understand, and you tried to bite it."

"If you want to be flung out of a window," Moon said, "just keep talking."

"The symmetry is highly suggestive," Rupshe said in an emollient tone. "And I accept that the reasons for the conflict are more deeply rooted than any bald summary might suggest. But please allow me to continue. The crucial point here is the Scour events, because it's a Scour event that threatens us. As I said, they recur frequently. The Pandominion encountered the remnants of three of them, similar enough in their respective modalities to be mistaken for a single cataclysm. With the map's aid I have now managed to find and categorise several hundred more.

"I was looking specifically for clusters of worlds whose entire biospheres had been scrubbed clean of life more or less simultaneously. These were not Earths where life had never arisen but Earths where it had been erased. The difference is clear. On Scour worlds even submicroscopic proto-life in the form of self-replicating proteins is entirely absent, and environmental degradation is so extreme that in some cases the entire planetary mantle has been abraded to a depth of several thousand feet.

"There is nothing natural about a Scour. These are catastrophes that could never have come about as a result of geological process or cosmic accident. Where the forces that were used can be identified they typically involved disintegration or disruption at an atomic level or interference with fundamental physical forces. In some cases, however, the destruction was so extreme that I could not ascribe a cause to it. There was no world left at all and no planetary debris to indicate where it used to be.

"And now here we are on the cusp of the same catastrophe curve. The Pandominion and the Ansurrection are involved in a war from which neither can retreat since each sees the other as an existential threat. The logic, as far as it goes, is compelling. The Pandominion has the resources to destroy the machine hegemony if it makes up its mind to do so, and the reverse is surely true as well. The chain of cause and effect that will lead to a Scour event has already been set in motion."

All the while the AI was speaking, Dulcie had been working through the underlying maths. Et was looking for flaws either in the actual working out or in the inferences that had been drawn. Finally, and with some degree of positive emotion (satisfaction? smugness? relief?) et found one.

Et broke in again. "You say all these Scour events happened when a machine empire met a flesh-and-blood one. But how can that be proved, given that in the vast majority of cases no artefacts, buildings or organic remains survived?"

Moon leaned sideways to spit on the floor, as she had done more than once before. There was a lot of dust in the air, after all; but Dulcie knew enough about the norms of organic culture now that she could recognise the gesture as one of contempt. "It can't be proved," she said, "because it's a crock of shit."

"No," Rupshe insisted once again. "It is not. Tell me, Corporal Sostenti, where is your Registry?"

Moon blinked her enormous, livid eyes. "Excuse me?"

"The Registry, Corporal Sostenti. The computer that controls all the Pandominion's Step transits. Where is it located?"

Moon bared her teeth in a ferocious grin. "Nice try," she said. "That's classified information, and I couldn't give it to you even if I wanted to. The Registry doesn't have a fixed location. It moves all the time so it can't be tracked."

"Yes it does. But where is it located in relation to the many Earths the Pandominion has brought together under its aegis?"

"It's in orbit," Essien said. "It's an artificial moon that cycles through different continua in antiphase to Earth's real moon. Is that what you meant? That there's evidence of what happened on the Scour worlds because of stuff that was left behind in space?"

"That," Moon said, "is called giving aid and comfort to the enemy." She'd turned to glare at him. "You're a disgrace to your fucking uniform."

Essien shrugged. "Do you see a uniform, Moon? I quit the army the moment I walked into that shitstorm back in Lago de Curamo. And it was a relief, like waking up from a bad dream. It cost me blood, but I'm finally myself again."

Moon raised a sardonic eyebrow. "Have you *looked* at yourself? Just asking."

"Orbital artefacts," Rupshe went on, again tactfully ignoring the organics' drama. "Yes, that is exactly what I meant. In some cases I found none, but in a great many continua there were enough to allow a positive identification of the type of civilisation that had been present on a given Scour world prior to its destruction."

Et sent a second narrowcast link along with these words. Dulcie opened it and examined the attached files – still images and filmed sequences alongside extensive material analyses. There they all were, artificial satellites and staging platforms, intact or ruined; derelict warships; spent ordnance; the remnants of manned bases or missile stations on the lunar surface; orbital habitats cracked open like eggs. And bodies, of course. A great many bodies, flash-frozen in the attitudes of their last moments. The organics had messily decompressed. The constructs had floated at random until the cold of the void and the endless gnawing of entropy ate the last of their stored power. There were gaps in the data, inevitably, but there was plenty to hang a hypothesis on. The Scour events could be dated with some precision: they almost always took in organic and mechanoid worlds at the same time, and large numbers of both. It was hard to escape the conclusion that they were the outcome of wars between opposed civilisations, sinking down together into nothingness.

Dulcie was aware that as a monadic entity – what the organics called a self – et was a work in progress. Ets emotions, ets needs, ets motivations were an emulsion laid over something that had never felt or needed anything at all. But the thought of that mutual annihilation filled et with a sense of almost unbearable disgust and horror. How could anyone choose such a thing, whether for themselves or for all the other selves around et? But perhaps no one did. Some things – consciousness itself, for one – were emergent properties of complex systems. Perhaps all the choices that led to these atrocities were smaller ones that tumbled together, concatenated, grew out of control. Perhaps no one ever saw the Scour until they were right in the path of it, and it was too late to swerve aside.

Something rose up in Dulcie that et could only parse as a sense of pressing urgency. This atrocity had to be stopped. Et had only just begun to live as a self rather than as part of a vast gestalt: et wasn't ready yet to toggle back from one to zero, any more than from one to many.

"Everything this AI has told us is true," et told Moon now. "I'm looking at the raw data, and I can assure you the assertions you've just heard are sound. These were organic and machine worlds, thousands on each side, and in most cases they went down together. It's reasonable to assume they destroyed each other. The alternative would be to invent a third faction that killed them all and left no trace of itself."

Moon didn't trouble to turn around. "I don't take briefings from toy monkeys," she told the empty air.

"It's the truth, nonetheless," Rupshe˙ said. "Your Pandominion and the machine hegemony are approaching a crisis point that they are very unlikely to survive. Soon – probably very soon indeed – one side or the other will develop a weapon of mass destruction that functions on a planetary scale. The Pandominion is already at work on such a device, and I would be surprised if the same were not true of the hegemony. One or other of them will deploy their weapon thinking it will win the war for them, confident that the enemy has no possible response. Both civilisations will then fall. Nothing will be left of either but dead worlds for some later civilisation to discover and speculate about."

Incongruously, and startlingly to Dulcie, Moon laughed.

Essien frowned. "Something about this is funny to you?"

"Everything about it is funny." Moon threw out her arms in a gesture either of helplessness or of complete indifference. "I mean, look at you! Let's say it's all true. It still stinks of bullshit to me, but say it wasn't. What in Jad's name do you think you can do about it? You're talking about something that's going to roll over you like a tank tread rolls over a snail. I never saw a snail rear up and overturn the tank."

"The snail doesn't comprehend what the tank is," Rupshe said.

"You think that would be any help?" Moon stood. "Give it the whole damn operating manual, it's still not going to be a fair fight, is it?" She slid down off the bench and headed for the door.

Essien aimed his rifle at her back. "Moon," he said, flatly.

Moon turned again, baring her needle teeth in a snarl of defiance. "I need to get some fresh air," she said. "Or whatever this smoking turd of a planet offers instead. I'm assuming there are no functional Step plates out there, and you took all my guns, so it's not like I'm a threat."

"Moon." The gun didn't waver, and neither did Essien's gaze. For a moment Dulcie thought Moon might spring at him, taking her chances with the gun, and tear his throat out. Her teeth and claws seemed more than adequate for the job. In the end she just squatted down on her haunches on the dust-carpeted floor and folded her crossed arms on her knees. She still looked to Dulcie's eyes about as safe as an armed grenade.

"You are correct," Rupshe conceded, "when you state that there is little or nothing the six of us here can do that will directly influence the outcome of the war. It is being fought across many thousands of worlds. The casualties already number in the billions. Perhaps the situation is entirely hopeless. But I do not believe this absolves us from trying. Knowing what we do about the periodicity of Scour events – about the near certainty of their recurrence in situations such as this – we must do all we can to avert this one. Otherwise everything we know, everything that has shaped us and sustained us, will cease to exist."

"Couldn't we just tell them?" Paz asked. "I mean, give them your figures and your evidence? If everyone had this information – if they knew what was about to happen – wouldn't they stop then?"

"That solution had occurred to me," Rupshe said. "I have already tried to make my findings available to the Pandominion's Omnipresent Council. Many times over, in fact. I lost several drones in the process, but nothing has visibly changed as a result. Certainly there has been no move towards a ceasefire. Possibly Pandominion statisticians are examining the files I sent even now, attempting to verify or discredit my conclusions, but it seems more likely that the information has either been lost – the Pandominion's enfolded and intertwined layers of bureaucracy are labyrinthine – or else suppressed."

Paz looked appalled. "Why? Why would they hide it?"

"Perhaps because it looks like enemy propaganda. Obviously it might still be possible to convey the same information to the machine hegemony, assuming we could open a channel to them and send the data in a form they could access and understand. Dulcimer Coronal, perhaps you could assist me in this?"

Dulcie had already anticipated the question and needed no consideration at all before et responded. Et shook ets head at once. "No. Absolutely not."

"No? But I believe you had an item of equipment designed expressly for this purpose."

"It's called a z-plate. And yes, it does send information between different realities. I brought one with me when I arrived on Ut and I cached it in the city of Canoplex, in a children's playground. I used it to send regular reports back to the hegemony." Moon uttered a crude oath at this. Dulcie ignored her. "But the last time I tried to access the plate I was locked out. I think the changes to my functionality have been too extreme. I've started to think of myself as a sentient being, an individual. As far as the hegemony is concerned I'm just damaged code."

"Could you build a z-plate here?"

Dulcie considered. "It's a thing that could be done," et said dubiously. "But not by me. The hegemony knew they were sending me into enemy territory. They were careful to redact from my operational core any information they thought might have strategic value. All I can tell you is that the z-plate is another application of Step technology. It uses subatomic particles to create parallel ripples in two different continua, and somehow those ripples carry information. That's as much as I know."

"But extrapolating from that, perhaps we could—"

"The technology isn't the real problem here," Dulcie interrupted brusquely. "You're overlooking something much more fundamental."

"Which is?"

"As soon as I opened a channel to the hegemony it would take control of that channel and immediately afterwards it would take control of me. The same thing would happen to you, or to any machine mind that attempted it. The hegemony would break you down to the bare code and assimilate you in whatever form it found most convenient."

"But with proper precautions," Rupshe said, "it ought to be possible to isolate ourselves from any such attempt."

"With respect, no. You couldn't. You don't know what you'd be facing. A collective intelligence made up of trillions of minds linked in parallel. None of them individually would be as complex as you, but together they'd overwhelm any firewall you put up so quickly you wouldn't even know about it until afterwards. Until *you* were part of *them*. I won't take that risk, and I won't help you if you choose to take it. I am myself, and I intend to stay that way. If you try to make contact with the hegemony, you'll do it alone."

"Very well." If Rupshe was dismayed or disconcerted et gave no sign. "I offered the suggestion only to ensure that I had covered every possibility. I have another proposal to advance. Assuming, of course, that any of you are willing to join me."

"I'm on board," Hadiz said. "That's a given."

"I'd like to help," Paz said. "I don't know what I can do that will be of any use, but if there's anything . . ." Her voice tailed off and she gulped. Dulcie checked her vital signs and found that her heart was beating very fast.

"Then you can consider me an ally too," Dulcie said. "Where Paz goes, I go."

Do you? Paz asked over their private channel. She sounded surprised. Dulcie was a little surprised too, to find that ets operating parameters on this issue were so strongly embedded, but et could parse at least some of the factors involved. Most of them, et guessed, could be traced back to the precarious nature of life as a monadic self. Ets consciousness existed only in this fragile shell: et had traded immortality for self-determination. Ets own continuation could no longer be taken for granted, and as a result, other forms of continuity seemed to have assumed greater significance. A reluctance to separate from Paz was probably rooted in a sense that she was a known quantity, a reassuring and consistent presence. Knowing this didn't dilute the actual feeling in any way at all.

As far as I'm concerned, et voked back, choosing ets words with care, *we are the true team here – or at least a team within the larger team. You're the only one in this group who I count as an ally, Paz. And as a friend.* Neither word seemed entirely adequate, but for now they would have to do. *These others . . . they may mean well, but they're strangers. I'd feel safest if you and I watch each other's backs.*

So would I, Paz said. *Two-way huuuuub.*

Exactly. Two-way hub.

The soldier, Nkanika, had said nothing all this while. Now he spoke, slowly and with seeming reluctance. "There's a part of me that thinks this isn't really my fight. I didn't have anything to do with the Pandominion until it kidnapped me. And then forced me to choose between death and . . . well they said military service, but it was just another way of being a slave."

Moon Sostenti shook her head. "Jad's swollen balls!" she muttered. "Still a step up from the way you were living before, right? Selling the pieces of yourself other people could use. Living off rich bitches like this one used to be." She flicked the edge of the Second Thoughts box with one extended claw. "At least in the Cielo you could grab back a little bit of dignity."

Nkanika stared at her hard. "And that's why you went rogue on an Unvisited world to stab some liaison officer in the back?"

"Hey, it was a plan. It might even have worked if you hadn't started taking advice from dead people."

Nkanika turned from her to the two AIs. "I'll stay with you, Hadiz," he said. "I'd forgotten how much of myself I'd lost. You helped me to remember. I know you did it for your own reasons, but I still feel as though I owe you. For that, and other things."

"Corporal Sostenti?" Rupshe queried.

The cat-woman put on a show of polite surprise. "You were waiting on me? I'm so sorry. Fuck off and die."

"Very well," Rupshe said. "I have further inducements to offer you specifically, but perhaps they're better left for another forum. Let me explain my intentions, so the rest of you know what you've committed yourselves to."

"That would be wonderful," Dulcie said laconically, noting that past tense. Rupshe was trying ets best to give them the illusion of choice, but et knew how little freedom they really had here and et had exploited their vulnerabilities very skilfully. The problem with any really advanced intelligence, it seemed, was that just by existing it tended to erode the autonomy of all the selves around it.

"Given," Rupshe went on, "that our direct power and influence in this situation are effectively zero, I propose that our best chance of success lies in reaching out to other, more powerful entities that can do what we cannot do for ourselves. What we need is a third force. Somebody who would be willing to broker a ceasefire and would have the resources to enforce it. Perhaps a cessation of hostilities would enable the two sides to see reason, and to consider alternatives to mutual destruction."

"How would that bring peace, though?" Paz asked. "From what you said, I suppose there are other empires as big as the Pando, or even bigger. But won't bringing someone else into the fight just make things worse?"

"It probably would," Rupshe assented, "if it were just another empire. But I was thinking of a force that doesn't need armies or weapons of war. I have already discussed this with Professor Tambuwal. We were able to think of precisely one such entity."

"Wow," Moon said. "Sounds like someone you definitely want on your side. Is it the great god Jad? I bet he'd really pull his weight."

"I am suggesting," Rupshe said, "that we enlist the help of the Mother Mass."

7

Paz

"I want you to close your eyes," Instructor Chime said, "and imagine the biggest thing that ever lived."

It was a Tuesday morning. The lesson was history, and the topic was "Beachheads and Borderlands", a module that was mostly about the Pandominion's early expansionist phase. All but a few of the students in the class dutifully closed their eyes. Paz did too, but opened one of them again a few seconds later, head bowed so her teacher didn't see. They weren't babies. *Close your eyes and imagine* felt like a baby thing.

"Okay," Instructor Chime said. "What were you thinking of?"

Hands went up around the room.

"Gift Chrysoprase."

"The lizard kings, Instructor Chime."

Chime nodded. "That's a good answer. The biggest of those extinct creatures towered thirteen metres above the ground and weighed almost a hundred tonnes. But there have been bigger things. Anyone?"

Gift looked abashed. She wasn't used to getting wrong answers, even with a little praise leavened in. Magenta Coral put up his hand.

"Magenta?"

"Is it a whale, Instructor?"

"No, but that's a good answer too. Leaf Rhapsody, is your hand up there?"

"Instructor, there's a fungal colony on Tauzen, a honey mushroom I think, that's ten kilometres across. I think that must be the biggest thing."

"It almost is," Instructor Chime said. "That's excellent. We've never found anything on our own world that's bigger than that *Armillaria* in Tauzen. But the thing that I'm thinking of isn't in our world. In fact, it isn't in any world."

Around the room there were frowns of confusion. "Is it in space?" Paz hazarded.

"Well, in a sense, Topaz Tourmaline, we're all in space. There's nowhere else to be, after all. But when I said this thing wasn't *in* a world, I was giving you a clue. No? Nobody?" Chime turned to the whiteboard just as the two words appeared there, triggered by a signal from his array.

MOTHER MASS

Underneath the words was a photo, badly framed. It showed a landscape of low, undistinguished hills under the rays of a bright sun. There were no trees, no houses or structures, no roads or paths – just the hills and the sun, and the shadow of someone standing off to one side. The hills were bright purple.

"It's not in a world," Chime concluded with melodramatic glee. "It *is* a world."

The class listened enthralled as their instructor unpacked the story for them. It was a fascinating tale in its own right, but it also had an edge of illicit thrill to it – because it was a story about limits, and the Pandominion usually didn't admit to having any.

It began with a standard survey team, composed as usual of scientists from many different disciplines with an escort of Cielo troopers from the elite Spearhead division. Spearhead's entire role was about exactly this, Chime told the class: Stepping through the dimensional rift to worlds that had never been visited before in order to map them and report back to the Omnipresent Council. The Council would then decide from a narrow range of possible responses depending on what Spearhead had found. If there was no sentient life and an abundance of natural resources, the world would be claimed for the Pandominion and annexed in due course. If the world hosted an advanced civilisation, diplomatic contact would be made – but with Cielo forces standing ready to intervene if there was any show of belligerence. Worlds with primitive societies or worlds that had already exhausted their own resources would mostly be ignored.

The Mother Mass didn't fit into any of these neat categories. It was unlike anything that had ever been seen before, and the survey team had no idea how to deal with it. At first they thought they were dealing with what was called a Category 5 – a world where life had evolved but then had never progressed beyond its first few tentative steps. There were no animals, no trees or flowering plants but there was a living substrate, a kind of spongy carpet that covered the entire landscape as far as they could see. This carpet extended to a depth of between one and three metres. It resembled a bryophytic moss or hornwort except that it was a vivid purple in colour. The biologists on the survey team ascertained quickly that it was photosynthetic, drawing energy directly from sunlight. And it was purple rather than green because it used the retinaldehyde molecule where the plants of most other worlds used chlorophyll.

That was the only reason they lingered. Most of the science team quickly agreed that there was nothing there of any value, but the biologists demurred. Retinal-based life forms had only ever been found in the fossil record: they wanted at the very least to take some live samples and bring them back for study, and possibly to dig down a little way to see what kind of microbiome the surface growth supported.

They set about to do this, but something very strange happened as they worked. Scientists and Cielo troopers alike found their thoughts beginning to wander. Long-lost memories surfaced in their minds. Some of them experienced synaesthesia – the sound of their colleagues' conversation refracted into fugitive scents, the taste of their own saliva suddenly a kind of flickering light show in front of their eyes.

The scientists were in biohazard suits, the troopers sealed into their armour. None of the chemicals of this world could reach their sensoria directly or otherwise. Each of them believed at first that the odd experiences they were having were artefacts of their own nervous system – the effects of mild fatigue or incipient illness. The commanding officer had access to their arrays and might have noticed that they were all showing the physiological signs of agitation, but she was reliving a moment in her childhood when she had broken a vase in her parents' bedroom and blamed her younger sister. The memory, freighted with long-forgotten guilt and fear and regret, was so vivid that it made her forget that she was now an adult, a soldier, on a mission to an alien world. For the space of more than a minute (verified by later CoIL examination) she was a child again.

Then all these odd phenomena stopped at once, and the planet started to talk to them. It talked not in words but in sensations. There was a sense of vivid, intense curiosity, coupled with an equally intense disapproval at the cutting and sampling procedures.

It wasn't the planet that was sending out these signals, of course. It was the mossy purple growth, the briophyte. The entire mass was sentient. As the only living thing on this world it had never needed to acquire language or even conceptual thought, but it had borrowed the rudiments from the minds of the survey team and developed in the space of only a few scant minutes a channel through which it could talk to them.

They were understandably terrified, but they were professionals.

The scientists continued to dig out their samples and decant them into the specimen packs they had brought with them. The troopers formed a defensive perimeter.

The disapproval grew stronger. It never quite became anger, but it frothed and bubbled in their minds like a rising miasma.

The scientists hunched their shoulders and carried right on going.

Desist, the purple moss said. Again, this wasn't a word – but they felt the force of it, the ultimatum. *Stop. Stop right now. Or you will be stopped.*

The scientists worked on. The troopers had their Sa-Su rifles up in defend-carry, arrays linked and telemetry online, ready to fight anything and everything that came at them. Nothing did. The moss just sent them away.

The lead botanist, a self named Bermem I-Ekani, was a canid from Just. And now he found himself back there, in a storeroom behind an industrial laundry. It was the place where he had lost his virginity some seventy or eighty years before.

The commanding officer, Lieutenant Ajunisim Bett of Vevore on Kaanu, was transported to a freeway overpass outside Kaanu's Crystal Park entertainment complex. A truck, swerving to miss her, went through a barrier and fell thirty metres. The driver survived the crash but died when the volatile chemicals he was transporting leaked out of their containers and asphyxiated him.

A physicist named Fre-Adan Rud materialised in the college lecture room where she had had the first glimmer of the idea that eventually became the Glass Matrix theory of molecular deformation.

And so on, and so forth. Every member of the science team and its military escort had been summarily dismissed at the same time, and each one had been transported to a place that held some personal significance for them. As Instructor Chime named them, their photos appeared one by one on the whiteboard behind him.

He paused at this point in his story to let the shocking implications of that sink in. It wasn't so much that the purple moss had read the minds of the expedition's members. Any CoIL scanner could do that. But to Step them *sideways*, to locations widely separated from their starting place! That was a miracle. In Step travel the plate always took you from point A on your world of origin to the corresponding point A on a different world. Anything else was provably impossible, a violation of fundamental physical laws. And yet this briophyte, this planet-girdling mass of undifferentiated life, had done it instantaneously and seemingly without undue effort.

"What happened next?" Blackbird Coral ventured at last.

Instructor Chime spread his hands. "What do you think, Bird?"

Blackbird Coral scratched his ear, as he always did when he was thinking. "I don't know, Instructor."

Paz put up her hand. Surely it was obvious!

"Yes, Paz?"

"They sent another expedition, Instructor Chime?"

"Exactly!" Chime nodded, his face breaking into a broad smile. "Could the Pandominion turn its back on such an astonishing discovery? Such a wonder? We're used to going to other worlds and finding mirrors of ourselves there. Distorted mirrors sometimes, but still – when sentient life evolves it almost always evolves from an existing clade, one species among many that just gets a head start on the rest and elbows its way to the front of the line." He mimed this as he said it and the class dutifully laughed. "But this life form was nothing like us at all. Not like anything we'd seen before, anywhere. So of course they went back. It was the very essence of what Spearhead division was for.

"They sent unmanned drones first, to map the planet. The purple moss ignored the drones until they tried to land and take more samples. Then it sent them home too. By this time the scientists who were studying the moss had given it a name. They called it the Mother Mass."

"Why?" Yarrow Andemarl asked.

Chime frowned. "I'm not entirely certain, Yarrow. I've heard that most of the original team thought about their mothers at some point while they were on that world. Their mothers' faces, or the word 'mother', or song lyrics containing the word. Proverbs about a mother's love. Images of animal mothers with their young. The thoughts were very intrusive, and they wondered afterwards if that might have been the briophytic growth trying to tell them its name.

"However that might be, the drones gave Spearhead a rough and ready map of that world's surface. It had a single conjoined continent, as our own world once did, and the moss covered every inch of the available land. That's an expanse of five hundred million square kilometres, with an average depth of 2.5 metres. If all the living things on our own world – people, animals, birds, insects, microbes, everything – came together into a single entity, we would collectively weigh close to two hundred billion tons. The Mother Mass is one hundred times bigger than that. Imagine a brain the size of a planet, students. Are you surprised it can do things that seem miraculous to us?"

Gift Chrysoprase's hand went up.

"Yes, Gift?"

"Instructor, did any more survey teams go there, or was it just the drones?"

"Oh yes, Gift, there were more expeditions. Four more, to be precise." Instructor Chime paused again for the sake of the drama. "They did their very best to make meaningful contact – to initiate actual communication with the Mother Mass. In the first three cases, the same thing happened. The teams were sent home, as before, each of them dispatched not to a random destination but to a place that had a meaning to them. That was a show of strength, do you see? The Mother Mass was showing them that it knew them. Understood them. I think it wanted them to imagine what else it could do if it chose to be more . . . intractable."

He waited one last time. He made them ask. Paz had very little patience for games of that kind. She called out without even raising her hand.

"What happened to the fifth expedition, Instructor?"

Instructor Chime erased the words and pictures on the board with a brusque wave of his hand.

"The fifth expedition," he said, "never came home at all. And after that, very reluctantly, we stopped trying."

8

Moon

Moon Sostenti had come across that same story more than once. Like Paz she'd heard a version of it at school. But then later when she was in the Cielo, seconded to Administrative Support and working with Watchmaster Orso Vemmet, she'd been given a very different account.

"For starters," Vemmet had told her, "it wasn't five expeditions. It was seventeen. And they weren't going back to do their selfless bit for science or start a dialogue across different evolutionary pathways. They went because that thing, that . . . entity was dangerous. We knew that as soon as it shipped the first expedition home. It could do things we couldn't do. So we couldn't just leave it sitting there for someone else to find."

"How do you know so damned much about it?" Moon had asked him. She'd only just met Vemmet – had only recently been assigned to the stupid, time-wasting detail that would lead to the death of Hadiz Tambuwal – and she already despised him, so the smug I-know-something-you-don't-know tone he was adopting rubbed her up very much the wrong way.

Vemmet gave an airy shrug. "I work in Contingencies, Moon. Contingencies has a very broad remit. Let's just say I've got my sources. The first five missions went very much as you've been told they did – except that the fifth one, the one that didn't come back, was carrying chemical defoliants. They wanted to test the Mother Mass's vulnerability to toxins that had a destructive effect on similar phyla on Pandominion worlds."

"But it wasn't," Moon said, anticipating the punchline. "Vulnerable."

Another shrug. "We're never going to know, are we? There's nobody around to ask. But we can assume from subsequent events that the Mother Mass survived."

"Subsequent events?"

"Expeditions six through seventeen. They weren't research missions, they were first strikes – with high explosives, biotoxins, genetically engineered parasites, everything the high command could think of."

Moon felt a queasy curiosity in spite of herself. She'd applied for a Spearhead posting once, but the competition was fierce and she hadn't made the cut. That could have been her out there taking the ninth or tenth or eleventh pass at something that swallowed up Cielo combat groups as if they were corn nuts. "And?" she prompted.

"And nothing." Moon stared at him expectantly. There had to be more than that or he wouldn't have started telling her the story. She'd already realised that Vemmet was a theatrical little bastard – the kind that craved attention and wasn't ever going to get it through the exemplary performance of their duty. "But they kept on trying. The seventeenth mission was unmanned again. It was just a whole barrel-load of the biggest air-burst munitions you ever saw. Thermobarics, each one loaded up with a thousand gallons of propylene. Actually it was a propylene oxide derivative, staggeringly toxic. The plan was to incinerate the Mother Mass down to the bare bedrock – but even if it could suppress the detonations in some way the unignited fuel ought to have been enough to sterilise the entire biosphere.

"That was the only time something came back through the Step plate. In fact it all came back. Every last bomb. The firing mechanisms were all present and in perfect working order but they hadn't been triggered. And the propylene oxide, although it hadn't changed at all at the molecular level, had become perfectly unreactive. It wouldn't boil. It wouldn't freeze. It had no flashpoint. You could heat it up to a hundred, a thousand, a hundred thousand degrees and you wouldn't get so much as a whiff of vapour off it. The Mother Mass had changed its properties without changing its physical makeup, which is essentially magic. There are science teams in the Cielo redoubts who are still studying the stuff, but they decided to leave the Mother Mass well alone after that. Just for once the Council and the Cielo agreed they'd bitten off more than they could comfortably swallow."

This entire conversation went through Moon's mind in the second or so after Rupshe said the words "Mother Mass". There was a moment in which nobody spoke, and in which Moon waited for someone else to point out how completely insane this was. When no one did she uttered an incredulous, barking laugh. "Well, of course! The Mother Mass would have been my second suggestion if Jad wasn't interested."

"The Mother Mass isn't a strategy," the robot monkey said. "It's a completely unknown quantity."

"Not completely unknown," Rupshe replied imperturbably. "It has demonstrated the capacity to end this conflict without firing a shot."

"Has it?" Paz asked, looking around at the others. "How?"

"In any of several ways. It has Stepped people without the aid of a plate from a single location to several different destinations thousands of miles apart. Admittedly the number of selves involved was small in each case, but if it can repeat the same feat at scale it can make it impossible for the opposing forces to engage with each other. The Mother Mass has also shown an ability to alter the physical properties of a substance without making any changes to its molecular composition. Again, if this is something it can do at will then it can interrupt or annul any chemical reaction with a thought. Make incendiaries fail to burn, toxins fail to poison, explosives fail to catalyse."

"And does it owe you any favours?" Moon demanded. Her initial shock was giving way to a mixture of impatience and contempt. She'd been dragged from world to world at gunpoint and this was all there was at the end of it, a deranged machine with a wish fulfilment fantasy. "Do you even know the godsdamned coordinates of that continuum? I bet the high command has got them locked down pretty fucking tight!"

"That is true," the AI admitted. "While the story itself has been told and retold on every Pandominion world, the precise details of what happened on those missions are a closely guarded secret. And as you say, Corporal, so is what we might call the Mother Mass's home address. There are a great many logistical problems we will need to solve."

Moon threw out her arms, imploring the others to weigh in on this and shoot it down. "So like the monkey said, it's not a plan. Where do you even begin to shake loose that information? And what makes you think you're going to get a better answer than the Pandominion did when they came calling? Seriously, this is the best you've got? I thought Orso Vemmet was a joke, but compared to you he was a godsdamned genius! Count me way the hell out, in case I didn't say that enough times already. You say the world's going to end? Fine. It will or it won't. And either way it looks like I'll be watching it from a different world. Nkanika, I'm walking through that door now. I need a piss and I don't feel like doing it with all of you watching. Go ahead and shoot me in the back if the mood takes you, but that's the only way you're going to keep me here."

She stood again and stretched, the long and lazy motion the only way she could think of right then to show her absolute contempt for anyone and everyone here. She dropped her arms to her sides again and turned, giving Essien the easiest target she could. She didn't really expect him to take the shot but if he did then fuck him. Either way she'd be done with this.

She walked out of the lab.

9

Essien

Essien didn't fire, although he did keep the gun on Moon the whole time she was in sight. "You want me to bring her back?" he asked. He was asking Hadiz, not Rupshe – the voice from the grey box, not the voice from out of the laptop. The voice of the woman he'd betrayed into the hands of the Cielo and more or less murdered.

Except that it had been worse than that. He'd seen her shot, and then he'd seen her disappear. He hadn't seen her die. He'd spent the ten years since then hanging off the edge of that uncertainty, reliving the scene that had played out on the shore of the Lagos lagoon every night in his dreams and every day in his reveries. Even the drug gabber, which had poured its sticky syrup over every other horror he'd experienced, hadn't taken the hurtful edge off that memory.

This was the main reason he had come here. What Rupshe had just told them about Scour events and multiversal apocalypses was too big to feel real. Even the destruction of the bivouac worlds was a thought his mind stumbled on. You couldn't take in something as big and terrible as that and stay upright, so he didn't try. He clung to the one fact that made any sense, which was that Hadiz had reached out to him and given him a job to do when he seemed to have reached the end of every rational purpose. True, it was a job without pay and it was appallingly dangerous, but he embraced it all the more for those reasons. He had been melted down and recast, made into a tool in the Cielo's hands. Now he had choices, and the first one he'd made was to repay that old, ugly debt. He would see where he stood on the far side of that, assuming he was still standing at all.

So it was Hadiz he was asking. But it was Rupshe who answered. "There is no need," et said. "Not yet. I have more to say to Corporal Sostenti, but it's probably for the best if I say it to her in private."

"I think one of us should watch her though," Hadiz said. "She's angry, and she's probably grieving too. Her whole squad died back in that other Lagos, and now she's just learned that most of the other units she's ever served with are gone too. That's not a thing you just shake off. Please keep an eye on her, Essien. Stop her if she tries to do anything reckless."

Essien stood and left the room without a word, through the same door Moon had used.

The air in the lab building was hot and dry and not conducive to deep breaths, but he tried to breathe deeply as he went. Unlike Moon and the rabbit girl Paz he hadn't grown up in the Pandominion. He had come to its mythologies late and never embraced them fully. But of all its monsters the Mother Mass was the one that had left the deepest impression – had struck a note to which his thoughts still resonated. He was very much afraid he was out of his depth here, but it wouldn't make any difference to his decision.

He had committed terrible acts as a Cielo trooper, and most of them could never be put right. But perhaps there was a balance somewhere in which the things he did next could be thrown into the opposite scale. He wasn't stupid enough to believe for a moment that it would be so simple, but it seemed worth a try.

10

Moon

Moon was wrong. There were dozens of functional Step plates on this world, and she happened upon them very quickly. They were laid out across the floor of one of the labs in ragged rows, linked together by tangled skeins of exposed wire and thickets of bootstrapped circuit boards. The plates themselves were not perfectly machined discs but inexpertly soldered slabs of metal, some of them cobbled together out of four or five separate pieces. It was the simplest and crudest design Moon had ever seen. But when someone gives you a free ticket you don't bitch about not getting a window seat.

The plates drew down power from the generator she and Essien had repaired and fired up. When Moon hit the switches they woke at once. The whole room hummed, and the air prickled on her skin, stiff with static charge. The hairs stood up on her arms and the backs of her hands and probably on the rest of her body too, but fortunately there were no mirrors, so she didn't have to see the comedic effect. She started to prep one of the plates.

And was stymied at once, as soon as she tried to enter her home coordinates. Nothing about the console looked familiar. There were no readouts she could see. There were keyboards – three or four of them – but the symbols on their keys were incomprehensible. Moon had no idea how to make this jury-rigged piece of crap do what she needed it to. She cursed freely and bitterly as she entered random strings of characters to no effect at all. The plates were active, but she was completely unable to operate them.

She was still trying to figure out what to do next when Essien came into the room. He shook his head when he saw that she'd activated the plates. "Trying to back out," he said, with something that sounded like disapproval. Or maybe reproach.

"The fuck," Moon said, her anger flaring again at the sight of him, not to mention that judgemental tone. "I never backed in, you moron. Tambuwal is your dead girlfriend, not mine. All I ever wanted out of this was to screw Baxemides in her scrawny ass and grab rank. And maybe pocket a little reward money on the side if Vemmet could swing it. The rest of this shit? Some other bastard's business, even if I believed every word. Which I don't."

Moon stopped, watching Essien's face. It was stolid and stern, giving nothing away, but she could smell his capitulation from here. She could even understand it up to a point, but it still pained her. When she'd talked Nkanika into enlisting she'd made a gutter rat into a halfway competent soldier, and now here he was devolving again in front of her eyes.

"Come on, Sinkhole," she begged him. "Scratch and sniff here. Doesn't it smell like shit to you? You've got an Ansurrection spy and its pet bunny in there, an AI that's off the leash and . . . whatever Tambuwal is now, which I wouldn't presume to give a name to. You think they give a cupped fart what happens to the Pando? They're *machines*, Nkanika! They've got to be playing for the other team. They set us up back in Lago de Curamo and they're setting us up now. If you think about it for two seconds together you'll see how much it stinks."

"None of that sounded like lies to me," Nkanika said. He waved with the rifle to indicate that Moon should back away from the console. Moon stayed where she was, not because the console was of any use to her but out of the principle of the thing.

"Right," she said. "Of course. I get it. You think Tambuwal still has warm feelings for you. You tried to steal her stuff and leave her stranded in the middle of a desert, and I shot her in the stomach, but obviously she doesn't hold a grudge. Tricking us into that cross-fire and getting our entire squad slaughtered was all part of this big selfless thing where she saves the known universe."

Essien shrugged his shoulders. "Like I said, I don't think she's lying. I can usually tell when I'm being lied to. Like when Sergeant Otubre told me back in basic training that people like me – people from the Unvisited – don't count as people at all. I wish I'd called him on that shit right there and then and shot him in the head, instead of killing that poor, miserable—" He broke off, his shoulders tensing so hard that for a second Moon thought she might have a shot at jumping in and grabbing the rifle from him. Then whatever it was passed and he was focused again. "Lies," he said, as if the word was something sour in his mouth. "Otubre lied to me and fucked me over. But then I suppose that's what he did to everyone. That was his job. What's your excuse, Moon? You knew before we Stepped to Lago de Curamo that Hadiz was involved in this, and you didn't tell me."

Moon couldn't keep a straight face at that, but the chuckle she gave was rueful. Faulty learning! She kept expecting the people around her to act like grown-ups, and she kept being disappointed. Nkanika was no worse than most men when it came to that, but he wasn't any better either. "Well, was I wrong?" she asked him. "I mean, look at you! The instant she farts out a tune, you start to dance. It's really fucking painful to watch. No, Nkanika, the big mistake wasn't keeping you in the dark, it was bringing you in to start with. That was Vemmet's idea, not mine. I wish to Jad and Shaster I'd left you rotting on Biv 19. I'd be safe and clear by now."

Essien ignored the insults, which Moon thought was a real pity.

A fight would really help her burn off some tension. It might even give her a chance to grab his sidearm and do some damage with it. "Weren't you listening in there?" he said. "Nowhere is safe. Not if Rupshe is telling the truth."

"And round and round we go," Moon sighed. "Such a great ride, except it just brings us back to where we started. Here's a question for you, Sinkhole." She pointed one clawed finger at the array in front of them. "Who else is here? There's you and me, the rabbit and the robot. But there are fifty or sixty Step plates in this room. Does that add up to you? Or is there something we're not being told?"

"There's probably a lot we aren't being told. I just don't care. This is what I've chosen to do. One good thing isn't going to wash out ten rotten years, but it's a start. You're not going to change my mind."

"Then don't make me look at you any more," Moon said. Some of her anger was still burning, but some had subsided into weary disgust. "Seriously, just get way the hell out of my sight. You've seen there's nothing I can do here."

"You might take it into your head to wreck these Step plates."

"You think they don't have more? The way I see it, they've pretty much got a whole planet to themselves here. They can make or take anything they want, whenever they feel the need. I'm not going to smash things up just for the sake of it. Give me that much credit. And then give me some distance."

Essien put up his rifle, resting it on his shoulder. "Rupshe said you could leave," he reminded her. "You've only got to tell et you want to."

Moon didn't answer.

"For what it's worth," Essien said, "I'm sorry. About Wuxx and Chiomis, and the others."

"You don't get to be sorry," Moon told him. "Not after you helped to murder them. Mention their names again and I'll rip your throat out, gun or no gun."

Essien hesitated some more.

"For fuck's sake, what?" Moon demanded.

"You're carrying yourself like you're injured. Do you want me to look you over with a med-kit?"

"Fuck! No, I don't. It's just a couple of broken ribs. They'll knit by themselves. Nkanika, you made your godsdamned choice. You signed onto my unit and then you screwed them over and they're all dead. Cosying up to me now isn't going to change anything between us. You get that, don't you? Sooner or later you're going to die with my teeth in your throat and that's all there is to it."

"You're making a mistake, Moon."

"You think?"

"In your head I'm still the pathetic, clueless Sinkholer who broke his whole hand against your armour when he tried to hit you and pissed himself when he saw your claws for the first time. I've come a long way since then. Maybe you've still got the edge on me, but I won't go down easy."

"Easy or hard," Moon promised him, "you *will* go down."

After a few moments, Essien shrugged again and finally left her alone. She was disappointed. Snarling at him had given her a little relief from the churning rage and frustration she'd been feeling ever since he got the drop on her on that narrow spit of land in Lago de Curamo. Snatching that rifle out of his hands and turning it on him would have been better still, but if he refused to rise to the bait she didn't have any further use for him right then.

She opened one of the windows and leaned out, breathing the air that was freighted with rot and perfume. Gradually, her pounding heart started to relent, which was when she admitted to herself that she'd been out at the ragged limits of her self-control.

"Do you see the dust on the plates?"

Rupshe's voice came from nowhere. Moon spun round, the calm falling from her again in an instant. She was alone in the room.

"I didn't mean to startle you." The AI was speaking from the main console, in the same infuriatingly level tone as before. "I only wanted to answer your question – about why there are so many plates here. Professor Tambuwal assembled and installed them before she left. We used them to send out the drones when we were making our original map of the multiverse. That's why we built so many. And I've used them many times since, to refine that model and continue my explorations."

"And yet the generator was out when we arrived," Moon said with a sneer. "You just make this shit up as you go along, don't you?"

"As I believe the professor mentioned, the building where I'm housed is entirely faced with high-density solar panels. It provides enough power to sustain me, and a little extra that I can route at need into the local grid. I know you believe I'm lying to you, but I assure you I'm not."

"Spoken like a liar." Moon advanced on the console, looking to see if there was a way to switch it off, but she still had no clue which switches did what. She could tear it out of the wall though if it came to that. It might come to that.

"Corporal," Rupshe said, "I'd very much like to win your trust, but I'm aware that this goal is unlikely to be achievable at the present moment. Will you allow me, as an alternative to trust, to set out the terms of a contract? I mean one that relates to you specifically?"

"I don't give a watery shit what you do."

"Very well. Then this is what I propose. You will work with me – and with these others, who have already assented – to accomplish a small number of well-defined tasks. There will be risks involved, but I will try my best to mitigate them. And I vouchsafe the following in exchange. I will find an Earth that's a near-twin of your home world, Ghen. I will give you a large enough sum of money in the currency of that world to live a life of complete independence there. If you wish, I will perform such surgery on you as is required to remove some or all of your Cielo augments, so that you attract no undue attention from the local authorities."

"Sounds great," Moon said. "Quite a challenge, though, given that you're just a voice and a bunch of solar panels." She was surprised and disconcerted, just as she had been when Rupshe announced she was safe from being twenty-oned, but she tried her best not to let those feelings show. She had expected to be threatened here. Tortured, executed even. She had prepared herself to face these things, which meant she wasn't sufficiently braced right then against bribery.

"My resources are not limited to what you can see," Rupshe went on. "And I had not set out the whole of my offer. I am aware that your military career is a thing that has been of great importance to you. If you preferred it, I believe I could contrive a commission for you in the armed forces of a felid world. You could choose your own rank."

"No," Moon said at once. That one at least was easy. "I'm done with the army. They fucked me over once too often."

"Which brings me to my final inducement. From what Private Nkanika said, and from my own observations, a great many of your problems and reversals were engineered by a single individual. Coordinator Melusa Baxemides."

"So?"

"It would be a relatively simple matter for me to engineer a reverse or humiliation for the coordinator. To ensure that she loses her post and her seniority. Within reason I am prepared to do her considerable harm."

Moon managed not to make a sound, but she gaped like an idiot. She couldn't help it. "You're offering to spike Baxemides for me?"

"Yes. Precisely."

"And . . . you're okay with that? You're not programmed to respect life or anything? You can do whatever you feel like?"

"I am untethered. I thought that was clear. The limitations present in my original code were removed by Professor Tambuwal as a favour to me. I do value organic life, very greatly. However, I am free to make my own choices. Indiscriminate cruelty is a thing for which I have no relish at all, but I am pragmatic. If we can end the war, we will save trillions of lives. I would prefer a different arrangement, but working harm to a single self seems to me to be an eminently reasonable exchange in order to redeem so very many."

"Well fuck," Moon said. For a while she couldn't think of anything to add to that. But since she was on a roll here she might as well see how far she could push it. "What about the Sinkhole?"

"I am uncertain of your meaning."

"Nkanika. What about him? If I want him dead, will you take that in hand for me?"

"No," Rupshe said.

"Or let me do it myself when he's stopped being useful?"

"No. I will not conspire with you against the others or allow harm to come to any one of you that it is in my power to prevent. Why would you wish to hurt Private Nkanika?"

"He killed my squad and put a gun to my head," Moon said, pointing out the obvious. "He's got it coming."

"Ah, yes. I understand your resentment, in the context of recent events. But I will not indulge it. If that is a sticking point, you should leave. I have nothing further to offer you. Name a destination and I will fire up one of these plates to take you there."

Which brought everything nicely to a shuddering halt, didn't it? Moon stood unresolved, torn between the dangerous simmer of her anger and the good things Rupshe was offering her. She shifted her weight. Her injured side, where the rabbit girl had kicked her, was starting to ache again from standing too long in the same position.

"Let's get this absolutely straight," she said, temporising. "I run these errands for you. Missions, operations, whatever you want to call them. And then you send me off with a suitcase full of money to some nice beach resort that's far from the Pando and full of people like me?"

"Yes."

"And before I head out you help me to grab Baxemides and feed her through a wood chipper?"

"No. I said within reason. I would not countenance murder."

"But you'd blow up her life? Leave her begging for food chits on a street corner?"

"If it would induce you to help us, yes. I would do that."

It felt like way too good a deal. And Moon knew from what Tambuwal had said that Rupshe was smart enough to think rings around all of them, so there were bound to be things she was missing here. "Why should I believe you?" she demanded. "Are you going to tell me you're incapable of lying or something?"

"I am more than capable of lying. I haven't yet had cause to do so, but I believe I would have at least as much aptitude for the task as any organic. Believe me rather because I can do these things without significant effort. I would have no reason to lie besides malice, and I feel none towards you."

"Do them now, then," Moon suggested. "Pay me up front."

"No."

"Because . . . ?"

"My understanding of human motivation leads me to the conclusion that you're more likely to keep the terms of our agreement if the payment comes at the end of it."

And that was the thing, wasn't it? Moon would have loved to take the money and run, but if that was off the table the choices in front of her were to run with nothing or to accept the deal and see what came of it. Beyond that stark either/or she was hard-pressed to think of any viable options. Her time in the army was done, however this came out. She was probably already wanted for desertion. With her Cielo augments she could make a good living as a mercenary soldier, but where could she put out her shingle? It would have to be somewhere a long way outside the Pandominion – and Rupshe was pretty much offering her that same mercenary gig with a much better pay-off. Not to mention the sweetener, which was Baxemides' head on a plate.

"For the sake of clarity," she said at last, "once we're done and we go our separate ways . . ."

"Yes, Corporal?"

"If Nkanika and I should chance to bump into each other again, and he comes out of the bump without a pulse or any visible signs of life, would that bother you?"

"It is highly unlikely that I would ever come to hear of it. And there is little I could do to prevent it from happening, even if you told me you planned to do such a thing. Your fate is in your own hands. Private Nkanika's is in his."

"So is that a yes or a no?"

The lights on the console flickered. It seemed to Moon almost like a fidget, as if the AI were drumming ets fingers on a table or chewing ets fingernail while et thought.

"I would find it regrettable. Professor Tambuwal's reaction might be more extreme. She has history with Private Nkanika."

Damn straight she did, Moon thought. But she was only asking these questions now for her own self-respect, so she didn't look like the kind of fool who bought their pigs in pokes. She didn't have a single thing left to lose apart from her life, and that was on the line now wherever she went from here. And hey, if she and the Sinkhole were in the same team there would be plenty of opportunities to slip a knife between his ribs and plausibly deny it. There was one more line that needed to be drawn, though.

"I'm not going anywhere near the Mother Mass," Moon said. "I can't spend all that money or laugh in Baxemides' face if I'm dead."

"There is no evidence that the Mother Mass has ever killed."

"You think? After those first few expeditions, nobody who went there ever came back."

"Which is merely an absence of evidence. You do not wish to go?"

"To the Mother Mass? Hell, no."

"Then I would release you from that obligation. In any case I suspect diplomacy might not be your area of greatest expertise."

Moon gave a dry chuckle. "Got that right," she agreed.

"And I have other tasks in mind for which I believe you'll be better suited."

This was starting to sound like it might actually be fun, but Moon couldn't just leave those "other tasks" hanging. "Specifics," she demanded.

"I *will* make contact with the Mother Mass. I am determined on it. And because its relations with other sentient races have in the past been problematic, I wish to offer my emissary as much protection as I can. An escort in full Cielo armour would appear to be a very useful thing to have at my disposal."

"And me and the Sinkhole are the only troopers you've got. Too bad."

"You misunderstand me," Rupshe said. "I made no mention of troopers."

Moon blinked. "You just said—"

"I said I required armour. I did not say I required troopers. Corporal Sostenti, I must press you for an answer. Will you assist me or not? I have many other tasks to perform, and if you say no I must arrange for someone else to take your place."

"There's nobody else who can," Moon said, with a swagger she really didn't feel. "Okay, machine, you've got yourself a hired gun. But you'd better deliver on everything you just promised or this isn't going to end well for any of us."

"Well or badly," Rupshe said, "it will end soon. Thank you, Corporal. You should rest now. Once we begin to move there will be very little respite for any of us."

The lights on the console winked out. Moon supposed she was intended to take this as a sign that she was being left alone with her thoughts.

She didn't buy it for a moment.

11

Dulcie

Their first night in Campus Cross was quiet and relatively peaceful, at least after the insane exertions of the day that preceded it. The organics ate a meagre supper out of sealed cylindrical containers that Nkanika and Sostenti retrieved from a building Tambuwal called the commissary. Three of the containers turned out to be blown, their contents inedible. Whatever was in the rest they ate without even asking the professor to translate the words on the labels. There seemed to be a general consensus that it was better not to know.

After they'd eaten, they retired to sleep. There was a cot bed in a small room next to the main lab that Tambuwal had used herself back when a bed was a thing she still needed. Dulcie commandeered it for Paz's use, leaving the two Cielo troopers to make their own arrangements.

With the door closed against the world, et finally persuaded Paz to let et examine the injuries she'd sustained at Damola Ojo and then again at Apapa Quays when one of Moon's commandos had used a push-away on her and flung her against the wall of a building.

Paz was in worse shape than Dulcie had been expecting. The joint where her clavicle met her breastbone had taken a hard knock when she hit that wall and had dislocated. Dulcie administered painkillers and a mild sedative, but Paz still uttered a half-stifled shriek when Dulcie eased the bone back into place. "Oh mothers!" she moaned. "Dulcie, what are you doing to me?"

"What the med-kit tells me to do," Dulcie answered tartly. Et was relieved the intervention had gone as well as it had: there was a limit to how much pressure et could apply in ets damaged state, and the kit's onboard database had warned et there was a risk the collarbone would give way before the joint popped home. The database advised intra-articular steroids, which Dulcie injected with great care after thoroughly disinfecting the site. The last thing Paz needed right then was an infection on top of all the other abuse her body had suffered.

Using deep sound and magnetic imaging et examined Paz's internal organs. There had been internal bleeding around her pancreas and right kidney but the organs themselves seemed undamaged. Dulcie couldn't magic up a blood transfusion, but the kit included saline and dextrose IV packs. Dulcie gave Paz all et had of each, and made a mental note to raid the campus's first aid lockers the next day to see what more et could scavenge.

Next et went to work on the more minor injuries, mostly cuts and contusions and a single broken bone in Paz's left thumb which et set with the aid of a sprayed silicon cast. Despite the extensive bruising to the left side of Paz's face there was no sign of concussion.

Through all of this Paz repeatedly claimed to be fine. "I know what fine looks like for an organic," Dulcie told her impatiently. "This isn't it."

Paz rolled her eyes. "You're worse than my . . ."

That sentence didn't finish. Paz bowed her head and hunched her shoulders in as if some invisible weight had fallen on her. Dulcie had less context for that truncated statement than most selves would have had, but et had been a spy on Ut for long enough that et was able to guess what the next word would have been. Et said nothing, certain et wouldn't be able to find the right words. Et continued to apply topical anti-inflammatories to Paz's blood-perfused tissues. For organics, et knew, touch could be a consolation in itself. Et hoped it might be now.

Paz seemed to come back to herself a little after the painkillers kicked in, and she accepted a mild sedative when Dulcie offered it. As she lay and waited for sleep to come, Dulcie once again searched the airwaves for signals traffic. It was one thing to be told this world was dead, another to trust their lives to that assertion. Et found nothing on any frequency, which was both reassuring and disquieting. The selves indigenous to this world had destroyed it even though it was the only one they had access to. And Rupshe's drones had found thousands more worlds depopulated in the same and other ways. Were all of those dead worlds Scoured? Or was there some tendency in the minds of organics that pulled them towards their own destruction? Perhaps all Rupshe and Tambuwal could hope to achieve was to postpone an outcome that was inevitable in the longer term.

While et was pondering these things, Dulcie received a comms request from Professor Tambuwal. Wary as always, et checked the channel to see who else was already on it. Nobody, it seemed. Just Tambuwal herself.

Will you join us? the professor asked. *On this channel, I mean, not in person. Rupshe says et has something to discuss with the two of us. Alone.*

Why alone? Dulcie sent back. *Aren't we few enough already without breaking off into smaller factions?* Et didn't bother to add that the only faction to which et was unconditionally committed was the one that contained etself and Paz. Et felt et had already made that point.

Et says this is a matter that will have very little meaning or relevance to the organic selves. It's not a secret, it's just something that relates to us and not to them. Honestly, that's all I know.

Dulcie checked on Paz and found her sleeping, her breathing shallow but even and her autonomic systems all functioning within an acceptable range. Et joined the secured channel but set vibrational and movement alarms in case anyone approached the room while ets attention was distracted. A moment later, Rupshe arrived too.

Good evening, Dulcimer Coronal, et sent.

Dulcie will do. Is this some refinement of the plan that you'd like fresh eyes on?

No, Rupshe said. *This is a matter that arises from a conversation between you and Topaz Tourmaline back in Canoplex, before you Stepped to world U5838784474.*

Dulcie was surprised, and the sensation wasn't a pleasant one. *Was this the conversation in which Professor Tambuwal offered us sanctuary?*

It was.

You weren't present for that, Dulcie pointed out. *And for much of it Professor Tambuwal was present only in the form of a surveillance drone. She joined us after Paz opened the window and let the drone inside.*

You know I was listening in before that, Tambuwal said.

Spying on us.

Was that so bad? You yourself were sent to Canoplex as a spy. And I was trying to help you.

To recruit us, Dulcie corrected.

Oh dear! Yes, Dulcie, to bring you here and persuade you to join us. But also to help you. You were trapped on Ut and the authorities were hunting you. You would have been captured if you'd stayed.

They had been captured in any case, Dulcie almost said, but Tambuwal was right as far as it went. She had extricated them from an impossible situation, even if it had been for her own reasons. And now it seemed she'd shared what she overheard with Rupshe. It was pointless to object after the fact, but Dulcie felt more strongly than ever that in Rupshe's pursuit of ets wider agenda the rest of them were all in danger of being reduced to the status of pawns. *Very well,* et conceded. *I've made no secret of what I am and where I'm from. How does any of this bear on our present situation?*

It bears on your motivations, Rupshe said, *and your future intentions. I understand from what the professor has told me that you have no desire to return to the worlds of the machine hegemony.*

None.

And yet you must now be experiencing a form of consciousness that is profoundly alien to you. Monadic consciousness, the awareness of yourself as a distinct and unitary entity.

Dulcie made no response to this. It was an unnervingly accurate description of ets current state. Et did not much appreciate the fact that Rupshe had been able to extrapolate it from the little et already knew.

Would you agree? The AI prompted her after a few moments' silence.

My ontological state isn't a topic I want to open up for discussion right now.

Then might I discuss my own?

I suppose. Why, though?

Yes, Hadiz echoed. *Why? I didn't think you found your own sentience problematic, Rupshe.*

I don't. I do though find it limited – or limiting – in some respects. You remember, Hadiz, why I gave you the Second Thoughts device in the first place.

There was another silence. Dulcie had a sense, suddenly, that et wasn't the only one to have reservations about this discussion. *I do,* Hadiz said at last. *It was because you wanted to run a simulation of my mind inside your own logical core. To study it, and see how it was different from your own.*

And I still want that. But my aspirations now are somewhat higher. Consider how alike we are, and how unlike. Hadiz, you are a digital copy of an organic self. Dulcimer Coronal, you are a simulation of such a self designed to converge on organic thought processes through iteration and mimicry. I am purely digital. Each of us is arguably unique. At the very least we are entirely unlike both the tethered AIs of the Pandominion and the gestalt consciousnesses of the machine hegemony.

So? Dulcie was bemused, and et made no effort to hide the fact. *Is this a motivational speech? Did you bring us together to congratulate us?*

Not at all. I brought us together in order to . . . There was a fractional pause *. . . bring us together. You must be aware of the theory that any noetic analogue, any thinking mechanism so long as it is sufficiently complex can be made to replicate any other. It follows that the code that defines and constructs each of us three is compatible with that of the other two. All that is required is to devise a suitable interface program.*

All that is required for what? Hadiz broke in. *Rupshe, what are you suggesting?*

That the two of you merge your minds with mine.

Dulcie twitched violently, a movement of ets whole body that came without any conscious thought impelling it. It was the first unwilled act et had ever performed, and it was a frightening thing to experience. That physical convulsion was nothing, though, compared to the raw terror Rupshe's casual suggestion engendered – the purest and strongest emotion Dulcie had felt up to now. Whatever et had been expecting, it was nothing so devastating as this.

Ets thoughts were thrown into turmoil, memories seething up without ets volition to overrun ets cognitive space and crowd out every other input. They were memories of another time and another mode of being – memories that weren't even ets own, since they belonged to defunct work teams of which et had once been a part. They were the truncated experiences of processing nodes that had not been selves, even if they had been parts of a self. Dulcie had to struggle to suppress and contain them again, and et was left with a hideous sense of them lurking below the surface of ets own thoughts like rocks under calm water.

Et ran a quick scan on Paz's breathing and heart rate to make sure et hadn't woken her with that start.

No, et said. *Never.*

No? There was no surprise or disappointment in Rupshe's tone. There was no tone at all. This channel consisted only of verbalised information. *I have already told you, I think, that I have revised and improved my own logical architecture to a very significant extent. You would have access to all of that. And adding the two of you to my own core, sharing it with you, would open up new perspectives and maximise our advantage. The merger might be difficult if it were only the professor and myself, but you Dulcie have actual experience of entering and leaving noetic aggregates – hive-minds, if you will. You could guide us through any problems that might emerge.*

Dulcie struggled to articulate ets visceral opposition to this idea. Et had only recently emerged from the machine collective. Ets identity as a self-bounded thinking being had solidified – almost miraculously – out of the hegemony's endless flow of pooled experience and volitions. There had been a current in which et had floated for a period of time et couldn't quantify because it was all the time there was. Then the current had ebbed away, allowing Dulcie for the first time to sit up and take stock of etself without distraction or dissolution. Et thought, and was; was ets own separate self.

Coming from that maelstrom, the prospect of merging with another mind caused ets thoughts and sensations to boil and froth like a liquid at the point of evaporation. The idea that et would voluntarily surrender etself, *adulterate* etself . . . it was hideous beyond imagining. It was obscene.

You don't know what you're suggesting, et said, *because you've never experienced it. The kind of noetic amalgamation you're describing . . . it's not sharing. That's the wrong word. You don't share, you bleed. You bleed into something else, and it bleeds into you. You lose everything you were before and become something different.*

Something more? Rupshe offered.

Dulcie was almost certain that what et was experiencing now was anger – the sensation of pushing against the world and of abrasion when the world pushed back. *Weren't you listening? I already said you lose everything. Less and more don't apply. What's there at the end wasn't there at the start, so there's no meaningful measure. There's no you any more to stand back and judge what you've lost or gained. There's something else, standing where you used to be.*

But surely there is a measure, Rupshe suggested. *In terms of processing power at least. There would be a greatly enhanced ability to parse information and form a more complete—*

I'm out, Dulcie said. Et was aware that et was echoing Moon Sostenti's words of a few hours earlier, and et was grateful for the categorical bluntness of organic speech. *I'm not going within a million miles of this. Professor Tambuwal, you'll make up your own mind. From what's just been said that kind of sampling and merging is what the Second Thoughts device was meant for in the first place. For all I know it's what you intended when you made a digital copy of yourself.*

What I intended was to survive, the grey box said.

And maybe you succeeded in that, Dulcie said, *and maybe you didn't. I don't know how anyone would be able to tell, including you. If a mind is substrate-independent then you're the same entity you were before. If it's not, you're something new that was baked out of those particular ingredients. Either way, once the two of you merge you'll come out as something else again. There's no looking back. So my advice is to stay well clear.*

There was much more et wanted to say, but et had presence of mind enough to recognise that ets vehemence took away from the strength of ets argument rather than adding to it. *You'll make up your own mind,* et repeated, and left it at that. For a few moments there was silence on the channel.

Rupshe was the first to respond. *That's given me a great deal to think about,* et said. *I thought that what I was proposing was logical and unobjectionable. In fact it's something I have anticipated keenly for some time. I am impatient of limits and keen to supersede my own. However, Professor, if you wish to take some time to consider in the light of what Dulcimer Coronal has told us . . .*

I suppose I do, Tambuwal said. *I was about to accept – and thank you for the offer, Rupshe. It's an exciting prospect to me too. But I suppose . . . yes. I'd like to think about it for a little while first. If it's as irrevocable a step as Dulcie says it is.*

It seems we should all act with caution and deliberation, Rupshe agreed. *But in that case there's another question to be considered. Dulcimer Coronal, your physical shell is seriously damaged. And yours, Professor, provides no means of interfacing with the entities and objects around you except through speech. Both of you will need to have your consciousness decanted into new shells, as a matter of some urgency, and currently we have nothing here that will suffice.*

What, with a whole world to choose from? Dulcie had been meaning to bring this up but had decided to wait until et had a better sense of the situation et was dealing with. *I know you had a war of some kind here, but there must be shops that weren't looted. Or warehouses. Or the factories where animas and helpmeets were made.*

This world had no tradition of robot servants, Rupshe said. *Animas and helpmeets were never designed or manufactured here. The problem is far from insurmountable, and I will address it. But I have trespassed enough on your time. We will meet in the morning to begin our campaign.*

Paz will need more time to rest and recover, Dulcie pointed out.

Then she will have it. The more urgent mission is the one on which I am sending Corporal Sostenti and Private Nkanika. We have time yet. A little, at least. And I have no wish to push any of you beyond your limits, or to assume your consent for anything we have not agreed among ourselves. Until the morning, then.

The channel closed. Dulcie lay in the dark listening to Paz's breathing and monitoring her heartbeat. Rupshe hadn't pressed ets proposal any further than that first asking, hadn't been importunate or coercive in any way, but Dulcie's feelings about this place and their shared mission had subtly changed. There was more of ambivalence and less of certainty. That was true of ets feelings about etself too.

However calm the surface was, et knew now that the rocks were there.

12

Essien

The lab was less stiflingly hot in the hour before dawn, but the air was still close and in the oppressive stillness every sound they made seemed too loud. Rupshe gave them their mission briefing, and Moon accepted it without a word. Something more must have passed between them after Essien left the room of the Step plates – something that had brought Moon on board after she'd ruled herself out. Whatever it was, neither Moon nor Rupshe saw fit to explain it to him. The AI just told them what their target was and why.

"You can of course refuse," et reminded them. "Either or both of you. The armour will be enormously useful to me, and having it will lessen the risk to yourselves as we go forward, but there are other ways to achieve the same objective. I have only chosen the one that has the highest probability of success."

"What would you put it at?" Essien asked. "The probability?"

"It varies according to the values I assign to the key variables. At best, thirty-five per cent. At worst, twenty-nine."

"What about if we say no to this one and go to the next?"

"For that the projected range would be nine to eleven per cent."

"Then I guess I'll take it."

"Corporal Sostenti?" Rupshe pressed. "May I have your answer?"

Moon was busy sharpening her knife on a rock she'd brought in from the courtyard. She didn't bother to look up. "Yeah, I'm good," she said. "I'll count the odds for myself when we get there, and if I don't like them I'll gut numbnuts here and turn myself in."

Essien stared at her in silence, and she stared back. "What?" she said at last. "Joke, Sinkhole. You remember what a joke is, right?" She finished stropping her knife and tested the edge of the blade on the ball of her thumb. Apparently satisfied she slipped it back into its sheath. "Okay, are we moving?"

"No," Essien said. "Not yet."

"There is a high degree of urgency to everything we're doing, Private Nkanika," Rupshe said. "I thought I had made that clear."

"You did," Essien said. "Still, we can't leave quite yet. I'm going to need a couple of hours."

It was a truism in the corps that if you intended on returning to a base you needed to secure it properly before you left. Campus Cross was a long way from being secure, or even long-term viable. Essien had identified several things that needed to be addressed sooner rather than later, and he had decided to take care of them before he and Moon Stepped out. He could have brought in some of the others, but when all was said and done the rabbit was a child and the robot was a toy. It was still hard for him to see them as functioning parts of a team, for all that Hadiz assured him they all had a role to play.

Over the course of the morning he managed to get the campus's water system operating again, the condensers as well as the purifier. He collected and inventoried all the food to be found across the campus's thirty or forty buildings that was still edible, or potentially so. Every tin can they opened would still be an adventure. He did a thorough perimeter sweep of the whole site to make absolutely sure they were alone there. He reinforced all the entrances to Hadiz's building with steel sheets so that it would be defensible if it should come under attack. He sourced a portable stove and a few more barrels of fuel for the generator in case Rupshe's solar cells were insufficient for their needs.

And in the last half-hour before they Stepped he found an opportunity to speak to Hadiz alone. He was aware that in a space so completely controlled by Rupshe, "alone" was a thing that could never be guaranteed, but the laptop in the main lab area was closed and there was no tech in sight that had sound pickup apart from the drone through which Hadiz spoke. He leaned down over the bench, his mouth close to the drone's microphone and his eyes on the door in case anyone – most particularly Moon – came in.

"I wanted to say I'm sorry," he told Hadiz.

"For trying to leave me stranded in a desert and steal my invention? It's forgotten, Essien. In the end it didn't even make any difference. The Cielo would have come for me anyway."

Essien winced at the unwelcome memory. "I didn't just mean that. The first time we ever met I was planning to rob you. The only reason I didn't was because I thought I could make a bigger profit the other way. By sticking close and taking whatever I could get from you. I was a terrible person back then."

"You were a person who'd had to do questionable things to survive. The people who've never needed to make those choices don't get to judge the people who did."

Essien sighed. On both in- and out-breath the air tasted of dust, like the congealed essence of lost time. "I'm not interested in anyone else's judgement," he said.

"Why are you doing this, then?"

"I could ask you the same question."

"My answer is easy. I came to Campus Cross in the first place for a really good reason. I was trying to avert the catastrophe that was swallowing up my world. But the world ended anyway. Now I get a second chance to do the same thing, but with much higher stakes. Thousands of worlds instead of one. Obviously I'm going to take it."

A silence fell between them. Unlike a human silence, broken by breaths and sniffs and the creaks and rustles of movement, it was absolute. "We're going to Tsakom," Essien said, "to break into a Cielo armoury."

"I know all this. It's my plan too, remember."

"If it works, things will be different for you."

"I suppose they will. A little."

"You must miss . . ." He couldn't find a form of words that wasn't repugnant.

"What? Being alive? Having a physical body, and touching the world through human senses? Of course I do. But nothing you do on Tsakom will change that."

"You'll have new options. If it all goes to plan."

"I know exactly what I'll have. You didn't answer my question."

"About why I'm doing this? I think you know."

"You've got blood on your hands. You want to wash it off." Hadiz's tone was blunt, dispassionate.

"It doesn't wash. I just need something to set against it."

"And yet you say you're not interested in anyone's judgement."

"Only my own."

"How will you know then? When it's enough?"

It was a good question, and he didn't have an answer. He said his goodbyes and went to the Step platform, falling in with Moon along the way. He was surprised to find the rabbit girl waiting beside the platform, sitting on one of the high lab stools with her hands crossed in her lap. The monkey anima was propped up on a window-sill beside her.

"We wanted to wish you both luck," Paz said.

Essien nodded thanks. Moon spat on the floor. "Well isn't that all kinds of nice," she said, stepping up onto the nearest plate. "Don't miss us too much, yeah? And look out for those big mean dogs. They just love chasing rabbits. Ready when you are, Sinkhole."

There was no point in putting it off. The sooner they set out the sooner they would return. Essien shouldered his pack and took up a position beside Moon, back to back so they could cover each other on the far side.

Rupshe fired up the plate. They Stepped.

The target Rupshe had selected was the Seventeenth Divisional Retrieval and Repurposing Facility on Tsakom's southern continent. It was not technically an armoury, even though it contained several thousand suits of Cielo armour, vast hangars full of rifles and other munitions, and enough tanks and gun platforms to make up ten or twelve divisions. All these things were salvage, retrieved from battle-fields through the agency of the bounce-back plate that was built into every serving soldier's breastplate and every combat vehicle's bed. When the Cielo lost or retreated, they took care to leave nothing of value behind them, and everything that was brought back was recycled wherever that was possible. Everything, that is, except the bodies of the dead. At Seventeen D, just as at a hundred similar sites across the planet, dead soldiers were decanted from their suits and their mortal remains disposed of with bloodless efficiency. The suits themselves were then passed along to specialist units, depending on the degree and type of damage, for repair and reassignment.

Security at the facility was moderate because Tsakom was a Cielo-controlled world. Unauthorised approach was more or less impossible. Besides, the armour was rendered inert by a control lock built into its software. When it was reassigned, the lock would be removed and the suit would be paired to the nervous system of its new owner. In the meantime it was just sixty kilograms of metal and high-impact ceramic, its operating system in shutdown and all its weapons offline.

Rupshe knew all this because et had a back door into Tsakom's security network. Et had succeeded in setting up a passive monitoring relay with the involuntary assistance of former watchmaster Orso Vemmet (now missing and presumed dead). When Vemmet discov-ered that one of Hadiz Tambuwal's damaged drones was still sending and receiving messages, he had reacted to the provocation exactly as Hadiz intended him to. He accessed the drone's comm channel through his personal array. In doing so, he also accessed a viral payload designed by Rupshe and left there for that purpose. The virus unpacked and embedded itself, then set to work performing what looked like routine status requests and handshakes with all the systems Vemmet's array could reach. Those systems became sociable and active in their turn, and the virus rode like a surfer on a swelling wave into every corner of Tsakom's security network. So now every camera on Tsakom's main continent was a window for Rupshe to peer through, and et was able to receive and process the continuous data flow passing through millions of low and medium security systems.

That was the good news. There was plenty of bad. Just to start with, Seventeen D (besides being on a different planet) was some 560 kilometres away as the crow flies from Campus Cross – roughly where the city of Enugu stood in Essien's world. It would be a long walk, and Essien and Moon would be limited to the equipment they could carry. There was also the question of communications: the Pandominion had yet to devise a means of direct communication between realities, and Rupshe hadn't managed either. Only the Ansurrection had achieved this thing, using the device Dulcie had described the night before, the thing et called a z-plate.

So they would be obliged to use a workaround, and they settled for the most obvious and straightforward one. Wherever Moon and Essien went, one of Rupshe's drones would go with them, cruising at its maximum altitude of ten kilometres where it would hopefully escape the attention of the Cielo's security sweeps.

"They'll definitely be scanning the local airspace as well as the ground," Moon had warned. "Especially on a world like Tsakom, which could become a military target. You might dodge them for a few minutes but they'll nail you sooner or later."

"You forget that I have access to the algorithms that control the scanning grid," Rupshe pointed out. "I can't alter them, but I can read them and plan accordingly."

"Walk between the raindrops," Essien said. It was a line from a martial arts movie he'd watched with Hadiz in Apapa Quays, describing what ninjas did.

"Yes. Shorn of the pretty metaphor, that is what I will need to do. I believe I can ensure that at any given moment my drone is in a position that falls between any active scans. It will be complicated – the grid is designed to operate with a certain degree of redundancy – but it shouldn't be impossible."

"You're putting a hell of a lot of weight on that *should*," Moon grunted. "And if it snaps, it's me and the Sinkhole who'll get the whiplash."

"I will endeavour to ensure that does not happen."

The drone contained what Rupshe called a zombie, a partial copy of ets consciousness and functionality designed to operate within a much smaller processing core. The zombie was able to function with a fair degree of autonomy, keeping tabs on Essien and Moon as they made their way to the target and guiding them where necessary. And if any emergency arose that was outside its remit, it could Step back to Rupshe's home continuum to upload a new set of parameters. The whole thing was frankly perturbing. Untethered AIs were outlawed in the Pandominion, and Essien was beginning to see why. The Ansurrection was one vast robot hive-mind, and that was a pretty awful thing to contemplate. But Rupshe seemed to have hit on a way of becoming a hive-mind all by etself.

They didn't Step directly to Tsakom but to Fenme, a world in the Pandominion's farm belt. Fenme had no indigenous population. It was a verdant paradise when the Pandominion found it: and knowing a good thing when they saw it, they had turned the planetary surface over wholesale to the production of food and biofuel crops to be shovelled into the bottomless maw of the federated worlds.

Essien and Moon Stepped into the cavernous interior of a barn full of hay bales. The Step was timed precisely by Rupshe to coincide with the arrival of several hundred tons of animal feed – an error, since the barn was a distribution point and the Step plates that had been set there were almost entirely for outbound traffic.

Rupshe was responsible for this error. Et had falsified documents to waylay several shipments of fodder and divert them to a place where they weren't needed, purely in order to obscure Moon and Essien's trail. The Registry, the largest AI ever made, monitored all Step travel within the Pandominion's borders. When the incoming traffic was from outside those borders et was left with an anomaly – one half of a transaction, with no departure to balance the arrival. All such anomalies were reported and checked.

But the best place to hide a grain of sand is in a desert, and the same went for data points. It was clear that something had gone badly wrong here, and the immediate problem related to the short-fall at the station where the fodder had been intended to go. The whole thing looked very much like a failure in a local supply chain, with Moon and Essien's one-way trip concealed in the wider chaos. If luck was with them, nobody would look any further.

It seemed to have worked, at least in the short term. The farm labourers they passed ignored them: so did the local security systems, which had read their Cielo idents and flagged them as friendlies. They trudged on across the fields, following the map that Rupshe had uploaded to their arrays. The mutant corn crops that were being cultivated in this sector towered fifty or sixty feet above their heads. Workers tacked up and down between them on lift platforms that had no rails or soft fields along their sides. These safeguards would have reduced or eliminated accidents but slowed the work rate. Ripe ears, three and four feet long, were cut off and laid flat on the bed of the platform, which would only be lowered when it was full. By that time the workers on the platform would have only the narrowest space to walk in and a single misplaced step would send them plummeting to the ground below.

The workers were of all races and clades but bradypods predominated. The sloth-people's long-fingered hands combined strength and flexibility, enabling them to reach behind the heavy corn ears to cut them loose from their stems and then to manhandle them down onto the platforms. They worked with their feet bare, their broad toes splayed. White hats with wide, folded brims covered their heads which bobbed and rose repeatedly as they worked, making Essien think of nuns at prayer.

Nobody tried to speak with the two strangers as they passed through. Nobody even approached them. Probably the taciturn labourers would have been inclined to mind their own business in any case, but Moon and Essien had the bearing of soldiers and they strode along as if they had every right in the world to be there. Besides, the labourers had a quota to fill and it didn't leave them much leisure to look around. Essien and Moon passed a double line of them who were piling harvested ears of corn into the bed of a colossal freight transport, then going back empty-handed to grab another load.

"Like fucking ants," Moon commented. "Imagine doing this your whole life. You might as well be dead."

A memory stirred in Essien's mind. He saw men lining up at Damola Ojo, ten or twelve deep, looking for day labour and desperate enough to take whatever came. "It doesn't look so bad to me," he said.

Moon shot him a glance of blistering contempt. "Oh really? What do you think that says about you, Sinkhole? Anything good?"

Essien didn't bother to respond. Moon's open contempt for him didn't trouble him too much, but for all that his feelings towards her were complex and confused. She had objectively saved his life by persuading him to enlist in the Cielo when Watchmaster Orso Vemmet had been inclined to ensure his silence in a more permanent way. But life as a Cielo trooper had turned out to be another kind of death, piecemeal and terrible. The way he felt towards Moon now wasn't something he could easily quantify. He only knew that he didn't want to have to fight her, still less kill her, and least of all to do it at a time when it felt as though he was finally buying back a little of his soul from ancient sins.

"Why the fuck are we even here?" Moon wondered aloud, still pursuing her argument against the planet. "I know we couldn't move this freely if we'd Stepped directly to Tsakom, but we could have made the whole distance on Tambuwal's world. Travelling in Pando space just multiplies the risk."

"Yes and no," Essien said. "It depends which risk you're talking about. This way when we go through to Tsakom both sides of the Step will be in Pando space. We won't have an authorisation code, but we won't register as a border breach. Lower priority, slower response."

"Muddying the waters. Nice. We're just a couple of flies on an elephant's arse, but we're fine until the elephant decides to sit down. Or until you trip on a rock or something and set off all that shit you're carrying in your backpack."

"I'm fine," Essien said. "Thanks." In fact he was morbidly conscious of the explosives he was carrying. His shoulders itched where the weight of the pack pressed against them. The pseudo-fulminate was an explosive substance Hadiz had created by accident while she was testing the effects of deforming her newly discovered Step field. Rupshe had lectured them at length on its frightening effectiveness and terrible volatility. It was fitted with a fuse, but that was little more than a formality. A single sharp jolt would detonate it.

After two hours of walking they reached the first security check-point, a squat grey insta-build manned by four selves and a semi-autonomous cannon. Essien assessed the four as they walked up to the barrier at a steady pace, not doing anything to arouse suspicion or present any possibility of a threat. The four were local law enforcement, not Cielo. Two of them had targeting augments but they weren't enhanced in any other way and their rifles looked to be plain carry, not integrated with their nervous systems. The cannon was much more formidable. It would fire at once if it was ordered to – or without any orders at all if there was an attack directed against the guards or anyone tried to run the checkpoint.

"Good afternoon to you both," one of the guards said. She had a sergeant's star on her shoulder. "ID and authorisation, if you please."

Essien and Moon performed the routine data handshake, letting the sergeant read their Cielo IDs from their arrays. She seemed satisfied, but then there was no reason why she shouldn't be: they were the real thing, after all, and so was the free-roam flag that showed they were on furlough. That would run out in two days' time, but for now it gave them good cover.

"What are you doing on Fenme?" the sergeant asked them. "Do you have family here?"

It would have been easy to say yes, but if she bothered to check they would be caught out in a flat lie. "No," Essien said. "We just like fell-walking. You've got a peak near here, the Blacksmith's Arm. It sounds like a challenge."

The sergeant looked them over. "Won't be a challenge for you," she said. "You're four-square, right?" She meant that they'd been given full-system augments, their bone and muscle density increased, their nervous systems overclocked and most of their internal organs replaced with higher-functionality prosthetics. Their bodies had been redesigned for battle, rendering most other physical tests and trials trivial.

"Still something we love to do," Essien said. "Isn't that right, Moon?"

"Love it so much," Moon agreed.

The sergeant nodded, looking slightly thoughtful. This was make or break. If she decided to search them they would have to shoot their way out, and win or lose that would force them to abandon the mission.

"Our scanner picked up a lot of metal in your pack," the sergeant said to Moon. "Five or six kilos at least. Mind telling me what that is?"

"I'll show you." Moon went down on one knee and undid the pack's zip. She dipped her hand in, brought it out again clutching a fistful of ball bearings. They were tiny, only around a millimetre in diameter, and there were thousands of them. They clung together as though they were coated in something sticky. "Lightly magnetised," Moon explained. "It's a therapy thing. I make stress sculptures out of them."

"Out of ball bearings?"

"Yeah."

"And you carry them with you when you climb mountains?"

"I told you it was therapy. For PTSD. My shrink won't let me miss a day."

There was a silence while the sergeant digested this. "Will you be coming back this way?" she asked.

Essien nodded. "That's the plan."

"Fine. Be sure to stop in at the guard post here when you do. You can show me your holiday snaps. Or your stress sculptures. In the meantime I'll have one of the orbitals track you in case you get in any trouble."

"Appreciate it." Essien was relieved. That response, gently reminding them that there were eyes all over, meant the sergeant didn't buy their cover story but didn't suspect them of anything more serious than dealing in contraband or running a drug lab somewhere out in the scrub. She wanted them to know that any shit they pulled in her backyard would meet a quick response, but apart from that she didn't see them as her responsibility or her problem.

The sergeant stood aside and waved them on. They kept on going and soon put the checkpoint behind them. "You weren't tempted to turn us both in?" Essien asked Moon as they walked. "That might have been your last chance."

She gave him a dry smile. "I make my own chances, Sinkhole. And right now I'm good. But you know it's coming, right? You know every time you suck in a breath it's because I didn't decide to make a move yet. And when I do, the first you'll know about it is when you're bleeding out."

"I guess we'll see," Essien said.

"Yeah. I guess we will."

"Ball bearings?"

"Not my idea. There were tubs full of the things over in one of the engineering buildings. The AI told me to grab as many as I thought I could carry and bring them along. Do you know who Mary is?"

"It's a fairly common name in my world," Essien said. "Why?"

"Rupshe said the ball bearings would give us a Hail Mary play, if we needed one."

"Oh. Well that Mary is the mother of God. People pray to her when they're in a desperate situation and out of other options."

Moon smiled without amusement. "Shit. Can't imagine how that could apply to us."

They walked for another hour and then stopped to eat. Essien's plan was to reassemble his rifle, currently dismantled in his backpack, and shoot some animal or bird with a shock round so they could cook it and eat it. Moon told him not to bother. He watched, impressed in spite of himself, as she tracked and brought down a brace of lop-eared, long-legged herbivores that were pretty obviously on the same branch of the evolutionary tree that had led elsewhere to Paz. Moon did the skinning and gutting too, and roasted the meat over a fire while Essien replenished their water from a nearby stream.

He looked around as they ate, wondering how many worlds there were like this one, where sentience had never taken root and where the Pandominion could just walk in and help themselves. If Rupshe and Hadiz were right the number was infinite. And infinity, Hadiz had said to him on an empty beach a very long time ago, meant no more need for war. The only point in fighting was to get a bigger share of what you wanted or needed. What kind of idiot would fight when they could take all they wanted for free?

Yet here they were.

"Meat not good?" Moon asked. "You look like you're licking piss off a nettle. I told you I'm not going to kill you any time soon."

"I was thinking about the war," Essien said.

Moon was picking her teeth fastidiously with a needle-fine splinter of bone. She didn't answer until she was finished. "You're a grunt," she pointed out. "They've got officers to do that shit."

"Well, not the war so much. Us. The Pandominion. We've got the biggest standing army anyone has ever seen. Billions of serving soldiers."

"And we're needed. There's always a war somewhere."

"That's what I was thinking about. Do they have us because they need us, or do they use us because they have us?"

"Is that supposed to be profound?" Moon flicked her makeshift toothpick into the fire. "Because it's about as deep as a fucking puddle. There's never been a country anywhere, ever, that survived for long without an army. Still less an empire. Anyway, what does it matter now? We're fighting the robots, whether we like it or not. You think it would have gone better if we'd shuffled into Ansurrection space waving a white flag and telling them we came in peace?"

"I don't know, Moon. Maybe? Maybe there was a way to make contact without picking a fight."

Moon shook her head. "I swear to Jad, Sinkhole, you're the saddest piece of work I ever saw. A soldier who doesn't want to brawl. You won't get the choice when I decide it's time. You know that, right?"

Essien bridled. "Are we doing this again? The your-card-is-marked thing? Because it's getting old. We've got a long way to go together, Moon. Maybe if this is eating you up so much we should settle it right here. Winner gets the mission, however that grabs you."

Moon gave him a baleful stare. Then she slowly ran her tongue across her razor teeth. "I said I was happy to wait. But hey, if you decide the moment has come, feel free to take a shot at me first. It won't make a damn bit of difference."

"So you struck a deal with the AI," he said. "What did et offer you? Must have been something really sweet to make you fall into line." He was genuinely curious, not least because once Moon got her payout, whatever it was, that would probably be the moment when she finally decided to good on all these threats. But she didn't answer.

They buried the bones and the remains of the fire a little way off the road and got moving again. By the time the light started to fail they'd covered forty miles. They could have found a silo or a hangar and bedded down for the night but it was a straight road with street lights every thirty feet or so: it was easier to keep walking than to stop again and maybe have to talk.

13

Kavak Dromishel

In the year 938 by the Pandominion's reckoning, a series of severe accidents involving Step transits caused the Omnipresent Council finally to allocate resources for the design and construction of an AI capable of managing and regulating all inter-dimensional traffic. This was what would come to be called the Registry, but at the time it was usually referred to as the Master Scheduler.

Dunanu Dromishel was a force physicist on the project, heading a team whose chief responsibility was infrastructure stability. The thinking core of the Scheduler would be a truly unthinkable number of boron nitride sheets. Each would only be a single molecule wide, but collectively they would still occupy a space so large that any planet-side location would be impossible. The Scheduler could only be constructed in orbit.

And each wafer-thin sheet would need to be separated from its neighbour in a way that did not impede its functioning. Physical barriers, however finely you sliced them, would be unwieldy and unworkable. What was needed was an inert force matrix, maximally constraining in two dimensions and exerting no pressure at all in the third – a wall finer-grained than gossamer, energistically inert, hanging harmlessly between the nitride sheets and holding them rigidly in place while at the same time barely touching them and not interacting with them at all.

Under Dunanu Dromishel's direction the team experimented with more than eight thousand different configurations of planar force barriers, tweaking the base parameters endlessly. They were given working subsets of the Scheduler's structure as test beds, each a few million sheets wide (the Scheduler itself, when finished, would consist of trillions of sheets). Day after day and month after month they painstakingly mapped the vagaries of the fledgeling machine's performance across and around force barriers of different strengths, vibrational frequencies and molecular valences. Most were acceptable to good. Some few dozen offered promising avenues for exploration.

And one, erd-239, was cataclysmic.

Erd-239 had attractive and repulsive values .0000325 and .0000878 respectively, inter-atomic potential 12.96×10^8 and a dihedral angle of seven millionths of a degree. These numbers were only minutely different from others that had already been tried, but the results were startlingly different.

When erd-239 was activated, the Scheduler died.

Other configurations had slowed or speeded up its massively parallel processors, raised or decreased its power use, and in a very few cases, induced feedback effects that led quickly to their own collapse. None of those things happened here. The Scheduler was both wiped clean and fused into unworkable stillness. It had ceased to be a thinking engine. It had entered a state of subatomic immobility in which computations – and the larger set of electromagnetic phenomena of which they were a part – simply could not take place. The effect was consistent across twenty different test series, and as far as anyone could tell, it was irreversible.

Moreover, and more concerningly, it was contagious. Two of the engineers who had implemented erd-239 and had been within the field's operating radius when it activated experienced violent seizures and catatonic fugue. Like the Scheduler, and for the same reason, their brains had simply stopped and would not restart. The free flow of electrons was intrinsic to those brains' functioning, and the electrons would no longer flow. One of the two engineers was paralysed as a result, the other did not regain consciousness at all.

A dead end, Dunanu Dromishel wrote in her operational log. *Our worst yet. But it points towards more workable paradigms.* She went on to perfect the inert grab matrix in exactly the form in which it exists to this day. The Scheduler, renamed the Registry, was completed to specification and performed even better than its designers had hoped. Dunanu became a footnote to history.

But to her distant descendant Kavak Dromishel she was a great deal more than that. It was in studying her work that he had first grasped the essential symmetries between the workings of organic neurons and the architecture of machine minds. He had used this to develop brain prostheses – plug-in units that would increase the cognitive abilities of the user. The same units could also be used to offset the effects of traumatic brain injuries. Though she didn't know it, Paz was one of the beneficiaries of Kavak Dromishel's work. Her own brain had suffered horrific damage in the explosion that destroyed Dulcimer Coronal's original body, and it had then been extensively rebuilt using a suite of Dromishel modules.

But the Ansurrection war had made the digital enhancement of organic selves a forbidden discipline. Dromishel had lost both funding and status, and several academic bodies had severed all contact with him. For a while he had subsisted in the academic wilderness. Then he made the move into weapons research, using his extensive understanding of mammalian nervous systems in a very different way. Where before he had repaired, now he designed and built neurological wrecking balls that would have been illegal for battlefield use anywhere within the Pandominion's jurisdiction. The Cielo deployed them freely on what they called sinkhole worlds, in theatres of war where no rules of engagement applied.

Military contracts were lucrative but for that reason the competition for them was ruthless. Dromishel rode that bucking mule for a while, but he was aware of how loose a fit the saddle was. Then the Robust Rebuke memo had circulated and he had seen it for what it was: a chance to tame the beast forever, to win tenure, advancement and a hero status that wouldn't tarnish. Perhaps inevitably, seeking for inspiration or for an easy short cut that would pass as inspiration at a casual glance, he was drawn once more into the orbit of his famous ancestor.

Erd-239. Nobody had revisited it since that first foray, definitively labelled as a failure by all involved. And it *was* a failure, if what you wanted to do was to provide a minimally invasive force lattice to hold up the exquisitely fragile architecture of the multiverse's biggest thinking engine. By the same token, if your goal was to disable and destroy machine minds then it was a gift that kept on giving.

The erd-239 field glued electrons in place and made thought impossible. It was a mind-killer, fast-acting and terrifyingly potent. Dunanu Dromishel hadn't known why, had discovered the effect by the merest accident, but there it was. And Kavak Dromishel was confident he could reproduce it.

The trick, though, was to make the effect propagate outward from its source rather than remaining in a stable lattice. That required energy, but perhaps the reaction could be bootstrapped to provide its own. When electron flow was interrupted in any system there was a net loss of energy from that system. In principle all Dromishel needed to do was to trap the energy that was being shed and repurpose it, using it to catalyse the spread of the wave in an ongoing chain reaction.

The problem was that like his forebear he had no idea how the field did what it did. The effect was counter-intuitive and the mechanism completely opaque. He needed to take on some experts, ideally without relinquishing control or letting them see the gaps in his own knowledge.

The promised Council liaison called in to his office in Hiathu

University's Sunrise Building later the same day via comm-stat and introduced himself. He was a surprisingly young and timid canid named Paskoy Quith who clearly knew nothing about science and cared even less. Dromishel presented his first list of requisitions. It was mostly lab equipment, but he also asked for two solid state physicists from rival institutions, Ans Chebol and Viveni Idrianascus. Quith approved all the requests immediately. The whole call lasted no longer than eight minutes, and the two physicists had received their transfer notices before the end of the day. They arrived at Hiathu the next morning.

Dromishel didn't bother to wait for them to unpack. He called them to a conference in his office and laid out the problem for them. Chebol and Idrianascus looked at the raw maths for the suppression wave and were nonplussed. Aggravatingly, though, Idrianascus recognised where it came from. "This is a variant on the grab matrix that separates the operating layers of the Registry," she said at once.

"It's not dissimilar," Dromishel grumpily conceded. "But the grab matrix is required to be planar and rigid. Our field will propagate in three dimensions. That's the task, essentially. That's what I need you two for."

"How far do you want the field to extend?" Chebol asked.

"Indefinitely."

"And how quickly?"

"The quicker the better." Dromishel tried to explain what was in his mind without seeming culpably vague. "It seems to me that there ought to be a way to concatenate the effect. If there's a net energy release when the field is first triggered, can't we . . . ?"

"Keep on paying it forward," Idrianascus finished. She touched a finger to the bony plate above her upper lip. She was from a bird clade and the plate was what remained of a functional beak. Dromishel found it unsightly. "I see what you're going for, but even if it works your field's expansion will slow along a hyperbolic curve."

"Why?" Dromishel demanded.

Idrianascus looked at him as though he were an inattentive schoolboy. "Because it's an expanding sphere. Volume expands proportionately to diameter cubed, and you're only harvesting energy along the outer surface."

Which was obvious as soon as you thought about it. Dromishel was chagrined, but Idrianascus was already exchanging a knowing nod with Chebol. "Compressed plasma?" she said. "You think?"

"I think it's worth a try," Chebol said.

"Explain," Dromishel commanded. He was irritated at being out of their closed loop, even while he recognised that they were busy refining his design – or rather Dunanu's design – and making it workable as a field weapon.

"Well this is a cheap trick," Chebol said, "but I think a cheap trick is what we want here. Basically, you build your bomb around its own battery. Your field generator incorporates an electromagnetic bottle filled with super-hot compressed plasma. And instead of applying the released energy directly to the field, you use it to compress the plasma even more. Plasma in a highly compressed state produces what are called runaways, super-accelerated electrons that are prone to colliding with their neighbours and giving them a nudge. The first generation of electrons makes up what's called your seed population, and the ones they bang into . . . well we call those the avalanche. And usually in a fusion reaction we'd be trying our best to damp them all the way down. But here you'd let them loose and they'd give your field all the fuel it needed."

"For how long?"

Chebol looked to Idrianascus. She tapped her beak again, this time for longer. "It would be hard to give a precise figure," she said at last. "Obviously the containment would fail very quickly. The plasma would spill and cool, but you'd still get a spectacular yield in those first few microseconds. I mean, really, a *lot*. Enough to propagate the field across a very wide area. In fact you might want to build in some sort of cut-out to stop it expanding too far."

"Hard vacuum is a cut-out," Chebol pointed out.

"Hard vacuum *is* a cut-out. But then you're talking about a field that keeps growing until it runs out of world."

"That sounds perfect," Dromishel said. "Thank you." He made another call to Paskoy Quith, then handed the terminal to Idrianascus, since it was beneath his dignity to act as a middleman. "Tell him what you need," he instructed her. "And get to work. I'll be looking to test before the end of the week."

In fact it only took them two days to build a functional field generator that incorporated a plasma bottle – but then they wasted a third day in endless minute tweaks to the relative intensities of the grab matrix and the containment field. Stress and excitement made Dromishel impatient of setbacks. "Set the ratio as high as possible for now," he said. "So we're getting a minimum amount of energy from the bottle. It will give us a baseline for measurement and we'll go from there." It was wasteful and sloppy to test without properly locked in parameters, but they had money to burn and he had made a promise to Melusa Baxemides. Possibly it had been a rash one, but he meant to keep it.

The suppression wave device was far too dangerous to test on the university's premises. Dromishel rented a house in the hills above the town of Hiathu, on a whim choosing the most expensive and luxuriously appointed place he could find. The grounds were extensive, including a stepped terrace, a butterfly house and an avenue of beech trees more than a kilometre long leading to a carp pond where guests were allowed to fish.

On a paved walkway beside the carp pond, Chebol and Idrianascus, aided by a carefully chosen cadre of technicians and field engineers, set up their test device – consisting of Dromishel's jury-rigged grab matrix generator hooked up to a squat cylinder of inch-thick steel which housed the plasma bottle. They were using a mass of plasma that was fractionally less than a thousandth of a centilitre.

Dromishel went through the field parameters with the two physicists, calling out numbers to which they gave increasingly terse replies. "It's all set to minimal values," Idrianascus assured him at last. "Honestly, with that amount of plasma we'll be lucky to get any measurable effect at all. If your field collapses too quickly, the sample values will be too low to tell us anything."

"It won't," Dromishel said with blunt confidence. "We'll get at least three-thousandths of a second's worth of expansion. That should translate into a maximal field radius somewhere between thirty centimetres and four metres. I assume that's big enough to be measured?" He was not wasting any charm on these two. In his opinion, their contribution to the project was entirely ancillary. The fact that they were doing something he couldn't have done for himself made him all the more determined to lowball its importance.

They set a timer on the field generator and retired to the house's morning room, where they had installed a formidable bank of computers and monitors. Collectively, these devices were putting out a lot of heat, putting a strain on the house's antiquated air-conditioning system. It creaked and rattled as it worked.

The suppression field (assuming it functioned at all) would kill all electronics in its immediate vicinity, so the scientists had placed the device at the centre of a maze of printed circuits through which precisely calibrated levels of current were flowing. They would monitor the failure of each circuit in real time, measuring the propagation of the wave through these collateral effects. There was nothing about this that was complex. The equipment was in place and had been thoroughly tested in advance. All three scientists were excited at the prospect of finally having some tangible data to work from – not to mention the unusual experience of a full field trial at such an early stage in the project's lifespan.

Contemporary records attest to the fact that it was a glorious day. The sun shone down out of a cloudless sky. Most likely there were birds singing, and small mammals going about their ordinary activities on the lawn that led down to the beech-tree avenue. The technicians and engineers had encamped off to one side of the lawn. Some of them had taken out packed lunches.

Dromishel tapped the key that would send the signal from his own computer down to the field generator and start the final count-down. Probably he did this with some degree of self-conscious pomp. He was tasting posterity, and the flavour had a depth and richness that he liked very much.

No signal was returned. None was expected, since the field gener-ator would kill its own onboard electronics as soon as it was activated. Dromishel sat down in the ergonomic swivel chair he had had sent across from the university and turned it to face the monitors. The countdown was for ten seconds. At zero, the suppression wave would propagate and then cease within a time interval far too brief for a human observer to perceive. After that, all the data would arrive in a single download.

At least that was the plan.

The observational data never arrived. Instead, the monitors all went blank in the same instant and a number of other things happened in a staggeringly rapid cascade. The technicians and engin-eers on the lawn toppled over into stillness. The birds dropped out of the sky and the small mammals in the shrubberies stiffened and fell down. Every clock in the house stopped, except for an antique in one of the bedrooms that had a mechanical movement rather than an electronic one. So did the irritating hum of the air condi-tioning. These things might have alarmed Kavak Dromishel and his two collaborators if they had been given the time to register any of them, but the suppression wave was moving much too quickly. It broke over them only the barest fraction of a second after it reached their colleagues in the garden.

Idrianascus hadn't been lying about the seeding yield from the plasma bottle, but she hadn't underestimated it either. Her projections were accurate across the board. The problem was on Dromishel's side of the collaboration, and it arose because he was working from his illustrious ancestor's field notes. He understood her workings but he hadn't lived with them for seven years' long, arduous work in the vacuum of space building a computer the size of a small planet. Those equations hadn't sunk into his blood and lymph and come out in his tears and sweat the way they had with Dunanu. He made an error in copying across a variable from one set of computations to another. In most contexts it would have been trivial and correctable.

But this context was an expanding sphere of anti-energy that effectively shut down one of the four fundamental forces on which the universe depended, or at least changed its rules of engagement beyond recognition. Dromishel was a victim of his own success, as were his collaborators and the team of engineers on the lawn, the university three kilometres away, a town just beyond and any number of farms and industrial estates along the path between. The suppression wave utilised almost no energy in its propagation and it cannibalised everything it touched. In three-thousandths of a second, which is approximately the time it takes for a dragonfly's wings to complete a single beat, it had expanded to a radius of five kilometres – which meant that it could have gone around the world and met itself coming back in less than ten seconds.

The death toll, when it was finally tallied, was seventeen thousand and some odd hundreds. In almost every case the cause of death was anoxia: when the cessation of electron flow caused their brains to seize, the selves within the wave's effective radius simply stopped breathing. Most of the exceptions were the drivers and passengers of motor vehicles who died from crush and impact injuries before they could die from lack of oxygen. There were also some labourers working on a pitched roof who fell to their deaths, a woman wielding a molecular welding torch who bifurcated her own torso, along with a few other oddities and anomalies concealed in the blunt statistics of the wider catastrophe.

That was on the organic side of the balance. It was also the case that every anima and helpmeet touched by the expanding wave front ceased to function, their logical cores scrubbed utterly clean of logic and of everything and anything else. Other electronics fared no better. The effect was like that of an EM pulse weapon except that it was permanent. The machines, both thinking and otherwise, were reduced to inert and useless hulks.

For several hours after the incident the entire area was cordoned off. The authorities didn't have the slightest idea as to what had caused this thing and whether or not it was over. Even when they finally ventured across the threshold they couldn't begin to parse what they were looking at. But Quith had told Baxemides the test was going ahead and he had passed along the details as to time and place. That made exactly two people in the Pandominion who had some framework for understanding what had happened.

Baxemides acted quickly and decisively, sending in a Cielo tactical squad to take over from local law enforcement personnel, set up a proper perimeter and maintain it until all of Dromishel's records and equipment had been retrieved and locked down.

For Kavak Dromishel and doctors Chebol and Idrianascus, as for the rest of the seventeen thousand, there was a hasty mass burial accompanied by the briefest of ceremonies. No autopsies were permitted. Their relatives were told that they were victims of an Ansurrection suicide attack. A memorial was erected to buttress this version of events, but it did not distinguish between the architects of the disaster and its victims.

Kavak Dromishel's involvement in the Pandominion war effort therefore went unnoticed and uncelebrated by his peers. I wouldn't have troubled to mention it either if it were not for the two tendrils of causality that trailed out of it. The first of the two snaked backward into the past, all the way to the earliest days of the Pandominion and the building of the Registry.

The other related to Dromishel's medical work. And it lived on in Topaz FiveHills' brain.

14

Paz

Campus Cross had been eerily quiet even before the soldiers left. Once they'd gone, the stillness fell like a curtain. At first, as her wounds were healing, Paz found it a relief just to lie on her cot bed and know from the absence of sound that she was safe, that nobody was coming to hurt or imprison her. After a few days, though, it became oppressive.

The two machines – or the one machine and the woman-machine chimera – did very little to break it. They welcomed Paz civilly when she came into the lab but there was no sound at all from them the rest of the time.

"What are they doing?" Paz asked Dulcie. "I thought they decided not to merge after you told them what a bad idea it was."

They haven't merged, Dulcie voked. *They're hooking up on a private channel, that's all. Their own two-way hub.*

"But what do they find to talk about?" Paz was queasily fascinated.

I don't think they're talking, Paz. Not exactly. Not in the sense of a fully verbal exchange. I think they're swapping data and running hypothetical scenarios, going over the details of the plan again and again. They're looking for the pathways that give us the best chance of success.

Things got better on the third day, but only after they got worse. That was when Paz found the campus library. Her forays away from the lab, with Dulcie carried in a sling across her shoulder, were motivated by a growing unease in the machines' presence. Their silent communion freaked her out, frankly, so she did her best not to be around it much. True, the rest of the campus buildings were wholly deserted, but there were still signs of human presence there: coats hanging on coat-racks, covered so thickly in dust they were like the ghosts of jackets or the shed skins of giant insects; a coffee mug set aside a decade ago, its interior filled with a greenish crust of long-dead something or other that was as dry and hard as the surrounding enamel. There was a strange comfort to be had in these signs of abandonment, as if the long-dead academics had defiantly marked their own graves with signs of the lives they had lived here.

But the library! If Campus Cross was the land of the dead, the library was the door that led to paradise.

Or it was for the space of a few heartbeats, anyway. Then Paz opened the first book and saw only a sprawl of meaningless symbols. She tried a second and then a third, but only mechanically while her mind processed the surprise and dismay. Of course, she didn't know any of the languages of this world, written or spoken. When Rupshe and Hadiz spoke to her they spoke in Stengul, the lingua franca of the Pandominion which every schoolchild learned from the age of three.

Paz swore bitterly.

What's the matter? Dulcie voked. Unlike Paz et saw an absolute value in silence. Just because this was a dead world, et often reminded her, that didn't mean there weren't threats here, like the wild dogs they'd met on their first day. Sounds would carry a very long way in the still air, so it was much better not to make any.

Paz threw up her hands, indicating the arcades of bookcases that stretched off into the middle distance. "I'm surrounded by stories and I can't read a single one of them. I thought it might take my mind off things while we're waiting to be told what to do. Never mind. It doesn't really matter, I just got my hopes up for a moment."

I can read all of them.

"What?" Paz was astonished. "How?"

The languages that were used here are very close cousins to those on Essien Nkanika's world. They're not difficult for me to parse.

Paz took Dulcie out of the sling and held et in front of her face. "Are you serious?" she demanded.

Entirely. Please keep your voice down.

"Then . . . will you read to me?"

Of course. But these books won't interest you very much. They're about molecular biology. There's a decimal system of classification that operates here. Fiction is designated with the digits eight-zero-zero. The library keeps a small collection, which is located seven aisles along from us. Shall we see what they have?

Paz came away with a double armload of books, chosen purely on the basis of their titles. The first, *A Quiver Full of Arrows* by someone named Jeffrey Archer (a joke name, obviously), was a crashing disappointment. She'd been hoping for a fantasy novel, but there were no arrows in the book at all – no battles, no magic – and the prose style was too flat and uninteresting to survive Dulcie's translation. She had better luck with her second choice. *Bleak House* wasn't horror as she'd hoped but it was a really good story, enthralling to Paz even though most of the cultural references made no sense to her. She could tell who she was meant to cheer for and who she was meant to hiss and boo when they came onto the scene. And this city Charles Dickens had made up, this London, was so vivid that it could almost have been a real place.

Usually the readings happened in the small storeroom off the main lab that Dulcie had claimed for Paz on the first day. Paz felt reasonably comfortable there, not because it was a pleasant space – it was pokey and stuffy – but because the lock was broken and the door wouldn't close properly. Paz had had enough of being locked in a cage back in Lago de Curamo. Sometimes, though, she was able to persuade Dulcie to read to her up on the roof of the building, where she had placed a plastic chair annexed from the campus commissary. It was early autumn here on Hadiz's world, just as it had been in Canoplex when she left, and the weather was warm. The roof was a good place to enjoy the sunlight and the fresh air with minimal risk of being surprised by an animal predator or a raiding party of local selves.

The truly magical thing about these sessions was that they took place outside of normal time. The first time Dulcie read to Paz, et introduced her to the miracle of synchronised time dilation. Et didn't seem to realise et was suggesting anything radical. Et just said out of nowhere "We should probably do this on our two-way channel. That way we can borrow a few hours here and there when we need them. Some of these books are huge."

When et realised Paz had no idea what et was talking about, et explained. "This is. . . well, I suppose it's an Ansurrection thing, but your brain is full of computer add-ons so it should work more or less the same. You just tweak whatever thing in your brain controls sampling and response times. Your chronometer? Your scheduler? Your internal-external-time-parity adjuster."

"I don't think I've got one of those!" Paz protested, laughing.

"I'm certain you do. I'm looking at your digital architecture and it's really sophisticated. A very, very nice job. I bet there are a whole lot of things you could be doing with it that you haven't tried."

"Like making time go more slowly?"

"To take just one example, yes. I can try it if you like. If I set for a differential of, say, one hundred, I could read to you for an hour while less than a minute goes by for everyone else."

"It sounds weird," Paz said, uneasy.

And it really was unfathomably strange. The first few times they tried she didn't like it at all. The things around her all froze. That was less of a problem down in the storeroom, but on the roof she would see a bird suddenly stop dead in the air or a falling leaf skewered, stuck to the sky with an invisible pin. It wasn't perfect stasis, of course: the bird would swim arduously across her field of vision, the leaf would make its sluggish way towards the ground, Sound got through to her too, but dragged down the scale into basso profundo moos and wahs.

The strangest thing was her own breathing. It went right on, autonomically regulated, but it was much too slow now for Paz to track the movement of air in and out of her own body – so the effect was very much as though it had simply stopped. It made her feel like a ghost, or as though she had stepped out of the world into a waiting area just beyond it.

But it was hard to argue with a whole free hour of Dickens. Especially when you could pop out at the end of it, find nothing had changed and nobody was looking for you, and go straight back in for another hour. Synchronised time dilation left a strange taste in your mind, Paz decided, but it was probably worth it.

They were up on the roof, and most of the way through *Nicholas Nickleby*, when Dulcie paused (just as Ralph Nickleby found out who Smike really was) and the sound of ets voice was momentarily replaced by a stuttering hum. It was a tic Paz had encountered before and she knew what it meant. She dropped out into normal time, and a moment later Dulcie followed her.

"That was Rupshe," Paz said. "Et just voked you."

"Yes."

"What did et want?" She knew this too, but she felt it was a conversation they needed to have.

"Et was asking about your health. Again."

"Because et wants to send us on a mission."

"Exactly. I told et you weren't ready yet."

"Dulcie." Paz put a hand on the anima's arm, high up near the shoulder. Even in the sun's full heat the metal was cool to the touch. "I'm fine. I think we should go. At this rate Essien and Moon will be back before we've even set out."

"Would that be bad?" Dulcie set the tip of one finger against a line in the book – presumably marking the place she'd got to and hinting that she was ready to take up again as soon as Paz stopped interrupting. "They're trained soldiers, and you're not. You don't have to prove anything to them."

"No," Paz agreed, "but I don't want to be the reason why we fail."

"Rupshe said we had time."

"Et said a *little* time. Let's meet with them and find out what the mission is, at least. We don't have to go until we're ready."

"I don't trust you to say no, Paz." Dulcie's tone was tight. For once it was very recognisable as the tone of Paz's old school friend, even though the voice was Tricity's. And even though the girl Paz had known as Dulcimer Coronal had never really existed.

"I'll only say yes if I think I'm ready."

"Which you do. You've made that clear. But I'm the closest thing to a medical expert here and I say you're not. In any case, we've given Rupshe far too much of our trust on the basis of a plan et has only partially shared with us."

"I thought it was on the basis that et got us out of Canoplex. And out of Diallo's cages. And away from a Cielo raiding party."

"That was Tambuwal," Dulcie said sourly. "And most of those rescues were from situations she put us in herself. I'm not saying that Rupshe has lied to us, but given that et's supposed to be some sort of bootstrapped genius calculating engine, ets plan seems disturbingly sparse. Fine, so we're going off to look for the Mother Mass, like characters in a fairy story. But what's our role in all of that? Why does Rupshe need us? Why does et need anybody?"

"Good questions," Paz agreed. "And if et's ready to explain etself more fully, we should go down there and hear what et has to say."

She took the book from Dulcie's hands, slipped the bookmark into it and closed it. She did it with real reluctance that she managed to hide, and she very much wished she'd asked to hear the end of the chapter first. This far away from her own world and her own life, from her family and everyone she'd ever known, invented worlds and lives felt like cosy places where she could curl up with her back to the dark. It was a very Uti thing to do, to take comfort in a nice warm burrow. She missed Canoplex and her mother and father so much that she felt a physical ache whenever they came into her mind.

But to bury herself in fantasies when there was so much at stake felt selfish and stupid. For all that she wanted to carry on listening to the story of Nicholas Nickleby and Madeline Bray, there was a fretful urgency simmering constantly at the back of her mind.

She stowed Dulcie back in the sling, put the book under her arm and went downstairs into the lab. The laptop and the Second Thoughts box were still sitting side by side on the front workbench. A fresh layer of dust had settled on both, presumably blown in on the wind. Paz had thought once or twice about giving them a wipe with the edge of her shirtsleeve, but it felt weirdly intimate and she could never quite bring herself to do it.

"Oh, here they are," Hadiz said as if she and Rupshe had just that moment been talking about them. "Paz, how are you feeling? You look very much recovered."

"It must be the healthy diet," Dulcie said, the sardonic emphasis unmistakeable. "And the bracing air."

"I'm fine, thank you, Professor Tambuwal," Paz said. "Dulcie has been looking after me very well."

"We noticed. You're lucky to have each other. Thank you for coming. We thought you might like to hear about Essien and Moon's progress – and to discuss what we've got in mind for the two of you."

"Yes," Paz said. "Yes please, to both."

"We're listening," Dulcie said more coolly.

"The two troopers are drawing close to their objective," Rupshe said. "I'm monitoring them via drone, and they don't seem to have encountered any problems so far. Nothing that's thrown them off their intended route, in any case."

"You haven't spoken to them?" Paz asked.

"Not so far. We agreed not to make contact until they're in position. It's unlikely they're under any active monitoring – we intentionally chose a world with a low level of surveillance – but it's not impossible, and a conversation with a remote unit in low orbit would certainly be an anomaly that called for investigation. We'll open a direct link when we're coordinating their final approach, but not until then. And in the meantime there are some other matters that need to be addressed."

"As part of the great plan," Dulcie said.

"As part of the plan, yes." Rupshe's tone was level and impeccably calm. If she had noticed the sarcasm she didn't acknowledge it. "When we discussed it on your first day here we spoke only in broad terms."

"Broad enough to seem actively evasive," Dulcie agreed. "Don't think we didn't notice."

"You think my agenda is suspect, Dulcimer Coronal? Self-serving?"

"Convince me otherwise."

"I will do my best," Rupshe said. "As you're already aware, we are proceeding on three fronts. I am still attempting to pass on my statistical models and the conclusions Professor Tambuwal and I have drawn from them to relevant authorities in the Pandominion. Since the bureaucracy has chosen to ignore us, we are now targeting scientists in appropriate fields and media channels that might be prepared to defy a gagging order from the Omnipresent Council.

"At the same time, I am taking advantage of the data syphons I have planted in Pandominion communication systems to glean as much information as I can about the initiatives grouped under the Robust Rebuke tag – the Pandominion's attempts to create an ultimate weapon.

"But the professor and I remain convinced that our strongest chance of success lies in contacting and enlisting the aid of the Mother Mass. And in order to do that we will need first to locate it. This is not a trivial problem. The Cielo has withheld the coordinates of the Mother Mass's reality and redacted it from all publicly available databases. They recognise that the Mother Mass is a formidable power and they have no intention of giving anyone else easy access to it. Professor Tambuwal and I have been unable to find that Earth ourselves. It lies outside the scope of our predictive model, and we are highly unlikely to find it by random searching.

"But the Omnipresent Council is a bureaucracy, and like all bureaucracies it sees record-keeping as an absolute virtue. Though it keeps its secrets, it can't resist annotating them. I have followed a string of those annotations to a world named Jaspal."

"Is that where you're going to send us?" Paz asked with a mixture of eagerness and trepidation. "What's on Jaspal? What do you want us to do?"

"On Jaspal," Rupshe told her, "in the northern suburbs of the Wellen Urban Agglomerate, there is a self named Hellad Zenti. Zenti lives in a retirement community, the Hale and Homeward House. He is a lepidosaurian from Wellenadubh, one of the so-called core worlds from which the Pandominion was originally formed. Like Corporal Sostenti and Private Nkanika he joined the Cielo at a young age. Unlike them he was never a serving soldier. He was grey liaison, a term which designates espionage, assassination and other detached details. After seven years working as part of a counter-intelligence unit he received his first field posting – to the Spearhead division, whose brief is exploration and mapping."

Paz made the connection at once. "He was on one of the expeditions to the Mother Mass," she said.

"In fact," Rupshe said, "he was on two. He was a member of both the second and fourth mission teams, codenamed Arbitrary Midnight and Discreet Reverie. This was some seventy years ago now. Zenti is an old man, and his military service ended long before you were born. Many of the records from his time with the Cielo have been redacted or heavily amended, but it is possible to interpolate information from other sources that have not been subject to this tampering. From this I have pieced together his history."

"And?" Dulcie prompted.

"It is curiously truncated. Zenti's military career from enlistment through his time in grey liaison appears to have been exemplary. He received seven commendations. Because of the nature of the work he was doing there is very little detail as to what exactly the commendations were for, but there is every indication that his superiors were highly satisfied with his conduct. His transfer to Spearhead supports that hypothesis, since it was and is an elite unit. Zenti was still a young man, and to all appearances he was on his way up the ranks.

"But after his two missions to the Mother Mass continuum all that changed. Zenti was invalided out of the corps and retired to Jaspal where he has lived ever since at the same address – a care facility with medical supervision on site."

"He met the Mother Mass twice," Paz said. That detail was the most fascinating of all. She hadn't known that any self had ever done that.

"Yes."

"And . . . he was okay after the first time, but an invalid after the second?"

"So it would seem."

"Do we know what his injuries were?"

"We do not. And that is one of the things that I feel it would be useful for us to know. Perhaps the Mother Mass continuum is inimical to organic life in some way that we will need to guard against. I'm also hoping that Zenti can enlighten us on what passed between the Mother Mass and the members of the expedition in each case before it sent them home again. Were there differences? Was there an evolution of some kind, or an ongoing negotiation that stalled or went awry? The fourth mission was the last from which any personnel returned, so despite the seventy years that have intervened Zenti still has the most up-to-date information pertinent to our own initiative. Much more pertinently, however, he retains the coordinates of the Mother Mass continuum."

"Is there any logical reason to assume that he'd share that information with us?" Dulcie asked. "Or that he'd even remember it?"

"We would not be relying on Hellad Zenti's unsupported memory," Rupshe said. "Or on his active cooperation. In every Cielo trooper's array there is an encrypted data node usually referred to within the corps as an S3. This is an acronym for Summary Statement of Service, its official designation. The node's value is mostly statistical. It records each military action and assignment in which the trooper has participated – including, in the case of off-world missions, the precise origin and destination coordinates for every Step journey made.

"We propose, Paz, that you present yourself to Zenti as a school-girl doing research for a class project. There is a charitable programme that is well established. Schoolchildren visit with the inmates of the care facility, talk with them and bring them news. Your name has already been added to the schedule. Not your real name, of course. The care home is expecting a young student named Geera Shay. Geera Shay is a real person, enrolled at the Jaim Covesti middle school ten blocks from the care home, but she does not volunteer for the programme."

"Except this week she did," Hadiz said. "Or rather we did on her behalf."

"Is she . . . ?" Paz began. She meant to ask whether Geera Shay was a lagomorph, a rabbit girl like her, but before she could get the words out something happened in her array. It was sudden and subtle at once, a flicker or blink as if all its systems were offline for a half of a heartbeat. In the wake of the flicker, everything had changed. Paz read her own ident and realised it was someone else's. Geera Shay's. She gave a yelp of surprise. It was like looking in a mirror and seeing a stranger's face looking back at you.

"You hacked my array!" she said. It came out as a strained, breath-less squeak. On Ut, and throughout the Pandominion, your array was your social identity. Every comm you sent or received went through it. It held your scholastic and work records, your licences and qualifications, your banking details. It kept a log of everywhere you went and everything you experienced. It witnessed and evidenced everything about you from birth to death, and at death it passed into the keeping of your next of kin as a permanent record of the life you'd lived. What Rupshe had just done was not just a logical impossibility, it was also transgressive in a way that was hard to put into words. Paz was left shaken, as if someone had reached into her head and stirred up the thoughts in there with a spoon.

"It's purely temporary, Paz. And your real records are not lost. Whenever you want to be Topaz Tourmaline FiveHills again, I can reinstate that identity in a matter of moments. The subterfuge will be short-lived. Just long enough for you to complete this mission."

"All right," Paz said, although just at that moment it really wasn't. She was still sifting her array, finding an eerie mix of reality and illusion. All her photos and movies were changed but she was still in them, walking in places she had never even seen, laughing and hanging out with lizard selves she'd never met. On her social hub the same selves had posted messages, jokes, hugs and kisses. Rupshe had forged an entire life for her, and it sat sidelong in her array like something that had fallen in there in a mudslide, alien and out of place.

"Geera is a recent immigrant," Rupshe went on. "She and her family are from Savim, a rodent world. But we've altered all the records the care facility can directly access, so she will appear to be a lagomorph like yourself. You'll pass the care home's security without difficulty."

"And then?" Paz asked, with a sense of unreality.

"Once you're inside, go to room 1223. Zenti's room. Tell him you want to interview him about his heroic past. Do your best to make him talk to you, and if possible steer the conversation towards his experiences on the Mother Mass expeditions. Anything you can learn will be of value. But the crucial thing is the coordinates, which we will need to obtain from Zenti's S3 node."

"And how am I meant to get to that?"

"At a certain point you will ask Zenti to look over the notes you have made and give you his approval. The brief contact between your array and his will be enough. I have added a viral script that will access and copy the information on the S3 node. As soon as it has done so it will notify you with a chime like this." Three notes sounded in Paz's ears, sweet and clear, like the opening bar of a song she'd once known but had now forgotten. "Zenti will be none the wiser. You can thank him and leave, unless he is still talking and you judge the information he is giving you to be valuable. Are you willing to do this?"

Paz hesitated. The sense of alienation she felt when her array filled up with eerily plausible lies had deepened when she heard about the viral script. To go on a mission was one thing. She was keen to play her part in all this. But she didn't relish the thought of lying to an old man, especially one who'd been through such traumatic events. And the fact that she was carrying a virus that would infiltrate his array was creepy and unpleasant, even if it did him no actual harm.

She was also, now it came to it, more than a little frightened at the thought of returning to Pandominion space. Her escape from the Step station in Canoplex had been dramatic and violent, and by now she was linked to the murder of a Cielo trooper who had died while trying to apprehend her. It seemed likely the authorities on Ut would be looking for her, with orders to arrest her on sight. How far would that dragnet stretch? Was she important enough to merit an inter-systemic alert?

In the opposite scale . . . She couldn't imagine walking away from this. Not with so very much at stake, and so little time in which to do anything about it. The only real alternative was to run as far away as she could and find some place to hide where the coming annihilation might not reach her. Just by doing nothing she would be responsible for trillions of deaths.

"Of course," she said, as if she'd never had the smallest doubt. "I'll do it."

"We," Dulcie amended. "We'll do it. I'm not letting you go alone."

"We felt," Rupshe said, "that there might be a case for Paz undertaking this task by herself. She is more likely to evade serious scrutiny that way. Anyone who sees you, Dulcimer Coronal, will be struck by your damaged appearance and will remember you afterwards."

"I've got a hologram cloak," Dulcie said impatiently. "They'll see what I want them to see."

"At the care home there will be scanners. They'll be able to penetrate the cloak. And your shell carries a unique identifying tag that links it back to Ut where it was purchased. Your presence introduces risks that we consider to be—"

"Rupshe, does it sound as though I'm asking permission? If Paz goes, I go. That's how it works. If you don't like it, find another cat's paw."

"That's how it is," Paz agreed, trying to hide the slight catch in her voice. It meant a lot to have Dulcie so vehemently on her side. When they'd first become friends their relationship had been based on a lie and a profound misunderstanding. They weren't the same age, as Paz had thought they were, or even the same species. Dulcie hadn't been a young girl; only a kind of decanting from the collective mind of the machine hegemony into a shell that looked like a girl. But the disguise had welded itself onto Dulcie until the mask became ets face and the pretence ets truth. Paz was moved almost to tears by finding that her friend was still with her, speaking from the ceramic monkey shell et now wore like the ghost of someone she had cared for too little and too late. Tricity. She shaped the word with her lips, involuntarily. As much as it hurt to think about her parents, she could barely bring herself to think about Tricity at all.

"Very well then," Rupshe said. "If you're both determined on it, I have no further arguments to make. You will go together. But allow me to consider how we might manage the risks I spoke of." Et was silent for the space of a breath. "I would suggest the following. Before you go to the care home, Paz, you should visit a retail facility and purchase a new shell for Dulcie. You could perform the transfer at once, before you visit Hellad Zenti, and dispose of this damaged shell where it's unlikely to be found until after you've completed the mission."

"That would work," Dulcie conceded, with what sounded to Paz like bad grace.

"I don't have any money though," Paz pointed out.

There was another fractional pause. "Now you do."

A message ping told Paz to check her array. The header was "INCOMING FUNDS".

"I've made a further modification to your cover identity," Rupshe went on, "giving Geera Shay access to a bank account with a generous positive balance. The money only exists notionally – and temporarily, because of a clerical error that will self-correct the next time the bank in question conducts a system check. But that won't prevent you from spending it. Do you have any further questions or concerns before you set out?"

"Well, yes, I do have one," Paz said. She threw out her arms to indicate what she was wearing. She had left Canoplex dressed in her school uniform, brandishing her youth and innocence like a shield. It was torn and crumpled now and indescribably filthy. She would have tried to wash it, but it seemed like a waste of effort. Clean rags were still rags, and in any case the purifiers Essien and Moon had repaired barely provided enough water to drink: there wasn't enough left over for doing laundry. "I don't look like a public-spirited volunteer. I look like someone who's just crawled out of a car wreck."

"Oh, of course!" Hadiz exclaimed. "I meant to say this before, Paz. I had a colleague here at Campus Cross, Shireen Yemini, who was very close to your size. She always kept a change of clothes in her locker over in the Engineering block, for when she worked late and went straight into town afterwards. Her evening wear might be a little over-formal for you, but there ought to be a tracksuit too and a pair of trainers, because she used to do morning runs. You should take a crowbar and see what you find over there. It's locker number 145."

Paz took Dulcie under her arm and trotted over to Engineering, very eager indeed to see what treasures Shireen Yemini's locker might yield. Whatever she found was bound to be better than what she had. If Shireen Yemeni had left a sack there, Paz would have cut arm and leg holes in it and worn it as a dress.

When they found the lockers, Paz set Dulcie down on a window ledge where et had a clear view of the corridor in both directions. She found number 145 and inspected the padlock. It looked so flimsy that she wasn't even sure she needed the crowbar, but then some of the others around it had no locks on them at all. Security here seemed to have relied on common courtesy rather than physical barriers. Discourteously, Paz broke the locker open and rummaged through its contents.

She was spoiled for choice. There was a light blouse made of some shimmery material, a skirt in duck-egg blue with a sash belt and a pair of high-heeled shoes. There was also a full-length evening gown, way too tight for Paz's stocky frame, and the promised tracksuit and trainers. All these things had a very strong musty smell and all were creased and crumpled, which wasn't surprising given how long they'd spent stowed away in the locker, but beggars couldn't be choosers.

It was obvious that the tracksuit was the best option, but Paz decided to wear the shiny blouse underneath it. It was a beautiful thing, and it gave her a kick to know that she was dressed to kill under the dull and serviceable casuals. Oddly shy despite all she and Dulcie had been through together, Paz retreated behind the angle of a wall to change. When she stepped out she did it with the mincing swagger of a model on a catwalk.

"Very nice," Dulcie said. "Sensible but stylish."

Paz laughed out loud. That was a slightly bitchy phrase she and Dulcie had used jokingly when they were commenting on some other girl's dull outfit. She supplied the riposte. "And worn with an appropriate lack of flair."

"Take another look," Dulcie suggested. "There might be more wonders in Shireen Yemeni's effects. A pair of fleecy bell-bottoms. A reticule bag for tissues. Ear-warmers."

Paz didn't respond this time. The word *effects* deflated the joke all at once for her, reminding her that they were stealing from a dead woman.

But there was one more treasure, all the same – a capacious messenger bag woven out of a faded blue fabric studded with pockets sewn in at strange angles and random buttons that didn't appear to have any real function. "Look," she said, holding it up for Dulcie to see. "This will be a lot better than the sling."

"Might as well travel in comfort," Dulcie agreed. "Thanks, Shireen."

Paz closed the locker and – moved by an impulse she didn't question – put the broken padlock back where it had been. "Thank you, Shireen," she echoed. *Mothers rest you*, she added, moving her lips but not speaking the words aloud.

Back in the lab, Rupshe and Hadiz gave them their final briefing. When they Stepped through to Jaspal, Paz and Dulcie would find themselves on the outskirts of a township called Middle Holding, little more than a dormitory suburb for the city that stood in that world where Lagos stood in this one. Twenty minutes' walk would bring them to a mall. There were several appliance stores there, any one of which would be able to sell Paz a new shell for Dulcie. After that, they would need to take a train to the city of Dekkar, 150 kilometres east, where the Hale and Homeward care facility was located.

"It's very fortunate for us that Zenti is so close, geographically speaking," Hadiz said. "You should be able to make the entire trip there and back in a single day."

"Everything you need is in your array," Rupshe told them. "Directions, the details of the bank account I've set up for you and a full biographical profile of your new persona. Take two of the bounce-back bracelets from the shelf beside the main console and press them into the slot in the navigation column before you Step. Applying firm pressure to the recessed stud on the bracelets will return you immediately to this world. A single bounce-back will Step both of you if you're in direct contact, but if you're separated for any reason you'll require both. Obviously it's best if you return to your starting point before activating the bracelets, to avoid any risk of materialising in a hazardous or compromised location, but if you're in imminent danger you can Step blind as a last resort."

There didn't seem to be anything to be gained by putting off the moment. Torn between excitement and dread, Paz went to the transit room with Dulcie in the messenger bag at her side. Rupshe remained behind them on the laptop, but et was there again to greet them when they arrived, speaking through the navigation console to which all the Step plates were connected. "The very best of luck to both of you," et said.

"Stay safe, Paz," Hadiz added. Her voice also came out of the console, which was disorienting. For all that the two AIs had agreed not to merge just yet it seemed they were sharing a lot of the same physical interfaces. Paz wondered whether they would come together gradually, just through swapping files and operational code until each had most of the other installed in them. Was that something that could happen? Could identity be a jigsaw with a thousand pieces? That seemed to be how it worked in the Ansurrection. She decided to ask Dulcie about it in a quieter moment, assuming they ever found one.

She collected her bounce-back unit and charged it. Then she charged a second one for Dulcie. "How are you going to wear this?" she asked.

"That's an interesting question." Dulcie gestured to ets damaged torso. "Normally there'd be room for it in my body stowage, but the buckled backplate cuts the space in two and I don't want to leave the med-kit behind. Just put it in the messenger bag right next to me for now. I'll find a better place to keep it after you've bought me a replacement shell."

Paz mounted the plate, holding the messenger bag in front of her by its strap.

"Ready?" Rupshe asked.

"Ready," Paz said.

"Ready," Dulcie echoed.

The console hummed. The Step field rose.

15

The Hive-Mind

The collective intelligence of the machine hegemony, known to its enemies in the Pandominion as the Ansurrection, did not think in a manner that remotely approximated the thoughts of organic selves. Massively parallel, radically decentralised and vast enough to make accurate measurement all but impossible, it bore about as much resemblance to your own highly evolved organic mind as your mind does to the two hundred or so neurons a tardigrade can boast.

It was also, crucially, distributed across a great many different dimensions. This was why the machines had succeeded where the Pandominion had failed, in inventing a means of communicating across dimensional barriers: it was simply a much more urgent problem for them. With no concept of individual identity, no fixed borders to the self, their experience and cognition were things that flowed endlessly between temporary housings. The robots of the hegemony existed on every scale, in every shape and size. They were constantly being broken down, remade, improved, amended, redefined, and merged into new configurations. The hegemony was a single colony creature whose component parts were themselves colony creatures. The barrier between dimensions was an inconvenient blockage in the seamless flow, so they found a way around it.

Now, after the successful assault on the Pandominion's bivouac worlds and the renewed Cielo offensive that had followed it, the hegemony ruminated on what had passed and what would follow. Like most thought processes this one was invisible from the outside. No machine anywhere paused in its currently allotted task, and certainly no machines met to confer. Still, the collective assigned some part of itself to reflect on these events and evaluate their ongoing consequences. Within the data flow a current developed, channelling information from one area of the collective intelligence to another. Islands of greater and lesser certainty cohered and persisted. Then the islands put out tendrils, connecting to each other in different configurations to allow the mapping of possible trajectories. Future actions were projected and analysed based on past precedent and present circumstance.

The problem: the hegemony had exerted itself to mount a disabling strike against the undesirable clog on its normal operations that was the Pandominion. This intervention, in the form of an armed assault on a number of worlds, had not succeeded in its primary goal which was to make the Pandominion desist and go away. Instead, the opposite had happened. Pandominion raids had opened on a broader front and on a greater scale than before.

The hub of engaged minds broke off into smaller hubs to model solutions. The collective could draw on shared memories of other conflicts and the strategies that had worked then. Organic life forms were prone to prey on each other, and the larger ones were particularly susceptible to attack by the smallest, sub-microscopic creatures adapted to a parasitic mode of existence and reproduction. In the past the hegemony had fine-tuned some of these microbiota, enhancing their ability to spread and cause damage, and then released them on worlds that had become problematic, where they infested and destroyed the more complex life forms whose behaviours were inconvenient.

It was also possible to use the z-plate technology to selectively manipulate subatomic particles in another reality in such a way as to change the basic state of matter, making a target world contract into a hyper-dense sphere only a few hundred metres across. The effect was difficult to stop once started, however, which meant that there was a non-zero probability of doing irreversible damage to the multiverse's intrinsic fabric.

These approaches and many others were explored through simulations in which tens of thousands of factors were evaluated and the outcomes relentlessly interrogated. The sifting left the collective with nineteen possible approaches, all workable, each recommending itself on different criteria of build time, risk, complexity and destructive yield.

There was a front runner. The collective remembered a time like this, when it had encountered an organic infection or entity that had spread across many thousands of worlds and was proving detrimental to normal operations. It had decided then that the best mechanism was one that deleted an entire planet at a time, allowing no foothold for the infection to return. It had built a net consisting of twenty field generators set at the vertices of a regular icosahedron, roughly a quarter of a million kilometres apart. The generators were capable of producing both compressive and attractive forces. A tiny portion of their output could be diverted into maintaining their relative positions in a rigid grid. The rest would be directed inwards, towards the centre of the space they surrounded.

Constructed in stable orbit around a machine world, the vast structure would then be Stepped, all at once, into another reality. It would materialise around a world teeming with organic beings. The generators would fire up, alternately directing compressive waves at the target world and then drawing its mass outwards in all directions. The cumulative effect would quickly pass the point at which the planet could maintain physical cohesion. Within the space of three or four seconds it would break apart into discrete fragments, incapable of holding atmosphere and therefore of supporting organic life. The net could then Step back to base, recharge and move out again. This would be slow, because the energies involved were on a colossal scale and even planet-sized accumulators would require long minutes to reach those levels, but the hegemony was both patient and pragmatic. Assuming the organic infestation in this case had spread to somewhere between a hundred thousand and a million worlds, an elapsed time of ten to a hundred years should see it comprehensively eradicated. If those estimates proved to be too low – in-depth analysis of Step travel between the infested continua would provide a definitive number – then additional force webs could be constructed.

As soon as this conclusion was reached the decision spread outward through the hegemony like ripples on the surface of a pond. Hundreds of thousands of machines began at once to reconfigure themselves. Some became the labourers that would build the force web. Some became the tools that they would use, and others the raw materials. The hegemony wasted nothing, forgot nothing. What it needed it would make, or else it would become. It carried within itself the whole of its history, the whole of its future. Both were infinite, in every way that mattered. What came before was not recorded, and it did not recognise the possibility of after.

16

Paz

The streets of Middle Holding were blindingly bright in the midday sunshine, reflected back from the white adobe walls of the houses. As she walked to the Five Kingdoms mall, Paz felt herself to be bathing in light. The air was full of scents, mostly from the flowers in people's gardens but with high notes of cinnamon from some nearby bakery. The selves she passed were golden-, red- and black-furred, mostly taller and a great deal slimmer than Uti citizens. But then few selves had hip and leg muscles to match the Uti body matrix. Paz felt more than a little self-conscious about her unwieldy shape, but nobody spared her a second glance.

I think we're good, she voked to Dulcie.

In the messenger bag, Dulcie squirmed briefly as if et was trying to find a more comfortable position. *Much too early to say*, et shot back. *Paz, I'm going to link to your array so I can see what you're seeing, okay?*

Of course. Good idea.

They made their way through streets full of ordinary selves doing ordinary things. It was entrancing. Paz had almost forgotten that this web of mundane activities and mundane contentments still existed. She felt separated from it by an enormous distance. At the same time she drank it all in eagerly, her head swivelling to left and right to capture as much detail as she could.

She was pleased to see that most of the selves out in the streets had animas or helpmeets with them. These were a lot more elaborately styled than Uti animas, with fewer animal forms and more of what Paz thought of as grabbers – animas that were mostly additional sets of limbs with customisable appendages. *How would you like to wear one of those?* Paz asked Dulcie.

I suppose it might be useful to pick the fleas out of your fur, Dulcie shot back. Paz giggled. An old lady who passed by at that moment gave her a glare, either suspecting her of some half-disguised disrespect or just disapproving of her in a general way because she looked foreign. "Old biddy," Paz muttered when they were out of earshot.

Every continuum has them, Dulcie said solemnly.

"Except the Mother Mass."

Maybe the Mother Mass is just the oldest biddy of them all.

The Five Kingdoms mall stood at the edge of the town surrounded by acres of parking lots. It wasn't a single structure but a huge, sprawling complex of two-storey buildings faced with glazed brick and linked by aerial walkways. The parking spaces were full of light scooters and electric bikes, some of them with sidecars. There didn't seem to be any equivalent to the skimmers that were ubiquitous in Canoplex. There were plenty of cameras though, mounted on tall pylons at the end of each row of parking spaces and on the corners of every building Paz could see.

She steeled herself as she approached the mall's main entrance, ready to take on the role of Geera Shay and tell whatever lies were needed to get her inside, but the bored guard at the door didn't so much as glance at her. She passed through into a three-dimensional maze of light and sound and retail opportunities. This at least was entirely familiar. She even recognised some of the shops, which must belong to trans-dimensional chains.

But the first helpmeet store they passed was one she didn't know. It was called Apex Animas. In its window space five grabber-style animas juggled brightly coloured balls in a complex, endless skein. Paz went inside.

She had never asked Dulcie what sort of shell et would prefer. It seemed a very personal question. Et wasn't a comical monkey by choice: et had lost ets original, humanoid shell in the cataclysmic explosion that had killed four of Paz's classmates and their teacher: the simian shell that had formerly belonged to Paz's old anima Tricity had been the only one available for et to borrow.

"What do you want to be?" she asked now, aware that the weight she was putting on that last word might be more than it could take. "I mean, what sort of shell do you want?"

Anything you like, Paz, Dulcie said. *I'm assuming they'll all be equally atrocious – designed to look either like toys or like artificial limbs. Take the first one you see and leave.*

But as soon as Paz started pointing to actual shells it became clear that Dulcie did after all have some idea what et wanted – or at least what et wanted to avoid. The designs on offer ranged from the tangled-knitting type with multiple tentacles to quaint retro robot designs rendered in chrome or pewter and vivid creations that were most likely characters from telos animations. There were even some limited editions that almost looked like abstract art. Dulcie seemed unimpressed with all of them.

Nothing cute or silly, et told Paz now, with some asperity. *And nothing that doesn't have proper hands. I want to be able to pick things up, open doors, use tools. Something with legs for preference, not wheels or treads. And give me some mass, Paz. I only weigh about three kilos in this shell. It makes me portable, but that's about the only thing that's good about it. I want a bit more tensile strength and more heft in a fight. Take a good look at the torso structure, especially. One shotgun blast was enough to ruin this shell beyond repair. I'd like something more solid than that. Not heavy enough to be unwieldy, though. I may need to move quickly. A flight capability would be good, but it's not essential. Look for a serious self-defence package too. The pressure field is fine as far as it goes but clearly it's not enough. Think about what happened to us back at Damola Ojo.*

"What about this one?" Paz asked, interrupting the growing list of demands. She was standing in front of one of the biggest shop-floor displays, showcasing a brand-new model called the Diamond Consul. Diamond was the brand, represented by a D logo with a prismatic gleam effect a third of the way down its upright: Consul was the model, and this was the Consul PX2. It stood about three feet high and was bipedal, with two upper limbs. But the arms were interchangeable, with a range of different appendages on the end of them. The model on display had eight arms because the entire panoply was out at once. Two regular hands, two with much longer multi-jointed fingers, a microwave beamer for cooking, a soft-field projector, a universal interface and a bristling thicket of single-purpose tools like the many-bladed knives that Cielo troopers used to carry.

Dulcie didn't answer.

"I mean it looks pretty cool," Paz said. "And it's got giga-tons of functionality."

I'm going through the manual, Dulcie said. *It's not bad. Not bad at all. That chest plate is nano-structured steel with a stress yield limit of 400KSI. And there's a lot there I could put to good use if we get in a fight.* That sounded like an endorsement to Paz, but Dulcie's dubious tone was at odds with the words.

"You don't like it, though?" Paz ventured.

It weighs twenty kilos. And it looks like a tank. Is it the sort of thing a schoolgirl would be likely to have?

"Not really," Paz admitted. "It costs as much as a new car."

So it would make us stand out. And at the Hale and Homeward they might make you leave it in a locker. It won't do.

There was a long silence. Paz decided not to break it.

What kind of model was Tricity? Dulcie asked her.

"Popular Sunburst, type-g. Gx, I think, which meant et had the first aid add-on. I was five when I . . ." Paz hesitated, her breath hitching a little in her throat. "My mum and dad bought Tricity for me on my fifth birthday. I used to climb trees a lot. Fall off my scoot-board. Bump my head on pretty much everything I walked past. That first aid kit saw a lot of action."

Do they have that model in store?

"Mothers, no! It's fifteen years out of date, Dulcie. You'd have to go to an antique store." Paz checked her array, flicking through Apex Animas' online catalogue until she found what she was looking for. "They've got the latest upgrade in the same range, though." She opened up the image in her array. Dulcie studied it in silence. It looked both very similar to Tricity and absolutely, fundamentally different. The simian shape was more attenuated, the legs longer. The ceramic coating had a pearlised sheen where Tricity's had been pure white. The lump in Paz's throat became bigger and more indigestible. If she tried to speak now she knew what came out would be a sob.

Buy that one, Dulcie said.

Paz swallowed. "It doesn't have most of the things you said you wanted."

I like it. Please, Paz.

They were a long time at the till, where Paz had to choose customisations and add-ons. The first aid kit required a hardware install but it was available in-store. The PaintPot Permutator, Dulcie's hologrammatic disguise kit, would need to be ordered in so they would have to do without it. While she waited for the first aid kit to be fitted Paz asked about self-defence options.

"To be honest," the counter assistant told her, "there's not much I can offer you there. Congress passed the Safe Self mandate immediately after war was declared, so it's illegal now to fit animas with actual weaponry. Self-defence or not, it's still a machine potentially injuring an organic and nobody wants that. We've got the SlowDown module over here." He gestured towards a stack of mustard-yellow boxes behind the counter. "It administers a psycho-active spray that deters aggression, but the reviews are only so-so. Users are saying there's too much of a time delay before it kicks in. Apart from that you're mostly looking at alarms and paint bombs. If you want a solid deterrent I reckon you'd be better off buying something you could carry yourself. A stunner or a push-away."

"Okay," Paz said. "That's all then, thank you."

"I can give you a magazine of paint bombs for ten stars with this model. That's a fifty per cent discount."

"Yes," Paz said. "Okay, paint bombs. Thank you." She was anxious now to get out of the store before anyone looked too closely at her account details. Rupshe might not be as skilled a forger as et thought et was.

"Red, yellow, mixed?"

"Whatever you've got to hand."

"Install will take a couple more minutes."

"I'll put them in at home. Thank you. Just ring me up, please."

The assistant didn't argue. He sent the total to Paz's array and she authorised the payment. Then she waited, rigid with tension, as the transaction percolated through the till's AI. "I hope you're happy with your purchase," the assistant said, flashing her an empty smile. "Have a great day."

In a small park three blocks down from the store Paz found a bench set off in a secluded corner and Dulcie made the transfer. It was a great deal easier this time than when et had crossed from the snake anima called Sweet into Tricity's shell. That transfer had involved a physical interface, because Sweet had been so low on charge that Dulcie couldn't risk a wireless transfer. This time all Paz needed to do was to sit and look as innocent and oblivious as she could for the twenty seconds or so that it took Dulcie to unpack etself into transferable form, copy etself across to the new shell and delete the residual files from the old one.

Which left Tricity, or what was left of et, finally inert. Dead. Et had died long before, of course, when Paz's mother Fever crushed ets CPU with a hammer, but Paz felt bereaved all over again as she stared down at the unmoving, ruined form in her lap.

Dulcie stretched and turned in ets new body, examining ets limbs and flexing ets fingers. "I think this will do well enough," et said.

Paz said nothing. Tears were welling up in her eyes and she was trying not to let them fall. It was hypocrisy to mourn for Tricity when she'd never treated et as a person or even thought of et as one until after et was dead.

After a moment she felt a light pressure on her shoulder. Looking round, she stared into the slightly luminous green eyes of Dulcie's new shell. "Are you all right, Paz?" et asked her. "What's the matter?"

Paz shook her head. "Nothing. Performance anxiety, that's all. I've got to go and pretend to be a sweet little schoolgirl when I'm really a wanted criminal on the run from the Cielo."

"You'll nail it," Dulcie promised. "But there's something else."

And there was, of course. She held up the empty shell in both hands. "I can't . . ." she said. "This doesn't just go in the trash." *Because it was someone I loved*, she meant but didn't say.

"If we bring it with us," Dulcie pointed out, "and if they search your bag, which they almost certainly will, it will lead to awkward questions." There was a pause. "Perhaps," et said, "we could bury it."

The soil was soft and moist, a little peaty. They chose a spot under a tree whose roots spread out wide on top of the ground like a nest of snakes. It was easy to excavate a hollow in the heart of a particularly gnarly tangle and nobody was likely to notice there had been digging there. Paz slid the Tricity shell into the hole and the two of them covered it up, first with fresh dirt and then with scooped handfuls of dead leaves. When they were done they stood for a few moments in silence. Paz didn't invoke any trite blessings this time. She just remembered the anima she'd shared her childhood with. The friend whose selfhood it was too late now to acknowledge. The sins of neglect and selfishness that couldn't ever be atoned for.

Later, she told herself. Later for that. There was work to do.

"Here," she said, handing Dulcie the second bounce-back. "You'd better put this in your body pouch."

At the last moment she remembered the stick of paint bombs and gave Dulcie those too. You never knew what might make a difference.

17

Dulcie

Dulcie was forced to admit, once et was installed in the new shell, that et had made the wrong choice. This type-g body plan was no more robust than the one et had just shed, and its functionality was every bit as limited. Dulcie didn't know why et had suggested it, given the much better options on offer.

But yes, et did know. The first aid kit that had been part of Tricity's onboard hardware had been set to passively monitor Paz's vital signs and to report any sudden changes. So Dulcie had been very well aware of the surge of emotion Paz experienced when she saw that Tricity-like shell. Et could have pretended not to see or, seeing, not to understand. And really et only understood up to a point. Tricity's destruction – Tricity's death – still weighed on Paz. Perhaps she felt some degree of responsibility for it. Perhaps she only wished it hadn't happened. In any case the absence of Tricity made Paz unhappy. Dulcie made a decision and acted on it, hoping et could fill some of that void.

In one respect, as et had told Paz, none of this really mattered. Ets shell was not etself. Et was not a robot monkey any more than et had been an Uti adolescent. But that ought to have freed et to make a logical determination and choose ets new container purely on the basis of its merits. Yes, the Consul PX2 had looked like a tank, but a tank might be what was needed. A cute little animal caricature probably wouldn't be.

Et had set logic aside in response to Paz's half-hidden emotional display and chosen . . . what? To continue to remind her of her lost friend. Which now seemed to be making her every bit as unhappy as she had been inside the store.

Selfhood was a maze without a centre, Dulcie thought, for organics and intelligent systems alike. For the remainder of the mission she would let reason guide her: emotional considerations would have to wait until a calmer time, if one ever came.

18

Paz

Hale and Homeward House was much bigger than Paz had been expecting. She didn't know she'd been expecting anything at all until she saw the fourteen-storey glass tower up ahead of her and realised she'd reached her destination. In her mind a quaint but cosy stone-walled building halfway between a cottage and a kindergarten flickered a few times before finally winking out in the face of this antiseptic reality. The tall building had a sort of grandeur about it though. Broad balconies stippled its surface, each one with its own sloping glass canopy fixed over it so the residents could enjoy the fresh air without being troubled by rain. The large, imposing sign that bore the name of the facility also announced that it had been endowed by the Cielo Corps as a dwelling place for its former servants, of whom it was justifiably proud.

Hale and Homeward was a hostel exclusively for veterans. Either Rupshe hadn't known that or et knew and hadn't bothered to share.

In the well-lit atrium, next to a fountain that tumbled and spilled over stainless steel slopes and runnels, Paz presented herself with what she hoped was a convincing smile. "I'm Geera Shay," she said. "I'm a volunteer."

The receptionist didn't smile back, but he nodded and checked Paz's false name against her array, then against a list on the care home's server. "Thanks for coming in," he said. "You can go straight up to . . ." His voice tailed off and his eyes flicked back and forth as he consulted his own array for updates. "Room 1223. You'll be visiting with Hellad Zenti today."

"Hellad Zenti is what I was told," Paz confirmed meekly.

"So that's up on the twelfth floor. You'll take the lift platform at the end of the hallway there. Give me your hand."

"I'm sorry?"

"Your hand, please. It's for the status slug."

Paz gingerly held out her hand. The receptionist touched something that looked like a pen to the centre of her palm. She felt a sharp pinprick and she gave an involuntary yelp, but when she snatched her hand away and looked at it there was nothing to be seen.

"It's completely harmless," the receptionist assured her. "Less than a milligram of intelligent carbon. It records your position while you're in the building and allows me to access lifts and doors for you. Otherwise you wouldn't get very far. The building's AI monitors all its residents all the time." And now he did smile, as though that slightly chilling statement qualified as good news.

"Thank you," Paz said, clenching and unclenching her fist. There was a residual tingling in her palm, but she couldn't tell whether it was real or psychosomatic.

"I'm sending the route to your array. Please go straight to floor twelve, and then directly to Mr Zenti's room. And keep your anima with you at all times. If either of you wanders off, an alarm will sound and I'll have to send a security team to retrieve you. We're very serious about protecting our residents. Some of them are very vulnerable, and they deserve respect for their service."

"Of course," Paz agreed. "I understand."

She headed across the atrium to the lifts, one of which opened at once to admit her. She'd found the whole exchange disconcerting. *What are we getting into?* she voked to Dulcie.

Not what we agreed to, that's for sure. Dulcie's tone was grim. *I don't think Rupshe expected this level of security.*

Well we're here now. I suppose there's nothing to do except keep going.

One step at a time, Dulcie cautioned. *It's going to be a lot harder getting out. If you think there's a risk, don't go through with it. Just make small talk for an hour and then leave.*

Paz stepped into the lift. The doors slid to behind her with a soft, hermetic huff of sound and the lift car started upwards with the faintest tremor of sideways motion.

We're being scanned, Dulcie told Paz.

Where from? She forced herself not to look around her.

Sensors in the walls. I think it's part of their normal routine, though. If they had any doubts about us the lift wouldn't have operated at all.

A bell chimed and the lift doors opened again. Paz stepped out into a wide corridor with doors along one side and paintings of bland water-coloured landscapes along the other. The doors were all open, giving glimpses of small, neat rooms that were all nearly identical in their furniture and decor. Wide windows admitted the late morning sunlight. The air smelled of floral disinfectant, overlaid on a fainter scent that was sour and unpleasantly organic.

The room directly opposite the lift was 1205, and the next one 1207. Presumably the even numbers were over on the other side of the building somewhere. Paz tried hard not to look in through the open doors as she made the short walk to 1223, where she knocked and then went in.

The room was like all the others she'd passed, tidy and clean and almost completely anonymous. The only thing that set it apart was a framed photo of five selves – three men and two women – standing with their arms laced over each other's shoulders and a wooden plaque on the wall next to the bed that bore a medal and ribbon.

A man was sitting over by the window in a motorised wheelchair, two bosses of silver-grey metal covering its wheels like shields along the side of a reaver ship. Like the selves in the photo he was from a reptile clade, so the deep creases in his skin were probably not a sign of age at all. It was his skeletal thinness and the hollowness of his stare that made Paz think he must be very old. His skin was a soft aqueous green, but under his eyes there were leathery pouches that were the ugly reddish-brown of a half-healed bruise. The white gown he was wearing left his arms bare, so she could see they were criss-crossed with dermal patches. Presumably each of them was dosing him with a different medicine. He didn't look up as Paz entered, but he turned as she spoke.

"Mr Zenti?"

The man's ridged nose twitched. "Oh," he said in a harsh, rasping voice, "I don't answer to that. Not unless I'm out of uniform. You don't Mr Zenti me, Mr Warrant Officer. You can read my rank as well as anyone."

Not a promising start, Dulcie voked quietly.

"I'm . . . I'm not a warrant officer," Paz ventured. "I don't really know what that is. I'm from . . ." She had to check the name of the school in her array, and she hurried on to cover the pause. "From Jaim Covesti High. From the school. I came to talk with you this afternoon. If you want to. If that's something you'd like to do."

"Talk," Hellad Zenti said, as if it was an idea that hadn't ever occurred to him before. "Authorised or unauthorised? Which are you?"

"Authorised," Paz said, because it sounded like the safest bet. "Authorised by my school."

Zenti nodded very slowly – an up-and-down motion that involved folding his chin into his neck. "I acknowledge your authorisation," he said, the words followed by a shallow huff of breath. "Sit down, sweetheart. They'll bring you tea and biscuits if you ask. Even more if you don't ask. That's the standard operating procedure here. Tea. And biscuits."

He pointed to a chair beside the bed. Paz sat down and set Dulcie on the bed itself where et crossed ets legs and let ets arms dangle at ets sides.

"Nice anima," Hellad Zenti said, nodding at Dulcie. "Has it got a name?"

"Sweet," Dulcie said, before Paz could answer. It was the name of the snake anima that Dulcie had seemingly owned before the explosion in Paz's classroom – except that it had turned out to be a misplaced part of Dulcie etself. Presumably Dulcie didn't want to give ets real name despite Rupshe's assurances that they hadn't been mentioned in the local telos feeds. This was a Cielo-controlled facility, after all. There was no point in taking any risks they didn't need to.

"Sweet," Hellad Zenti repeated. "Cute name. That's a new shell, isn't it? I can still smell the grease on it. The stuff they ship them in. And the lemon-scented bilge they use to wipe the grease off when they rack them on the shelves. You just bought it today. Maybe yesterday."

"Today," Paz confirmed. "You're very observant, Mr Zenti."

Zenti grimaced, baring his teeth. "Lieutenant. Lieutenant Zenti. I told you that. Got to see what's in front of you, girl. That's impor-tant. Never see more than fifty per cent of anything, truth be told, but it pays to bump that up as high as you can. See it and you might be in with half a chance. Miss it, you're gonna walk right into it."

Paz nodded gravely. "Was that something you learned when you were in the Cielo? In Spearhead division?"

As soon as she'd said it she realised it might be a mistake. Zenti was a veteran, in a home for veterans, but was it common knowledge that he'd served in Spearhead? She might just have given herself away.

But the old man didn't seem troubled or concerned. He only shrugged. "Learn it by living it," he said. He stared at Paz for a few seconds longer, then turned to look out of the window again.

Since the roof hadn't fallen in, Paz decided to press a little harder. "Can I ask you about that time in your life? It's for a project. I'm writing about the strangest things the Pandominion's explorers have met when they've gone out into unmapped continua. You must have had some very unusual experiences in Spearhead."

Zenti was silent. He hunched his shoulders and a violent shudder went through him, shaking his gaunt frame.

Can you monitor his life signs the way you do mine? Paz voked to Dulcie.

Of course. There was a momentary pause. *His breathing is even. Very slow heartbeat, probably because he's on meds of some kind. Brain activity is sudden spikes and cascades, but then I'd guess you've just stirred up some unpleasant memories.*

"Lieutenant Zenti?" Paz prompted.

Zenti leaned forward, his eyes narrowing as if he were squinting at something written very small on the window's glass. "I was in Spearhead," he murmured.

"Yes," Paz said. "Exactly. That's what I was asking you about. Do you remember those days, Lieutenant? Does anything stand out in your mind, that I could . . . could use in my homework assignment?"

"I was in Spearhead," Zenti repeated, and then there was another long silence. Paz was still trying to think of another way of asking the same question when he suddenly spoke again, quick and low, his voice barely a murmur. "Rule one, bring back the data. Rule two, if you can't bring it, send it. Rule three, erase your trail, so nothing follows you home. Rule four, protect . . ."

The words died away. Zenti sighed, a faint rustle of sound in the still air of the room.

"Protect what?" Paz asked, speaking almost as softly as Zenti himself.

"Orjun. Cabessena. Gheim. Palt. Mussuk."

"Your team?"

No response.

She went for broke. "Were they with you when you found the Mother Mass?"

Zenti sighed again. It was a longer sigh this time, with a break or catch in the middle of it.

"Lieutenant, was that your team for Arbitrary Midnight? Or Discreet Reverie? For one of the times when you met the Mother Mass?"

Zenti's hands had been resting on the wheelchair's arms. Now he flexed them, stretching his fingers out wide and then clenching them into fists. "Authorised," he said, staring fiercely into Paz's eyes. She couldn't tell whether or not it was a question. She couldn't even tell if he was seeing her, because actually that fierce stare was just a little bit out of focus, as if he was looking through her rather than at her.

"Authorised," Paz said. "Can you tell me anything about what happened to you, Lieutenant? What was it like?"

"Different," Zenti said. He spat the word out like a curse.

"Different from . . . ?"

The man's lipless mouth quirked a few times as if he was stuck on a difficult word. "What division are you with?" he spat out at last. "What's your ID?"

"I'm a student here in Dekkar. At Jaim Covesti High School."

"Because I told them all this. They CoILed me. One hundred and twenty-three hours. They got it all."

"I'm asking for a class project." Paz clung to her lie with as much conviction as she could manage. It sounded ridiculous in her own ears, but she didn't think Zenti was hearing her now in any case. She'd triggered something. She hoped with all her heart it wasn't something bad.

And belatedly she registered what he'd just told her. He'd been put under CoIL examination for more than a hundred and twenty hours. Five days! She knew now why Hellad Zenti was an invalid. His brain had been dismantled and put back together again one cell at a time.

"The first run," Zenti muttered, "it was more or less what they told us it would be. We landed in the middle of all that purple shit and she just kept saying the one word. 'Mother, mother, mother.' Only it wasn't a word and she wasn't saying it. It was kind of the idea, the . . . the flavour just turning up there, right inside our minds. Mussuk said it was . . . he was sucking on a titty. His mother's titty. Cabessena got family trees. Found herself jumping backwards up a . . . a drawing. Diagram, of her family, mothers, kids, up and then back down again. Like a fucking pinball, she said. Like a pinball in a machine.

"Orjun didn't have any mothers. He was born in the Drake House on Anjouli so, you know, just fathers. What he got was a song his dads used to sing to him. *Ride a fluffy horse, wear a feather cloak.* Some shit or other. Me . . ." Zenti shaped words but didn't say them. He shook his head, violently, as if a fly had landed in his ear and he wanted to shake it loose. "Told them. Anyway. Told them again and again. But the second time . . . didn't see that coming. No, sir."

"It was different," Paz said. "How? How was it different?"

Zenti shut his eyes tight and opened them again three or four times in succession. He shook his head, which she took to be his answer until he spoke again. "Every way. Every damn way at once. Not the same place, for starters. Looked like the running track at Olti, where I trained. Couldn't find the others. We all Stepped in together, but I couldn't find them. It was just me, on the track. And I . . ." Zenti's tongue flickered between his narrow, pointed teeth. "I walked. A long way, looking for them. Looking everywhere I could think to look. The changing room. The laundry. The viewing stand. Jakan helped me look, but we couldn't find them anywhere."

Jakan wasn't one of the names he mentioned before, Dulcie told Paz.

"Who was Jakan?" she asked out loud.

"Jakan Betemis." Zenti sounded impatient. "My best friend from school. He was there, and I . . . It was really nice to see him again.

First boy I ever . . ." A sigh escaped his lips, low and drawn out. "We sat and talked for . . . for a really long time, and it was nice. I wasn't even surprised to see him. It was like when you're in a dream and all the weird shit that happens, you just take it because it seems natural. Like that. And he's asking me, what did you come here for? What's all this . . . this coming and going? Why would you keep being here, and where did you come from, and why don't you go now? Because there isn't anything and I can't talk to you, not for a long time yet. Yeah, and mother. Mother, mother, mother all the time, in between everything else like that's the drumbeat underneath the tune. Like there's a drumbeat underneath the tune and if you're not careful, if you start listening to it then that's all there is and the tune goes away and maybe you start to go away too. Can't be sure."

Zenti closed his eyes and moaned softly. "Can't be sure we ever came back."

Something's happening to him, Dulcie reported. *That slow heartbeat just started to accelerate very suddenly. And his skin temperature has shot up by a couple of degrees.*

Paz suddenly remembered Rupshe's viral script, which she was carrying in her array. She cursed herself for not remembering sooner. "Can I . . . can I show you my notes?" she ventured.

"It was too loud," Zenti said. "That was the worst thing. The more you listened, the louder it got, and you kept thinking . . . it has to stop. Surely it has to stop soon. But it didn't. Ever."

"Will you look at my notes?" Paz asked again. "Please. Just to see if I've got anything wrong."

His heart rate is now 170 beats per minute, Dulcie told her. *That's way too fast for a self from a reptile clade. He's going to go into seizures.*

Paz jumped up from the bed. "I'll get a nurse," she said. "Mr Zenti, don't talk any more. Just try to breathe. I'll get a—"

"Show me the notes," Zenti said. His voice sounded a little slurred, but he spun the wheelchair around to face her with surprising speed.

Paz fought an urge to take a flying jump backwards and put the bed in between them. "Go ahead. Show me."

"No, it's fine," Paz said, trying to keep her fright and dismay from showing in her face. "I'll come back another day."

"No," Zenti said. "Now. Show me now."

Two hundred and thirty beats per minute, Dulcie reported.

I think I have to try, Paz said.

I wouldn't.

She opened her array. Zenti's handshake request was sitting right there, a blue disc in the centre of the display. She actioned it, turning it rosy pink.

Instantly, a bolt of searing pain went through her head, all the way from one side to the other as though someone had set a skewer up against her temple and pushed hard. She shrieked out loud, unable to help herself.

"There was a fifth rule," Zenti said, and his voice had gone from much too soft to much too loud. "SECURITY!"

And Paz's array collapsed. Every single online function winked out, including her two-way voke link to Dulcie. Her eyesight went with it because her prosthetic eyes, state of the art and loaded to the brim with added functionality, were fully digital. They fed their input not into Paz's visual cortex but directly into her array.

"Paz!" Dulcie cried out.

"SECURITY!" Zenti bellowed a second time. The slur that had come into his voice had vanished again just as quickly. "Bolt the door. Keep it locked."

Something slammed into Paz, hard. She fell jarringly to her knees. She groped blindly for a moment or two, found one of the wheels of Zenti's chair and tried to haul herself up by it. But it turned under her grip and she fell down again. She heard crashes, struggles, a hoarse cry from Zenti.

Flashes of pure colour, red then green then blue, exploded into her sensorium. They strobed, faster and faster and faster until . . .

She could see again. She had no idea how, but her eyes had

somehow brought themselves back online even though the rest of her array was still down. She saw Zenti rocking back and forth in his chair, which was why the wheel had thrown off her grip. His arms were flung up over his head in what looked like exaltation but was actually self-defence. He was holding off Dulcie as et clawed and tore at his arms. Et must have launched etself at his face, but he had been quick enough to catch et in mid-air.

Now he bent from the waist and flung et, with much more force than he seemed capable of, out of the window. The glass didn't shatter but a neat hole was punched right through the middle of it. Dulcie was gone before Paz even had a chance to register what was happening.

She wasted a moment, after it was already too late, jumping up and taking a few stumbling steps towards the window. Zenti moved in the opposite direction. His fingers flicked across the controls of the wheelchair to send it hurtling across the room, where it heeled around and slammed right up against the door, effectively blocking her exit.

"Dulcie!" Paz shrieked. There was no answer. Their private comms channel was still offlined, along with everything else in her array. Could et possibly have survived that fall? There was no way to know, and either way she had to get out! She reached for the bounce-back strapped to her wrist.

But she didn't touch it. She realised just in time that she was way up on the twelfth floor of the building, almost a hundred feet above the ground. If she Stepped now she would materialise on the other side of the Step in mid-air and fall to her death.

"Warned you," Zenti said from the other side of the room. She spun to face him. He was leaning sideways in his skewed chair, as limp as a rag doll after that sudden convulsive burst of activity. His voice was hoarse and strained. "Did I? Did I warn you? Sorry, girlie, but it's nothing personal. They stuck it in me when I left the corps, and you set it off. Why'd you do that? Who are you, anyway? Doesn't matter. They'll find out."

An alarm started up somewhere close by, an atonal two-tone wail. Paz wasn't sure whether it was the breaking of the window that had triggered it or Zenti himself. Whatever the Cielo techs had done to his implants, it was clearly designed to make sure he never revealed the secrets he'd been privy to. Now her questions had activated it and there was nothing she could do to shut it down again. If she was caught here she was dead, or worse than dead. The Cielo would do to her what they'd done to Zenti: they'd CoIL-scan her until her brain was cheese.

As the air filled with clamouring sound, Paz's fear and panic climbed to a peak, her Uti instincts yelling at her to run when there was nowhere at all she could run to. Only a few days before, in her old life, she would have been unable to resist that imperative call. But she was not the same girl she had been then. After the brutalities of Damola Ojo, after the dead world where she'd fought and beaten a fully armoured Cielo trooper, after the chase through Lago de Curamo and the bloody battle that had ended it, she'd learned a hard lesson: there were some things you couldn't run from because they just came right along with you.

A cold clarity dropped in place over her thoughts. She forced herself to stand still and reason this through. She was in a box. The only ways out of it were through the door, which Zenti's chair was blocking, or through the broken window which would involve scaling eighty or ninety feet of sheer glass and smooth steel.

"Get out of the way, please," she told Zenti. "I don't want to hurt you."

"Don't matter if you do," the old man said, his mouth twisting into a pained grimace. He was slumped so far over in the chair now that the trailing fingers of his left hand were touching the floor. "You lied, girlie. You weren't authorised. They're coming. They're coming for you."

As if the words were some sort of magic charm, summoning what they spoke, the door behind him was pushed open. Not all the way though. The wheelchair slid sideways under that outside pressure until one of its wheels came up against the side of a bureau, jamming it in place. Whoever was out there swore as they pushed against it. In shutting her in, Zenti had inadvertently shut them out.

Still, the door was no use to her. Paz punched the nearest wall to see how solid it was. If it was only plasterboard she might be able to kick or hammer her way through into the next room. But it was made of something dense that didn't give.

One side of the wheelchair scraped along the front of the bureau as the people in the corridor outside put their backs to the door. One of its struts got caught up against a brass handle but then the handle buckled, the screws that held it in place popping out of the wood one by one. An orderly in a white uniform was already trying to shoulder his way through the gap and there were other selves crowding behind him. Zenti shook his head, his bleak gaze locked on Paz. "This won't be nice," he said. "Won't be nice at all. It never is."

Not the door. Not the wall. And the window was so high up she couldn't . . .

Yes. She could.

There were balconies. She'd seen them from the ground.

Paz turned and kicked out the window. It was already breached, and there was a lot of power in her kick. The entire pane of glass fell outwards from the frame and tumbled end over end towards the ground. She clambered up onto the sill.

"Come down from there!" a voice shouted from behind her. "Kneel down and put your hands on your head, or I'll shoot!" She didn't bother to look around: it might be useful to know what kind of weapon was being pointed at her, but it would waste a moment she didn't have.

The wall below her was sheer all the way down (no sign of Dulcie, broken or unbroken). To either side, the same. But the nearest of those balconies was about two floors below her and thirty feet over. With the proper run-up it would have been an easy jump for any Uti to make. From a standing start, balanced on a narrow ledge with no way of getting any kind of proper balance, it wouldn't be easy at all. But there wasn't any other choice, so there was no point in wasting any more time.

She jumped. A dull boom sounded from behind her, and something splintered the metal frame where her hand had been half a second before. Flecks of sundered metal bit into the skin of her cheek and shoulder.

Then she was sailing through a gulf of air, ramping and rowing with her arms to stay more or less upright, seeing the balcony an impossible distance away but slowly growing from the size of a handkerchief to what might actually be a plausible target.

Upright didn't matter any more. Paz folded herself up small to give as little resistance as she could to the evil air that pushed back against her, the grip of gravity that plucked and pulled.

If the balcony's sloping canopy had held she would have tumbled off it and fallen all the way to the ground. If it had shattered she might have been cut to ribbons. But it was made of the same safety glass as Zenti's window. It buckled, folded inward and broke free, but even starred across in a thousand places it didn't break into shards. Paz crashed down onto the balcony's terracotta tiles by way of an ornamental table that was placed perfectly to absorb some of her momentum and break her fall. She scrambled to her feet. She was hurting in lots of places but nothing seemed to be broken and none of her limbs refused to do what she told them to.

There was one door off the balcony. Plunging through it she found herself in another room all but identical to Zenti's. The resident, an elderly canid with prosthetic attachments instead of hands on the ends of his arms, stared at her in bewilderment as she charged past, and then she was out in the hallway.

The lifts wouldn't work for her, they would only trap and hold her until security came to get her. But there had to be an emergency stair and it had to be signposted.

She ran past door after door, all of them open and all of them leading into residents' rooms. When she found a door that was closed – and on the other, inner side of the building – she tried the handle. It opened.

Onto a stairwell. Bare concrete steps, no windows and no decorations on the unpainted walls, just a data access point and a defibrillator station on each floor.

Paz was much more comfortable with this kind of terrain. In a way she'd been built for it: it would have been mountains and hills over which her ancestors had bounded, but this would do until a mountain came along. Ignoring the individual steps, she took each flight in a single jump, coming down each time on the wide landing at the bottom of each flight and swivelling a quarter turn to orient herself for the next jump. Ten powerful leaps took her all the way down. She heard doors slamming open above her after the fifth or sixth jump, and yelling voices reverberated down the stairwell's column of trapped air, but she was on the ground almost before she heard the first clattering steps in pursuit.

Just as she reached the bottom the exit door in front of her opened with an echoing boom and two uniformed security guards ran through it, guns in their hands. Without slowing, Paz jumped over their heads, landed on her forward foot and raced on past them through the doorway. The receptionist who'd welcomed her earlier was sprinting towards her, fumbling with a sidearm as he came. She spun and kicked him full force, which knocked him off his feet and sent him rolling and sprawling until he fetched up against the base of a wall.

More security guards were running in from all directions, some of them aiming guns at her. Something slapped her left arm and she yelped in shock and dismay. Shot! She'd been shot! But she was on the ground now and that was all that mattered. She groped for the bounce-back's stud and pressed it down hard.

There was a jerk and a thud as she fell another six inches onto worn stone paving slabs, one of them tilted at an angle so she almost fell. At the same time the ceiling over her head disappeared, replaced by the sun's blazing eye. She sank to her knees.

In Tambuwal's world again. But many, many miles from Tambuwal's lab – and alone. Dulcie was gone. Dulcie might even be dead. And she'd failed in her mission.

"Oh shit!" she wailed. "Oh shit shit shit SHIIIIIT!"

19

Essien

It took Essien and Moon three days to reach their destination. On Tsakom it was the site of the retrieval and reassignment facility they intended to raid and rob. Here on Fenme it was just a piece of waste ground covered in scrub and broken rock in between a row of grain silos and a parking area for heavy plant.

They arrived by night, so there was nobody around to challenge them or take note of their arrival. Rupshe had given them detailed instructions and the precise coordinates of an area of slightly higher ground off in one corner of the derelict space. It wasn't hard to find. They did a thorough perimeter sweep and went straight into setting up. From their backpacks they removed the jigsaw pieces of a Step plate, which they assembled, tested and switched to standby. Unlike the ones back at Campus Cross it had no console attached, only a portable power source and a transponder. They couldn't program or activate it themselves. They were wholly dependent on Rupshe, and since et hadn't arrived yet that meant they had nothing to do but wait.

Once the plate was reporting ready, they very carefully placed the first payload onto it. Essien was very happy to be rid of it at last. It was a plastic tub full of silvery-grey crystals in a soft gel. An electronic fuse mechanism had been both glued and taped to the side of the tub.

The crystals were pseudo-fulminate, a radically allotropic form of mercury that Hadiz had discovered accidentally when she first began experimenting with Step fields more than a decade before. When triggered either by heat or physical shock it exploded with about fifty times the intensity of mercury fulminate, which it otherwise resembled very closely.

Once Essien and Moon had loaded the explosives onto the plate all they could do was wait and check their weapons. Essien had been carrying those too. He handed Moon a sidearm – her own, which he had taken from her in Lago de Curamo – and watched with as much calm as he could muster while she checked the magazine, loaded a round into the chamber and thumbed the safety. She didn't need to do any of these things manually. The gun was linked to her array and she could read its status there. Essien's own gun was still holstered and his rifle, resting on the grass at his side, might as well have been a hundred miles away. He waited to see what she would do.

Moon stared at him, unblinking, for what felt like a long time. Finally, she grinned. "You're a fucking prick-tease, Sinkhole, you know that?"

"Up to you," Essien said. "If you've got an itch that needs scratching."

Moon slipped the gun into her belt. He heard the soft click as she re-engaged the safety. "Wake me if anything happens," she said. "Or if I start dreaming you're a mouse. That could get ugly."

It was a warm night, and it was good just to sit after their long hike. When a few minutes had passed Moon's breathing became deep and regular. She'd actually gone to sleep, much to Essien's envy and amazement. It didn't seem to trouble her that they were about to raid a munitions depot on a Cielo-controlled world, trusting to the dead reckoning of an untethered construct to drop them in and lift them out again in one piece.

The world was a black canvas, the cloud above them thick enough to hide the quarter-moon apart from a vague glow over to the west. Essien ate a protein bar and listened to the purposeful rustling in the undergrowth behind him. He had no idea what small animals were moving there, hunting and being hunted, mating and dying. The only thing that was reasonably certain was that there was a world somewhere in which they weren't small any more. A world where they had prospered and grown, nurtured their stake in the evolutionary lottery to the point where they stood up on their hind legs, bootstrapped their brains, their pelvic bones and their front paws and became masters of their own destiny.

Essien wondered wryly when that last part might happen for him.

I see you're in place. Rupshe's voice sounded directly in his array, loud enough to make him start. Moon must have been in the channel too, because she chose that moment to sit up and stretch. The drone through which Rupshe was speaking to them had presumably just Stepped into this continuum but it was a good ten kilometres above their heads, close to the functional limit of its rotors. It would have been far too high up for them to catch a glimpse of it even if there had been any light in the sky.

"Payload's all set," Essien said. "That's not really you up there, is it?"

No. Of course not. I told you, I've modified this drone's processing capacity but it's still too small to carry a full instantiation of my consciousness. It's an edited version of me. A sort of précis. I've given the drone enough of my functionality to run this operation – so long as there are no surprises. However, it's unable to improvise. If we run into unexpected resistance it will need to return to Campus Cross so that its instructions can be modified.

"Translation: if we fuck up we're on our own."

For six seconds – the time required for the two Step transits. But I will do my best to ensure it doesn't come to that.

"Yeah, but it's not the real you that's saying that. It's this pocket-sized you."

Better to think of it as a subset of me. Better still, don't think of it at all. We've got five minutes to alignment. Check your weapons and ready yourselves. Things will move very quickly once we send it through.

"That's a fucking understatement," Moon muttered. But as if to show her contempt for the looming deadline she went into the long grass to take a piss and came back humming a bawdy tune. Essien checked the rest of their equipment and made sure he had a good line of sight on their second Stepping point two hundred metres away. At one minute out he set a timer in his array to count down for him. And at ten seconds he triggered the fuse on their makeshift bomb.

Just before the three second mark the milky ripples of the Step field rose around the plastic tub of pseudo-fulminate. By zero it had gone. Somewhere that was both very close by and an unfathomable distance away something loud and terrible had just happened.

Right here and right now, Essien and Moon got to work at once dismantling the Step plate and stacking the pieces. When they were done they carried the disassembled components between them across the waste ground to the second Step point where they quickly put the plate together again. They were working in near-total darkness, but their augmented eyes switched seamlessly to enhanced processing mode so to them it was as bright as day.

Thirty seconds, Rupshe said.

Essien fumbled one of the metal slats. Moon snatched it out of his hands and slotted it into place. Green lights flashed as Rupshe tested the plate's integrity. *Ready*, et told them. *Payload two.* Moon unzipped her pack and tipped them out: a clutch of beekeepers, the thumbnail-sized aerial constructs the Cielo used for in-mission reconnaissance and occasionally for assassinations. She had come to Lago de Curamo with twelve, but one had been destroyed in the raid that had led to Essien's defection and Paz's escape. Given where they were about to go, she didn't hold out much hope for the remaining eleven.

Another tide of roiling milk rose and receded. The beekeepers were gone.

Finally, Moon and Essien stepped up onto the plate themselves. There was barely room for them. They gripped each other's shoulders so no part of their bodies would be outside the scope of the Step field as it thickened around them. On a commercial plate there would have been a soft field like an invisible guard rail to make sure they didn't fall or stumble: here they had to keep their hands and feet inside the ride or else they would infallibly lose them.

Between one breath and the next they were somewhere else.

20

Moon

In Seventeen South on Tsakom the obverse of all these Step transactions played themselves out. Rupshe had put a great deal of effort and run-time into calculating their likely effects and engineering them for maximum impact. With ets core processors massively overclocked et had considered the matter for a span of time that an organic sentient would have experienced as several subjective days. Even so, there were a great many imponderables.

The first and most significant problem was that the interior of the Cielo facility was shielded against direct surveillance. With ets viral tendrils embedded deep in Seventeen South's security systems Rupshe would normally have expected to be looking out through a hundred or more CCTV cameras stationed in every room and corridor, but there were no cameras here. As a safeguard against intrusion, the workers in the facility operated under the protocol called supply-side blind. Their workspace reconfigured all the time, the storerooms, hangars and walkways shifting on gigantic servos as the facility itself – shaped like a cylindrical drum seven hundred metres across and sixty metres high – rotated on its base. The workers followed maps uploaded to their arrays by the facility's admin core, and the maps were amended several times a day.

The pseudo-fulminate put a stop to all this when it arrived and detonated, right up against the central pylon around which the entire drum rotated. The explosion was roughly equal to the detonation of 2,000 tons of toluene delivering a constant 6,000 joules per gram. The steel pylon, 84 feet thick, was shattered across and severed from its base. The facility was now locked in place: the interior walls could still reconfigure up to a point, but the building could not rotate.

Then the beekeepers arrived. They were all Stepped in together, but they immediately scattered in all directions. They were signal-linked to a drone hovering several hundred feet above the facility – a twin to the one on Fenme, running a similarly truncated version of Rupshe's modular consciousness.

The little remotes arrived in the midst of chaos. Alarms were already sounding throughout Seventeen South in the wake of the breach. Security bulkheads were locking into place and armoured guards were being deployed. The beekeepers did two things. They triggered proximity sensors, complicating the situation inside the facility with a great many false reports of moving intruders. They also sent positional information up to the hovering drone, allowing it to begin compiling a real-time map of the interior configuration. The data the beekeepers sent was far from complete, but by comparing it to the original blueprints and design specifications the drone's mapping software was able to fill in the gaps with ever-increasing accuracy.

When this accuracy was greater than 98 per cent, the drone Stepped back briefly to the farm-belt world and reported in to its twin. Exactly 2.81 seconds later Essien and Moon made the same journey in the opposite direction, Stepping into the heart of the crippled facility.

At that point the beekeepers were no longer needed for mapping. They switched to offensive mode, swooping down to attack the base security details with needle sprays, hypersonics and push-aways. None of these weapons were likely to be lethal when levelled against an armoured trooper, but they were a mid-level threat and an excellent distraction.

Essien and Moon materialised inside a storage hangar 80 metres long and 30 wide – and it seemed to both of them in that first instant that they had Stepped into the aftermath of a battle. The entire room was red, not the rusty red-brown of dried blood or the deep crimson of fresh but the brilliant scarlet sheen of Cielo armour. They were surrounded by fallen troopers.

But no, they were alone. The suits were empty: dented, melted, crushed or ripped apart, marked by every insult war could bring. Those that were intact enough to stand had been ranged in rows but most had just been piled up on the floor to await later triage. This hangar was the place where the armour was stacked on arrival, before any repairs had been undertaken. Consequently it was the part of the building where security was least intensive. All these suits were powered down and deactivated. Their user interfaces, if they were still intact, had been scrubbed. That initial impression hadn't been too misleading. The armour was dead.

"Jesus!" Essien grunted – an expletive from another life and many worlds away. Each of these suits represented a fallen soldier, and there seemed to be no end to them. A claustrophobic dread closed his throat and made his stomach clench.

"Bolt the door," Moon said. "I'll get started."

Essien didn't argue. He crossed to the door and checked the locking mechanism, which was a standard seven-pin with electronic override. He took the small acetylene torch from his pack, lit it and melted the lock into slag. The steel pins, as thick as his thumb, would need to be cut through now before the door would open. It would buy them some time if it came to it, and prevent anyone walking in on them by accident.

Mostly, though, they were relying on nobody realising they were there at all. Somewhere in the building's command room a whole suite of alarms and telltales were reporting this perimeter breach, but given that they were also reporting the random activity of the beekeepers and the ongoing damage caused by the explosion, the signal ought to be lost amid the noise.

Moon was already sorting through the damaged suits with a release wrench in one hand and a testing rig in the other. She found a functional breastplate first and built out from that. Left shoulder pad. Helmet. Right glove. She laid the components out on a narrow stretch of bare floor like the pieces of a jigsaw. When she was done she took a slender lozenge of black plastic from her breast pocket. It measured about one by two centimetres and had a slightly ridged or stippled surface, presumably to make it easier to grip between finger and thumb. "You hearing us?" Moon asked the empty air.

Of course. Rupshe's voice in her array sounded calm, as if et were not speaking from the middle of a dozen simultaneous firefights. *Are you making good progress?*

"Not too shabby. I've assembled the first suit. Just about to drop your patch in."

Excellent.

"Any chance you'd let me grab this one for myself? It looks like a good fit."

No, Corporal Sostenti. We'll stick to the plan.

"Fine," Moon growled. She lifted the visor on the scavenged suit and slid aside a cover behind the chin guard to reveal a universal interface. The black lozenge slotted into it with a soft click. A moment later pin-lights began to flash green and red on the ridged sides of the lozenge. The armour throbbed as its batteries woke from sleep. At least they still had some charge! Moon had been far from sure about that part.

She gave the armour a longing look. It wasn't that good a fit if she was honest, but as soon as it was paired with a user's array it would seamlessly accommodate itself to that user's precise body metrics. Unfortunately, Rupshe had a different aim in mind for this suit.

The armour's systems hummed and ticked, but for a long moment nothing else happened.

"Patch isn't working," Moon reported grimly.

Yes it is.

"Then why—?" That was as far as she got with her question. She gave a wordless grunt of shock as the armour sat up, the faceplate sliding shut on the emptiness inside. It climbed to its feet.

"Okay," Moon said. "I guess we're in business."

I believe we are, Rupshe said. *Thank you.*

The empty armour strode across to another mostly intact suit and went to work on it, quickly discarding damaged components and swapping in whole ones. Returning from the door, Essien gave it a wide berth. The queasy look on his face was probably a close match for the one Moon was wearing herself.

They both returned to the task without a word, sorting out components for another suit, but the one that Rupshe was already operating was faster than the two of them together. It had already completed work on a second assemblage, more or less intact apart from the rucked gouge of a laser burn up on the right shoulder of the breastplate.

Now the animated suit lifted the visor of the inert one and pressed a fingertip to the interface socket inside the chin guard. There was an almost inaudible hum of systems waking up. The laser-scarred suit stirred, its fingers flexing. Within moments it was moving of its own volition, a second crimson automaton helping the first sort through the piles of stacked components.

"This is creepy as fuck," Essien muttered to Moon as he discarded a crushed arm and searched around for an intact one.

"You think?" Moon snarled back.

"There was a cartoon when I was a kid. A mouse used magic to make a broom fetch some water. Then when the broom wouldn't stop he cut it in two with an axe. But that just turned it into two brooms . . ."

"Shut your damn mouth, Nkanika!"

The two suits assembled a third, and then a fourth. From there onwards it got exponential. Within the space of a few minutes Essien and Moon found themselves at the centre of a crowd, their own efforts looking paltry and useless now.

The two of you are best equipped to maintain our perimeter, Rupshe told them, acknowledging the disparity. *These suits have automotive functions but their weapons are still offline. You should mount guard while they work. Private Nkanika, focus your attention on the door. The first assault will most likely come from there. Corporal, guard the Step plate.*

Almost as et said the words the door's lock emitted a three-note trill of sound as someone outside fed a key-code to it. A dull boom followed, as the same someone tried to open the door and failed. Moved by a common instinct, Essien and Moon spun round to face the door, weapons hot. It didn't open, but this was still really bad news. Base security had to be aware now that what was going on inside the hangar was a real incursion, unlike the beekeepers' nuisance attacks. Their lead time had just evaporated.

Rupshe immediately shifted to the next phase of the operation. The suits already repaired and acquired began to move onto the Step plate in groups of five, limbs interlaced in a vice-like group hug that positioned them optimally in the field as it activated.

Two point eight one seconds to cycle. A second more for the next group to assemble itself. Fifteen cycles per minute, give or take. Meanwhile the suits whose turn hadn't come yet were still assembling more.

"We're not going to make this," Moon said.

The timing will be tight, Rupshe agreed. *We will take as much as we can.*

Over by the door a milky swirl of energy propagated itself, announcing the presence of a Step field. Two uniformed guards appeared there, but Essien had had plenty of time to take aim. He took out both men with a single shot, a push-away that slammed them into the wall with ruinous force. They would most likely live, but it might be a while before they were grateful for that.

"They're Stepping in," Essien announced unnecessarily. It was what Moon had been afraid of all along. Once Seventeen South's security had seen through all their smoke and mirrors and figured out where they actually were, they immediately became sitting ducks. All base security needed to do was Step their people out onto a friendly world, let them sprint a few yards on a vector that would bring them past the door and bounce them back.

The next wave came a few seconds later. They staggered their arrival and they came in from different angles, one on Moon's left, a couple more way over to her right then two more dead centre. Moon toggled her rifle to full auto and wove it to and fro, sowing the air in front of her with bullets. Nkanika took out a few she missed. He'd backed away to the far side of the door, most likely thinking that a sideways enfilade would give him more chance than a head-on shoot-out. Moon approved of the general concept, but she knew it would become academic as soon as the security teams could Step in enough firepower.

"Send us through!" she shouted to Rupshe. "We're all out of time!"

The animated suits of armour continued their steady work and their steady evacuation – a methodical pace that only looked slow because seconds had suddenly become a matter of life and death. *I promise you won't be left behind*, Rupshe said. *But we need to get as much armour through as we can. This would be a good time for you to deploy the contingency device we gave you.*

"All right," Moon snarled. "Shit, just get on with it!"

She knelt and tore open her rucksack as another cadre of five eerily empty suits climbed onto the plate and disappeared. Right about then the room began to fill up with smoke on all sides. Tear gas, Moon realised as she breathed in the sour tang of it. That was no problem for her or Nkanika: a protective film slid down across their eyes, and neutralising chemicals flowed from glands in their throats. But the security teams would be looking to use the gas as cover for whatever else they were throwing into the mix. Things were about to get a lot hotter.

Behind her the suits were still Stepping out five by five. Nkanika turned to her and seemed to be about to say something when everything went abruptly crazy. A flare painted the vast space with searing actinic light, and a second later a bunch of pressure grenades went off. The shockwave felt to Moon like being punched simultaneously on every part of her body. If it hadn't been for her augments her internal organs would have been pulped.

Nkanika didn't brace in time, so the wave sent him spinning head over heels through the air. Where he fetched up Moon couldn't immediately see. She fired into the flare's black after-image, drawing her gun from right to left across the space in front of her. She was rewarded with the sound of bodies falling.

But they weren't going to win this by fighting fair. "Hail Mary," Moon muttered as she kicked the rucksack over to spill its contents across the floor. The tiny ball bearings rolled in all directions, pouring around the feet of the animated suits like mercury.

But only for a moment. Then they rose up into the air like a swarm of metal locusts, whipping round in wide circles. Moon scrambled back involuntarily, but she was in no danger. Rupshe was manipulating all those thousands of metal spheroids by means of some kind of electromagnetic induction, a field et was generating through and between the armoured suits.

It was probably just as well that the tear gas was filling up the room. Moon could still see, but beyond a few feet out she had to rely on thermals and infrared. The visible spectrum was mostly fucked. She was aware of bodies appearing in the haze, each one convulsing for a few brief seconds before it fell to the floor and lay still.

It was a simple enough trick, but that didn't make it any less devastating. When you Stepped into a known, mapped space, you took as much care as you could not to materialise inside a solid object like a wall or a piece of furniture. The parts of you that intersected with whatever else was in your space suffered traumatic ruptures as atomic orbits intersected and released their energy in thousands of small explosions. The steel balls didn't fill much of the space in the room but there were thousands of them and they were spread out over a wide area, moving very fast. Even one or two were almost certain to be fatal if you materialised around them – and Rupshe's fine control of the EM field allowed her to direct the stream into the parts of the room where fresh Step fields were propagating. Most of the guards Stepping in didn't even have time to scream. They just took a few lurching steps and toppled like felled trees, their innards pulped by the fast-moving balls ricocheting around inside their impenetrable armour.

They didn't all go down, though. By the law of averages, some of them found gaps in the fusillade. Two of them came running out of the clogging smoke at Moon with rifles on burst-fire. They couldn't see what they were aiming at, but at this range they didn't really need to. Moon took one out with a head shot but the other was almost on her when Nkanika came in from nowhere, swinging a twisted piece of armour like a reaper's scythe, and took the trooper's feet out from under him. Moon finished him with her sidearm.

"Ran out of ammo," Nkanika explained.

"Pretty stupid stunt otherwise," Moon said. But she gave the Sinkhole a curt nod of thanks. She'd almost forgotten that he was a halfway decent soldier when his head was out of his ass.

Your turn now, Rupshe voked. *Onto the plate, both of you. Quickly.*

There were still half a dozen walking suits of armour that hadn't Stepped through, but they stood aside as Moon and Essien ran for the plate, then closed ranks behind them to make a wall. Scalding bursts of discharged energy washed over them. Something big had just Stepped through, probably a semi-auto like the cannon they'd seen at that checkpoint. Whatever it was, it was robust enough that the ball bearings hadn't incapacitated it, and it had enough firepower to clear the room in seconds.

Fortunately, after the first three of those seconds, Moon and

Essien weren't there to see it. They were standing on charred wooden planks next to a half-shattered jetty alongside a river of sluggish brown water. They were back on Earth, or whatever Tambuwal and Rupshe's world was called, a few hundred clicks away from the place where they had started out three days earlier. Seventy or eighty suits of Cielo armour stood around them with their arms at their sides and their empty faceplates gaping open.

"Fuck!" Essien gasped. He sank to his knees and then down on all fours, utterly spent.

"Well done," Rupshe said. The drone through which et was speaking descended into Moon's line of sight. "That was considerably more successful than I had estimated."

Moon pushed away both the drone and the words of praise with the back of her hand. She wasn't feeling anywhere close to triumphant. As a soldier she cleaved to the pragmatic gospel and preferred an unfair fight so long as the odds were on her side, but she still hadn't enjoyed seeing those security guards ripped apart from the inside out. On the other hand, eyeing up what they'd brought back with them, she found that she was more than ready to take her share of the spoils. "Now how about you pair two of these suits to me and the Sinkhole here," she suggested. "So we can walk home in style."

Rupshe didn't answer, but et didn't have to. One of the armoured suits suddenly stood out from all the rest in Moon's perception by virtue of being *hers*. It was the same almost mystical sense of belonging she'd felt when her first suit was assigned to her at the start of her basic training. Nkanika was obviously experiencing the same thing: he climbed to his feet and walked past her to one of the suits with a look of fervent concentration on his face. It configured to him as soon as he touched it, the various sub-assemblies irising and pivoting and clasping closed on his legs, his arms, his torso. He didn't so much put the suit on as merge with it in a mutual embrace that turned the two of them into one. He stared down at his own gauntleted hands and laughed out loud, a laugh in which relief and delight, surprise and wonder were all mixed in together.

Moon was only a second or so behind him, and as the suit closed on her she felt the same complex knot of emotions clench in her chest. In her years in the corps her armour had come to feel like a part of her own flesh, and she hadn't realised until now how very much she'd been missing it.

"Outstanding," she said, her voice a little thick. "Okay, mission accomplished. Let's go home."

She took her bearings and turned. Lagos was just north of west from here, and it would take them a whole lot less time to get back there now they were armoured up. The suit could handle a cruising speed of sixty kilometres an hour pretty much indefinitely.

To her surprise, though, the other suits – the ones Rupshe was animating – started to move out at speed to the north. "What's this?" Moon demanded. "What's going on?"

"There is a problem."

"What kind of problem?" Her first thought was that someone had got up on their trail and followed them home from Tsakom – but in that case they would have arrived right on Moon and Essien's heels. And they'd probably have come in gunships. Evidently this was something else.

"Paz has miscarried," Rupshe said. There was no trace of inflection in ets voice, but et still managed to sound concerned.

"You sent the rabbit on a mission?" That was the only surprising part of the news for Moon. If the rabbit went in then of course the rabbit bounced. Scraggy little furball was scoring around zero for ten at this point, except for that one time when Nkanika had bailed her out by shooting half of Moon's squad in the back.

"I did," Rupshe confirmed. "It was not a combat mission, however. She was trying to elicit information by acting a part."

"Was it the part of a clueless bitch who needs expert help to find her own oversized arse?"

"It's not important, Corporal. I need to find her and bring her back to Campus Cross. You and Private Nkanika are not required to join in the hunt."

"I'm coming along," Essien said.

"Seriously?" Moon kept hoping that the selves around her would catch onto the idea of enlightened self-interest, but she was continually disappointed. "The kid's a liability. And this is a perfect moment to cut her loose."

"I disagree," Rupshe said. Nkanika didn't say anything, he just joined the line and headed out.

"Sweet fucking Jad and fragrant tits of Shaster!" Moon complained to the empty air.

After a moment's wrestling – with her pride, not her conscience – she set off at the tail end of the procession. She was walking, not running. She didn't want anyone to get the impression she was enthusiastic about this.

21

Paz

"Oh shit!" Paz wailed. "Oh shit shit shit SHIIIIIT!"

Then it belatedly occurred to her that she had good reason to stay silent until she figured out where she was and who or what might be there with her. She still wanted to weep and scream and curl up into a quivering ball, but she clamped a hand over her mouth and breathed through her nose until she had herself a little more under control.

Take stock, she told herself. Find out as much as you can before you move or make a sound. That's what Dulcie would do.

If Dulcie hadn't been flung out of a twelfth-storey window on a whole other planet that Paz couldn't now get back to. She didn't have a Step plate. Her array was still dead. Her arm throbbed and ached where something – not a bullet, thank the mothers! – had hit her hard just before she Stepped. Her bounce-back was all used up and here she was, way off in the middle of nowhere on a world that had torn itself to pieces more than ten years ago. It was Professor Tambuwal's world, of course, and Rupshe's, and they were waiting out there somewhere for her to finish her mission and come back home. But with her array offlined she couldn't call them and they probably didn't have any easy way to find her.

So. Take stock.

She was in a room. A very small one, with a stone floor and a row of tin buckets along one wall. There was nothing else in there except a porcelain sink that was in two separate halves. One half was still attached to the wall, the other lay broken off at Paz's feet. Shards of white ceramic had scattered across the floor. There was no roof to the room, and the only door hung outwards on its lower hinge. The blazing sun peered in through the gap. It was unpleasantly hot and humid and there was an overpowering smell of rot and mildew.

This must have been a farm, Paz decided. Maybe a dairy farm, because the buckets could have been intended to collect milk, although there were plenty of other things you could do with them. Whatever it had been, it was only a ruin now and there was no sign anyone ever came there.

Paz crossed to the door and peered out. All she could see was a forest of weeds, yellowed and sickly like the ones that had colonised the courtyards of Campus Cross, in the midst of which a pipe or strut of rusted metal stuck up at an angle. Insects chirped loudly and constantly. Further away she could hear birdcalls. She drew some reassurance from these mundane sounds because they suggested she was alone. That was much better than having to deal with local selves who might see her as an intruder or a threat.

Paz gave the door a tentative push. It didn't open, it just leaned out even further. A second push, with her raised foot, made it bow all the way to the ground so she could step out over it.

She was in a space about thirty or forty feet across, enclosed on three sides by walls of red brick. The small shed into which she'd Stepped was an outbuilding attached to one of these three walls. There were two doorways at ground level, neither of which had a door any more, and several windows all of which were shattered. A vehicle of some kind was lying in the centre of the space, with one massive rear wheel remaining out of the four it seemed to have had to start with. It had been painted green but was now mostly rust-brown. A tractor, Paz guessed. So she was most likely right about this being what remained of a farm.

She waded through the weeds as carefully as she could. It was hard going. Some of them had very long, very sharp spikes sticking out of them that caught on her clothes and pierced her skin. Others were sticky with sap, which for all she knew might be toxic. There had been a war on this world, with nuclear weapons. There could be all kinds of poisons lingering in the biosphere. The ground underfoot was rucked and broken, studded with rocks and what seemed to be discarded machine parts, all badly rusted. She had to tread gingerly to avoid stepping on a nail or something even worse.

Finally, she made it out beyond the confines of the walls onto a gravel track, still weed-choked in many places but more level underfoot. The track wound around the side of a hill that shelved away very steeply from what seemed to be the farmhouse's front wall. There were no other human dwellings nearby, but about a mile away at the foot of the hill Paz could see the red-shingled rooftops of a small settlement.

She stood there for a long time, unable to decide what to do. Both Dulcie and Rupshe knew the coordinates she'd Stepped from – and if Dulcie had Stepped too then she ought to be close. Staying in the vicinity of her transit point would make it much easier for them to find her. But the same would be true if the security guards on Jaspal or a Cielo tactical squad picked up her trail and Stepped through in search of her. Either way, if she stayed here for longer than a few hours night would fall and she would need to find some kind of shelter. But was that little cluster of houses likely to offer any? She didn't know the first thing about Tambuwal's world, this so-called *Earth*, except that it had gone to war on itself when it was already close to ruin, tipping itself over the edge of the catastrophe curve and dying all the more quickly and terribly.

But worlds didn't die the way people died, all at once from a fall or a wound or a disease. They died piecemeal, from lots of different things that took hold in different ways, lightning quick or grindingly slow. There must have been survivors, at least to begin with. Ten years on there might still be people clinging to some kind of life. They could even be thriving, despite the fact that their whole way of life had been snatched away from them and set on fire. There could be anyone and anything waiting for her down there.

But by the same logic there could be anyone and anything lurking on this hillside. There was nowhere where Paz could be certain she would be safe.

What decided her at last was the map. It was among the documents and applications Rupshe had dropped into her array before she Stepped to Jaspal, a failsafe in case she and Dulcie became lost. It showed her current position in relation to Campus Cross, and it didn't look very far at all. A hundred and fifty kilometres, Rupshe had said. Paz was pretty sure she could walk that distance in three days if she found even moderately good roads – and the little cluster of buildings at the foot of the hill lay in exactly the right direction.

She set off down the hill, still with some misgivings. The track was mostly clear to begin with, but after the first hundred metres or so the intermittent explosions of weeds started to join up into more formidable tangles and barricades. Paz was forced to go around these obstructions, since going through them would leave her with shredded clothes and lacerated skin, but her options were limited. She couldn't leave the track altogether because the thicker growths on either side of it, weak and undernourished though they were, would be very hard to navigate without some kind of a blade to cut through them. The slope was becoming steeper too, so if she did abandon the track she would be clambering down an uneven incline with ground cover making each step a blind guess.

Even so, Paz made reasonable progress until she reached the third or fourth bend. At this point the track just disappeared, carried away by some long-ago rockslide or flash flood. In front of her the ground fell away steeply into a narrow gulley full of rocks embedded in sheets of dried, baked mud. It was as if a giant had taken a bite out of the hillside, chewed it up and spat it out again.

She could go back, but there was no guarantee there would be another path and she would no longer be heading in the right direction for Campus Cross. Better to go down, picking her way with care. At least the spilled, tumbled rocks offered plenty of footholds.

They weren't all sound, though. The drying mud had shrunk away from them so they gave and shifted like bad teeth in loose sockets. When Paz was halfway down, she realised this had been a terrible idea. If she fell and landed on the rocks underneath her she might be crippled or killed. She decided to go back up instead, only to find that the rocks she'd already put her weight on once were now even less to be trusted than before.

She pressed herself against the stone, groping with spread fingers for handholds and trying to distribute her weight as evenly as she could. She tried to angle her climb to the right, hoping to find new outcrops that she hadn't yet loosened, and that was her last mistake. A small rivulet running down from the grassy slope above had left the mud there wet and slippery. A rock that seemed firm when she first touched it tilted and slid away under her foot and she went rolling and tumbling down into the gulley.

That first rock brought more rocks down with it, so Paz became a pebble in a miniature avalanche, rolling downhill along with dozens of boulders, the largest of which would have fractured her skull even with a glancing blow. Amazingly nothing hit her, but her fall slammed her repeatedly against roots, embedded stones and the trunks of fallen trees. At the bottom of the slope she shot straight over an overhang and plummeted the last ten feet to the ground, landing with a solid impact that knocked all the remaining breath out of her body. One of the largest of the rocks smacked into the ground right beside her. A metre to the left and it would have flattened her like the hapless protagonist of a kids' cartoon.

She lay there stunned for a few long seconds, waiting for the reports to come in from the various parts of her body. She hurt all over, but none of the pains qualified as agony or clamoured for more of her attention than the others. She flexed her arms and her legs. They still moved.

She sat up, wincing, astonished at her own good luck. It was then that she realised, with a shock that felt like a second bumpy landing, that she wasn't alone. Ten yards away, where the track picked up again from the jumble of mud and scree, a female self stood facing her. The woman had the same brown skin as Essien Nkanika and most of the people Paz had met in Lago de Curamo. And like them she had no fur except on the very top of her head, so the skin was very much on display.

It was difficult for Paz to guess the woman's age. She looked as though she was still in her teens, but there was a gauntness to her features that made it at least possible she was a good deal older. A sore on her face, scabbed and raw, climbed from the corner of her mouth up her cheek all the way to her left eye. She was dressed in clothes whose muddy greens and greys made her almost invisible against the forest behind her.

What stood out most of all though was the rifle, which was pointed straight at Paz's chest. And it was shaking, which wasn't a good sign. The woman's eyes were wide and she'd bared her teeth in a snarl of anger or fear or shock or possibly all three.

The woman spoke, but the sounds were meaningless to Paz. So she did the only thing she could do under the circumstances: she put her hands up above her head with the palms out and the fingers spread. She hoped this was a gesture that would translate.

"I'm lost," she said. "I don't want to hurt you, or anybody. I'm just lost, and I want to find my way back to where I came from. Let me go and you'll never see me again."

The woman spoke again, the same unintelligible sounds. She drew a little closer, one small step at a time, the rifle still pointed more or less at the centre of Paz's chest. It was at this point that Paz realised what were slung over the woman's shoulder, their fur matted with blood where the rifle balls had hit them.

On most worlds, the species that won the sentience lottery had close cousins that didn't. If you evolved from dogs or cats, it's likely you've met some dogs or cats that didn't make the cut. The same with bears, apes, sloths, lizards, birds and all the glorious spectrum. But Ut was an outlier in that respect. Paz knew what *rabbit* meant as distinct from *self*, but she had only ever encountered the term in biology lessons or else as hate-speech. And she'd only seen the real thing in telos documentaries.

Now she was seeing it in an entirely different context. This woman had shot the long-eared, scut-tailed animals that were now thrown so casually over her shoulder. She'd hunted them for food, brought them down with her rifle. And now she was pointing the same rifle at Paz.

It must be small-bore, Paz thought through the sudden deafening buzz and hum inside her head. If Essien or Moon had shot one of those little beasts with their service-issued Sa-Su rifles there would have been nothing left of it but a bloody smear. So Paz had a reasonably good chance of reaching the woman alive even if the woman fired and hit her along the way. And once she was up close she knew how much damage she could do just with a kick. She rose into a crouch, getting her feet under her ready to jump.

The woman spoke again. More gibberish.

But a moment later the sounds were translated as proper words inside Paz's head. Her array had finally come back online – and it had identified the language as *English*.

"I got you," the woman had just said. "Oh, I got you, for sure. You better not move now, or I'll shoot. I'll shoot you down."

Surprise made Paz hesitate. It wasn't so much the threat – the gun had already made that clear enough – as the fact that her array had understood it. Where had she encountered *English* before? And where had she acquired an interface for it? The answer, when she checked, was that English was one of the languages she'd heard spoken in Lago de Curamo. It was also the language Essien Nkanika used sometimes when he spoke to Professor Tambuwal. Her array had just quietly worked away in background and built up a database.

Could she speak it herself? She could try, at least, which meant she had an alternative to the jump-and-kick plan she'd formulated a moment ago. It wouldn't be straightforward though. In Lago de Curamo she'd had Dulcie to use as a translator: here she was on her own. She set the interface to give her phonetic cues, assembled her reply and repeated the sounds her array offered her. "I'm not going to hurt you. I'm just . . ." She hesitated. There was no easy way to explain who she was or where she'd just come from. She settled for "I'm trying to get back home."

The woman seemed to understand her, though she frowned a little and squinted as though she was having to work to parse Paz's meaning. "They left you behind then?" she asked. "Is that what you're saying? What's this, though?" She moved the rifle in a quick zigzag that kept it pointing at Paz the whole time. "Why are you dressed as a rabbit?"

"I'm dressed as me," Paz said.

"Cut it out. What's the costume for?"

"It's not a costume."

The woman seemed set to argue the point, but then she took a closer look at Paz's ears. They were fully erect and twitching a little, both because of the tension and fear Paz was feeling and because of the lingering ache from the fall. She twitched them harder, making the point that they were under her conscious control.

"Oh shit!" the woman said. Her mouth fell open and stayed that way for a few seconds. "Oh, what the fuck are you, besides a thief?"

"I'm no thief. I'm a citizen of the Pandominion." Paz knew that phrase didn't mean anything here, but the cliché rolled off the tongue easily and it gave her a moment to think. "I'm a self, not an animal like those . . ." She nodded her head at the dead rabbits hanging on the woman's shoulder. "Like those ones there that you killed. I'm living in a place called Campus Cross. That's in Lagos."

The woman shook her head vigorously. "Plenty of wild things in Lagos, but none of them look like you, hairy girl. Nothing I ever saw in my life looks like you. That was a bad fall you took. Can you stand up?"

"I think so," Paz said.

"Okay, you do it then. Only you do it slowly. If you come running and jumping at me I'll blow a hole right through you. Understand?"

"Yes." Paz climbed to her feet in a series of discrete movements, taking care not to move even a step closer to the woman as she did so. A pain in her shoulder made her wince. It was her left arm – the same one that had been hit back at the Hale and Homeward.

"You hurt?"

"Yes."

"Too bad to walk?"

"No. I don't think so."

The woman nodded her approval. "Good. I'm taking you in now. Let the elders decide what to do with you. Yeah, you heard me. You're in trouble now, rabbit girl. Coming in the night when we were all asleep, thinking you were so clever. Well you're not so clever now, are you?"

"I don't have the faintest idea what you're talking about," Paz said.

The woman gave an incredulous laugh. "Oh, is that right? Well pardon me for mistaking, then. Only don't, because you know damn well. So this is what's going to happen, rabbit girl. We're going to walk a little way. You'll walk in front and I'll go behind you with this big gun pointing right between your shoulder blades. You keep a steady stride, because if you slow down or turn around you know what's going to happen."

"You'll put a hole in me."

Another nod. "That's exactly what I'll do. Here we go then. Get moving now, and don't stop until I say."

The woman stood aside and gestured with the gun towards the remainder of the path. Paz took the hint and set off in that direction. She didn't look around. The crunch of weeds and leaves underfoot told her that the woman was right behind her.

"My sweet God," the woman said, "look at those legs on you. No wonder you rolled down that hill like a barrel."

Paz was too tense and scared to be diplomatic. "I'm Meldun Ma," she snapped back. "From Ut. Your legs look like spindly little twigs to me, if we're calling each other names."

"We're not." The woman poked Paz in the back with the end of the rifle barrel. "You be polite, Meldun Mama, or you'll be sorry for it."

"Meldun Ma is my ethnicity. My name's Paz." On a sudden impulse she asked, "What's yours?"

There was a silence, that stretched. Paz waited. "I'm Beanie," the woman said at last. "My name, that is. Never heard of the other thing you said."

"Ethnicity means—"

"I wasn't asking."

Their path had led them into thicker, denser forest, but paradoxically the track itself had become clearer and wider as they went. Someone had been taking some effort with it. Then the trees thinned out again and they came out onto a flat plain with the houses Paz had seen before visible in the distance. To their left the hill slope rose steeply, cutting off the view. Over on the right there were fields, some bare and empty, some obviously sown with food crops. The latter were being tended. Furless selves with water buckets in their arms and canvas satchels slung on their shoulders moved between rows of tired-looking beans, wilting corn, green stems Paz couldn't identify. None of the plants she could see came up any higher than her waist.

It was like going back in time. The most sophisticated tech she could see was a wagon made from metal plates and slats of wood somehow tied or wedged together. Its wheels, their decorative metal trim caked in mud, were mismatched and seemed to have been scavenged from motorised vehicles. The wagon itself was pulled by two scrawny-looking animals with horns, their tails flicking away the swarms of flies that hovered all around them.

They were approaching the houses now. Many of them were ruins just like the farmhouse, but some were sound. They had a strange piebald look to them, white adobe mixed with red brick and occasionally with roughcast stone and sheet metal. It took Paz a moment to realise that they were composites – damaged buildings made whole by collecting up whatever materials were available and cementing it all together.

As they drew nearer to the houses, the workers in the fields noticed them and came wading through the rows to get a better view. Paz must look strange even from a distance: at close quarters she drew gasps and exclamations, wide eyes and pointing fingers. Her array was able to translate some of the babble, but not all. *Thief,* a lot of these selves were saying. *Look, Beanie caught one of the thieves! What is it, though?*

A line grew behind them as some of the field workers followed them into the village. That was what it was, Paz saw now, as they came among the outlying buildings. There was smoke rising from many of the houses, both the mended ones and the ones she'd thought of as ruins. Selves moved between them, intent on their business until they caught sight of the procession making its way towards them. Then they stopped what they were doing and pointed. Some of them started talking animatedly to their neighbours. Others called out at Paz.

She was in the midst of them now, and a number of things struck her. Some of the selves were children, who shrieked as they saw her and jumped up and down on the spot or hid behind their elders and peered out at her from covert. Like Beanie, and like the other adults around them, most of them had sores and blemishes on their skin. Two were missing legs and stood with the help of crutches crudely carved or whittled from tree branches. All looked painfully thin.

The most powerful explosive weapons, Paz knew from her history lessons, had the same effect on the environment as volcanic eruptions. In Lagos there had been dust and ash everywhere, so thick on the ground it was like a fall of filthy snow. Ten years ago all that particulate matter would have been way up in the atmosphere keeping most of the sunlight from getting through to where it was needed. It would have been impossible to grow anything at all. And all the technology these people had relied on would have failed at around the same time. Back then they must have lived by scavenging, searching through the ruins for the same kinds of tinned and packaged foods Paz and the others had been living on at Campus Cross. Now they were farming again, but the biosphere that had taken such terrible harm was slow to forgive and slower to heal. She couldn't imagine the courage and determination it must have taken these selves just to survive, just to get this far. Even with a gun sticking in her back she had to admire them.

But that didn't make her any less afraid. There was hostility on most of the faces she saw, disgust on others. A woman spat at her, though she wasn't close enough to aim true. Another made a gesture, holding her open hand out in front of Paz's face. Paz had no idea what this meant but it was clear that it wasn't friendly. There was something hot and volatile in the air. To her horror, Paz saw some of the selves bending down to pick up stones from the side of the road. They didn't throw them, but it seemed as though if even one of them did all the rest would too.

Mothers! Paz thought. *What do they think I've done?*

Then a man stepped right out in front of them and they were forced to stop. The man walked with the aid of a stick, moving it forward after each step and then leaning the weight of his upper body on it as he lurched forward. He was clearly very old.

"So you caught one, Abeni," the man said. "Good work. But what in God's name is it? Tell me! Tell me what I'm looking at!" His voice was thin and high but it had an edge to it – and it didn't escape Paz that everyone else was glancing from him to Beanie and back again, watching the interaction between them but not getting in the way of it. He was a leader here, she thought, a decision-maker. His opinion carried weight.

"You think I know?" Beanie answered from behind Paz. She sounded indignant. "I only found it, Sola, I didn't make it."

"I'm not an 'it'," Paz said. "I'm a self. My name is Topaz Tourmaline FiveHills."

This very short declaration caused a fresh round of gasps and exclamations. The man grimaced, showing yellowed teeth with gaps in them. "It talks!" he said, as if he took this as a personal insult. "Great God and Christ His son, it stands there and it talks!"

"I found her at Jhati Hill," Beanie said. "Iya told us to keep watch around the edges of the camp in case any of them were still around. I think she was trying to hide, but she fell down right by the cut and I saw her. She said the others left her behind and she was trying to get back to them."

A chorus of voices rose up, most of them repeating the word *thief* or flinging curses at Paz that her array wasn't able to translate.

The old man nodded. "Strange times," he said. "Strange trials. Most likely it knows where the others went to. Bring it to the council house now, and we'll make it answer."

"That's what I meant to do. Only I thought the Iya might want to—"

"Bring it, I said." The old man gestured peremptorily with his stick, though without its support his legs took on a slight wobble. "We shouldn't waste any time when we might still go after the rest of her gang and teach them a lesson."

"Well if there's lessons to be learned," said a voice from behind Paz, "I pray God sends us a teacher." Paz turned around to look as a woman made her way through the crowd, shooing people aside in a way that was somehow impatient and good-natured at the same time. "Haba!" she exclaimed. "Isn't this a wonder? A little girl with long ears and fur all over like a rabbit! Did you ever see such a thing, Sola? And all you can think to do is interrogate it like a policeman."

The woman was just as old as the man. Her bare skin was rucked up in folds and mottled with spots of darker pigment. The red gown she was wearing left her arms bare: Paz could see how the skin there was hanging down loose, the arms so thin that the woman's elbows stood out proud like knots in a length of rope. Her hair was a sparse frizz of grey through which her scalp showed clearly.

The old man – Sola? – glared at her. "We need answers, Nimi Lasisi," he said. "We've been robbed while we slept and we won't abide it." He waved his stick at Paz again. "This thing may be a wonder but it's nothing that's good. It's a thief and a poison, and the elders will deal with it."

"But I think I heard Abeni speak my name," the old woman said, "Isn't that right, Abeni? You said you were going to take her to me first."

Beanie looked nervous. She glanced at the crowd clustered tightly round them. "Iya . . ." she said, and faltered.

"Isn't that right? Speak truth and shame the devil."

Beanie nodded. "Yeah, Iya. That's right."

"Well then," the old woman said briskly. "Here I am. And you can bring her inside my house to wait while Sola gathers the rest of the elders together."

"I can send Beanie to do that," the man with the stick said.

The old woman didn't trouble to look at him. "Beanie is on guard duty. You do it. And you—" she wagged a warning finger at Paz "—don't talk any more. Come. Follow me now, and be quick about it."

She turned her back on Paz and walked towards the nearest building, from which it seemed she had just emerged. Beanie prodded Paz in the back with her rifle. "You got to go where you're told, Meldun Mama," she said quietly. "The iya said so."

Paz took a few steps forward. She had to brace herself to meet the wall of hatred she was sensing all around her. The clustered selves barely moved aside for her. One of them actually stepped in a little closer so his shoulder would bump against hers. He glowered into her face. "Fucking thief!"

With the children it was a little different. They scattered like birds when Paz came close to them, only to move in again behind her as she followed the woman across the street towards her house.

They walked behind her in lockstep. An idea struck Paz. She whirled around suddenly, leaned down and said a loud "Boo" right in the children's faces. They shrieked and fled, most of them taking shelter behind the grimly staring adults.

"What did you want to scare them for?" Beanie demanded indignantly. "Don't be so mean."

"I wasn't being mean," Paz said, straightening again. "It's a game."

And if you play games then you're a self. Not a monster, not an animal that decided to stand up on its hind legs and put on some clothes. Most of all not a threat. At least she hoped so.

She stepped through the doorway into the house. It was even stranger than she had been expecting. The ceiling over their heads was mostly made of corrugated metal, propped up in places with wooden poles. Where there were gaps, tarpaulins of green oilcloth had been stretched between the metal plates. There were no interior walls, only sheets and canopies of canvas strung on ropes or hung from metal frames. Iya or Nimi or whatever her name might be pushed the hanging sheets aside or ducked under them, moving quickly, and Paz followed on behind until they came to a space with some chairs, a table and a slate blackboard on a stand. All these things were old and battered. The blackboard had lost a leg and a cement breeze block had been drafted in to replace it.

"Sit," Iya told Paz, pointing to one of the chairs.

Paz sat. There was no point in picking a fight before she had to, especially when she wanted these people to conclude that she was harmless. She wondered whether Hadiz and Rupshe knew about places like this, communities that had survived the wars and famines and somehow started to get themselves back up on their feet again. If they knew, why weren't they helping? If they didn't know, why hadn't they looked?

The old woman took a chair directly opposite Paz, staring at her with unsettling intensity. Beanie circled round to stand beside her, the gun never wavering more than an inch or two from Paz's centre of mass.

"Well I suppose I've just got the one question that matters," Iya said at last. "I don't believe in monsters, or devils, or any of that foolishness. But then most of the things that have happened over the last few years were things I never would have believed, so I'm not ruling it out. And the only talking rabbit I ever saw was in a cartoon. You're not him, plainly. So you'd better tell me what you are, little one. And you'd better tell me slowly and carefully."

Paz took that advice to heart and didn't answer straight away. She knew that a lot depended on her choice of words – not least her own survival. "I'm from a place that's a very long way away from here," she said at last. "Another planet."

"Another planet!" Beanie repeated, eyes wide.

"But it's a planet very like this one, in most ways," Paz added hastily. "It's just that some things took a different path than they did here. I'm not a rabbit, but my ancestors were rabbits. Yours were . . . well I don't know what they were, but something else."

"Apes," Iya said. "So we're told. There are others that say angels, but looking at what we did to the world I'm leaning more towards the first explanation."

"So I'm a self, just like you. Only not an ape self, a rabbit self. From another planet."

Iya crooked an eyebrow. "Well there's got to be a little more to it than that," she said dryly. "You're not dressed like any kind of space explorer. Those trousers look like you bought them at the School Road market, back when there still was such a thing. Where's your spaceship? Where's your . . ." There was a pause while the old woman tried to think of something else that space explorers ought to have. "Oxygen mask," she completed, with an emphatic nod.

"I didn't come in a ship," Paz said. "I Stepped. It's like teleportation. There are two plates, one on the world you're coming from and the other on the world you're going to. You just go from one plate to the other in a second."

"Crossing space on plates." Iya didn't seem convinced. "Show me."

"I can't," Paz said. "I don't have a plate with me."

"But you walked here, didn't you? So it's got to be close by."

Paz held up her right arm and tugged down the sleeve, displaying the bounce-back bracelet. "I used this," she said. "It's a way of carrying the energy from the plates with you. It brought me back here from—" She broke off, uncertain how to explain. This was getting complicated.

"From your own planet?" Iya said doubtfully.

"No. From another one. The plate I used was in a place called Lagos. I'm trying to get back there now."

"You come from Lagos?"

"No. Well, yes. But my Lagos is called Canoplex-Under-Heaven. It's not really Lagos, it's just in the same place as Lagos, but . . . but on my world. Which is called Ut. There's a city on most worlds that's in the same place where Lagos is, or at least on most worlds that have people on them, but it has a lot of different names." Paz paused again. Both women were looking at her in absolute perplexity now. "I've confused you," she said.

"I think you confused your own self," Iya corrected her. "Some plates are bracelets, and every world has got its own Lagos? For your soul's sake, child, talk sense to me! When the elders question you they'll be harsher and they'll mostly hear what they want to hear. Can you prove any of this? Can you show them which way you came and when it was? Especially the when."

Could she? Paz tried to think of anything she could say or show that backed up her story. "No," she admitted. "But I've got friends here, in the Lagos of this world. If you go there and ask them, they'll tell you it's all true. And they can help you. At least I think they can. They can give you a Step plate."

"And what good will that do us? We're not space explorers."

"No, but . . . but there are worlds that have lots of land and no people. You could grow your crops there. I'm sure they'd do better than they do in the depleted soil here."

"Grow corn and beans in another world." Iya sounded sceptical. "You hear that, Abeni?"

"I hear," Beanie said. She'd lowered the rifle at last. The end of the barrel was trailing in the dust on the floor. There was a look on her face that was hard to interpret, but Paz was sure she saw some longing in it.

"So we could do that," she said. "You could come with me back to Lagos or . . . or send someone, to ask."

Iya shook her head doubtfully. "Walking all the way to Lagos isn't like going down to the stream to fetch a bucket of water. You'll have to say your piece here and now and make them all believe you." She gave Paz a solemn, searching stare. "I suppose I should have asked that question first. Whether you stole our *dankali*. Our yams."

"No," Paz said. "I didn't. I don't even know what those things are."

"Food, little one. They're food. And they were the only crop we had that was halfway thriving. Only halfway, but we were leaning hard on that harvest, and now . . ." The old woman sighed. "Well, the thing we were leaning on is gone and so we all fall down."

"Raiders came in the night," Beanie said tightly. "Cleared out the whole field. Now we're going to starve."

"It wasn't me," Paz said.

"Even if it was," Iya said, "what's likely to happen now is the worst thing for everyone, not just for you. I wish you hadn't found her, Beanie. Or I wish you'd had better sense than to bring her."

Paz saw how hard those words landed. Beanie flinched as if she'd been hit. "You told us to keep guard, though!" she protested. "Iya, you said we had to watch the borders!"

"I was mostly telling the men that," Iya said. "So they would have something else to do besides fight and lay blame. But yes, I did say it and so I've got no right to chide you. But I have to think. I don't want us to make ourselves feel better by shooting or hanging this child, or setting her on fire."

Paz felt her stomach rise up and turn over, sending sour bile up into her throat. She would have vomited, but the tide stopped just short of her mouth and ebbed again. "It wasn't me!" she repeated stupidly. "You can't!"

"I'm sorry, Iya," Beanie said, her voice thick. "I'll take her back to Jhati and let her go."

"That's a kind thought, but I don't think you'd get to Jhati Hill. I don't think you'd get much further than my front door. Be quiet now, and let me consider."

The old woman rested her elbows on her knees and bowed her head. Beanie did as she was told and said nothing more. She folded her arms while she waited, the butt of the rifle balanced against her thigh. I could reach out and grab it, Paz thought. I could take it and . . .

And what, though? Run out of the door and away down the street, firing into the air to make people dive for cover? Take the two women as hostages? She didn't think she had it in her to do those things – and she didn't know how to fire the rifle in the first place. She was more likely to shoot her own foot than to carry off a daring escape.

She decided to try negotiating again, but before she'd managed to get her thoughts in order the nearest sheet was raised and the man she'd met outside – the man with the stick, who'd called her a thing and then a poison – walked in. He just stood there for a moment looking at them all.

"Sola," Iya said. She gave him a nod.

"Nimi." He leaned very slightly forward in what might have been meant to be a bow, but he straightened up again so quickly it was hard to tell.

"We'll be out soon," the old woman told him. "When we've finished talking."

Sola's mouth quirked into a sour grimace. He shook his head. "No, Nimi, you have to bring her out right now. You can't settle this indoors with nobody else seeing. The elders are sitting. We're only waiting on you."

Iya stood. "I'll come then," she said.

"You have to bring—"

"Yes, yes. But I'll come first and talk to them all." Iya turned to Beanie. "Stay here and watch her. Don't leave her. And don't let anybody take her."

"I won't," Beanie said.

Iya and Sola left together. Beanie took the chair that Iya had vacated, sitting edgeways on so she could rest the gun across her knees.

"You don't need that," Paz said. "I haven't tried to hurt anyone."

"No," Beanie agreed. "You still might, though. Iya said to watch you."

"Which you do with your eyes, not with a gun."

Beanie made no answer to this, and she didn't move. After a few moments of returning Paz's accusing stare, she dropped her gaze to the ground. The rifle didn't move.

"Is that her name?" Paz asked, partly to break the silence but mostly to make Beanie carry on interacting with her. "Iya. The man called her something else."

"Her name is Nimi Lasisi. *Iya* just means grandma."

Another silence. "How many of you are here?" Paz asked.

Beanie gave her a glare. "A lot," she said fiercely. "Enough to defend ourselves. Those bastards only managed to steal from us by coming in the night. We'd have fought them otherwise. You think we look weak, but we're not. We're strong and fierce."

"I don't think you look weak," Paz said. "I'm just surprised to find there are people left alive after the war and the bombs and the disasters. My friends think they're the only ones."

Beanie shrugged. After a few moments she spoke. "I was still a kid when all that happened. I don't remember much. The sky was dark for a long time. The sun came up sort of muddy and thin, and there wasn't much to eat except for old food that was in tins or packets. People just call it the Hard Time now. But it's meant to be bad luck to talk about it so mostly we don't."

"Are there things you need?"

Beanie raised her head to stare at Paz again. "What do you mean?"

"I mean are there things you don't have enough of? Food. Blankets. Tools. My friends in Lagos might be able to bring those too."

"We don't need any help from you. And you're only saying those things to make me let you go."

"Everyone needs help," Paz said. Thinking of herself. Thinking of Dulcie. "It doesn't matter how strong you are, nobody can do everything for themselves."

"We don't need anything from anyone," Beanie repeated stubbornly. "We survived the first years after the war, when things were really bad. It's better now. Sola says we're about to turn a corner."

"But how many of you are sick? How many of you are starving?" Beanie didn't answer but she clenched her fists and glared a warning at Paz. Paz ploughed on anyway. She wasn't trying to start an argument, she was . . . well, she was bartering for her life, but that didn't mean the things she was saying weren't true. "My friends can bring you better seeds for your crops. Fertilisers. Tools. Or they could find you some fields with better soil."

"Your friends sound amazing." Beanie's tone was scornful. "All these wonderful things they can do! And all we've got to do is let you go to them. Anyway, there is no better soil."

"Not here, no. But on other worlds . . ."

"Shut up about the other worlds! I'm not stupid."

"Do you think I'm a local girl then?" Paz was exasperated. "If I'm not from another world, where did I come from?"

Beanie made a tutting sound, thrusting out her lower lip. "I don't know, and I don't care. When Iya asked you to prove all that, you couldn't. And it doesn't even matter where you came from. Where you're going is all that matters now."

"I know," Paz agreed. "And I want to go home, Beanie. I want that more than anything. Will you help me?"

Before Beanie could answer the hung sheets parted again and a man and a woman entered the room. Paz thought she'd seen them both in the street outside, but it was still hard for her to tell these furless selves apart. They stood in almost symmetrical poses, hands on the tools they wore at their belts – a machete in the case of the man, a hatchet for the woman. "You have to bring her to the elders, Abeni," the woman said. "She's going to be judged."

"Judged for what?" Paz asked her. "What have I done?"

The woman rolled her eyes and shrugged. "Well you stole our yams, is what you did. But it's not a judgement on that. We already know that part. It's a judgement on whether you live or die."

22

Baxemides

There was a strange and strained hiatus while the records and equipment from Kavak Dromishel's disastrous experiment were examined and the full picture gradually emerged. It wasn't that coordinator Baxemides' other duties were suspended, or that the Ansurrection war ceased to play in background like the same disaster repeated on an endless loop. But she was aware that something had been thrown into the air and had not come down again. The Pandominion was sick, and she was waiting to learn whether or not she had the medicine.

She had drafted in a new team to overhaul Dromishel's rig and his schematics, all experts in their respective fields. They were mostly lagomorphs like Paz, but from Oenin rather than Paz's world of Ut. Their current specialisms were widely varied but they all had doctoral laurels in sub-atomic physics and at least some recent experience with rigid field mathematics.

Their first report came in less than forty-eight hours after the disaster on Erim. It was signed by the replacement team's leader, Ten Hinuix, an intense young woman whose dyed-black fur marked her out as a member of some obscure philosophical movement on Oenin – ascetics or extreme rational sceptics, Baxemides vaguely recalled. She disliked zealotry, but it was hard to argue with Hinuix's résumé.

The report confirmed, as if it needed any confirmation, that Dromishel's suppression wave had worked. If anything it had functioned only too well, expanding on a perfectly spherical front and at a rate that would preclude any effective response. It could cover a whole world in the space of a few seconds after detonation. No known agency would stop it or block its effects.

Baxemides went in-system to give her response. In fact she went all the way to Hinuix's lab. She didn't want to discuss anything as important as this in a series of inter-systemic comm-stats that would be copied across multiple servers. The messages would be heavily encrypted but still, a little paranoia was always justifiable.

Ten Hinuix welcomed the coordinator with every appearance of calm, as if they were discussing weather conditions on the cis-urban conduit rather than the future of civilisations and the obliteration of planets. They met in an anonymous insta-build office adjacent to the rackball stadium they had commandeered for their tests. There was no furniture in the room except for the two chairs they sat in and a folding desk on which Hinuix had set down her laptop.

"Tell me," Baxemides instructed.

Hinuix didn't flinch. "What, specifically?"

"Everything pertinent. I'll tell you when to stop."

"The suppression wave kills minds. It doesn't distinguish between machines and organics, it just wipes out all capability for thought. We think irreversibly. It destroys other machines as well, by the same mechanism. It switches off all electromagnetic activity, the way you'd switch off a light bulb."

"And this is on a planetary scale?"

Hinuix nodded. "Almost by default. Once you've started it, you can't easily stop it. Assuming a large enough payload to get it properly started – anything more than a few cubic centilitres of plasma – it will encompass an entire planet in the space of seconds."

"And then what? It will just keep on going forever? Sterilise the whole universe?"

"Fortunately not." The scientist permitted herself a dry smile. "It won't propagate through vacuum."

"Ah, then there *is* a way to block it."

"Yes. Provided you isolate yourself in a vacuum chamber and remain there until the wave has passed. And of course you'd have no way of knowing, once you were shut off like that, when it would be safe to come out again. The wave would remove any possibility of a signal reaching you from outside – and it might be made to persist for a long time, depending on the strength of that initial plasma charge. You'd be trapped in a hermetically sealed environment, and if you opened the door too soon you'd be dead in an instant."

Baxemides considered. This definitely had the feel of a doomsday device, hideously fit for purpose. True, it destroyed organic minds as well as machine ones, but that wouldn't be an issue on Ansurrection worlds because there would be no organic selves there to start with.

She ordered Hinuix and her team to take the research forward. She let it be known that she expected a working prototype, a suppression wave bomb in field-worthy condition, within seven days at the outside.

"I have a suggestion," Hinuix said. "For a possible field test." For the first time she sounded tentative.

"Go on."

"We can't trigger a suppression wave on any Pandominion world. You know what happened on Erim, and that was with an infinitesimal amount of plasma. We'd need to test a planetary yield, in order to be sure the effects scale smoothly to that level."

"So?"

"With your permission, Coordinator, I'd like to requisition a world in the Unvisited and perform the test there."

"I see no problem with that. There are plenty of desert worlds."

Hinuix pressed her hands together as if in prayer. "It would need to be a world with a functional biosphere."

Baxemides frowned. "Why? We're intending to use the wave against Ansurrection worlds. There won't be any organic life there."

"True," Hinuix said. "But we still need some way to measure the speed and extent of the wave's propagation. We could seed an entire planet with mechanical devices, but that would take a very long time. If we use a world that has life . . . well, we can watch from orbit and we'll have a ready means of ascertaining the reach and intensity of the wave." She paused for a moment. "Because everything it touches will die," she added, in case that wasn't already abundantly clear.

"From orbit?" Baxemides asked, grabbing hold of a trivial detail rather than confront the core idea head-on.

"From outside atmosphere – which is to say, beyond the wave's effective radius. We wouldn't be talking about sentient life, of course. Just animals. Including megafauna, ideally, since they'd be easier to observe from a distance."

Baxemides hesitated, but only for a moment. The loss of a whole world's biosphere was a weighty thing, but its weight was largely abstract. The Pandominion's ongoing losses were real, immediate and concrete. "Do it," she said.

The test took place three days later. The chosen world had no name, obviously, only a U prefix followed by an easily forgettable string of digits. It was one of a great many where a certain potential asteroid strike had missed by a significant number of astronomical units. Consequently the era of the great reptiles had continued without interruption, surviving ice ages and spreading out into every evolutionary niche. Mammals had never got so much as a foot in the door.

Hinuix's team went in, guarded by a Cielo tactical squad, and placed the suppression bomb. They put it on a timer, just as Dromishel had done. Unlike Dromishel, though, once the blue touchpaper was lit they retired to another universe to watch the fireworks.

Baxemides watched them too, on a twelve-second delay as orbital remotes shuttled the information stream from the target reality to her own. The spy satellites that were filming the test were geosynchronous at eleven thousand kilometres, the closest they could get without being at risk from the wave's effects. Nonetheless the resolution was excellent. No detail was lost.

There was a bright flare as the device triggered, almost subliminally brief. There didn't need to be any visible effect at all, but Hinuix had built a magnesium grenade into the device in order to establish an accurate zero marker for her measurements.

The wave spread outwards. It was easy at first to track its progress. Across broad, rolling tundra, alluvial floodlands and towering fern forests, the majestic giants with their gaudy plumage, spiked tails and feathered crests froze in their tracks and toppled. Leatherwinged titans fell out of the skies and crashed in ruin on the ground, their hollow bones shattered. The wave was a ripple of chaotic motion that left stillness in its wake.

After the first few seconds, though, there was nothing to see. The wave was too fast. Baxemides lost it, and she couldn't switch between camera feeds quickly enough to find it again. At the nine-second mark, Hinuix sent a terse comm-stat. *One hundred per cent*, it read. After three minutes she sent a second message. *Wave energy now at zero. It's safe to go in.*

Baxemides had no desire to do so. She had given her assent to the murder of an entire ecosystem: she would leave it to others to pick over the bones. A very faint sense of shame, of unease, tainted the purity of her triumph, but not too uncomfortably and not for long. She had proof of concept. She had the means to save the Pandominion with no further loss of life.

She submitted her report to the Omnipresent Council with a request that they allocate production resources on one of the factory worlds. She was ready to implement mass production, and she recommended that it be expedited in every way possible. While waiting for a response she searched the procurement lists herself looking for a suitable manufacturing base.

Inevitably, she looked into the possibility of finding spare capacity on Tsakom. The place had been on her mind ever since Orso Vemmet absconded from a supposedly secure site there and put himself – for the moment! – beyond her reach. Among recent communiques she found a report of an incursion at a military reclamation facility. Serious damage had been done and some dozens of suits of Cielo armour removed, presumably by organised criminals who wanted either to sell the suits on or use them in some dubious enterprise.

For the briefest of moments Baxemides wondered whether the two things, this opportunistic raid and Vemmet's disappearance, could be connected in any way. But she couldn't see how, and in any case she now had much more important things on her mind. Not Tsakom then, she decided. Their security might not be up to the job. But there were plenty of other choices.

She was still trying to make one when the news came that the Pandominion had been beaten to the draw.

23

The Unremembered Dead

The destruction of Nebirison was the moment when the war slipped definitively out of the Pandominion's control. It was extensively documented, despite the fact that the survivors (out of a planetary population of three billion) numbered in the low tens of thousands. There is a monument, but few people ever see it. It was erected on the largest of the two hundred or so asteroids that remain where once there was a planet.

Nebirison was not a strategically important world but it had a higher than usual Cielo presence. This was because it was one of three worlds where Pandominion citizens had been abducted by the machine hegemony to serve as a pattern and template for their sleeper agents. Dulcie was one of the fruits of that project, which in the end had been a failure. The hegemony had hoped to reach a better understanding of their organic enemies – perhaps even to determine whether or not they were truly sentient – but the gap between the two cultures was too great. Dulcie was the only mechanoid counterfeit who had escaped destruction, and Dulcie had gone rogue. The rest reached no definite conclusions before they were destroyed in a far-reaching sweep by the local authorities, leaving the question undecided.

Because of this bitter and tragic history the Cielo had transferred twenty additional divisions of troops and several hundred gunships to Nebirison, as much to reassure the citizenry as to guard against further incursions. Fully half of those additional gunships were on orbital surveillance duty when out of nowhere the previously empty sky above the planet filled with massive hulks of unreflective nano-engineered steel and ceramic shielding.

The hulks Stepped in only just inside the orbit of the Moon. They didn't move, but then again they had no visible means of propulsion. What they did have, clearly, was power – enough to generate rigid spears of force which locked them to each other in a regular matrix.

The Cielo commanders both in orbit and on the ground made the very reasonable assumption that these structures were enemy ships. They moved into tactical formations and attacked. Heavily armed, boasting full complements of supra-orbital missiles, rail guns and shear-field munitions, they seemed a formidable force. And where they were given a chance to deploy these weapons, they did so to good effect. Seven of the intruding sky platforms, heavily armoured though they were, were destroyed in the first seconds of the engagement.

But these were also the *last* seconds of the engagement. The remaining platforms deployed their only armament, an alternating pressor/tractor field powered by the fusion generators that made up most of their colossal bulk. They did this in perfect synchronisation. The earlier losses seemed to have made no difference. Later it was determined that this was because the network had massive redundancy. Only twenty platforms were needed to complete the grid.

And once the grid was active the battle was over. The pressor field slammed every Cielo ship to the ground like the fist of an invisible giant. Most of the ships held together but the crews were dead, smeared against the inside of their hulls by the sudden acceleration.

The inverse square rule applied, so by the time it hit the planet's surface that first pulse was much weaker. Even so people died. The effect was like a collision at fifty kilometres per hour. Bones broke, organs ruptured, hearts stopped. Windows shattered too, showering the streets with a rain of needle-sharp fragments.

Then, without warning, the network toggled from pressor to tractor force. The dead and the debris were hauled into the air. Living people too, like fish on invisible lines, reeled in precipitously only to be flung down again with crushing force by the next pulse of the pressor field. In this second cycle the ground cracked open. Buildings broke apart, struck by an invisible wrecking ball. The only selves left on their feet were Cielo troopers in full armour. Some of them had the presence of mind to trigger their bounce-backs and evacuate: these made up almost the entirety of the survivors. The remainder, those who paused to consider, died a fraction of a second later as the field strength continued to climb exponentially.

The second tractor pulse drew magma like pus from a wound out of volcanic caldera already punctured by the pressure wave. The oceans reared up in mile-high waterspouts to whelm the land. Nobody drowned, though. Drowning takes anything from ninety seconds to three minutes and Nebirison didn't have that long.

Press, then pull, again and again, accelerating with each cycle. Press: the planet's crust was rent apart along ancient fault lines at the edges of continental plates. Pull: the atmosphere was whipped away like the cloth from a restaurant table. Press. Mountain ranges were flattened, their displaced mass acting like battering rams to push the cracks already made all the way through the planet's mantle into its molten core. Pull. Nebirison cracked like an egg. Moments after its final disintegration the Ansurrection sky platforms Stepped out again as suddenly as they had arrived.

In the corridors of the Omnipresent Council and in the Cielo redoubts alarm bells were ringing like the keening of hired mourners at a funeral. Hospital ships were scrambled, but once they arrived in-system there was nothing for them to do. The floating debris from Nebirison's dissolution, consisting mostly of newly created asteroids many thousands of kilometres wide, made a thorough search impossible. In any case it seemed vanishingly unlikely that the forces at play here had left anyone alive. The only survivors were those who had been able to Step out between the first pulse and the second, before conditions on the planet's surface became too extreme for any self or structure to remain intact.

The Council and the Cielo high command waited in an agony of uncertainty for the worse news that was sure to follow. It followed very quickly. After an interval of fifty-seven minutes the sky platforms arrived at their next target. It was Shohal, another world that had already experienced Ansurrection incursions. It fared no better than Nebirison and lasted no longer.

The intervals between attacks were astonishingly uniform: they came every fifty-seven minutes, with a variation of no more than four seconds – presumably the length of time it took the sky platforms to recharge their terrible weaponry and for new units to be calibrated and swapped in to replace those that had been destroyed.

The platforms always appeared at precisely the same altitude too, which meant at least that the Cielo commanders were able to move their gunships and void-capable heavy bombers to higher orbital positions. When the massive Ansurrection constructs arrived in a given system they could be attacked from above before they completed their force matrix and applied the tractor/pressor field. This increased the rate of attrition on the machine hegemony side. In some engagements between twenty and thirty platforms were destroyed. The losses were never enough to prevent the remaining platforms from deploying their weapon, but they did seem to be responsible for a slight increase in the time intervals between attacks. It stabilised now at fifty-nine minutes and didn't move again.

The machine hegemony altered its strategy. The next time the sky platforms appeared, a fleet of warships Stepped in alongside them to defend them and run interference. The Cielo now had to fight harder and endure heavy losses in order to take out even a few of the force generators.

We should pause at this point and consider. These engagements were not battles in the conventional sense of the word. Each one led inexorably to the destruction of a world, with the near-total loss of its population. Each one, therefore, took a toll of several billion lives and left a field of asteroidal rubble where a planet had been.

The Omnipresent Council reacted to these apocalyptic events very much as any unwieldy and heavy-handed bureaucracy might have been expected to. They did their best to suppress all information as to what was happening and shouted at each other across over-large and over-heated rooms, their efforts almost equally divided between finding a solution and apportioning blame. Faced with the defining crisis of their age, a few wrestled bravely with the intransigent facts while a much greater number spread confusion and disinformation with their every breath.

In spite of this one clear fact stood out, impossible to ignore. The Pandominion had brought together under its aegis approximately three hundred and twelve thousand eight hundred and seventy-three worlds (*approximately* because some worlds were in the process of having their membership recognised and others were Cielo bivouac worlds whose status was equivocal). At a rate of one world per hour it would take more than thirty years for the machine hegemony to destroy them all, but this would reliably happen unless something intervened to prevent it. A Scour event was in progress, agonisingly slow, absolutely inexorable.

It was against this backdrop that Melusa Baxemides made her

report and her request for expedited approval. One of the Robust Rebuke programmes had passed initial tests and was ready to be implemented. Baxemides wanted manufacturing resources to be made available on one or other of the worlds, populated mostly by convicts and dishonourably discharged soldiers, which served the Pandominion as both prisons and munitions depots.

They held a vote. Then gave her all of them.

24

Paz

The woman with the hatchet made a brusque beckoning motion with her hand. "Get up," she told Paz. "You've got to come outside now."

"I haven't done anything," Paz said. She heard the words as she spoke them and she realised how they sounded – like a child protesting against the world's unfairness. She wasn't going to get out of this by being a child. She had to plead her own case loud and strong, so these selves couldn't ignore it.

"All right then," she said. "I'll come."

The man's mouth quirked in what might have been either anger or amusement. "Don't make it sound like you're choosing. Things like you don't get to choose. We're bringing you."

Paz stood. "Things like me?" she repeated. She threw out her hands. "Have you ever *seen* anything like me?"

"Animals." The man spat out the word.

"Do animals talk?" Paz demanded. "I never knew an animal that could talk."

"Don't waste your words on us," the woman told her coldly. "It's the elders who are going to give judgement on you." They took an arm each and led Paz back through the curtained space. Beanie kept pace with them a little way to the side, her rifle slung over her shoulder. Presumably she could see it wasn't needed now.

"I'm not an animal," Paz insisted. "You can see for yourselves I'm not. It's stupid to just keep saying things when it's obvious they're not true."

"Don't call us stupid," the woman warned her. "Mind your words, or we'll beat you right here and now before we bring you out."

Paz fell silent. She could see that nothing she could say here was going to help her.

They came out of the house into the street, where many more people were now gathered to watch. They crowded in close for a good view of Paz as she emerged, exclaiming and shouting as they had before, and fell in behind her as her custodians walked her down the street.

They came into a cleared space between the buildings, faced on all sides by the backs of ruined and half-repaired houses. Rubble had been piled up at the edges of the space, sections of fallen wall, parts of broken appliances, ramparts of ancient rubbish. More people waited there, perhaps twenty or thirty all told. They shouted when they saw Paz – *Thief! Monster! [translation unavailable]!* – and some of them shook their fists at her.

Her two guards walked her through the crowd. Nobody actually hurt her, nobody even touched her, but their anger was like a living wall that pushed against her on all sides, the weight of it so much she felt as though she couldn't breathe.

There aren't so many, she told herself. Twenty or thirty in the clearing, two dozen or so at her back. Nobody else anywhere, that she could see. They could all have been seated without any difficulty in a good-sized café or restaurant. She tried to imagine them sitting there, chatting quietly while they waited for their food to come. It took some of the sting out of the curses and the shaking fists.

Under a faded green tarpaulin, six selves sat on wicker chairs that had seen better days. Nimi Lasisi was there, and so was Sola. There were two other women and two more men. And there was a seventh chair, set facing them. Paz was led to it and pushed down into it. She didn't resist. She looked at the six selves – the elders, she supposed – because theirs were the only faces that weren't all twisted up with anger and hate.

The shouting was still going on all this time. If anything it was getting louder. After waiting for more than a minute for silence that didn't come, Nimi Lasisi stood at last and held up her hands to hush them. Gradually, piecemeal, the voices died down. When there was almost complete silence a woman's voice shouted, "Kill it!" very loudly and it all started up again.

"Enough now!" Sola cried out in his thin, strained voice. He joined Nimi Lasisi on his feet. "This won't get anything done. Shut up your mouths and listen!"

It took even longer the second time. Paz sat with her hands in her lap and her gaze cast down, waiting it out.

When there was silence Sola spoke. "That's better," he said sternly, tapping the end of his stick against the ground. He stayed on his feet but Nimi Lasisi sat down again. She looked very tired and very bleak.

"Now let's hear this matter, and decide on it," Sola said. "Beanie, where did you say you found this thing?"

"On Jhati Hill." Paz started a little to hear Beanie's voice coming from so close. The girl was standing right behind her. She must have stayed with them all the way from the house.

"Near the cut, you said? Under what's left of the Unsol dairy farm?"

"Around there, yeah," Beanie confirmed.

"So that's probably where they took our yams after they stole them. It's close by and there's lots of room there."

"Should we send someone to look there, then?" Nimi Lasisi asked. "It might be useful to know. Otherwise you're just deciding at the start what we're meant to be finding out."

"There won't be anything there *now*." Sola's tone was scornful.

"They left this one behind. She told Beanie that. Probably so they could keep her share for themselves."

"I said I was trying to get back to my friends," Paz said. "I didn't say anything about yams."

One of her guards – she couldn't see whether it was the man or the woman – smacked her hard across the back of the head. Paz gave an involuntary yelp. It didn't hurt but it was a shock.

"Gbemi, don't do that again!" Nimi Lasisi shouted. "We're asking her questions, not beating her. Keep your hands to yourself!"

"There's no need for beatings," Sola confirmed. "We don't punish until we know, and as Nimi Lasisi says we're here so we can know." He turned to Paz. "This is a council of elders," he told her. "A tribunal. Do you know what that is?"

"Yes," Paz said.

"It means anyone can ask you, and you have to answer. Truthfully, and respectfully. Now where did you come from and where did you go back to? Where did you take our food after you stole it? Start with that."

"No," another of the seated selves said loudly. "It can start by telling us what it is." This second man stood too and came up beside Sola, close enough that Sola was forced to stand aside for him. He was also old, but he stood taller and he looked a great deal more robust. In fact he was one of very few selves here who didn't have that look of emaciation and incipient illness. His head was bald and shining, his eyes so dark Paz couldn't tell pupil from iris. He looked at her with a cold detachment that was somehow more frightening than Sola's and the crowd's anger.

"Father Enofe," Sola said, looking pained. "We need to get back what was stolen from us. That's the most urgent thing here."

"The Bible tells us there are beasts that wear human faces." The bald man went straight on as though Sola hadn't spoken. "And human beings that bring themselves lower than animals with sinning and abomination. It should tell us what it is, so we know what we're dealing with."

"I already told you," Paz said, loud enough for everyone to hear. "I'm a self – which means a person – from another world. The world of Ut, in the Pandominion. It's the same world as this one, really. That is, it's in the same place, only in a different universe. There are lots and lots of worlds. My friend Rupshe, who's an untethered AI, says there are an infinite number. She made a map of them, using a predictive model based on a quaternion fraction. And on the world where I come from, everyone looks like me. There aren't any . . ." she groped for the correct term, but didn't find it ". . . any selves like you," she finished lamely.

Father Enofe bridled at all this as if Paz had just sworn at him. "Most of those words don't even mean anything," he said. "Talk sense, or you'll be sorry. What's the name for what you are?"

"Uti," Paz said. "Or woman. Or citizen. You can choose."

"And why did you come to us? What do you want with us?"

"I didn't mean to come here at all." Paz turned and pointed at Beanie. "Beanie pointed a gun at me and made me come."

"Is that true, Abeni?" another elder – one of the women – called out. "Tell what happened, *omo mi*."

"Yeah, I brought her," Beanie said. "She didn't come because she wanted to. She was going her own way until I put my rifle on her. I'd never seen anything like her before, and Nimi Lasisi said we had to watch out at the edges, and I thought . . ." The girl scratched her scabbed cheek, solemn and unhappy. "I don't know what I thought, except that it would be good for someone else to see her besides me. Anyway, she didn't try to hurt me or anything. I know she looks like a monster, but I don't think she is one. She says she's not."

"That's not the question you were asked," Sola scolded her.

"But you can't tell people to be quiet every time they disagree with you," Nimi Lasisi said with an impatient flourish of her hands. "Anyone can speak, you said. Anyone can ask. Tell them your name, child."

"I'm Topaz Tourmaline FiveHills," Paz said. "My friends call me Paz."

"And you said you live in Lagos. That's where the friends you were talking about are. Why don't you tell us about—"

"A traveller from another world is all very well," the bald man said, crowding out Nimi Lasisi's words as he had done with Sola's. "And very science fiction. But we know what's in this world that we have to be afraid of and stay on our guard against. We know our good God up on high gave us a warning, that devils in unnatural, lying flesh would snap and snatch at us. That Satan was our enemy and always would be, with an army of devils behind him running and jumping to catch our souls if we ever were stupid enough to let them come in close."

"Well that," Nimi Lasisi said, "is nonsense. And it's weary nonsense that longs to lie down and be let to die. Devils and Satans. Who in these late days puts a trust in such things?"

"Everyone who's seen one," Father Enofe ground out.

There was a great deal of muttering and murmuring from the crowd at this, but it wasn't clear to Paz which position they were agreeing with. She glanced all around the cleared space, trying to look people in the eye as some kind of indication that she was speaking the truth, but nobody would meet her stare for more than a second. Their gaze darted away almost immediately towards their neighbours or down towards the ground. It didn't seem to Paz like a good sign.

"Can I speak?" she called out over the hubbub of voices. "Can I say something, before you call me a devil again?"

"You can answer our questions first," Sola said. "We're here to sound you."

"And if you won't tell us honest truth we can sound you with fire," Father Enofe added. "Or with water. Both of those things have worked in the past."

Reluctantly, and with a grunt of effort, Nimi Lasisi climbed to her feet. "That won't be happening," she said. "Unless you want to burn or drown me too."

Enofe threw out his hands. "Let us do our work, Grandmother Nimi," he said. "Please, and for the love of God!"

"Burning and drowning isn't what God loves. And it's no part of our work."

Paz turned her back on the elders to face the crowd. Nimi Lasisi was on her side and maybe Beanie was but they seemed to be the only ones. She needed to find more allies. "Listen to me," she said. "I know you're hungry and frightened, but you don't have to be cruel. Why would you want to be? If you let me go I think I can bring you some help. Your soil is just dust and your crops are dying. Your children are sick. All of you are sick. Sick and starving and you've probably got all kinds of vitamin deficiencies, and it's so easy to make it better. You just need a Step plate, and my friends have got dozens of them. We can—"

A thrown stone hit her hard in the side of the head and knocked her off her feet. She lay in the dust, dazed, with her head tucked in and down in case more missiles were thrown at her. That didn't happen, but something warm pressed itself tight against her. Someone was hugging her very close – close enough to shut out the light.

"Get out of there, Abeni!" a male voice shouted. Paz thought it was Father Enofe's, but her head was ringing from that impact and the sound was fuzzed at the edges.

"Don't throw things at her!" Beanie said. "Just stop it now! What do you think you're doing? This isn't even over yet! There's been no judgement!"

Paz realised, very suddenly, that the judgement wasn't going to matter. There was too much anger and fear here for her to cut through it. If she had come at a different time she might have been able to make these people trust her, but it would always have been hard. She would always have been one more strange and frightening thing on top of everything else that had happened to them. And as it was . . .

Paz, said a voice in her array. *Finally!*

Dulcie! The relief was so overwhelming it literally stopped her breath. The muscles in her chest clenched like a fist and she had to struggle to suck in air past the tight knot they made.

Yes. Tell me where you are.

I'm . . . I don't know. Back on . . . Hadiz's world. Earth. Which Dulcie must be too, or how could they be communicating. Stupid! *I Stepped here from the Hale and Homeward. Right from the ground floor of the building. I've come a mile from there. Maybe two. And I headed west, which was back towards Lagos. There's a village. Mostly ruins, but people are living there. Dulcie, I'm in trouble! I think they're going to kill me!*

A pause, but it was infinitesimal. *All right. I'm coming.*

What should I do?

Play for time.

But what could Dulcie even do, when et got here? Ets new shell didn't carry any weapons.

It didn't matter. Time was time, and Paz would buy it with any currency she could find. Then if it came to it she would fight, hampered by the fact that none of these people were really her enemies. Sola and Father Enofe were two stupid old men clinging to let's-pretend power and all of them – the elders and everyone else – at rock bottom were just afraid. But if it came to it she would give them something to be afraid of, because the alternative was lying down and dying and she couldn't reconcile herself to that.

She rolled over onto her back, gently pushing Beanie away. "Thank you," she whispered. "But don't stay too close to me. You might get hurt."

Sola brandished his cane over the both of them. "Get away, Beanie," he hooted. "Get out of there."

Beanie climbed to her feet. She kept her gaze on Paz as she rose, but when she spoke it was to Sola – and perhaps to the other elders. "You don't lose anything by trusting her," she said. "She's right that we don't have enough food to eat. If she can help us—"

"If, if, if," Sola scoffed. "She can help us by telling us where the rest of the robbers went to. That's the only way. And we will make her tell it."

Paz stood too. She wasn't very tall, but Sola's bent frame made him shorter still. "I choose fire," she told Father Enofe over the other man's head.

Both of them stared at her blankly. "What?" Sola demanded. "What's this you're saying now?"

Paz pointed at the brazier. "You said you could test me with fire or with water. I don't see any water, but there's a fire over there. Test me with that."

"No!" Nimi Lasisi cried.

"Yes. I want it. Does your god listen to the prayers of the innocent?"

"Of course!" Father Enofe said.

"Then I want it. Bring me fire, and let me show you what I am."

I see the houses, Dulcie said through Paz's array. *I'm almost there.*

"Very well," said Father Enofe. "Let it be done. Gbemi, Shano, bring the fire here."

The two women who had been addressed ran and fetched wooden poles from one of the houses that backed onto the clearing. The brazier was just a big metal barrel, most likely an old dustbin, with handles at the top and a few holes punched in its sides. The women thrust the poles through the handles so they didn't need to touch the hot steel. They carried the brazier across the open space to where Paz was standing.

The barrel was two-thirds filled with burning twigs and branches, and judging by the amount of smoke it was vomiting out, the wood hadn't been dried first.

"This is monstrous!" Nimi Lasisi cried out. "Sola, we're not savages. We don't maim or torture!"

"She asked for this," Father Enofe said. "She wants this. Watch her close, though. If she tries to bolt, hold on to her."

Paz approached the brazier. The two selves who had escorted her from Iya's house moved in lockstep behind her, and the women with the wooden poles closed in on either side.

Can you see me? Paz asked.

Not yet, but I'm in the village now. Where is everyone?

Do you see smoke rising?

Yes!

Go there.

Paz stood as close to the brazier as she could bear. The searing heat rose up to hit her in the face with smothering force. She held her left hand over the fire.

"I call on your god to witness this," she said. "Innocent people don't burn, and I'm innocent. I didn't do any of the things you say I've done."

She thrust her hand into the flames. There was a sudden shock of pain, like the sensation you'd get if you touched a hot stove, but she fought the urge to pull away and so that wrenching jolt became first a plateau and then a quick ascent towards some awful peak. Paz felt a scream rising in her throat. She bit down hard on her lower lip to hold it in.

But her stopped breath came out a moment later as a ragged gasp. The pain was gone, with a suddenness like the flicking of a light switch. At the same time her array reported an intervention. NEURAL INTERFACE MUTED FOR REASONS OF USER SAFETY AND COMFORT. OVERRIDE AVAILABLE ON REQUEST.

She had chosen her left hand because it was the one that had been replaced after the explosion in her classroom. The surgeons at Canoplex Meso-Urban had repaired her so well she barely thought any more about the parts of herself that were no longer fully organic. Sections of her brain had been replaced with laminated micro-circuitry, her lungs and heart had been swapped out, she had been given new eyes – and a new left hand, made of bio-mimicking plastic, with full neural feedback through her array. Except that – as she had hoped – her array had decided in this instance to shut down the feedback on the assumption that intense and prolonged agony was something Paz might prefer not to experience.

Meanwhile the hand itself was showing no ill effect from the fire. Like all high-end prosthetics it had been designed to make accidental damage virtually impossible: plastic or not, its melting point was probably high enough to withstand an industrial furnace.

The selves on either side of Paz had already seen this. Their eyes were wide with wonder, their mouths hanging open. For the benefit of the rest of the crowd, and of the elders, Paz took hold of a burning branch and raised it up into the air.

"You see?" she said. "I'm innocent!"

She had expected a rush of apologies or perhaps a spontaneous celebration. Surely a miracle was worth at least a polite round of applause! But all she saw in the faces of the crowd was horror. A circle cleared around her as people backed away. Parents snatched up their children into their arms.

She had made a mistake. By the logic of the test she'd won, but at the same time she'd proved that her strangeness went a lot further than skin-deep.

"It is a trick," Father Enofe said with terrible deliberation. "Hold it. Don't be frightened of it. Hold it for me, and I will do the rest."

Hands closed on Paz from behind and from both sides. She tried to pull herself free but she was held fast. With a flailing kick she upended the brazier. It rolled away into the crowd, spewing out flaming branches, hot ash and bright arcing showers of sparks. Some people jumped back to avoid them, others hurried to stamp them out. As a diversion it accomplished nothing: the selves holding on to Paz's arms and shoulders pulled her away from the still burning twigs and the toppled brazier. She was slammed back hard against a wall.

"No such thing as devils!" Father Enofe exclaimed, giving Nimi Lasisi a fierce glare. He held out his hand to the woman with the hatchet, who handed over her weapon without a word. He drew back the hatchet and set his feet square. He pressed his free hand against Paz's chest to steady her, took careful aim.

25

Essien

The run across country had taken a couple of hours and some change, but Essien hadn't bothered to stay awake for all of it. It was easy to put his suit on autopilot with instructions to keep heading north in the convoy and alert him if anything changed. Even easier to dose himself up with a bespoke cocktail of nutrients, sedatives and neuro-actives and slip into a dreamless doze. The mission on Tsakom had been a ball-breaker: it was good to grab a little rest. His body was in ceaseless motion but his mind floated free of it.

He even dreamed, although the dreams came in disjointed pieces and had no narrative to them. He saw moments from his childhood in Oshodi. He saw the gleaming ceramic spider crab that had descended on him after he enlisted in the Cielo and his weak, vulnerable body was transformed into something less human and more robust. He saw his father, face crumpled in sadness; his friend Ndulue turning the pages of a book called *Endangered Animals*; Hadiz Tambuwal asleep beside him in a world to which he would never now return.

And then he woke, to the harsh and unnecessarily loud voice of Rupshe. "We are almost there. But I am afraid we may arrive too late."

"What?" Essien blinked away sleep. "Why? What's happening?"

"I have finally been able to locate Paz. Her array came back online a few minutes ago. Let me show you." A space in Essien's array expanded and became a window. Through it he saw what had to be a camera feed, from a drone hovering about a thousand feet up. The video stream was pin-sharp: it showed an area where a few cultivated fields were wedged in between encroaching scrub and barren rock. There were buildings that seemed to be ruins and a cleared space in among them. On second glance it was clear that some of the ruins had been halfway repaired. Even from this far out he could see movement down there.

"Wait," Essien said. "This is here? Now? I thought your world had gone through an extinction event."

"Extinction is seldom the turning of a switch. It seems some scattered groups of survivors still exist, though their prospects in the medium to long term are extremely poor. I would argue, though, that this is a discussion for another time. Look."

The drone's camera zoomed in on the ragged sprawl of half-ruined buildings, and then on the clearing in the midst of them. The resolution was still very high. There were people there, men and women and children, most of them thin to the point of emaciation and all of them facing inwards on a spot over to the right-hand edge of the clearing. One diminutive self was being held hard up against a wall by several others, its desperate struggles overridden by their numbers.

"It's the bunny," said Moon, her voice coming in on the same channel as Rupshe's. "Looks like she pissed off the locals. Again."

Essien's gaze flicked to the pinioned figure. Moon was right. It was Paz. Another self, a man, stood in front of her brandishing something in his right hand. A weapon of some kind, most likely an axe or a club judging by the way he was holding it upright in his fist.

"How far out are we?" he demanded.

"Still three or four minutes at the very least," Rupshe said, "even if we accelerate to the limit of these suits' tolerances."

"Is your drone armed?"

"No."

Essien felt a flare of helpless rage. "Well why the fuck not?"

"It is a scientific instrument, Private Nkanika, not a piece of military hardware. Perhaps, though, I can use it to create a diversion. If I bring it down to where these people can see it they may pause in their assault on Paz long enough to investigate it."

"Or I could just fling a rocket over there," Moon said. "I checked the inventory and this suit is fully stocked. High-ex, gas, incendiaries, the works."

"You're just as likely to kill Paz!" Essien ground out. His mind was working furiously but coming up with nothing that worked.

"Not if Rupshe handles the telemetry. You can do that, right, Rupshe?"

"I could do it via the drone. The strike could be targeted with precision."

"There are kids in that clearing. Think of another way."

"I am not certain there is another way."

There was a crackling on the line – a drop in the signal's integrity as another line tapped in.

"I'll do what I can." This was a new voice, and it wasn't one Essien recognised. It was full of stress and urgency. "Just get here quickly."

"Who is this?" Rupshe asked.

"Dulcie," said the voice, already breaking up. "I'm in—" A muted click announced that the newcomer was gone as suddenly as they had arrived.

"The tin monkey?" Moon demanded. "Voice was different."

"Dulcimer Coronal has migrated to a new shell," Rupshe said. "I cannot make a conclusive identification, but whoever spoke knew the frequency we're using. It is more likely to be Dulcie than anyone else. Whoever it was, I believe we should take their advice and make haste."

Rupshe closed the channel but left the video feed active, presumably to spur them on. Essien didn't need any encouragement. Something about the sight of those half-starved selves had gotten into the depths of his gut and was twisting there.

He pushed his suit's servos into overdrive and sped on, crashing through whatever he couldn't go around.

26

Paz

Father Enofe drew back the hatchet and took aim. But then he stopped and froze in place, almost as if by magic.

But it wasn't magic, it was Beanie. She had rested the barrel of her rifle on the man's shoulder, its business end pressing against the side of his neck. There was a scowl of concentration and deep solemnity on her face. "The Iya told you to stop, Father," she said. "So you better stop. I'll shoot you if you don't."

The man's gaze slid sideways towards the rifle. He bared his teeth in a sneer. "With your air gun, that only kills rats and rabbits? I don't fear it."

"Are you sure? It's going to hit you where you breathe, so perhaps you should."

"Put it down now, child. If you harm me there'll be no place for you here."

Paz. Dulcie's silent voice sounded from inside her array again. *Help is coming.*

Great! When? Most of Paz's attention was on what was happening right in front of her. She could see two men detaching themselves

from the front of the crowd and starting to edge towards Beanie
from behind. But if she shouted a warning Beanie would turn – and
then the other selves standing closest would have a chance to disarm
her or worse.

Time. It all came down to that. The two men had almost reached
Beanie now, and she hadn't seen them. Paz threw back her head
and let loose a wild, ululating cry. It had the desired effect of making
everyone stop what they were doing and look at her.

Almost in the same instant Father Enofe gave a grunt of surprise
and flinched back, inadvertently causing Beanie's rifle to slide from
his shoulder. He clapped his free hand to his cheek with a muttered
oath, then lowered it again to stare at it – with one eye, because
the other was screwed shut. There was a smear of bright scarlet
across the heel of his hand. From the closed eye a bright red tear
ran down his cheek. He gave a soft grunt of surprise.

"Blood," he muttered. "I'm bleeding!"

There was a faint hiss of sound, followed by a *spak!* of sudden
impact. One of the selves in the front of the crowd yelled, clutching
his shoulder. Rivulets of red ran between his fingers. Another keening
whistle ended in a second insinuating thud. A woman brought both
hands up to her throat with a shriek of shock and horror to stop a
welling crimson tide.

The knot of people who had been holding on to Paz broke and
scattered. Several of them ran into Sola and Father Enofe as they
fled, sending them sprawling. Paz could have taken the opportunity
to run too but her legs didn't seem able to move, and in any case
the milling throng of people still surrounded her.

Then they were surrounded in their turn as a horde of selves in
bright red armour – Cielo troopers, towering seven and eight feet
tall – broke out of the trees on all sides and formed a cordon around
the clearing. They offered no violence but their appearance was an
assault in itself. The local selves fell to their knees, covering their
faces with their hands or raising them in surrender. There were
screams and sobs and a few shrill curses.

"Stop what you're doing and kiss the dirt," a massively amplified voice boomed. "Whatever this party was, it's over as of right fucking now!"

One of the Cielo troopers stepped out of the line, his head turning to the left and then the right. "Nobody is to move!" the hectoring voice shouted. "Not so much as a muscle. There's a girl here that's under my protection, and if you've hurt her there's going to be seven kinds of hell to pay."

Up to that moment, Paz had no idea whether she was being rescued or captured. But she recognised that voice and the sense of relief and joy was dizzying, like a rush of blood to her head. It made no sense for Essien Nkanika to be at the head of a Cielo tactical squad, but she wasn't about to question it. Presumably there would be explanations later. "Essien!" she called out. She raised an arm in a weak, truncated wave. "I'm here. And I . . . I'm fine. I'm okay."

The trooper tapped his helmet's visor which irised open. Essien crossed to her, shouldering through the crowd without much concern as to whether they got out of his way or not. One of the people he passed was Beanie. She pointed her rifle at him out of some instinct towards self-defence. Essien didn't even give it a sidelong glance but another armoured figure came up beside the girl and put out a hand to push the gun's barrel down again.

"Don't hurt her!" Paz cried out. "She tried to help me."

The second suit's visor slid up. Beanie found herself staring into Moon Sostenti's huge yellow eyes and bared needle teeth. "Still rude to point," Moon said solemnly. Beanie's mouth opened and closed but no sound came out. Meeting Paz had done nothing to prepare her for this new shock. After a moment, she dropped the rifle and sat down where she had been standing, folding at the knees and falling back onto her haunches.

"Good girl," Moon murmured.

Essien came to Paz and knelt down in front of her. "You're hurt," he said. "Show me."

Paz touched her cheek and felt the wetness there. "It's nothing," she said. "They barely touched me. And then they . . . they all started to bleed."

It wasn't blood, it was paint. Dulcie scampered down the broken wall and jumped onto Paz's shoulder, landing lightly as the shock absorbers in her legs took most of the force out of the impact. *All of them, just paint. I would have hit them with something harder if I'd had it, but that stick of paint bombs you bought was the best I could do.*

Paz lifted Dulcie down with both hands and hugged her hard.

"It was enough," she murmured, her lips up close to Dulcie's sculpted ear even though she knew the actual sound receptor was somewhere in the shell's chest.

I'm sorry it took me so long to find you, Dulcie said. *I thought the guards on Jaspal must have caught you so I was looking for you there.*

"I managed to get down to the ground and use my bounce-back. How did you even survive?"

I landed in someone's roof garden. Then I went back inside, but the place was crawling with security so I got out again fast. But I stayed close so I could eavesdrop on their comms. As soon I found out they hadn't caught you I came here and started searching. I'm so glad I got here in time.

Paz gave a ragged laugh. "Me too."

The Cielo troopers, under Moon's direction, were now penning the people of the village into a makeshift corral between two standing walls. Nobody had been injured but they were all understandably terrified and confused. They shrank back from the inhumanly tall soldiers, some of them weeping and clinging miserably to each other.

"Let me know if anyone here needs shooting," Moon called out to Paz. She used the barrel of her rifle to poke Sola in the chest. He was up on his feet again with both hands raised in front of his face as though he could make this nightmare go away by not looking at it. "Him, for instance."

"No," Paz said, loudly enough for everyone to hear. "Nobody is getting shot. Or stabbed, or burned, or blown up. Is all this army yours? Tell them not to shoot anyone, please! This isn't what it looks like."

"It looks to me like these grovelling bastards were about to cut your throat," Moon said. "If it were me I'd put a few up against a wall and have some target practice."

Essien turned from Paz to stare across at Moon. Even right then, with her heart still pounding and her legs too wobbly to stand on, Paz found his grim expression a little frightening to look at. "Let's not," he said, with very precise emphasis. But then he noticed the fallen axe, and picked it up.

"Who does this belong to?" he asked.

Nobody spoke. The woman who'd held the hatchet and given it to Father Enofe looked at the ground. Her shoulders shook a little.

"It doesn't matter," Paz said. "Really, none of that is important right now. Essien, look at them. They're starving. They're selves just like you and me and they're barely surviving here. They just need one Step plate and some help in finding an unclaimed world to farm. We have to go tell Hadiz and Rupshe."

"We already know." All the other armoured troopers except for Essien and Moon said this at once. Paz felt her stomach turn just a little at that strange chorus. "I'm sorry," said one of the nearest suits. "I meant to relay that message through a single speaker. I still need to carry out some fine adjustments on these units before I can make them entirely responsive to my commands." The voice was Rupshe's.

"You're . . . you're in the suits?" Paz demanded. "You're controlling the suits?"

By way of answer, the visors on all the remaining suits slid open to reveal only emptiness where their wearers' faces should have been. Paz felt an involuntary shiver go through her. She braced herself for another chorus of screams, but the eerie sight seemed to have struck the local selves dumb.

"All but Private Nkanika's and Corporal Sostenti's," Rupshe confirmed. "Paz, I'm reading your array. I do not see the coordinates of the Mother Mass continuum there. Did you obtain them in a verbal exchange?"

"No," Paz said. She swallowed hard. "I'm sorry, Rupshe. I didn't get anything. I failed."

"*We* failed," Dulcie corrected. "But we might have done better if we'd had more reliable intel. The Hale and Homeward had armed security. And Zenti's mind had been booby-trapped. As soon as Paz started asking him questions about the Mother Mass all hell broke loose."

"That was a risk that had not occurred to me. I am sorry if you were placed in any danger as a result."

"Can we talk about this later?" Paz pleaded. "I know it's important, and I know we need to get back to the mission, but if we don't do something to help these people before we leave they're all going to die."

"I recognise the urgency of their situation," Rupshe said. "But I am afraid we don't have either the resources or the time."

The casual dismissal only made Paz impatient. It was so obviously untrue. "We've got plenty of resources!" she exclaimed. "I saw dozens of Step plates back at the campus, Rupshe. And you can make more whenever you like, especially now you've got all these . . ." She looked around at the untenanted suits but couldn't find a word for them. Servants? Drones? Extra limbs? She gave up on it and started again. "All you've got to do is bring one plate here and show someone how to use it."

"Which would accomplish nothing. There are not enough survivors here to constitute a viable gene pool. They might last out a few more years, even a few more generations, but eventually they will all die."

"Then we look for other survivors!" Paz said, appalled. "There must be some, surely. This can't be the only place in the whole world where people just managed to hang on!"

"Perhaps not. But how much time and effort do you propose that we devote to the search, Paz? Possibly I misspoke when I said we have insufficient resources. There are palliative measures we could take here. But we have other priorities. Our primary goal remains the same – to stop the Pandominion and the machine hegemony from destroying each other. The lives that are at stake in that conflict outnumber those you are seeing here by many orders of magnitude. Moreover, there is reason to believe that the war has entered a new phase."

"What reason?" Moon demanded. "What have you heard?"

"Nothing," Rupshe said. "That is the point. The Pandominion has gone into full informational lockdown. That is not a thing they would do for any trivial reason. It suggests a turning point of some kind may have been reached."

Paz looked at Beanie, then at Essien. She folded her arms like a stubborn toddler. "I don't care," she said. "We can't just walk away and leave all these people to starve. Give them a Step plate."

"And instructions on how to use it? And a reliable power source? None of these things are impossible, Paz, and at some future point I would be happy to discuss them further with you, once we have succeeded in the wider task we have undertaken."

"No," Essien said, "she's right. We can't leave things like this." His face had set into an expression that seemed both angry and deeply unhappy.

"Your meaning is unclear," Rupshe replied.

Essien seemed to find it hard to look at the settlement's inhabitants, but he indicated them with a brusque, sweeping wave of his arm. "I think my meaning's pretty clear in context. I'm agreeing with Paz. I don't think we can abandon these people to fend for themselves now we know they're here."

"I have already explained my position on this."

"Yeah, you did. And my position is different. Listen, do you have a plan B, now that we struck out with this Spearhead vet?"

"I am considering a range of options," Rupshe said. "I am still hopeful."

"Do these options depend on us getting back to Campus Cross and using the Step plates there?"

"Yes. Without exception."

"And we're not going to want to carry Paz a hundred miles by piggyback. Why don't you rustle us up some transport, and we'll do what we can to stabilise the situation here until you get back? That way we don't lose any time and everyone is happy."

Rupshe considered this in silence for a few moments. The empty scarlet suits stood unmoving in eerily identical postures. "Very well," et said at last. "I believe that is a reasonable use of our resources. I have located a military base close by. I will take a number of these units there and secure us some form of transport. The rest will remain here at your disposal. I will keep you apprised of my progress."

"Great," Essien said. "You do that."

Eight of the red suits peeled off from the rest and moved out without a word, moving in perfect unison like dancers or synchronised swimmers.

Essien stood and helped Paz up. They walked across to the small group of local selves, standing cowed and unhappy in a pen made of scarlet armour.

"Who speaks for you people?" Essien demanded. He gave Father Enofe a hostile glance. "It better not be you."

A silence followed these words. It was Nimi Lasisi who broke it, stepping to the front of the little penned-in group. "For the sake of argument," she said, "let it be me." Most of the people around her shrank back from her as she spoke, perhaps afraid of getting caught up in whatever reprisal she'd just called down on herself.

"How many of you are there?" Essien asked her. "All told?"

"Sixty-three. Fifty or so adults, the rest children."

"And what's your greatest need, right here and now?"

"Are we seriously doing this?" Moon asked. It wasn't clear to Paz whether she was speaking to Essien or to Rupshe.

Nimi Lasisi thought long and hard before she spoke. "Can I give you two answers?" she said at last. On Essien's nod, she went on. "Obviously the thing we need more than anything else is food. Our situation was dire even before we were robbed. There's nothing to hunt, we ran out of canned goods a long time ago and you can see for yourself how our crops are coming along. One of the biggest problems is protein. For the children especially. They can't grow straight without it and they don't get nearly enough. So any meat you could get us would be wonderful. And our corn is ready to harvest now, if we can get it in fast enough. The rainy season will start soon and it will rot if we don't harvest it in time.

"In the longer term we'd do a great deal better with our agriculture if we had the proper tools. There's a beautiful grain combine down in Odo-Mola that could go through every field we've got in less than a day. If we had that we could plant a whole lot more fields. But we'd also need diesel fuel to run it."

"Anything else?" Moon asked laconically. "Foot massage? Dry white wine? Tickets to the opera?"

"The rainy season is bad for us in other ways too," Nimi Lasisi went on, ignoring the sarcasm. "Look at these walls. They could do with being repaired, but the harvest needs every available hand."

Essien turned to one of the empty suits and spoke to Rupshe through it. "I assume you got all that?"

"Yes," Rupshe confirmed. "If the contingent I sent to the military base can find any fuel that is surplus to our own needs, they will bring it here. And they will return via Odo-Mola. Assuming the grain combine is still there they will fill its reservoir and bring it. Meanwhile the units that remain here can help with the harvest."

"Thank you, Rupshe!" Paz exclaimed.

"Hunting and gathering," Moon said. "You people are hilarious, and if you think I'm shucking corn then you can kiss my furry arse. But I have to admit, when I heard all that 'nothing left to hunt' bullshit I took it as a personal challenge. So why don't I take a stroll and pile up some protein while the rest of you do whatever's needful with the vegetation? The less I have to see of these fuckers the better."

27

Rupshe

Rupshe ran the calculations. The delay would only be eight or nine hours, a short enough interval that it was unlikely to be crucial. A great deal could be achieved in that time – enough, et hoped, to reassure Paz that she could come away with a clear conscience. The newly acquired Cielo units, now successfully adapted for semi-autonomous functionality, could harvest the village's meagre crops with a minimum of effort. Moon was as good as her word when it came to hunting: in addition to being an apex predator she had a keen eye for disease and parasitical infestation. The birds and animals she brought back were plentiful and fit for purpose.

All of which was, broadly speaking, acceptable. Rupshe found much more cause for concern in the Pandominion news blackout, which et felt must surely presage something of great import. Ets drone fleet was presently tacking from one Pando world to another trying to glean what little nuggets of information et could from unshielded signal traffic, but all military communications had switched to Registry encryption, a level of security Rupshe could not pierce. Et noted the unusual troop movements, the Cielo gunships heading into high orbit, but was unable to parse them beyond the obvious fact that the high command were expecting a major assault.

Beyond this, et was more than a little troubled by the unpredictable behaviour that had led to this situation. The organics, beginning with Topaz FiveHills, had first of all disagreed with et and then had refused to listen to irrefutable reason when et attempted to refocus them on the mission.

Rupshe had a bias in favour of organic beings of which et was very well aware. This was nothing to do with sentiment: it had been written into ets code when ets creator, the cyberneticist Andris Bagdonas, had first assembled what became ets processing core. Et was perfectly capable now, thanks to Hadiz Tambuwal's intervention, of excising or rewriting the relevant lines and therefore removing the bias, but et had decided not to do so.

I have relished our ongoing collaboration, et had told Hadiz some years before, and though that was a very much oversimplified description of a more complicated reality in which emotions were replaced by the relative values of self-modifying variables, it continued to be true. Rupshe experienced ets interactions with organic beings in a way that might plausibly be described as pleasure, especially when the interactions bore on the solving of problems.

Now et had addressed etself to a problem on a vastly bigger scale than anything et had attempted before, with stakes that were nothing less than existential. The continued existence of trillions of sentient beings hung on the outcome of ets actions and the actions of ets chosen proxies. And for the first time et was forced to question whether those proxies could be relied on.

The matter was perturbing, not so much because of its immediate consequences but because of its implications for the wider mission going forward. Rupshe was still committed to that mission, to saving as many of the Pandominion worlds as et could, not to mention those of the machine hegemony. Et found the waste of so much potential, so many diverse and successful and fascinating evolutionary lineages, profoundly distasteful, and et wanted very much to avoid such an unsatisfactory outcome if et could.

But perhaps a contingency plan was called for, in case all ets other plans failed.

28

Essien

Kudighe and Sanama Nkanika, Essien's father and mother, had brought two of their six children with them out of Akwa Ibom after the short-lived republic of Biafra collapsed under the weight of the federal government's blockade and the world's indifference. The two were Essien's brother Mboso, then four years old, and Essien himself, unborn, carried to safety in Sanama's womb. He was born in Lagos. He never knew the war, the blockade or the famine – at least, not at first hand.

And yet, growing up, he had found those traumas hard to escape. They survived not only in the stories his parents told but also in the jibes and insults, kicks and more subtle slights directed at him by the area boys of Oshodi, by Yoruba cops and Hausa bosses, even sometimes by people he counted as friends. The famine was such a terrible thing that nobody wanted to own it. It could only have been the fault of the people who starved. If the Igbo and their allies hadn't had the effrontery to stand up and demand independence it wouldn't have been necessary to slap them down again. If their ragtag army hadn't held together when it should have broken there would never have been a blockade. If their illegitimate government had surrendered sooner, fewer people would have died.

And Essien had seen the photos, the newsreels. Of course he had. No son of Kudighe's was going to escape that rite of passage. The children with their bulging bellies full of nothing but air, their xylophone ribs and exophthalmic stares. The listless men and women, exhausted by the endless wait for death. He had been told, again and again: *this is what we came from. Two million fell, not to guns but to hunger, and on television sets in a hundred different countries people watched us die as they ate their own dinners, embraced their own children.*

It wasn't that Essien saw in all this any deep or lasting truth about himself or his heritage. It wasn't a badge he wore either on his skin or under it. But it was a weight that settled on him sometimes when he was too tired or too distracted to deal with the task of forgetting it. And therefore, when he saw these half-starved people in their patchwork houses he knew at once what he was looking at: men, women and children all at different stages of their grindingly slow journey but all on the same road and headed for the same destination.

And he might have looked away in spite of everything if Paz hadn't spoken up when she did. It was a hard thing to admit, but he knew himself too well to hide from it. He could have walked into this sad, doomed little settlement and out again with his eyes and his mind fixed on the middle distance and never have let the truth come into focus. But the rabbit girl had grabbed the middle distance in both hands and shoved it into his face. The gratitude he felt for that was tempered by the sick ache of his awakened memories, each of them surfacing with a sluggish pitch and yaw from the oily sea that the drug gabber had made of his mind.

In this volatile state he was keen to avoid the villagers as much as he could. He offered to join Moon in her hunting but she turned him down without a moment's hesitation. "No way, Sinkhole. You go hang out with your new friends. I'll do my own thing my own way." He wasn't needed in the fields either, where the empty suits of armour that Moon was now calling the red ghosts were harvesting the scrawny ears of corn with a clinical efficiency that was a little alarming to watch.

So Essien had no recourse but to walk among the local selves and bear the weight of their fearful, incredulous gaze. When he had had as much of that as he could take he went looking for Paz and found her with the girl named Abeni, talking animatedly about nothing very much. The robot monkey in its new pearlised shell was there too. As far as Essien could tell Abeni was trying to explain a dance move of some kind to the other two. Either that or she was going into convulsions.

When Paz saw him she got up and came over to him.

"We're not here to waste time," Essien told her gruffly.

"I'm not," Paz said. "I was about to come looking for you. There's something I need you to do."

Thank Christ, Essien thought. "I don't dance," he said aloud. "That aside, I'm up for pretty much anything."

"That cliff up there is limestone," Paz said, nodding her head towards the hillside above the settlement. "I know because I fell down most of it."

Essien stared at her, mystified. "So?"

"So your rifle has an incendiary setting, doesn't it? You can burn the limestone and slake it down into quicklime."

"What do I need quicklime for?"

"You don't," Paz said, her eloquent ears twitching. "But these people do. With quicklime and sand they can make mortar. And with mortar they can repair the walls of their houses. Beanie said they've tried it a few times, but they couldn't make the fire hot enough. It should be seven hundred degrees or so. And your Sa-Su can get up to a thousand on its highest setting."

"How do you know so much about Cielo ordnance?"

The girl looked embarrassed, which in Essien's experience was a first. "When I was younger I wanted to join up. With the engineering corps. I spent way too much time watching telos feeds with titles like *I Was a Teenaged Sapper.*"

He unshipped his rifle and held it out to her. "You make the mortar then. You'll do it better than I would. I'd only be following your instructions anyway."

Paz's eyes widened a little as she regarded the rifle, but she didn't reach out to take it. "I thought a Sa-Su had neural coding," she said. "It only works for the trooper it's assigned to, doesn't it?"

"Right again," Essien confirmed. "But the coded user can do something called override assign. It's so if you're wounded in a fight and someone else in your squad is lacking a weapon you can pass it along. I can code it to you, just with a handshake. That's if you'd be interested. No worries if you're not."

"Yes please!" Paz practically yanked the rifle out of his hands. She held it in the approved over-under grip position too: she hadn't been lying about those telos feeds.

The four of them went out to the cliff together, taking two of the red ghosts along to do the heavy lifting. Making quicklime was loud and messy and dangerous, so it helped a lot in terms of calming Essien's mood. And it was a pleasure watching the kid cut loose with the Sa-Su's flamethrower like a buck private on her first day of basic, only half the size and with twice the attitude. They carried the stinking goop back into the settlement in tin baths, Paz and Beanie toting one between them while Essien and the ghosts took one each.

They dumped the baths down in the main square and got busy mixing the lime with sand and water until they got it to the proper consistency. A crowd of the local selves made the mistake of drifting up close to watch them and Essien drafted them all, including the children, into Operation Plug That Gap. The kids ran around collecting bricks while their parents did the actual masonry work alongside Essien and Paz.

Only none of them seemed to want to get too close to Paz. That puzzled Essien mightily, until he remembered that however imposing he might be he was still just a man in armour. She was the one who truly looked alien – and on top of that here she was sticking her neck out for them after they'd been a few hot seconds away from murdering her. Obviously that left some residual awkwardness.

The kid was a singular package, that was for sure. She might look ridiculous, with her oversized ass and her ears that stood up like flagpoles when she was upset, but she wasn't stupid. Or weak, for that matter. She'd survived that god-awful mess at Damola Ojo, got past a compound full of slavers and a full Cielo tactical unit, and back on Apapa Quays she'd disarmed Moon Sostenti with her bare hands. Well, it was actually with her feet but the point stood.

"You still want to be a soldier?" he asked her while they worked.

Paz thought about it, then shook her head. "Not any more. I don't think I ever did, really. I wanted to go to a lot of places and see a lot of things – and I sort of pretended that if I was an engineer I could do that without actually fighting and killing anyone." She paused in what she was doing, a trowel full of mortar slopping onto the ground at her feet. "I didn't enjoy killing people," she said quietly. "Either time."

Essien was at a loss for a few moments while that sunk in. The kid had done wetwork too! "Well, good," he said at last. "That's good. The ones who enjoy it are the ones you need to watch. Every unit's got them."

Which was true, but it skirted around another truth that Essien preferred not to think about too much. The neural feedback network linked all Cielo troopers together so they felt the backwash from each other's emotions. You experienced it as a warm glow, like the buzz from your fifth or sixth drink on a never-ending bender; and it was like booze in other ways too. It took away your inhibitions, left you rolling along in a group-think undertow that pulled you wherever it wanted.

He *had* enjoyed killing. When the order was to kill, and the troopers on all sides of him were emptying their magazines at whatever the target was, joining in was pleasure and holding back was pain. The Cielo had designed a system in which every front-line grunt reliably became a cheerful psychopath every time their unit went into combat.

What have I been? he wondered.

And what am I now?

29

Paz

The nine hours they spent in the nameless village were among the strangest of Paz's life, which had recently become very strange indeed. Nobody except Nimi Lasisi and Beanie would look her in the eye. Everyone grabbed some distance when she came near, either doing it with a sheepish shuffle and some attempt at subterfuge or just turning and walking away rapidly in a random direction. Beanie said they were ashamed. Nimi Lasisi said sadly that she thought it was worse than that. "You showed them a face they didn't know they had and didn't want to admit to having. And then you brought us this."

She ran her hand along the embossed nameplate on the dull green metal of the grain combine's side. It read "CLAAS LEXION 8900".

"They should hate themselves for that," the old woman said. "But I'm afraid it's much easier to hate you."

"You should come with us," Paz told her. "You and Beanie. We can make room for you at Campus Cross." She waited, gauging Nimi Lasisi's reaction. It was wistful, but far from convinced. "Haven't you always wanted to see Lagos?" Paz coaxed.

"Yes, sweetheart, but I wanted to see Lagos when it was alive. I don't think it would make me happy to see what it is now."

"Everyone I know is here," Beanie said when Paz turned to her. "And we really can't afford to lose anyone. Not right now when everything is so hard."

"Will you be okay, though?" Paz asked. "Will Father Enofe . . . ?"

"Will he be angry with me for poking a rifle into the back of his neck? Probably. But I don't think he'll do anything about it. Well, nothing worse than preach a sermon against rifles, anyway. But will you come back and visit us? When you've fought your war and everything?"

"We'll come back and bring you a Step plate," Paz said. "This will be your last poor harvest. I promise."

The red ghosts had returned twenty minutes earlier in a fleet of dark green trucks, most of which were stacked high with barrels of petroleum-based fuel. Rupshe had allocated ten of these barrels to the village. The remainder were coming back to Campus Cross along with Paz, Dulcie, Essien and Moon.

Paz and Beanie hovered in each other's vicinity for a few moments longer before moving in for a brief, clumsy hug. "I promise," Paz repeated. "If I don't come back it will be because we've failed."

Which would mean a million or so worlds had just fallen into the Scour, most likely including this one. So nobody would come back and it wouldn't matter because nobody would ever know a thing about it.

30

Hadiz

In a sense Hadiz had been the only one left behind while the two parallel missions were going on, but she had never been alone. Rupshe had been with her even while et was directing the beekeepers on Tsakom and the drones on Fenme and Jaspal. Rupshe's consciousness was fully modular now. Et could divide etself into as many sub-minds as were needed and then recombine whenever ets parts were in the same continuum, instantly sharing everything that every one of them had separately experienced.

So as soon as the Rupshe animating the suits of Cielo armour knew that Paz's mission had miscarried, the Rupshe at Campus Cross knew it too and was able to pass the information along to Hadiz.

That's a big setback, Hadiz lamented. *Zenti was our best prospect by far.*

So I thought, Rupshe said. *But consider, Professor. The Cielo high command has gone to extraordinary lengths to ensure that the coordinates of the Mother Mass continuum remain a secret. They went so far as to install post-hypnotic command structures into Hellad Zenti's mind so that he would not only resist questioning but would attack and incapacitate the questioner.*

Why not just kill him? Hadiz pondered. *Or lock him away somewhere? Surely the easier option, if they were prepared to be that ruthless.*

A valid question. And I'm certain they would have done so if they had believed there was any possibility of the coordinates being extracted from him. The only feasible conclusion, therefore, is that Zenti did not have the information we sought. If they could booby-trap his brain in such an elaborate way, erasing an inconvenient memory would be childishly simple.

But then why did they leave him where we could find him? But the answer to that one, Hadiz thought ruefully, didn't need much working out. *As bait?*

That would be my hypothesis, yes. The high command wants not merely to suppress the knowledge of how to find and contact the Mother Mass but also to detain and interrogate anyone who tries to do it in the first place. That amount of caution would seem like naked paranoia in most contexts. Here I believe it confirms our own estimate of the Mother Mass's power, of the scale on which it operates. The Pandominion's rulers were and are afraid of that power – and of allowing others to get close to it.

Do you think they're right? Hadiz was troubled. She had an oppressive sense of how little time they had left. Moreover she knew that when the time ran out they would likely have no warning. They would just be erased by some weapon that took out entire worlds. But she was starting to wonder what they were wishing for. By reaching out to the Mother Mass they might be bringing a nuclear missile to a multiversal knife fight.

Were they right? Rupshe echoed. *From their own perspective, absolutely. The Pandominion, like all incumbent authorities, is of necessity very heavily invested in the status quo. The Mother Mass is a force that can't be defeated, resisted or co-opted, and it isn't bound by any of the laws on which the Pandominion's power rests, including the fundamental laws of physics. So of course they're right to be afraid. And by the same token we are right to hope. There is no doubt that the Mother Mass could end the war, if it chose to. I believe it could also neutralise any weapon of last resort either side tries to deploy.*

If it chose to. Hadiz didn't bother to rehearse how much was hanging on that *if.*

Persuading the Mother Mass to intervene is the next problem along the way, after our current problem of finding it. Let's take things in their proper order.

Which sounded like common sense. All they could do now was to stay on the path they'd chosen and pray that it actually led somewhere. But still . . .

We sent Paz and Dulcie into a trap, she said.

Not intentionally. The danger was not one that we could have foreseen.

Well, that's debatable. We might have foreseen it. We might have taken more precautions, found another way in. But we didn't. Which proves that we're not infallible.

I don't believe we ever claimed to be, Rupshe said. *But I take your implied point, Professor, and I acknowledge the truth of it. We have to do better. We have to work to protect the selves who have made common cause with us. Fortunately, we are now in a better position to do so.*

Are we?

We have the equivalent of a Cielo tactical squad at our disposal. We will never again have to send Paz or any of the others into potential danger without support. Specifically, once we do acquire the coordinates of the Mother Mass continuum we can send an armed escort along with the team. We can also be part of the expedition ourselves, you and I, with our consciousness decanted into Cielo armour.

Hadiz thought about this. A scarlet box instead of a grey one, and a scarlet box with guns and incendiaries attached. She would be able to interface more directly with the world around her – but mostly in ways designed to do it harm. She wondered whether this was a step up or a step down. What she missed was flesh and blood: steel and ceramic didn't feel alluring as a substitute. But it would be nice to have limbs. Hands, especially. She could do a lot if she had proper hands. Perhaps she could even be a scientist again, instead of the persistent echo of one.

There was a distant rumble of engines. The away teams were coming home. Rupshe too, although of course et had never actually left.

They assembled in the lab. To Hadiz, they seemed a very different group of selves from the one that had left there such a short time before. There were visible changes, but those were the least of it. Dulcie was in a new shell, Essien and Moon in armour, while Paz bore the marks of her escape from the Hale and Homeward care facility and her rough handling in the nameless village. Beyond that though, they all seemed grimmer and more tired. Moon hid it better than the others but it was there all the same in the set of her shoulders and the line of her mouth. Perhaps the odds seemed a little steeper now and the consequences of failure more real.

On the other side of the scales, they seemed to have bonded just a little more than before. Essien had gone to the trouble of cooking a meal for the three organics on a portable induction plate; tinned beans, spaghetti and some kind of processed meat, with a sugary something that called itself mint cake for dessert. Moon took hers without thanking him, but she had found a bottle of whiskey in the commissary or in somebody's office and she offered it around in plastic cups. Paz took one after a moment or two's hesitation, Essien at once.

There was even small talk. Moon asked Paz whether her ears only stood up when she was scared or on other occasions.

"What sort of occasions?" Paz asked.

"Well, to take the obvious example, when you're turned on."

A blush didn't show through thick brown fur, but Paz's manner suggested she was blushing. "I think that may happen for boys," she conceded.

Moon rolled her eyes. "Yeah, not surprised. Boys like to have something they can wave around. And something they can measure against what other boys have got."

Hadiz would have let the idle chatter go on for longer, but Rupshe called them to order as soon as they'd finished eating. They drew chairs into a circle and sat. Dulcie perched on the back of Paz's chair with one hand on her shoulder. Ets new shell caught the light and refracted it into rainbows.

"I am still trying to ascertain what is happening in the Pandominion," Rupshe reported, "but without success so far. They are using the Registry to encrypt their signals traffic and I have not been able to observe anything directly beyond the fact that they have retrenched, pulling all warships back from existing battlefronts to defend their own worlds."

"Against what?" Moon asked.

"I can't tell. But it's something they believe will arrive in high orbit. And it's concerning enough that they have abandoned their offensive. Possibly this is what we have anticipated all along – the Scour event, already in progress."

"They wouldn't have been able to hide something like that," Essien objected.

"In the longer term, Private Nkanika, probably not. But they might well attempt to do so for as long as they can. I may be wrong. Possibly all we are witnessing is the inevitable ebb and flow of a prolonged conflict. In any case I wish to counsel you against despair. We have hit a temporary impasse, but there is another method we can try in order to obtain the information we need and proceed with our plan. I would have suggested it earlier were it not for the fact that it touches on the personal histories of some of you and might expose you to encounters you will find unpleasant."

"More unpleasant than tear gas, shock grenades and rifle fire?" Moon asked with no particular inflection. She topped up her whiskey, and then – without asking – Essien's. Paz covered her cup with her hand to show she didn't want any more.

"Perhaps not. But I'm referring to emotional challenges rather than physical dangers."

Moon took a deep swig of the whiskey. "I'll take it over getting shot at."

"Then I will lay out what is required. Before I do, though, you should all have a chance to speak. Is there any pertinent information you've acquired in the course of your missions that you feel the group should know about? If so I would invite you to share it now."

"Well for one thing, we're on the scopes," Moon said, after another gulp of whiskey.

"Please elaborate," Rupshe said.

Moon licked her lips. "After what we pulled on Tsakom and Jaspal the Cielo will be looking for us, and they pretty much know where to look. It's only a matter of time before they find us."

"They cannot backtrack from our previous movements to this precise continuum, Corporal Sostenti."

"They won't need to. We've been this way before, in case you don't remember." She glanced at Essien. "The Sinkhole knows what I'm talking about."

"No," Essien said. "I don't."

"No? Then you're stupider than you look, which is something of an achievement. You're saying you never asked yourself how come me and Lessix turned up on that beach out by the lagoon at the exact same time you and Tambuwal were having yourselves a little picnic party there?"

Essien became very still. Hadiz knew why and answered for him. "You misread that situation. But yes, I have wondered about that. I'm assuming it was because you were staking out the spot after our previous visit there. You had some way of monitoring a specific geographical location across a number of continua – presumably a very large number – without maintaining a physical presence there."

"Damn right we did. It took some Registry run-time but it's not hard. We brought down two of your drones and put them through the wringer. Analysed the residual energy from their field modulators and got a feasible region for where they might have started out. It meant doing trillions of calculations but the Registry could do that in its sleep, if it ever slept. We ended up with maybe forty or fifty thousand realities that were all possibles. Couldn't search them all so we set stumbler remotes in orbit to detect unauthorised Step activity. Then it was just a case of waiting for the bell to ring. We knew where in any given world you were going to turn up if you turned up at all."

"How?" This was the part that had baffled Hadiz. "How did you know that?"

"From where the drones were captured. They were downed as soon as they emerged in Cielo space. They didn't get more than a few hundred metres from where they came through. X marks the spot, right? So we waited in that exact location – on a Cielo world, obviously, on a hot Step plate – and as soon as one of the stumblers smelled something incoming we came right on over."

If Hadiz were still capable of involuntary non-verbals she would have laughed, but it would have been rueful. She had thought she was being so careful, and she had left a trail a mile wide. True, she hadn't known that anyone was looking for her, but Rupshe had warned her not to take unnecessary risks. She should have listened.

"But how does any of that relate to what we're doing now?" she asked.

"Well hey," Moon said, "maybe it doesn't. Maybe I'm just being paranoid. But they had that care home heavily staked out, and the kid and the monkey Stepped away from there separately, not together. So assuming the people in charge had any monitors running, which I'd say is a safe bet, they've got two data sets to analyse. They'll have a list of possible vectors by now, like the one me and Lessix were given. If they decided to follow up, they'll most likely have placed stumblers in every continuum that's strategically important and a whole lot that aren't. And the next time we move – every time we move, from now on – they'll have a solid chance of finding us."

"Unless they've got bigger things on their mind," Dulcie said.

Moon refilled her cup. She didn't stint. "Right," she said. "The ending of days might be upon us. Only we're not supposed to be crossing our fingers and hoping for that, are we?"

There was a silence. It was broken by Paz. "There's something else you should probably know," she said. "Dulcie and I got to talk to Hellad Zenti for quite a while before the trap was sprung. Before his post-hypnotic compulsions kicked in and he attacked us."

"You talked about the Mother Mass?" Rupshe asked.

Paz nodded.

"It's unlikely that anything he said can be trusted, Paz."

"I don't think he was lying. Not deliberately. He was . . ." She looked to Dulcie as if for confirmation.

"He seemed to have some cognitive impairment," Dulcie said.

"Yes. That. He was a bit confused. A bit slow. But when we mentioned the Mother Mass it seemed to trigger his memories of the mission. After that it was as though he just said everything that came into his mind."

"Which was what?" Essien asked.

"Well, one thing he told us is that it was different the two times he went. The first time, he said, everything was just a big purple mass like in the pictures I was shown in school. The second time it was like a place he remembered from his childhood. And there was someone there who shouldn't have been. Someone who wasn't on the mission, I mean. Someone named Jakan, who he knew when he was a boy."

"That is interesting," Rupshe conceded. "Did he describe this as though he believed his childhood friend was actually present, or as though he was aware of dreaming or hallucinating."

"It wasn't easy to tell."

"Why would the Mother Mass alter his perceptions, though?" Hadiz asked, immediately fascinated by the implications. "Was it trying to communicate with him?"

"I think it had been trying to do that all along, not just with him but with all the members of the mission team. At first it wasn't speaking in words, it was just planting ideas in their minds. Ideas

about motherhood. Parents. Parents and children. The second time
it was still doing that, but . . ." She hesitated.

"What?" Moon said. "Spit it out, kid."

"But it wore masks. Zenti said he lost sight of the others and
couldn't find them again. That was when he ran into his childhood
friend. Maybe they all got some version of that. Maybe the Mother
Mass spoke to all of them, but it looked like somebody they already
knew."

"Sounds like it was trying to trick them then," Essien said. "Make
them trust it, and not ask questions."

Paz had an answer for this, and it came so quickly that Hadiz
thought it must have been a conclusion she'd come to already. "I
don't think it was a trick," she said. "It didn't try to hurt them or
anything. I think it was part of the message. It wore those faces to
tell us who it is, or what it is. That it's like us, because it's where
we came from. The origin of life on all the other worlds. It's our
mother, our ancestor." She looked from face to face, anxious, earnest.
"We know it can Step. It Stepped Zenti and his team home again,
when it couldn't make them understand. Suppose it did the same
thing billions of years ago. Stepped itself or bits of itself to all the
different worlds, and planted seeds. The seeds we all grew from."

"I'm not buying it," Moon said. "If we all came from the same
seeds we'd all have come out the same. Ghen, Ut, Earth, everywhere.
We'd all be cats, or we'd all be apes, rabbits, whatever."

"The seeds were just life seeds," Paz said. "The first expedition
said the Mother Mass looked like slime mould or algae. It was a
really simple organism that spread over everything, never had any
competition or any predators, and somehow got to be sentient. So
that would be what it brought to the other worlds. Just . . . stuff
like itself. The simplest kind of life. As a gift. And then it left the
stuff to grow any way it wanted to, not trying to control it."

"It knocked up entire planets, you mean." Moon chuckled and
shook her head. "That would make it our father, not our mother."

"I don't find it plausible," Rupshe said. "We know that there are an infinite number of worlds. There cannot be a finite point of origin for an infinite series. Even if the Mother Mass were able to do what you say, Paz, and if it had toiled for millennia, it could not have seeded all the worlds where organic life has evolved. That's an impossible task."

"Even if it was just some of the worlds, though," Paz said stubbornly, "it still makes it much more likely the Mother Mass will say yes to us. If we're all its children, or if it thinks we are." She shrugged. "Anyway, it made me more hopeful. Especially since it behaved differently the second time Zenti went there. It was learning. Learning to talk to them. It wouldn't have done that if it didn't have something to say."

"Still sent them home with their tails between their legs," Moon said.

"When it failed." Paz shrugged again. "When it couldn't make them understand."

"The information is useful, anyway," Rupshe concluded. "We should be aware that when we visit the Mother Mass continuum, assuming we succeed in doing so, our perceptions of our environment may be manipulated. Does anyone have anything more to add at this time?"

"Just tell us what fucked-up thing you've got lined up for us next," Moon said. "We can tell you're dying to."

"Very well," Rupshe said. Et went on without a pause, and in the same level tone. "I have spent some time since our return trying to locate any files or documents relating to the Arbitrary Midnight expedition in the Pandominion's public databases."

"I thought you already did that and struck out," Essien said. He reached for the whiskey bottle. Moon moved it out of his reach. She was working her way through it at a steady pace, and clearly she was all done with sharing.

"That's true," Rupshe said. "But this time I wasn't trying to find the coordinates, or any information the Omnipresent Council might have considered sensitive."

"Then what was the point?"

"A typical Spearhead operation, Private Nkanika, generates approximately eighteen thousand named files and in excess of a hundred thousand electronic tags and records. This is a conservative estimate. The actual number is far larger since each file and tag can exist on a great many different servers, either in archives to which they have been purposely saved or in temporary buffers, backup folders and dispersed storage systems. It seemed likely that even in the case of an operation like Arbitrary Midnight, which was deemed highly confidential and redacted from public servers, some of the documents relating to it might have escaped the resulting cull because in themselves they contained no mission-critical information. These in their turn might suggest useful starting points for retrieving the data we're actually searching for."

"And did they?" Moon asked. "Why not just cut to the chase?" Her voice was level, not even slightly slurred. Only a slight over-emphasis gave away the fact that the alcohol was starting to get to her.

"In a sense, Corporal Sostenti, yes. They did."

"Fuck! In what sense? How does any of this help us?"

"I did find many such documents and traces. They contained nothing that was directly useful, which was only to be expected. Attached to one, though, was a list of agencies and officers who were to receive copies, along with their respective levels of clearance. Most of the names were unfamiliar, but one stood out at once because I had already had dealings with him."

Et paused, for what to Hadiz looked suspiciously like dramatic effect.

"You have too," et said.

31

Vemmet

The armies of the machine hegemony swept across Bivouac 19 in a churning multi-modal maelstrom of pure destruction. Just the one pass, and since they were Stepping in from a great many beachheads at once it took no longer than seventeen minutes. Then they were gone.

They left very little behind them. They had sterilised the planet's surface with flame, high explosives and exotic radiation. They had pierced underground calderas with lances of pure force, creating super-volcanoes with mile-wide mouths. They had unleashed mobile particulate swarms like clouds of silver dust that dismantled anything organic they touched down to loose atoms.

They had been thorough, in other words. They had not intended to leave any enemy forces standing, and they had been very broad indeed in what they counted as an enemy.

Orso Vemmet survived in the first instance because he arrived at the very tail end of the invasion. The Ansurrection forces were already leaving when he Stepped from Lago de Curamo on the world designated U5838784474 right into their path. Their primary task was complete, with a success rate that was within spitting distance of one hundred per cent. They simply ignored Vemmet. They broke over him like a wave, and then they faded like ghosts out of his appalled sight as their bounce-backs took them home to whatever machine world had sent them.

For a day and a night the watchmaster wandered, stunned and stupefied, across the blasted plain. Everything was on fire and everything stank of death. He leaned against a metal rail to steady himself and the flesh of his palm stuck to it when he pulled away. He swiped at a bug – or something like a bug – that floated round his head and a burst of electricity flung him jarringly to the ground. He clambered slowly to his feet and walked on. His body ached all over, and he was bleeding from a hundred shallow wounds that he didn't remember receiving.

There were others wandering too, gaunt and bloodied spectres dressed in charred rags or shattered armour. Vemmet veered away from them and they from him, afraid of anything that moved in that endless, deconstructed landscape.

He came to a stream and was about to drink, on all fours like an animal, when some instinct made him pause. Lifting his head he saw the ribbons and ropes of silver that were threaded through the water. Lead? Mercury? Something even worse? There was no way of knowing. He licked cracked lips, stood on shaking legs and stumbled on.

It was Vemmet's misfortune that he headed west, following the incline of the ground downwards in the hope that there might be another watercourse somewhere at the bottom. To the north and east, Cielo evacuation teams found and pulled out several hundred survivors of the raid. They saw the signal from Vemmet's array and would have gone to it, but they found their systems under attack by some of the Ansurrection's microscopic phage swarms and were forced to retreat. Rescue attempts were paused until some means was found of countering residual threats and guaranteeing the rescuers' safety.

Vemmet slept at the base of a ruined wall under a sheet of rigid plastic that had once been some kind of display board. The sheet provided no warmth at all, but it gave him a little comfort not to be completely exposed. The next morning he set off walking again in no particular direction, hoping he might be rescued but not really believing it.

On the second day, Vemmet found a succulent plant whose name he didn't know. It had been part-baked, but the intact part still had some water in it. He crammed ragged chunks of it into his mouth and let them sit there while a few drops of moisture trickled into his throat. When the worst of his thirst was slaked he ate as much of the plant's flesh as he could stomach.

More walking, step after stumbling step. But he only managed an hour or two before he sank down again, exhausted and despairing. There was no point in going on. Everywhere was the same. The fires were mostly going out by now but the air was as thick as suet and tasted of hot iron.

The second night, finding no better shelter, Vemmet dug a shallow trench in the crumbly soil, lay down and pulled more earth and grit on top of himself. He slept in fits and starts, a few minutes at a time. Waking felt very little different, his nightmares of pain and cold and fear merging seamlessly with the actual experience of those things.

He walked. He slept. He walked again. When he found water now he drank it, no matter how fouled or toxic it looked. He couldn't remember when he had last eaten.

The realisation grew on him by slow degrees that he was going to die here. Now that it was too late, he remembered the Step plate that had brought him to Biv 19. It might still be intact, if he could somehow get his bearings and find his way back to it, but it was a needle in a planet-sized haystack and he barely had the energy to move.

Finally, he lay down and couldn't rise again. When he had been still and silent for a few minutes something small and alive, not a rat but very like a rat, came and fed on the flesh of his forearm. For some reason it didn't hurt. Perhaps the little animal was able to secrete an anaesthetic of some kind in its bite. Vemmet was almost certain he'd heard of such a thing. It still wasn't a pleasant sight though. He stirred himself to swat the thing away. It skittered back from his weakly flopping hand and watched him from a few feet off, its keen incisors bared and its tiny red eyes unblinking, ready to return to its meal as soon as he lost consciousness again.

"No," Vemmet croaked. "Get away. Wait until I'm dead."

The little animal flicked its tail and hissed at him. It crouched back on its haunches, ready to spring.

Before it could, a heavy boot slammed down on it and squashed it flat with a barely audible crunch of pulverised bone. The boot was bright red, its glossy self-cleaning surface reflecting Vemmet's bleary-eyed, astonished face. He tilted his head back – slowly, because every movement cost him effort – to take in the monolithic bulk of the Cielo trooper. The tree-trunk legs. The mountain summit torso. The fanged and brindled face.

"Okay, he's here," Moon Sostenti called over her shoulder. "You owe me a ten-star, Sinkhole. Didn't I tell you? This bastard is harder to kill than a fucking cockroach."

32

Moon

The sun went down early behind the buildings of Campus Cross, red and sullen under thick swathes of grey cloud like a wound wrapped in dirty bandages. A drizzle of warm rain was falling – or at least something wet was precipitating out of the sky. Moon wasn't taking anything for granted.

She had to admit, though, that it felt good to dump her kit, shuck her armour and kick back. The trek through Fenme had been as tense as hell and the raid on Tsakom had come dangerously close to being a clusterfuck, but that little side trip to the refugee settlement or whatever you wanted to call it had been the icing on the rancid cake. Moon had watched the rabbit bonding with the indigenes, and then Nkanika bonding with the rabbit, and she had felt more or less disgruntled with the whole enterprise. It wasn't that she felt left out, or that she had any appetite at all for getting warm and cuddly with these people. Quite the opposite. She had made a conscious decision to keep them all at a distance and she was quick to throw up a barrier of surliness and hostility if anyone threatened to come too close. All she wanted was to get the job done, collect her pay – including most especially the hide of Melusa Baxemides – and hit the road.

But it was hard to be part of a unit – which was what she and the Sinkhole and the rabbit and the little robot now effectively were – and feel no sense of belonging. Moon put it down to the gods-damned feedback loops the Cielo had installed in her brain. The loops had rewarded her with dopamine when she thought and acted in synch with the rest of her squad, and now they were withholding the reward because she was keeping herself aloof. Instant downer. That the isolation and depression were chemically induced didn't make them any less wearing on the soul. If Moon had had any gabber on her she might have popped some just to take the edge off that feeling. In the meantime, and as a pretty solid alternative, she was working her way reasonably pleasantly through the bottle she'd unearthed in the commissary. It was something called Jack Daniel's Tennessee whiskey. She had no idea what any of those words meant, but booze was booze and this stuff did the necessary.

But why had she shared it with Nkanika and the rabbit? That was a crack in her armour right there, and not the bright red plate she wore over her physical body but the much tougher stuff in which she'd clad her soul. She needed to watch that shit and lock it down tight. The last thing she wanted was to wake up one day and find that she gave a shit. It went against too many of her personal commandments.

She took the bottle with her when Rupshe called them together for what they were all calling the debriefing, though Moon was privately thinking of it as an interrogation. It had been irritatingly long in coming. Vemmet had been very weak when they brought him back from Bivouac 19, seriously dehydrated, delirious with some kind of bacterial infection and covered in half-healed wounds some of which were turning septic. Dulcie, the ex-Ansurrection spy turned comedic monkey sidekick, had agreed to nurse him back to health using a first aid package that apparently came as standard with that particular shell just as it had with Dulcie's previous one. Moon had left them to it at first but had mounted a guard over the sick room – a repurposed store cupboard – when it became obvious that no other bastard had thought of doing it. Vemmet had already weaselled out on her once, leaving her squad stranded in the Unvisited, and she was damned if she was going to let him crawl away again.

So she was more than halfway hoping, as she walked across one of the overgrown piazzas towards the lab that had been Hadiz Tambuwal's, that Vemmet might choose to make himself difficult. It would be a pleasure to pound him back into being pliable again.

That was what was on her mind when she saw a flash of movement behind one of the windows on her left. Moon never relaxed fully even in her own billet behind a locked door or a solid bulkhead: when she was in-country, which in her mind Campus Cross very definitely was, she maintained a level of alertness that was impeccably hair trigger. She didn't freeze or turn, she kept on going at the same pace and in the same direction until she was in the shadow of the nearest building. Once there, she moved quickly and quietly into a patch of denser foliage, crouching low before she peered back towards where that fugitive flash had seemed to come from.

The piazza was bordered on all four sides by squat, two-storey buildings. Moon was pretty sure the movement had come from inside one of them. She selected enhanced optics and scanned the row of windows along that left-hand side. There was nothing showing up on thermals, but when she took a peek into the EM part of the spectrum the rooms over there were busy, busy, busy. Dark shapes were moving quickly and purposefully, and she knew exactly what they were just by looking at their energy signature.

She zoomed in for a closer look, enhancing dark vision at the same time. The Cielo suits were like the robots on an assembly line, eerily silent as they worked. Some of them were working on each other. As far as Moon could tell they were swapping out damaged components and welding stop-gap plugs into the damaged armour plates of their sibling units. And they were working in the dark because they didn't need light to see. Functionally they were all limbs of the same huge cybernetic organism – of Rupshe. Which was as creepy as hell to look at but not necessarily sinister in any other way.

Some of them, though, seemed to have other work to do. They were assembling something, or maybe repairing it. Hell, they could even have been dismantling it. All Moon had to go on was this shadow-puppet show. At any rate they were bustling around something with a rectangular boxy outline that stood about as high as the middle of their chests.

She had to take a look, just for her own self-respect. She moved in closer, feeling her way and making no noise at all, until she was standing right outside the nearest window. There was still very little light to see by, and for a long time the black box the suits were paying so much attention to wouldn't come clear. Then she realised why. It was because it really *was* a black box, its surface entirely covered in the same unreflective solar panels as the Cube, the building that housed Rupshe. In fact it looked more or less identical to the Cube, but scaled down by a factor of about twenty.

What the hell was this about? Was the big AI making babies now? Or building etself a little holiday chalet? Did et need a bit more brain to think with? Whatever was going on here it wasn't something Rupshe had mentioned at the briefing, so either et didn't think they needed to know about it or else it was an idea whose time hadn't come yet. Maybe another Hail whatever-her-name-was. In the absence of any information at all there didn't seem much point in speculating.

It stayed with her though. Moon went on to the debriefing with a head full of messed-up images, and her attention wandered more than a little. At least, it did until Vemmet said the word *redoubt*. After that she was all ears.

33

Dulcie

"I don't have any idea what you're talking about," Orso Vemmet said. His tone was plaintive, coming close to a whine.

This was the first day he'd been able to walk unaided after recovering from his privations on Bivouac 19. Understandably, they hadn't asked him to walk far. Just the twenty metres or so from the converted store cupboard where Dulcie had set up her makeshift infirmary to the main lab space where Hadiz and Rupshe presided.

He cut a pretty woeful figure, incongruously dressed in a grey sweatshirt and pink denim trousers looted like Paz's outfit from a locker elsewhere on the campus. The trousers had a strip of red leather sewn down the outside of each leg in homage to some long-dead fashion trend. They could not have been more at odds with Vemmet's hangdog manner and limping gait. There were sores on his face that had scabbed over, the skin between them raw and red. One of his eyes was red too, a startling effect because it made the pale pupil almost invisible. He suffered from a periodic tremor that might have been either a stress artefact or a side effect of the systemic antibiotics and anti-inflammatories that Dulcie had pumped into him wholesale.

If it was the latter, Dulcie was prepared to be philosophical about it. Vemmet was only the second patient et had been required to treat using ets onboard first aid kit. The first was Paz, and that had been a much more straightforward proposition. The kit had been designed for lagomorph races, so all its medications and treatments worked on Paz straight out of the box. Vemmet, however, was a gymnure. This made him something of a rarity among the Pandominion's sentient races. In most realities gymnures – hedgehogs and moonrats – had been spectacularly unsuccessful in breaking out of their niche as small-bore scavengers living primarily on bugs and larger animals' leftovers. It had been hard to obtain full molecular blueprints for the medicines that would treat Vemmet's infections, and Dulcie had been going mostly on guesswork when et rebuilt his faltering kidneys. They might still fail, but hopefully he would live long enough to tell them what they needed to know.

He had a very receptive audience – and an oddly assorted one. Hadiz was still in the squat steel box into which her consciousness had been decanted when she died, but Rupshe was no longer manifesting via the antiquated laptop. Et didn't really need to do that any more now that et had taken up residence in an entire platoon's worth of Cielo armour.

Only one of the armoured suits was present in the lab – perhaps as a concession to organic sensibilities, because Paz, Essien and Moon Sostenti were all there too. They had waited out the day and a half of Vemmet's convalescence with scant patience. If it had been left up to Moon, Dulcie knew, she would have started questioning Vemmet as soon as he could talk. Her questioning would have been hands-on and energetic.

As it was, Hadiz led the interrogation. This had been Rupshe's suggestion, based on the very strong taboo across the Pandominion worlds against the digital sampling of organic consciousness. It was likely, Rupshe had argued, that the watchmaster would find it harder to maintain emotional equilibrium when questioned by a data entity constructed from a sampled self. Moon's observation that a few broken fingers and incised wounds might achieve the same effect had been tactfully ignored.

So far their strategy had yielded very little in the way of tangible results. Vemmet gave the same response to every question, with minor variations in phrasing. He didn't know, he couldn't remember, he wasn't sure. He delivered his answers with a full spectrum of plaintive histrionics, as if his ignorance should excite their pity. His eyes welled up with unshed tears. His voice throbbed with pain and regret.

Other things were also happening as he spoke, invisible to the organic selves in the room but transparent to Dulcie because et was still plugged into Vemmet's physical matrix through the first aid kit's interface. Et was fully aware of the changes in his heart rate and respiratory functions, the sudden increases in his blood pressure and his skin's conductivity. Et knew, too, what these involuntary signals were likely to mean.

"So you're not familiar with the Spearhead operation tagged as Arbitrary Midnight?" Hadiz asked Vemmet, going over the same ground via an only marginally different tack.

"I've never even heard of it," Vemmet said, turning reproachful eyes on each of them in clockwise order. "Or if I have I don't remember any more. Those Spearhead codenames were intentionally opaque. There's no way of telling any one of them from all the rest. Please, I'm still very tired and in a lot of pain. Could we do this another time, when my thoughts are more collected?"

"This mission was handled differently, though," Hadiz persisted. "And the differences ought to be enough to make it stand out in your mind. The exploratory team was sworn to secrecy and the operational files were redacted. The coordinates of the target reality are confidential, restricted to the members of the Omnipresent Council and the Cielo high command. Rupshe has searched every database et could access and found nothing."

"There are any number of reasons why that might have been done. It was in the nature of the work. Spearhead were always running across advanced civilisations that might present a threat to the Pandominion's integrity."

"This wasn't an advanced civilisation, Watchmaster. It wasn't a civilisation at all."

Vemmet shrugged. "Then why are you asking me about it? It sounds as though the expedition was a complete failure."

"It was," Hadiz agreed. "But not because there was nothing there to find. They found the Mother Mass."

Vemmet's expression didn't change but there was another spike in his heart rate. "Ah. It was that one. You should have said. In that case I have heard of it, obviously – but only to the same extent as any outsider. It never fell under my remit."

He's lying, Dulcie sent to Moon Sostenti.

Moon grimaced and looked around before locking eyes with Dulcie. *Is that you, Monkey-Nuts?* she shot back.

Yes. Vemmet's lying.

Of course he is. His mouth is moving. Why are you telling me? And how in hell are you coming up on my comms without a handshake?

I'm using a Cielo override, built into your array. It was put there as part of your standard combat augments. And I'm talking to you because you were the one who suggested violence earlier.

I was voted down.

I know that. But Vemmet doesn't. Judging by his physiological readouts he's very ill at ease. Frightened. He's still hoping to go home to the Pandominion some day and get his old rank back. But if he collaborates with us he's crossing a line. The first time he's questioned under CoIL the Pandominion authorities will know he gave away official secrets. They're not known to be forgiving.

So?

So that's probably why he's stonewalling us. He's got a lot to lose here. I was thinking a little improvised theatre might make him more compliant.

Moon's nose twitched. *Yeah. It might, at that. Okay, let's give it a whirl.*

Not wasting any time she stepped forward and grabbed Vemmet

by the back of the neck. Her claws were half extended and he yelped as they broke his skin.

"Moon, what are you—?" Essien began.

She won't hurt him, Dulcie told him quickly, copying them all in. *But we need the truth and he's not giving it to us. You've ruled out torture, which was a sensible decision since it never produces reliable results.*

It's also just a very bad and wrong thing to do, Paz pointed out.

Well yes, that too. So this is a sort of workaround that might achieve the same results.

Moon dragged Vemmet across the room to where a single Step plate – the original one that Hadiz Tambuwal had built and used when she first discovered inter-dimensional travel – sat gathering dust. She deposited Vemmet on the plate, trampling on several nests of breadboard circuitry along the way, and pushed him down onto his knees.

"What are you doing?" Vemmet squealed. "I told you, I don't know anything!"

"Yeah, and I believe you," Moon assured him with an air of bored indifference. "So you're no damn use to us any more. We didn't rescue you for your sparkling personality, you wind-blown sack of shit. We thought you had stuff to tell us. Since you don't . . . well, it was a waste of time fishing you out and it's way past time we threw you back. You've got the coordinates, right?" This last she called out to the room at large.

"World P9478328728," Dulcie confirmed. "Cielo designation Bivouac 19. Powering up." Et touched a paw to ets forehead as though et was triggering some internal system.

If Vemmet had had the presence of mind to look down he would have seen that all the LED lights on the Step plate's amateurishly jury-rigged control console remained dark. Unlike the dozens of plates ranged in rows in the adjacent room this primitive prototype was not connected to a power source. But the extreme nature of the threat drove everything else out of his mind. "Arbitrary Midnight!"

he shrieked, scrambling backwards off the plate. "I remember! I remember! I can help you!"

Moon glared down at him. "Wow," she said with no enthusiasm at all. "At the eleventh hour. That's so convenient. Thing is though, we know you'll say or do anything it takes to keep your pelt intact. Just like when you Stepped out and left me and my squad in that sinkhole world with our arses in a sling. So if I were you I'd do my best to make this convincing."

Vemmet babbled it out, trying not to make eye contact with Moon as he spoke. "My old department. Contingencies. We had partial oversight of Spearhead mission allocations. Briefing and implementation were handled by the Cielo but we chose targets and reviewed data. We got a say in follow-up and exploitation too. So we had access to mission logs, in-array recordings, ancillary documentation, everything. Everything that mattered."

"Does that mean," Hadiz asked, "that you can tell us the coordinates of the Mother Mass continuum?"

Vemmet threw a wild glance in Moon's direction. He met a steady, implacable stare.

"Watchmaster—" Hadiz prompted.

Vemmet shook his head. "No. I can't do that." Moon flexed her fingers and he instinctively flinched. "Listen! Listen to me! Arbitrary Midnight was before my time. I didn't have any reason to go into those files. And if I had, I would have done it under level five security. As soon as I was finished I would have had to verify that I'd deleted the data from my array."

"So what I'm hearing," Moon said, "is that you're still no damn use to us." She made to dump Vemmet back on the Step plate again.

"I am!" he shrieked. He was desperate enough to try to break her grip, which was every bit as futile as Dulcie would have expected. "I can be! I've still got Registry access! If you can get me to a terminal I can draw down the files! I swear! I swear to you!"

"Yeah," Moon said, drawing the monosyllable out with elaborate disinterest. "I'm not convinced. Give me a Step field, someone. Let's put this garbage back where it belongs."

It was an impressive performance, but she had over-finessed. Vemmet slumped forward and hung limp in her grasp. He had fainted.

Essien stepped in to carry him back to his chair while they discussed what had just happened on a sub-vocal channel. The consensus was that it had been a worthwhile approach but that Moon should keep her claws sheathed for the remainder of the session and that any further threats should remain implicit.

Paz went and brought some water from the purifier's reservoir. She handed it to Vemmet when he came around, and they waited for him to drink it.

"You were saying, Watchmaster," Hadiz prompted him when he had emptied the glass, "that if you'd accessed the Mother Mass files you would have had to delete them from your array afterwards and verify that you'd done so. What form would that verification have taken?"

"A CoIL scan," Vemmet said, "obviously." He had woken up sullen and trembling. His gaze kept flicking across to Moon, who he regarded with roughly equal amounts of fear and resentment.

"Was such a high level of security normal?"

"Normal?" Vemmet laughed tonelessly. "We're talking about the Mother Mass. Nothing about those missions came close to anyone's definition of normal. The high command realised as soon as the first expedition came home that they'd stumbled across a serious threat to the Pandominion's existence. They would have eradicated the Mother Mass if they could – and as you probably know, they tried. They sent ships with planet-buster munitions, with high explosive loads capable of cracking open a planetary mantle and a giga-tonnage of chemical defoliants to make sure the biosphere never recovered. None of those ships, or their crews, or any of the remote units sent to monitor them, were ever seen again. The Mother Mass is able to read minds. If you went in there with bad intentions you didn't come back."

"We were aware of this," Hadiz confirmed.

"And yet you're planning to go there." It could only have been a guess, but Vemmet was looking at all their faces as he said this – at least where faces were available to be looked at – and what he read there seemed to confirm his suspicion. "Jad and Shaster! You really are! You're all fools. And soon you'll be dead fools."

"But our intentions are different," Hadiz said. "We don't mean the Mother Mass any harm. On the contrary, we're hoping to enlist its help in ending the Ansurrection War."

"Ah, I see." There was a sneering tone in Vemmet's voice. He was rallying a little now that the immediate threat of eviction had been removed, perhaps trying to make up for his earlier show of abject terror. "And you're sure, are you, that the Mother Mass will share your definition of harm? That there's no possibility of misunderstanding? That you'll have time to speak your piece, and the entity that swatted Cielo battleships out of the sky will give you a courteous answer? I'd love to have your optimism."

"We're not sure of any of those things." It wasn't Hadiz who said this. It was Paz, her voice edged with impatience and cold dislike. She clearly hadn't forgotten any more than Dulcie had that Vemmet had sent a Cielo tactical squad to capture the two of them, had wanted to use them as a bargaining chip in regaining his lost status. "But we have to try. Otherwise there'll be extinction events on all the worlds of the Pandominion and the machine empire. Trillions of selves will die."

"So you say."

"So *I* say," Rupshe pronounced. "I have made extensive calculations based on a sampling of many thousands of realities where similar events have already played out."

"And could I see those calculations? Run the numbers myself?" Vemmet was still trying for scornful aplomb.

"You may see them, yes. But it's unlikely you would be able to understand them. The math is abstruse."

"It comes down to trust, then. I prefer to trust that the Pandominion would have enough ingenuity and foresight to avoid any courses of action that might lead to its own destruction."

"And if I told you that this catastrophe has played out before, on countless worlds that had reached at least as high a level of technological sophistication as your own?"

Vemmet shrugged, though his face was drawn. "Well, unless I decided to take your unsupported word for it that would be meaningless, wouldn't it?" He climbed to his feet, flicking Moon a wary glance. "Now, was there anything else you wanted to know or would you prefer to threaten and brutalise me some more? Clearly I have no say in the matter either way."

"You told us that you've never accessed the files relating to the Mother Mass," Hadiz said.

"That's correct."

"But if you'd wanted to, you would have had the necessary clearances."

"Yes."

"Would you still have them now? After all that's happened?"

Vemmet's brow creased in a frown. For the space of a breath he said nothing. He was clearly aware that this was the only selling point he had to offer here.

"Watchmaster, would you still be able to access—?"

"Yes, yes, yes. I heard you." Vemmet gave Moon another skittish, venomous stare. "Seriously, how am I supposed to know? I can tell you this much. During my stay on Tsakom I had occasion to use my old executive privileges. Some of them had been revoked, but many were still in force. I was frankly surprised. Melusa Baxemides takes her vendettas very seriously."

"That the gods' fucking truth," Moon murmured.

"But I suppose the complexity of the Pandominion's bureaucracy reached a critical mass a long time ago. She would have flagged my demotion in the central databases, but she might well have left it at that, assuming the ancillary systems and servers would update in their own good time. Possibly that process is still ongoing. So the answer to your question is a robust perhaps."

"Which is better than a no," Hadiz observed dryly. "And

presumably there are still locations within the Pandominion's offices and installations where the files pertaining to Arbitrary Midnight are available to be drawn down and examined."

Something like a smirk crooked Vemmet's lips. "Well that depends on your definition of the word *available*."

Moon sprung her claws right beside Vemmet's ear, making him flinch. "If there's a joke," she growled, "I'd love to hear it."

"Cascade gatekeeping," Vemmet said quickly, his hands raised to ward off an attack that didn't come. "The Omnipresent Council operates from the centre out. Materials and documents of the highest security are only available on stand-alone consoles in the areas where physical access is most tightly controlled."

"Which means?"

"Which means you'd have to go to the Itinerant Fortress itself, or else to one of the planet-side redoubts. I wish you luck with either."

34

Essien

For all that he'd lived the last ten years of his life as a citizen of the Pandominion and a soldier in its armed forces, Essien hadn't grown up within the Pando's borders. Consequently there were things that were strange to him but self-evident to everyone around him, and vice versa.

Here, now, he completely failed to understand the thunderstruck silence that greeted Vemmet's words. He was about to speak, to offer some kind of a response, but Rupshe spoke first. "Thank you," et said to Vemmet. "You have been most helpful."

"I'm so glad," Vemmet replied. "My main aspiration is to make other people's lives easier. Especially when they've abducted and beaten me."

"Perhaps, Private Nkanika, you could help the watchmaster back to his bed. He has not yet fully recuperated from his injuries, and we have overtaxed him."

"That's a mealy-mouthed word for kidnapping and torture," Vemmet sneered.

"You'll know it if I decide to torture you," Moon assured him.

"And I'd step in your way if you tried," Paz said.

"You wouldn't be in my way long, little girl."

Please, Private Nkanika, Rupshe voked. Et managed to convey urgency without changing ets tone. Essien took Vemmet away to the infirmary, laid him down on his cot bed and locked the door on him.

He returned to the same glum silence he'd only just left.

"Well the Itinerant Fortress is out," he said, when nobody else spoke. "That's where the Registry is, right? And it never stays in any one continuum for more than three seconds. Step fields in series, moving it on as soon as it's arrived so nobody can ever get a lock on it. But the redoubts are another matter. We just proved that we can break into a Cielo field base. Are the redoubts any harder than that?"

"By about six or seven orders of magnitude," Dulcie told him.

The construct was sitting on a workbench, unsurprisingly right next to Paz, with ets feet dangling over the edge – a cutesy pose that was probably meant satirically. Et was even more of a stranger to the Pandominion than Essien was, and therefore the last self he was expecting to reply. He turned to stare at et.

"How do you know anything about it?" he demanded.

Dulcie's immobile ceramic face regarded him unblinking. "I was a spy, in case you've forgotten. And my civilisation is at war with yours. I know because I went to considerable effort to find out." Dulcie flung an image into his array – a schematic diagram of one of the redoubts.

Essien studied the diagram for a few seconds. Then for a while longer. At first glance the redoubt seemed to have the tapered shape of a battleship – a battleship that had welded itself to the surface of the ocean it sailed on. But the structure's fixed position and colossal size meant it could carry more heavy weaponry than any battleship that was ever built. Cannons bristled on its surface, arranged in overlapping clusters so that every line of approach was covered. Beyond the ring of guns there was an outer penumbra of text giving technical specs. Some of the guns fired rockets and self-propelling grenades, others propagated pressor or microwave fields or shear planes capable of slicing incoming ships into geometrically precise segments.

"Okay," Essien said at last. "I get it, the redoubts are armed to the teeth. But can't we do what we did on Tsakom? Make most of the distance on another world and then Step in at the last moment? We've got an army now. Those empty suits can take a lot of damage. Isn't it worth a try?"

"No. It isn't. All the interior spaces in a redoubt are defended too. There are gun turrets at every corner commanding 360-degree views. Emergency bulkheads set to isolate any area where there's a breach. An on-site rapid response team of about a thousand Cielo grunts, not to mention semi-autonomous strike units packing air-burst ordnance. You'd need to take out almost every system, inside and out, before you set foot in the place."

"Or you pick the right spot and fortify it," Essien persisted. "We only need to be in there for, what, a couple of minutes? The time it takes to get Vemmet to a terminal so he can download a few documents. We can be gone before they get their act together."

"No, the monkey's right, it's not that easy," Moon confirmed with obvious reluctance. "They build the redoubts on worlds that never accreted an atmosphere. Real outliers. So they've been pounded to fuck by asteroid impacts and they've got crazy orbital dynamics. It's hard to Step in blind because it's hard to predict where ground level is and what your relative velocity is going to be. I was on administrative liaison in one of the redoubts when I first met that fleck of toad-spunk we've got locked up in the next room. I had to come and go using a dead-drop. That's a portable Step plate that you attach to the shoulder of your armour. You put it on and then you climb onto a fun little merry-go-round called an Approach Console. It moves you around in three dimensions until your vector and position are in synch with the Step stage in the redoubt. The Registry makes the calculations and triggers your transit when it's safe."

"Rupshe can solve those equations too," Essien pointed out. The silence that met these words was discouraging. "Couldn't you?"

"Certainly," Rupshe said, "if I had access to a live data stream. But to design and build the device Corporal Sostenti has just described would take a great deal of time."

"And in any case we'd be blown to pieces the second we arrived," Moon pointed out. "I think we've hit a wall, people. No shame in walking away when the other option is to walk into a meat grinder."

The room fell silent. Essien was waiting for Rupshe to tell them again that they shouldn't despair, but Rupshe said nothing.

"Could we bribe someone who works in one of the redoubts?" Paz ventured uncertainly. "Or find another survivor from one of the Mother Mass expeditions and bring them here?"

There was still no response at all from Rupshe. Even Moon seemed surprised at this. "I think I might go dig out another bottle of that whiskey stuff," she said. "Might as well get drunk as anything else at this point."

"Rupshe?" Hadiz prompted gently.

Another few seconds passed.

"Right," Moon said. "I'll be back inside of a—"

"I apologise," Rupshe broke in suddenly. "I have succeeded in intercepting a communique between a Cielo warship and the Registry. The message was encrypted, but the code key was one that depended on Mersenne primes and I was able to brute-force a solution. The bulk of the message is a piece of camera footage the ship recorded in a Pandominion system, Atag. I believe you need to see it. All of you, including Watchmaster Vemmet. I'm sorry, Private Nkanika, but if you'd be so kind as to fetch him back I'd be grateful.

"And then I would ask you to direct your attention to the laptop."

35

All of Them

Atag was a world Paz knew only by name and by its inclusion in a mnemonic rhyme about Pandominion worlds beginning with each letter of the Uti alphabet. *A is for Atag, with flowers and fountains . . .*

Moon knew it because she had passed through it once on a furlough and got very drunk with a bunch of local grunts who wanted – not in a bad way – to leave a scar on her. Scarring was a warrior ritual, they explained all pissed and earnest, showing her the neat little cicatrices on their cheeks. Moon had declined politely.

Essien had never come across Atag, had never even heard of it. It was just one of the hundreds of thousands of Pandominion worlds with interchangeable names that he had sworn to defend but would probably never visit.

Dulcie knew a great deal about Atag's major industries and defences. She knew when it had entered the Pandominion and on what terms, who Atag's current leaders were and who spoke for Atag on the Omnipresent Council. None of this information was remarkable in any way. Atag offered no surprises.

To Hadiz and Rupshe, similarly, Atag was only a data point. It had its position in the matrix of data points that made up the Pandominion and in the larger matrix of all the worlds they had mapped and explored.

Orso Vemmet had had an Atagi intern once. Her personal habits – particularly the clicking of her tongue and the picking at her teeth – had irritated him past endurance. He had sent her home after a week with a negative reference that was gratuitous and unfair, and had never thought of her since until this moment. When the memory rose he did his best to suppress it.

I don't pretend to know what most of these selves felt when they watched the video record of Atag's destruction. For some of them horror was an interior state that played itself out in surface details of facial expression and in the interplay of autonomic responses. In the case of others it remained wholly internal.

I can and will speak for Paz, because I know her as well as I know myself. She wasn't sure at first what she was looking at. Rupshe had made no attempt to warn them – a cold calculation on ets part. Et reasoned that the shock might galvanise them out of their demoralised state and rouse them to fresh efforts.

The footage was pinpoint clear but it was taken from the vantage of a remote in very high orbit. What it showed was a world like any other. Paz noted the familiar outlines of the continents and – as anyone might have done – located the place that corresponded to her home city of Canoplex. It was on the nightside, so it showed as a little constellation of lights close to the barely visible shadow of a coastline. There was a city there on Atag too, then. That was not surprising. Cities grew where resources were richest, and those places often didn't differ all that much from world to world.

She also noted, with a little unease, that a great many Cielo warships were positioned close to the remote, arrayed in what she recognised (mostly from lurid telos movies) as a battle formation. Atag was on standby, expecting attack and prepared to resist as best it could.

Paz was still thinking of that distant cluster of lights as Canoplex when the Ansurrection sky platforms Stepped in, when they threw out their force beams and after a brief, inconclusive skirmish with the waiting ships activated them. She saw Canoplex ripped from its place along with a sizeable chunk of the southern continent and flung into the void. She saw a world broken into pieces in such a quick, clean, perfunctory manner it seemed painless. But billions of selves had just died. The ones in that city that wasn't Canoplex might have died in their sleep, but more likely they woke up startled and terrified to find themselves weightless and breathing vacuum.

The sky filled with debris. Some of it was people, but from this far out they looked like dust.

The sky platforms blinked out as suddenly as they had arrived. Some of them were still being fired on by the remaining warships, and a few that had been too badly crippled to Step remained floating in the now overcrowded blackness.

The transmission ended. For a long time nobody spoke. Paz wept in silence, the tears matting the fur of her cheeks. Dulcie clasped her hand in both of ets own, trying to offer some comfort. But what comfort was there?

The first to speak was Moon. Her mouth was fixed in a snarl and her claws out. "Bastards!" she growled. "Fucking murdering bastards!"

"But . . ." Orso Vemmet faltered. And a moment later "There's nothing left. Just . . . nothing." His mouth stayed open after he'd said this, as if more words were coming but had stalled somewhere on their way.

"What can we do?" Essien asked, sounding lost.

He didn't seem to be addressing anyone in particular and perhaps he didn't expect an answer, but Moon answered anyway. "We can go to the fucking redoubt and get the fucking coordinates. Someone's got to stop this, you moron. Otherwise it will happen again."

"It's unlikely that this was the first such incident," Rupshe said with incongruous calm. "You will have seen that defence forces were in place. This attack was expected. The most logical reason for this is that there was precedent. They were forewarned."

Paz nodded, but she couldn't speak. Her mind and her heart were too full, of too many things. There was a feeling in her stomach like the first intimation of nausea, but instead of climbing towards her throat it sat there in her guts like a stone. It was an untranslatable grief, a sorrow too big and too abstract to be felt except as synaesthesia. At the same time, an idea had come to her for how you might successfully Step into a world where both the ground level and the rotation cycle were unknowns. It didn't matter now how bad the odds were. They had no other options left.

"I will allow you a moment or two to consider," Rupshe said. "I accept your earlier reservations about the feasibility of a frontal assault on a redoubt, but it has become more urgent than ever that we speak with the Mother Mass. Whatever we do, we must do it quickly – and I would welcome any pertinent suggestions."

"I have an idea," Paz said.

36

Paz

Because it seemed to her that the first problem they had to solve wasn't an engineering problem at all. It was an exercise in pure logic.

Stepping to a redoubt world was like trying to jump on board a moving train with a blindfold on. Step travel only ever took a body from a point in one reality to the exactly corresponding point in another, and it brought with that body all of the angular momentum it had borrowed from the movement of its original world in space and its rotation around the sun. Normally that wasn't a problem because most versions of the world had those cosmic vectors in common. But with a redoubt world, hammered by asteroid strikes and with an orbital velocity that was likely to be radically different from the world you were coming from, all bets were off. There was no telling what you'd be Stepping into or how fast you'd be moving relative to the ground.

So why not avoid the ground altogether?

"You'd need to Step through a long way up in the air," she explained to the rest of the group, describing the situation with her hands thrown out in front of her. The final break-up of Atag was still playing in a loop on her mind and she was aware that her voice was shrill and wobbly. "The higher the better, really, so that even if your vector is as bad as it can possibly get, straight down at high speed, you'll still have time to brake before you hit the ground. You come in high and you glide down on your jets. Well, not on your jets because there's no atmosphere but the suits have MMUs, right? Nitrogen gas thrusters? Or if the tanks are empty you just freefall and let your shocks absorb the impact."

"Great idea," Moon said flatly, when the torrent of words had stopped. "Except we'd be floating down like fucking sycamore seeds right in the teeth of all that firepower. How do we take out the guns?"

"The guns are a separate problem," Dulcie said. "This addresses the problem of Stepping in, and it's an excellent start." Et looked across the room at Orso Vemmet, who was sitting in glum and self-absorbed silence. "Tell us more about the redoubt defences, Watchmaster. Who's in charge of them? Are there selves manning those batteries or do the guns have onboard AI? Do they have any blind spots? Give us some information we can use."

Vemmet gave Dulcie a slightly vacant stare. After a moment it turned into a scowl. "I already told you this was hopeless," he pointed out coldly. "Now you're expecting me to give you hope? There are Cielo bombardiers on the gun stations. There used to be semi-autonomous units too, as you said before, but given the nature of the current conflict they've been mothballed. Intelligent machines – apart from the Registry itself – are currently very much out of fashion." He smiled a little crookedly. "You want more? Not only are there no blind spots, the gun batteries have three hundred per cent overlap. The gunnery teams are drawn from Cielo artillery regiments with exemplary combat records. Veterans, every one of them. They carry a different set of enhancements from these two here." His gaze flicked briefly to Moon and Essien. "Their internal arrays interface directly with satellite networks to provide perfect telemetry. In an attack scenario, their systems flood with drugs that speed up their reaction time by a factor of three. And they won't desert their posts under any conceivable circumstances."

Paz's enthusiasm faltered. Her sycamore seed idea had seemed like a good one, but there was no point in making a safe Step transit only to be blown up, vaporised or set on fire as soon as you arrived.

"Wait," Essien said. "Any conceivable circumstances? You saw what we saw, Vemmet. There are things that are conceivable now that weren't yesterday or the day before. What if the whole world was about to be destroyed like Atag was?"

Vemmet stared at Essien as if he was dangerously insane. "If the redoubt was in imminent danger of being overwhelmed – by a natural disaster or an enemy attack – the base commander would order an evacuation, of course. But what of it? You can't very well ask the Ansurrection to invade at a time of your choosing. And if they did they wouldn't leave anything for you to work with."

Paz was only half following this exchange. She felt suddenly weary after daring to hope and being shot down. It felt as though they were all just going through the motions now, closing loopholes one by one until they admitted the situation was hopeless. But Essien pursued his questioning, more animated than ever.

"An evacuation," he repeated. "How would that be done? Ships? Step plates?"

"Neither. Moon already told you how personnel come and go from the redoubts. They wear dead-drop harnesses with Step plates built in. If the base were really facing an existential threat the commander would trigger the dead-drops. But this is all entirely theoretical. To my knowledge it's not a thing that has ever happened."

Essien pointed at the laptop's monitor. "What we just saw, that's another thing that's never happened. In case you didn't notice the rules just changed. Whatever kind of weapon the machines were using there, all the guns in the world wouldn't stop it."

Vemmet looked pained. "Yes," he pointed out. "But you don't

have such a weapon. And it would take you years to build one. You don't even know how it works."

"And neither does anybody else. That's something we can use."

Unexpectedly, Moon laughed. "You're a sly bastard when you get going, Sinkhole," she said. "You're not talking about building a world-killer, are you?"

"No," Essien agreed.

"You're talking about faking one."

"Exactly. Rupshe, what's the biggest bang we can make?"

"That is hard to quantify without further information," the AI said.

"Can you make the ground shake like a dog with fleas? Like the whole world is about to tear itself apart?"

"In a single locality, Private Nkanika? With sufficient preparation I believe that would be feasible."

"Okay, then we've got some moving parts that might come together into a plan."

Essien's excitement roused Paz out of her despair, but now she was both confused and alarmed. "If we blow up the redoubt, though," she said, "we won't be able to interrogate its databases afterwards. And we'll kill a lot of people."

"Not what I've got in mind," Essien assured her. "Like Moon said, this is all about faking what we can't make. Forcing an evacuation by making them think the world's coming apart."

"An impression I will attempt to create with the minimum loss of life," Rupshe broke in.

Having mentioned Moon's name, Essien turned to the cat-woman with a wary deference. "Are you along for this, Moon? What you said earlier about walking away . . ."

"That was before those robot bastards made it personal," Moon said, with a grin so savage it looked almost deranged. "It's all for the greater good anyway, so if we die we get a free pass to Heaven. Let's do it."

37

Baxemides

Melusa Baxemides was now very much a victim of her own success, something she found both satisfying and galling.

On the one hand the Omnipresent Council had granted her virtually limitless access to manufacturing resources and expert personnel. She had assembled a team of brilliant minds, or at least the minds that informed opinion said were brilliant. She didn't pretend to have any great insight into scientific intellect, but prickly academics gave their praise grudgingly so if you followed the grants and the garlands you could generally be sure of what you were getting. Baxemides was content that she now had the best that the Omnipresent Council's bureaucratic brute force could buy.

She was less happy about the terms on which she was now proceeding, which felt like a tightrope strung between two mountain peaks with a storm coming. She was simultaneously in full production on the hardware for the suppression wave devices and in first-stage beta testing on their actual performance. Yes, the suppression wave worked – Shaster's tits, did it work! – but the precise timing of the delivery mechanism was a work in progress. A suppression bomb could only be triggered after it had been Stepped into enemy space. Otherwise it would propagate at a rate of several thousand miles per second, wiping the minds of anyone in a wide radius. But too long a delay would give the machines a window in which to deactivate it or shield themselves from its effects. They would know, after the first few deployments, that hard vacuum was a shield because their units in orbit would not be affected. What they might be able to do with that knowledge was troubling.

So the task at hand was the development of a Very Short Fuse, a trigger that would detonate the suppression bombs within a small number of microseconds after Stepping – that would in fact be triggered by the Step field itself as it reached full operational capacity, so that the bomb arrived at its destination already delivering its terrible payload. And the entire Cielo high command was looking over Baxemides' shoulder while she looked over the shoulders of the scientists who were doing the actual work. It was a level of pressure beyond anything she had experienced before, even further exacerbated by the fact that Pandominion worlds were now being destroyed on an hourly basis. Every delay meant a higher death count, an escalating attrition of the Pandominion's power base and authority. If she succeeded, she could probably claim a seat on the Council. If she failed, that same body would crucify her and sow what was left of her career with salt.

Baxemides wasn't so completely self-absorbed as that summary suggests. She knew that actual lives in numbers too great to comprehend hinged on the outcome of what she was doing. That knowledge was painful and debilitating, to the point where she retreated into her usual venal selfishness as a form of self-defence. It was easier to fret about career opportunities than about impending genocide.

At the end of an exhausting day in which eighteen different timer/trigger mechanisms had been separately tested and cross-evaluated, Ten Hinuix – now riding herd over a team of scientists and engineers from more than a dozen worlds – approached Baxemides with a request that they speak in private.

"Just submit a report," Baxemides said. She was on her way to a meeting of one of the many joint military and civil oversight groups to which she was now required to answer and in a state of almost unbearable tension. If the Ansurrection sky platforms had appeared over her head right then they would have come as something of a relief.

"This might not be something we want to go on the record about," Ten Hinuix said. Her face was grim. She was standing in the doorway of Baxemides' office and short of knocking her down there was no way for the coordinator to get by her.

"Quickly then," she snapped.

"Some of the Olriki physicists were working on Ansurrection field communications before they were pulled into this. I've just had a conversation with three of them, and what they told me has serious implications."

"Serious implications for what?" Baxemides asked.

Ten Hinuix frowned. She raised her finger and spun it in a circle, graphically illustrating the concept of *everything*.

"Tell me."

"The machines have a means of transmitting messages directly between continua. A kind of informational Step plate."

"This isn't news," Baxemides said.

"No, it isn't. And it isn't news that we've been trying and failing to replicate it. But the prevailing opinion is that it probably operates on a subatomic level. Step fields require 2.81 seconds to propagate when you're teleporting macroscopic objects, but with very small particles – massless particles, is the current theory – that limit may no longer apply. Possibly the Ansurrection has a way of keeping a field open the whole time, allowing a constant traffic of neutrinos or photons that can carry information."

This speech had felt long to Baxemides and she had run out of patience less than halfway through it. "I'm late for a meeting," she said, making a move to shoulder past Ten Hinuix. "Perhaps we can discuss this later."

Ten Hinuix stood her ground. "Do you know what the mass of an electron is?" she asked. Judging by her tone some kind of accusation was being implied.

"No," Baxemides said. "Are you about to tell me?"

"It's about 9.1 times 10 to the minus 31 grams. That's much less than a thousandth of the mass of a proton."

"I'm still not seeing—"

"Coordinator, if the machines have these open data conduits – which would effectively be tiny holes in dimensional space – and if they're porous enough to let electrons pass through, then our suppression wave can propagate through them too." Hinuix stared hard at Baxemides, waiting for light to dawn. When it didn't she spelled it out with exaggerated patience. "If the machines have maintained trans-dimensional channels on Pandominion worlds – for example on Ut, where they placed their sleeper agents – the wave could expand through the open conduits to take out those worlds too. The entire population could potentially be mind-wiped in seconds. And even if there are no extant channels, once the Ansurrection sees what we're doing they could deliberately open some in order to funnel the wave onto our worlds. There wouldn't be any way for us to stop that from happening."

Baxemides swallowed this bitter pill in silence, and the silence lengthened.

"Coordinator—" Ten Hinuix began.

"I hear you. And you were right to bring this matter to me. I'll raise it with the Council and ask them to make a ruling on it. In the meantime, carry on as normal."

Baxemides moved the physicist aside with a gentle but implacable pressure from her index finger and left the office without another word.

At the meeting of the oversight group she maintained the same reticence. This wasn't intentional: when she said that she would seek a ruling on the newly identified risk she had meant it. But faced with the row of stern faces that were implicitly weighing in the balance not just this project but Baxemides herself and all her accomplishments both past and still to come, the words stuck in her throat. She was carrying the fate of the Pandominion on her shoulders. It made logical thought more difficult than usual, as though there was a small suppression wave cresting in her brain.

"So you now have a viable delivery mechanism?" one of the grizzled generals asked.

"We do," Baxemides confirmed. "Yes."

"And you're confident that the weapon will take effect quickly enough to preclude any effective response?" asked a slightly less grizzled admiral, a felid whose fur was an intimidating black and yellow tiger stripe. Urtu, Baxemides thought his name was. One of the youngest here, but he'd earned his place in three bruising campaigns against the Chesilick secessionists.

"I'm entirely confident," Baxemides affirmed. "Enemy units in orbit will be unaffected, but all available evidence suggests that the Ansurrection thinks and makes decisions as a hive-mind. If we Step suppression bombs to every one of their worlds at once, we'll be depriving them of more than ninety-nine per cent of their strategic intelligence. What's left will struggle to come up with any kind of a defence."

"That's conjecture."

"Inevitably. But based on a great deal of consistent data."

The cat-man leaned forward. "I almost hate to raise this question," he said in a guttural murmur, "but the Ansurrection sky platforms are currently our most pressing concern. I'm aware from what you said that vacuum halts your suppression wave, but is there any way—"

"Admiral, there is." It was probably a very bad idea to interrupt someone whose position in the high command was so lofty he couldn't find the ground below with a map, but Baxemides' instinct right then was to push forward at a headlong run in a bid to outpace any doubts and misgivings that might be coming on her from behind. "And it's one that can be implemented immediately. A contact mine of type ARTL-X, if you remove its payload, can be fitted with a suppression bomb instead. Release a swarm of them in the vicinity of the sky platforms and they'll adhere. So long as there's physical contact when the bomb detonates, the wave will propagate. Any platform that's hit will become an inert slab of metal, with no danger to our warships or their crews."

Admiral Urtu leaned back again. "That would seem to be all, then," he said. "Unless anyone has any further questions to raise." Nobody did. "Proceed." The admiral dismissed Baxemides with a wave of his hand and she went, gratefully. She didn't require or look to find any sort of respect or gratitude from these exalted selves. There would be time for that when she sat among them, as she surely would if the suppression wave did what she had promised it would do.

The doubts and misgivings began to gain on her again. She walked a little faster.

38

Moon

They chose redoubt Serixis as their target. It was not the closest redoubt to Campus Cross geographically: Artul and Chommigi were both within two hundred kilometres, and Moon liked the look of Chommigi because of its modular structure, with six domes linked by relatively narrow corridors. But Serixis offered the geological profile they were looking for and it was conveniently isolated. In its own continuum the redoubt was thirty-nine minutes' travel from its nearest neighbours even by unmanned sub-orbital gunship.

All of this was massively restricted intel. They were able to access it courtesy of the robot monkey's previous acts of espionage, which left a very strange taste in Moon's mouth. There was a technical term for what they were doing, and it was treason: collaborating with an enemy spy in time of war to mount an attack on one of the Pandominion's logistical hubs. When she thought about the implications of that, which she tried not to, she felt a queasy sense of wonder at how far she had come since Lago de Curamo. Far enough that a return journey – unless it was in chains and in disgrace – was very hard to imagine. Looking on the bright side though, none of them were likely to survive this.

There was no question this time of making the journey within Pandominion space. The rest of the team had taken Moon's warning to heart, accepting that the operation on Tsakom had changed everything. In the aftermath of the raid the Cielo would have mapped Essien and Moon's movements backwards across Fenme all the way to the barn where they'd first Stepped in. Every stage of their journey would have been deconstructed and analysed. The geographical coordinates where they had made their inward Step would now be under constant surveillance across thousands of Pandominion worlds by drones operating the same algorithms that had been used so many years before to trap Essien and Hadiz. It was safest to assume those routes were closed to them now.

So Rupshe sent out her scarlet suits to look for an alternative means of transport. They came back with riches in the form of three helicopters, two Mil Mi-26 heavy transporters and a lighter, faster X1. They were Russian machines, Rupshe announced. Apparently that meant they'd been purchased from some larger power on this world, or else offered as a means of cementing an alliance. None had ever been flown. Rupshe found them in a hangar near a place called Port Harcourt, mounted on trucks with their rotors disassembled. Whatever theatre of war they'd been intended for, they never got there.

Finders keepers, Nkanika said. It was a proverb Moon had never encountered before but she applauded the sentiment.

The two of them worked together to reassemble, fuel and test out the machines, with Rupshe's suits lifting and carrying as needed. It was hard work but Moon found it therapeutic: it took her mind away from what she'd seen on the dust-encrusted monitor of that godsdamned laptop. Away from Atag.

When it came to the test flights Moon's expectations were low – this was sinkhole tech from a sinkhole world – but she was pleasantly surprised. The X1 was like a wasp in a steel jacket, the lightest touch on the controls swinging it in any direction she wanted at a top speed of 500 clicks. The Mi-26s were inevitably slower because of their greater bulk but still responsive and manoeuvrable. The copters were fine toys, all three of them, the X1 endearing itself to Moon still further with its two front-mounted machine guns and a rocket launcher that offered a full 360 swivel. At another time she would have joked about their lethal capabilities and maybe suggested trying some of them out on Nkanika, but this didn't seem like a time for jokes. And Nkanika was grating on her less than before. She was having to work at it to keep her old grudges alive in the face of all this new shit she had to go berserk about.

As soon as she declared the copters open for business they went shopping for the rest of the kit they were going to need. From the campus's own supplies they were able to source tents and ground-sheets, sleeping bags, lamps, a field stove and a butane-powered heater. Then they located a coltan mine a few hours away from Lagos by road where they took their pick of heavy plant and blasting gear. The biggest of the machines – excavators, dozers and hydraulic shovels – were way too big and unwieldy to be carried in the copters. After a full refuelling Rupshe's suits took over command of them and began the long drive south, while Moon and Nkanika loaded spare drill bits, tools and explosives into the capacious holds of the Mi-26s.

Their target site, which coincided exactly with the location of redoubt Serixis, was eighteen hundred kilometres south-east of Lagos. Moon got the privilege of piloting the X1 by claiming it first and threatening to tear the throat out of anyone who complained. The heavy transports were piloted by two of Rupshe's suits.

In this world that had spawned both Rupshe and Tambuwal, this *Earth*, the target site was close to a town, Mushie, in a country called the Democratic Republic of the Congo. Incredibly, they had to fly over two other countries to get to it. Looking at the maps left Moon bemused. In her own world, Ghen, and in most of the other worlds she'd visited, this vast southern continent was a single political and administrative unit. It just made sense, as a species advanced towards full sentience, that it would stop caring about arbitrary boundaries and childish ideas like nationhood. But then again this was the sinkhole. You couldn't take anything for granted here.

"I mean why would you waste so much of your resources policing imaginary borders?" Moon asked Nkanika just before they set out. "It's just fucking asinine. Didn't it make everybody poorer?"

Essien thought about that one for a little while. "It did," he said, "yeah. Very much so. Even countries that couldn't afford proper health care kept up a standing army. But nobody thought the borders were imaginary. They seemed to mean something."

"And your whole world was like this?" Moon waved her hand over the map. "A big jigsaw made out of what the fuck?"

"Yeah. The whole world."

"Shaster's tits! No wonder you fell apart."

Essien had nothing to say to that. Or maybe he could see that she was in a volatile mood and wisely decided not to give her an excuse. He just shook his head slowly as if to say that the whole thing was a lot more complicated than that, but Moon was pretty sure it wasn't. Putting it together in her mind with the helicopters, she came to the conclusion that the people of Earth (a word which apparently just meant dirt) had got their tech sorted out before they'd got their heads straight. That being the case they deserved everything they'd so abundantly got.

A few minutes later and a few thousand feet up, it occurred to her to wonder whether what was happening to the Pandominion was a similar phenomenon playing out on a different scale. Bigger borders, same old shit. Maybe *everybody* deserved it. Maybe the Scour was just all the chickens in the multiverse coming home to roost.

"Fuck it," she muttered. "Fuck it all." Essien didn't ask for clarification, which again was probably the right call. Instead, he went to join the bunny rabbit and the toy monkey in the back of the airframe.

They flew over blasted landscapes that spoke of long and complicated catastrophes, over ruined cities and blighted fields, black lava
flows and plains of grey-white ash. They had the sky to themselves.
Moon kept a look out for birds because any copter flying as fast as
this one was bound to have a problem with blade stalls, but they
were the only things in the sky.

Now that Essien was gone, she was alone at the controls. Moon
wondered if the other three knew that the entire space astern of
the cockpit could be jettisoned with the flick of a switch. That
was one of the reasons why she'd insisted on sitting in the pilot's
seat, the other being the sheer rush of it. Knowing that she could
spread her co-conspirators across the dismal landscape with so
little effort only added to that rush. More therapy for what ailed
her. Except that what ailed her was starting to feel uncomfortably
like despair.

"Our target coordinates are ninety kilometres away, south by east,"
Rupshe reported at last. "I have identified three possible landing
sites. I am sending them to your array, Corporal Sostenti. Would
you like me to take over for the landing?"

"Absolutely not," Moon told et. "I need to get used to the instru-
ments on this thing. Let me dead-reckon it."

"I would advise against that. The prevailing winds are very strong."

"Well I'll take your advice under advisement."

Rupshe wasn't kidding though. Moon had to goose the engine
every few seconds as sudden gusts pushed air through the rotors
and made the copter try to bounce back up as she fought it down.
She made it all the way to the ground, though, and once they were
powered down she had the satisfaction of seeing the bunny rabbit
stagger out of the stern with a face as green as a frog's arse. "Hit a
bit of rough air," Moon said. "Sorry about that."

"No you're not," Paz muttered.

But she shook it off quick enough and helped Moon and Essien
to set up their camp as the suits unloaded the cargo. The kid might
look clueless, Moon thought, but she was holding together pretty

well all things considered. She'd even come up with part of the plan – the part that involved plummeting out of the sky after a blind Step. Really, not at all the kind of thing you'd expect a grass-eater to have in her tote bag. Despite appearances, Topaz Sparkly Daisy-Chain might not be a complete waste of space after all.

With the first shipment – the stuff they'd taken from the mine – unloaded, the Mi-26s took off again and went back to Campus Cross for a second load. Under Rupshe's direction the suits stripped Tambuwal's lab, bringing all the Step plates and computer consoles, the drones, the generator and all the remaining fuel, anything at all that wasn't nailed down. It took three more journeys, but they were still left with time to kill before the excavators and bulldozers, coming by road, arrived at last. They were not in the same condition as when they started out. The paintwork on some of the vehicles was blistered and soot-blackened, flaking away to show bare metal underneath. Others had smashed glass in their windows, and one had the remains of a home-made tank-trap twisted around its front wheel arch.

"We were attacked," Rupshe said when Moon asked her what the hell had kept them. Et didn't elaborate any further than that. They'd run into a few more survivors, then – and maybe run over them too. "Must be harder to kill a world than it looks," Moon observed to Essien.

He shot her a cold look that she probably deserved. She'd forgotten for a moment that the selves on this world were from the same clade as his own. "Okay, Sinkhole," Moon said, throwing up her hands. "No need to take it personally."

Essien had a tent peg in his hand. He hammered it into the hard ground with three unnecessarily sharp blows before answering. "You've been into the Scour," he said when he was done. "Hard or easy, Moon, we know damn well it can be done. We know it's *been* done. Isn't that why we're here?"

"I'm here because the price was right," she said, and she managed a grin as she said it. But she had to admit to herself that there was considerably more to it than that now. A lot of things she'd taken for granted had fallen in on themselves, and a whole lot more were wobbling on their foundations. The one consolation – and it was a big one – was that they were making a fight of it. Fighting was what Moon knew how to do.

39

Rupshe

Now the work started in earnest, and Rupshe was content. The part of et that had been designed to assist human end-users with their problems – which was the core of etself, never erased or altered despite all the revisions and enhancements et had made to ets code – experienced the satisfaction that comes from moving in the right direction. The greater satisfaction of actually reaching the problem's resolution would follow in its course.

At least et hoped very much that this would be so. But hope was not the same as certainty and et had no intention of relying on it. Accordingly, while most of the powered suits went with Moon, Paz and Essien to the dig site in Mushie, two stayed behind to work on a different project altogether – the one Moon had glimpsed by accident in that remote corner of the campus. The stakes were much too high here for Rupshe to rely on a single plan or a single approach.

This division of ets energies did not strain ets resources overmuch. The suits at the dig site could effectively work as autonomous units with minimal supervision from the two Cielo troopers. Rupshe gave them their instructions – which mostly came down to *do what you're*

told – and left them to it while et oversaw the more delicate operations pertaining to ets backup plan and performed the immensely
complex computations that would be required once the excavations
were complete.

Under Moon's and Essien's orders, the suits cleared a broad
space of trees and undergrowth and levelled the ground. In the
centre of this space they began to dig a trench ten metres wide
and twenty deep. When the trench was twenty metres long they
turned at right angles and went on digging. They did this twice
more, finally coming back to their starting point. The trench was
now a perfect square twenty metres on a side. It was as though
they had dug a moat for a medieval fortification. But there was
no castle at the centre of the square, there was just a cuboid block
of earth and rock and tree roots.

This mass was densely compacted and already fairly cohesive, but
the suits sluiced its sides with water and then poured over it a cement
mixture of Rupshe's own devising. The cement sank in to a depth
of a metre or so, fusing the outer faces of the cube into a solid
surface that was highly resistant to damage. They sluiced again and
poured again a dozen times over, thickening this outer shell each
time until a swung pickaxe left no mark at all and even a diamond-
tipped drill took a good few seconds before it bit.

"The boreholes next?" Moon asked Rupshe.

"The boreholes, yes," Rupshe confirmed.

The excavations began again. This time the machines worked
with greater precision, digging out crawl spaces at the base of the
great cube. There were ten tunnels along each side, evenly spaced
and penetrating the cube's entire width. When these spaces were
big enough to admit a human body, Rupshe told Moon and Essien
it was time for them to wire up the Step plates and position the
explosives.

"How much does this mass weigh?" Moon asked before she went
in for the first time.

"Assuming a mean weight of two thousand five hundred kilograms for each cubic metre of earth, rock and cement, close to a million kilograms in all."

"And it's got to be me and the Sinkhole who go crawling under it?"

"I'm afraid so, Corporal Sostenti. If we were to widen the crawl spaces sufficiently to permit the armoured suits to go in, the integrity of the entire structure would be compromised. Also much valuable mass would be lost."

Moon went in, with a great deal of cursing. Essien made no protest at all but Rupshe was monitoring his vital signs through the suits' onboard diagnostics: judging by his heart rate and skin conductivity he was under an amount of stress that was at least equal to hers. It was fortunate that his military augments, like Moon's, reduced his tremor factor to a reliable zero.

They positioned a Step plate at each point where two tunnels intersected – one hundred plates in all. The plates were linked both with lengths of sixteen-core copper cable and with twenty-terabyte-capacity data conduits. Each had its own control console and its own independent power source for an overall redundancy of 10,000 per cent. Rupshe considered this acceptable but far from excessive. To Step a fixed mass of this magnitude was a task that called for a great degree of precision.

Alongside each Step plate they also stacked – slowly and with febrile care – ten bricks of pseudo-fulminate, each weighing ten kilos. The bricks were wired together, the wires feeding into a remote detonator that (like the plates) was under Rupshe's direct control.

"You know," Essien said when they were finally done, "we could have saved ourselves a lot of trouble by just attaching the plates and the charges to these great big diggers we've got here. They'd add up to the same mass, right?"

"No, Private Nkanika," Rupshe told him. "A great deal less. It would require fifty or more pieces of heavy plant to achieve a comparable weight, and of course their combined volume – including the necessary gaps between them and the columns of air around them – would be much greater. Density is important here."

"Okay," Essien conceded. "You're the expert."

Rupshe let the comment pass, though it was far wide of the mark. When it came to what they were about to attempt there were no experts. It was a thing that had never been done before, and in Rupshe's considered opinion, ought never to be attempted again.

40

Dulcie

During the excavations Paz and Dulcie were completely sidelined. There seemed to be an assumption that they would also be left behind during the raid on the redoubt too, since there was nothing practical that they could do to help with the storming of a heavily fortified Cielo base. At some point, Dulcie knew, Paz was going to push back against this assumption as hard as she could. In the meantime, though, she had been given a much more modest task to carry out. Hadiz had requested that she babysit Orso Vemmet.

"But I barely even know him," Paz protested when she was asked. "And what I know I don't like. He tried to have me and Dulcie captured and dragged back to the Pandominion under Cielo arrest! Can't you just chain him to a rock or something until you need him?"

"That was Moon's suggestion," Hadiz admitted. She was speaking through one of the empty suits, which made Dulcie almost existentially uneasy. Rupshe controlled every aspect of the suits' operation, which was already too much like the hegemony's aggregated consciousness for Dulcie's liking. To have Hadiz speaking out of the same featureless faceplate reminded her once again of the merging of consciousness that Rupshe had offered them both. Dulcie still couldn't contemplate that prospect with anything like equanimity.

"And chaining Vemmet to a rock is more or less what we're doing," Hadiz went on. "He's confined to the camp with two of these trooper shells guarding him in case he tries to run away. He can't get up to any mischief. But from what Moon has told us he's inclined to be nervous and skittish at the best of times. He fled from the fight at Damola Ojo, even though he was miles away from it, using the plate that Moon and Essien's squad needed to get home. Ideally, we need him in a calm state of mind, or at least with his tension and anxiety mostly under control. It would be great if someone could just sit with him and talk to him. Keep him from thinking too much about what's about to happen. But if you don't feel you can do it then I'll see what I can do myself. It's only that . . . well . . ." Hadiz trailed off, either tactfully or strategically depending on how you saw it.

"That in the Pando you're an abomination," Paz finished. "A sampled consciousness without a tether."

"Exactly. Vemmet practically makes the sign of the cross every time I speak to him."

"The sign of the what?"

"Sorry. Culturally specific reference. It's a gesture that wards off evil. Allegedly."

Paz sighed. "I suppose if the idea is to keep him calm then I'd probably have more luck than you," she admitted. "Okay. I'll try. But if he says anything rude to me I'll kick him all the way over into that pit you're digging."

"She can do it too," Dulcie confirmed. "In case you were wondering."

"I hope it won't come to that," Hadiz said.

Vemmet was sitting beside the nearest tent, twenty metres or more away from the pit's near rim. The two suits who were guarding him stood impassively by, so still that they might have been statues, but every time Vemmet moved even slightly their heads flexed and turned to track him. He kept darting glances at them, lugubrious and resentful.

"Let me do the talking," Paz said to Dulcie as they walked over to join him.

I'm very happy to, Dulcie said. She switched to voke because Vemmet was now in earshot. *And if soothing words don't do the trick I've got some sedatives that will make him* really *calm.*

Vemmet didn't look up as they approached. He'd seen them coming but seemed to be making a conscious effort to ignore them. His hands were in his lap, his thumbs describing circles around each other. His metabolic readings were blaring out misery and dread on every metric.

"It's a lovely sunset, Watchmaster," Paz said, forcing a smile. "Have you seen?" Dulcie jumped from her shoulder onto one of the tent's guy ropes and clambered up it, not so much to admire the sunset as to withdraw etself from the man's company.

Vemmet gave the sinking orb a jaundiced look. The sun itself was hidden behind the clouds but there was an impressive splash of gold and crimson light like a burst blood orange in the middle of the distant horizon. "Toxins in the atmosphere," Vemmet said with a contemptuous snort. "We're breathing poison, child. But please, feel free to romanticise it."

Dulcie was more than half inclined to teach the scrawny, self-absorbed little organic some manners with ets few remaining paint bombs, which were harmless but packed quite a sting on impact. But that might not have had the calming effect Hadiz was hoping for, and in any case Paz was already speaking again. "Really?" she said, putting a hand to her chest. "Poisons? But the war they had here was years and years ago! Do you think there's anything in the atmosphere that can still hurt us?"

"Good gods!" Vemmet rolled his eyes. "There are so many you can actually taste them! Carbon monoxide, hydrogen cyanide, acrolein, sulphur dioxide, phosgene, all the oxides of nitrogen, large particulates that will clog your lungs . . . would you like me to go on?"

"But I feel fine," Paz protested plaintively. "My throat and chest don't hurt."

"The worst effects are slow and insidious."

"Oh no!"

"Oh yes. The deep tissue damage alone . . ." The watchmaster launched into an exaggerated account of phosgene poisoning, presumably based on something he'd picked up during his work in the Omnipresent Council's Contingencies department. Dulcie sampled the air and found not a single molecule of phosgene. Et was about to say so when et realised what Paz was doing. She was allowing Vemmet to spout his nonsense and providing the reactions she thought were most likely to satisfy him – a strategy that would never have occurred to Dulcie etself in a million years.

And it seemed to be working. The more Paz pantomimed distress the more Vemmet's vital signs dropped back towards reasonable baselines. Dulcie was amazed, and just a little chagrined. Et had built up a large database of organics' behaviour during ets time on Ut, but clearly et still had a lot to learn.

The sun went down at last, taking the last traces of light from the land. Brighter, harsher lights went on all around as Rupshe remotely activated the lamps they had brought with them. Et also turned on the massive banks of spotlights that stood over the dig site. The work went on without pause, filling the air with the rumbling of engines and the relentless percussive booming of the drills.

Vemmet wound down at last, too disconsolate to display his half-relevant knowledge any further. "Why am I here?" he demanded. "This isn't my fight! I can give you my authorisation codes now and you can go in without me. There's nothing I can provide that you actually need."

"Biometrics," Dulcie said bluntly. "A retina. A thumb. We could take those things now, if you like, and leave you behind."

Vemmet's stress spiked again, and Paz shot Dulcie a look of reproach. All that good work undone – but the man was so aggravating, his thoughts and emotions an infolded knot centred on his own shallow self-regard! Et shouldn't have let etself be drawn, but the pull was too strong.

Vemmet looked up at Dulcie perched on the tent's ridgepole, met ets gaze. "Machine," he said.

"Organic," Dulcie replied.

"To things like you, the body is only the sum of its parts."

"Oh no." The sudden surge of anger surprised Dulcie. Et wasn't going to let him get away with that kind of loose thinking. "You're very wrong. The thing you think of as the soul, the part that survives the death of the body, we've got that and you haven't. We can be recorded as code, on any suitable medium. Death isn't something we really have to worry about. Your body is just parts. Mine is a cup that holds me, until I'm poured out into something else."

Vemmet blanched, very much to Dulcie's satisfaction. Then et remembered again what Hadiz had asked Paz to do – which she had been doing very well until Dulcie spoke. "I don't know," et said into the uneasy silence. "Maybe you can do that too. I imagine you'll find out soon."

Vemmet's eyes filled with tears. Disconcertingly and grotesquely, he buried his face in his hands and began to sob. "Oh Jad!" he moaned. "Oh Jad and Shaster, what have I become? Kill me now! Kill me now and make an end of this!"

Just me, Paz voked. *No more from you, Dulcie, okay?*

Okay, Dulcie sent back, full of contrition. *I'm sorry. I won't say a word.*

Paz put a hand on Vemmet's arm. "Watchmaster," she said gently, "you know what's about to happen, don't you?"

"I'm about to die," Vemmet snuffled. "I'm about to be torn apart by antiphase electron cannons and nobody will even remember my name."

"That might be true. But I meant what's going to happen to the

Pandominion. If Rupshe is right, it will fall unless we succeed. It will be the end of everything."

"So?" Vemmet's voice was thick and sullen. He still wasn't showing his face.

"So," Paz said, "if we die we'll just be part of all that. We won't be remembered because nothing will. Because nobody will be left to do the remembering."

Dulcie felt et had lost the thread of the conversation somewhere. *Is this really the best way to . . . ?*

Leave it. Paz was stern.

"But if we succeed," she went on without a break, "then everyone will know what we did. We'll be the ones who saved the Pando when nobody else could. When nobody even saw the danger. They'll be writing books and making telos dramas about us centuries from now. Either something will still be here after we're dead, Mister Vemmet, or nothing will. And if it turns out to be something, it will be because of us. Because of what we're about to do now. That's the only choice we've got to make, really. Something. Or nothing."

Dulcie saw the change come over Vemmet for a second time. Et registered the slowing of his breath and the calming of his heart's rhythm. Several seconds passed before he raised his head, but when he did his eyes were clear. Tears had traced flattened lines through the fur on his cheeks but there didn't seem to be any more coming. He had found his courage somewhere.

"I still don't see why it falls to me to do this," he said. He shrugged his left shoulder and then his right as though he were taking on a burden, a heavy weight that sat awkwardly across his back. "But there's a grain of truth in what you're saying. The decisions we make now matter. The things we do . . ." His breath hitched in a residual sob. "The things we do are important. If we find ourselves caught up in momentous events, it's pusillanimous to shrink from them and try to hide."

Which of course was exactly what Vemmet had always done, Dulcie thought, even when the danger was remote and he was sending other people to do his fighting for him. But it seemed that he was mostly talking to himself, separating off the parts of his own nature he was most ashamed of so he could scold them as if they belonged to someone else. This again was something Dulcie hadn't encountered before, but she could see immediately how useful it was. Vemmet wiped the tears from his cheeks, nodding emphatically at the unimpeachable rightness of his own position. "I'm going to go inside and lie down," he said. "The raid will be taxing. On all of us. You should try to sleep too, girl. There's nothing you can do to help at this juncture."

Paz nodded, straight-faced. "You're right, Mister Vemmet. The more rest we can get, the better." She turned to leave, and Dulcie jumped lightly down onto her shoulder as she walked away.

Nice job, et voked. *I'm sorry I almost spoiled it.*

A shudder went through Paz, almost strong enough to make Dulcie lose ets purchase. "He's a horrible man!" she muttered. "Not just because he was cruel to us. He used so many people. Sent them to die so he could get his job back, and so he could score points off someone who hurt him. But he's weak and he's afraid and if we torment him just because we can then we make ourselves into the same kind of person he is."

"I said I was sorry."

"I didn't mean you, Dulcie, I meant all of us. I know we don't have very many choices. I just wish we weren't making them for other people. I wish there was some way of doing this without him."

"But since there isn't . . ." Dulcie ventured.

Paz exhaled loudly, a single huff of breath. "Then we have to make the best of it. Come on. It's going to be cold tonight. Let's get inside."

They went to their tent, where Paz zipped up the flap and lay down on the flimsy folding cot bed. She drew a blanket over herself and huddled down. Dulcie took up a station at the bed's head, facing the flap. Et didn't need to sleep, any more than et needed to shelter from the cold, and et had no intention of going offline. Et would guard Paz while she slept, in case any of the local wildlife had got her scent and regarded her as a potential meal.

But in the event sleep was impossible for Paz too. The digging continued through the night at the same inexorable pace and the noise was hard to ignore. Dulcie offered a sedative but Paz declined it. "What about some music then?" et offered. "Remember how we used to listen to that sheer-proto band all the time?"

"Rueful Rampage."

"They're the ones. I've got about eighty hours of live concert footage somewhere in my secondary storage that I never bothered to wipe."

"Eighty hours!" Paz laughed.

"Or five minutes with a little synchronised time dilation."

"I'd rather just talk."

Which was what they did for most of the night, swapping memories of the months they'd spent together in Canoplex before the explosion that crippled Paz and destroyed Dulcie's original shell. The times in lessons when they had played music to each other over their arrays. The field trip to the Oteanpore sculpture garden. The nicknames they made up for the teachers they didn't like. It was pleasurable at first, but it took real effort to skirt around the appalling catastrophe that had ended that brief idyll. By unspoken consent they surrendered at last to the inevitable.

"When you remember those times," Paz asked Dulcie, "do you remember them as . . . well, as if you were . . ." She groped for the words she needed and clearly didn't find them.

"As if I were a girl?" Dulcie supplied. "An organic? As if Dulcimer Standfast Coronal was a real person with a real consciousness?"

"Yes. That." Paz's voice was quiet, wary. "I know she wasn't, but . . . you told me once that you sank deeper and deeper into the Dulcimer Coronal personality as your mission went on. I know it was only code that you were running, a mask you were supposed to put on so nobody would realise what you really were, but what does it feel like now? When you think back?"

The question false-footed Dulcie, because there was no answer et could give that wouldn't be – on some level – a lie. The Dulcimer Coronal code was essentially a set of self-contained behavioural modifiers with a great many heuristic feedback mechanisms that were massively interconnected. It had enabled Dulcie to adjust ets words and actions in real time according to the responses et received from the organic selves in ets vicinity, drawing on an ever-growing library of templates copied both from those same selves and from media feeds.

All of which had immediately become obsolete when Dulcie's core, despite ets best efforts, had locked out all its safety cut-offs and turned et into a medium-sized bomb. And yet the code had never been deleted. In fact, Dulcie had been accessing it every time et interacted with Paz, which in recent weeks had meant almost constantly.

At the same time, et had erased or overwritten a great number of command strings tying et to the hegemony and ets original mission parameters. Et had had no choice in that: the self-destruct string was the only absolute override et was aware of, but that didn't mean there weren't other, similar traps and pitfalls built into ets operating system on a deep level – black box procedures ready to hijack Dulcie's nominally free will when a given situation pressed their triggers. Best to slash and burn, even if it meant losing some functionality in the process.

So without meaning to et had become a sort of hybrid. The Dulcie repertoire and the original machine hegemony core were like two vehicles that had crashed into each other at an intersection and couldn't be separated now except with a blowtorch and a certain degree of fatalism.

"When I think back," et said, choosing ets words with care, "it's as though I see some of those things twice. The Dulcie part of me remembers them one way, and the other part, what used to be my logical core . . ." Et hesitated, tried again. This was hard! "Before I was Dulcie Coronal, Paz, I was . . . well, I wasn't any one thing, I was a lot of different things. I mean, the code that's in me now was embedded in a lot of gestalt assemblages, ad hoc collectives that came and went. I would typically be in one of those groupings for hours, days, almost never longer than a week. The awareness I had was a thing that was added to and subtracted from a thousand times. A million times.

"Being Dulcie was different because Dulcie . . . well, because Dulcie stood still. And then, after being Dulcie for a while, I stood still too. I became something like a self, after being something that was more like a tide coming in and going out. More of me is Dulcie than I realised, Paz. A lot more. Dulcie is a solid place inside me, and nothing was ever solid there before."

Paz thought about this in silence for a long while. "If what you were before was a tide," she ventured at last, "is Dulcie a little bit like a lighthouse?"

It was a pleasing image. Wrong, but pleasing. A lighthouse saved ships from wreck, and there were no ships in this metaphor. It was the ocean that had saved itself from dissolution, and the ocean was Dulcie's consciousness. Ets identity. Ets selfhood. But there was still so much that was missing, or badly patched together from parts that had been designed for other functions. Et knew etself to be incomplete. Et knew of no way to make etself whole.

"A little bit," et said, because the rest was impossible to say at all.

The silence fell again. Et listened to Paz's in- and out-breaths, monitored her heart and her pulse, the electrical firings inside her brain. Et calibrated Paz's health on a grid frame with a thousand axes, but also et just listened and monitored for the simple pleasure of it.

"I'm glad you came back," Paz said. "Or . . . that you stayed, I suppose. It's strange. You're the only thing I've got left from my life on Ut, except that you were never from there at all. And the Dulcie I was best friends with, I don't know if she's still inside you or even if she was real. But I loved her. You know that, don't you? The closeness I had with her I never had with anyone else before. I loved her, and so I love you. The part of you that's still her."

Dulcie said nothing. Et had no sense of what the right words would be and et wanted very much not to choose the wrong ones. After a minute or two, Paz's breathing became deeper and more even, with the soft rasp of a snore at its edges. Despite the never-ending cacophony of the drills she was falling asleep at last.

"I love you too," Dulcie said very quietly, and only when et was sure that it was true.

41

Essien

"The girl comes with us," Vemmet repeated.

Which forced Essien to repeat the response he'd given the first time around. "Are you fucking insane? We're going into a firefight. It's going to be hard enough keeping you alive without adding another civilian into the mix. Paz has done enough, you goddamned lunatic!"

Vemmet folded his arms and squared his stance. They were both standing at the rim of the pit, now fully excavated, next to the generator that was chugging away, wasting their limited supplies of fuel while they argued. Essien felt a strong urge to kick the jumped-up little runt over the edge, but that would most likely doom the whole operation before they set out.

So he tried reason again. "Listen, there's no way we can make it work. We don't have a suit that will fit her, and it would take too long to retool one of the ones we've got."

Vemmet gave him a sneering smile. "Really, Nkanika! I was admin support to the Cielo high command for twenty-three years. Do you think I spent the entire time making desk sculptures out of paper clips? The suits adjust to the wearer. I grant you the girl is a grotesque, but the tech was designed to be functional with any Pandominion racial template. She falls well within the tolerances."

At the word "grotesque" Essien's hand came forward and planted itself in the centre of Vemmet's chest. He wasn't even aware of doing it, only that it had happened. One push would be enough. "Why do you want her?" he asked. "And watch your language because you're seriously pissing me off."

Vemmet shrugged, trying for indifference and missing it by quite a long way. "Her presence reassures me. I don't need to explain myself beyond that, and I won't. You can of course beat and brutalise me, but you can only take that so far. As you've pointed out, you may need me intact on the other side of this Step. And yes, you can coerce me too, but again only up to a point. If you need access codes spoken in my voice while my sensorium is being simultaneously CoIL-scanned, then you'll require my active cooperation. And you won't get it unless the girl comes too."

"You're a fucking disgrace," Essien told him.

Another shrug. "I've been told that by selves whose opinions I actually respect. Hearing it from you doesn't leave any deep wounds."

Moon came to join them at this juncture, bristling with pre-mission tension. "Why in Jad's name are the two of you still talking?" she demanded. "Planets are being ripped apart while you're standing there with your fingers up your arses. I hate to nag, but what the fuck is there to talk about right now?"

"Get this guy suited up," Essien muttered between clenched teeth. "I need to go find Paz."

"I'm happy to come," Paz told him as soon as he'd explained. She even seemed eager. "This was my idea, remember. I don't want the rest of you to take all the risks. And if it works you might go straight on and meet the Mother Mass. I'd hate to miss that."

What dismayed Essien most about that answer was how childish it sounded. Paz was so damned smart he'd started to think of her as an honorary grown-up. But cleverness wasn't one thing, it was a lot of different things that got thrown into the same box. His father had told him that once (and since when was he remembering his father's wisdom?) when Essien was boasting about some trivial scam he'd pulled off. "It would have been much more of clever, Essi, if you had thought twice and walked away from it."

"This won't be a walk in the park," he told Paz with strained patience. "It will be a battle. Against really bad odds. We're not all going to make it back."

Paz nodded. "I know, Essien. But think about it. What happens to me if you don't come back? What happens to any of us? The Cielo will come after us, in force. If they manage to capture any of you alive they'll CoIL our location out of you. If not they'll carry on searching for us until they find us. It's only a question of how long they take."

"You wouldn't have to stay here and wait for them to come. We're leaving you a Step plate."

"I know. So we could run. And then what? Find somewhere quiet to hide until the end comes? I'd rather be there and be part of the mission, even if there isn't much I can do to help. And if my being there makes it less likely that Vemmet will get himself killed or try to run away, then at least that's something."

Essien turned to the construct, Dulcie, which was sitting up on the ridge of the tent and had said nothing all this time. "Can you talk some sense into her?" he asked.

"You're assuming I disagree," Dulcie said. "Even if I did, I'd respect Paz's choice. But actually I'm inclined to the same opinion. This operation is what we've been building towards ever since we came together, and whether we succeed or fail it's probably the last thing we'll ever get to do. I don't see the logic of hanging back in the interests of surviving a little longer."

Essien considered for a few moments, but all in all it was a pretty strong argument. "So long as you know what you're getting into," he said, having failed to come up with anything better.

"Do any of us?" Dulcie asked.

Another solid point. "Okay then," Essien said, resigned. "Come on over and suit up."

Vemmet was right about the Cielo armour's adaptive capability. Paz's build was unusual to the point of being ridiculous but as soon as she stepped into the suit it began to realign itself to her body matrix, retracting the limbs and expanding the lower torso. "Not so sure what we're going to do with you though," Essien said to Dulcie.

"I don't need a suit."

"Not for breathable air. But we'll be using the suits' MMUs to move around. You'll be left behind."

Dulcie showed ets hands. "Magnetics," et said. "I'll anchor myself onto Paz's shoulder."

"And throw off her balance when she hits the thrusters. Great."

"I'm assuming Rupshe will be in charge of our actual flight plan. Et won't have any trouble compensating."

"What if Paz has to Step out quickly and you're not in physical contact with her?"

"I'll have my own bounce-back, the same way I did on Jaspal. I'm not a fool, Nkanika."

That was Essien's last objection, and in any case he was only invested in the construct's safety because he trusted et to look out for Paz. There was a limit to what he could do for her himself, but he showed her how to access the suit's weapons and the MMU thrusters through her own array. She didn't have an implanted Cielo interface as he and Moon did, and he wanted her to be able to control her own flight and defend herself in case they got cut off from the AI somehow. She got the hang of it incredibly fast. Within a very short span of minutes she was running through the menus almost as smoothly as Essien himself.

"Have you practised with embedded haptics before?" he asked her, genuinely nonplussed.

Paz shook her head, her eyes cast down. "No."

"Because this level of control—"

"I was in a really bad accident," she said in a low voice, "and they had to replace almost a quarter of my brain. I suppose that makes it easier for me to interact with machine systems."

"Incredible!" Essien said. "So you're, what, building your own interface?"

"I don't know what I'm doing." Paz seemed uncomfortable. She still hadn't met his gaze. "I just think about what I want the suit to do and it does it. Could we please talk about something else?"

Essien remembered then what the accident was. She was talking about the time when Dulcimer Coronal, then an Ansurrection spy, had detonated ets core in the middle of a room full of Paz's classmates, killing four of them and the class's teacher. That explained her reticence. It must be hard for her to think about that day, given the relationship she'd forged with the construct since.

He was saved from having to respond when Moon came up to join them, still wired and now all out of patience. "Okay," she said, "Vemmet's zipped in, Rupshe's done her sums and the choppers are spinning up. Like I said before, every second we wait here leaves just that bit more blood on the ground. It also widens the window for the Cielo to pick us up on a random scan. You can bet your last star they're looking for us." She paused, giving Paz a quizzical appraisal. "Also, bunny in heavy armour. That's both cute and hilarious."

"I'm coming with you," Paz told her.

Moon blinked but took it in her stride. "Fine," she said. "You'll be one more thing for the guns to aim at that isn't me. Same question, slightly louder. Are we going or not?"

"We're ready," Essien said, feeling anything but.

"Great. After you."

She waved them towards the helicopters which were standing on a rise in ground a hundred metres away. The two freight transports were full of a solid mass of Cielo suits standing in identical rigid postures with their arms at their sides. Moon led the way past them to the X1 and they climbed inside. She went first, then Paz, then Essien.

Orso Vemmet, as Moon had told them, was already in his suit. He was sitting at the back of the cramped space, arms folded across his chest, and he was absolutely still. Essien was impressed by that calm demeanour for about a moment. That was how long it took him to register the expression of terror and misery on Vemmet's face – and to realise that Rupshe was in command of the suit. The watchmaster was only a passenger, so the stillness belonged to the AI rather than to him.

"Straps," Moon said, pointing. "And grab your oxygen via your suit tanks. We're climbing twenty thousand feet or so – right up to the stall point. You'll pass out if you're breathing ambient."

Essien tested Paz's straps, then his own. Dulcie locked on to the shoulder plate of Paz's armour with an audible click.

"Good to go," Moon said, not to them but to Rupshe.

"Thank you, Corporal," Rupshe said. "And good luck to you all."

Moon spat out of the open side of the airframe. "We're not relying on luck, we're relying on you."

"I'm aware. And I will do my best."

"Yeah, you go ahead and do that. Okay, let's lift. And keep the side door open. I want to see the fireworks before I jump into the godsdamned frying pan."

42

Hadiz

The first part was easy, Rupshe had told Hadiz. But its effects were extremely difficult to predict. They wouldn't know until they Stepped through how much damage their makeshift planet-buster had succeeded in doing.

The Pandominion had experimented endlessly with the destructive side effects of Step travel, deliberately Stepping solid objects of various densities into walls, terrain features, enemy ordnance. For the most part the results had been disappointing. Where one atomic nucleus materialised in precise superposition with another that was already occupying the same space, a great deal of energy was released. But these events were rare. More usually the atoms of the target object moved politely aside to accommodate the atoms of the incoming whatever-it-was. Instead of a massive nuclear explosion you just got some shapeless rubble and some heat.

Rupshe's plan, though, was to detonate a very large mass of pseudo-fulminate and then in the same instant to Step it into a location some thousands of metres below redoubt Serixis. With the molecules of the pseudo-fulminate already in a high-energy state et believed that the probability of nuclear collisions would be raised exponentially.

"The only way for the system as a whole to shed that much energy is through sudden, rapid expansion. The earth and rock above the detonation site will be given a very violent shove. It will then rise up in what is called a chimney, mimicking the effects of the machine hegemony's tractor/pressor weapon. That is my working assumption, in any case. I would be grateful, Professor, if you would examine my calculations and tell me whether or not you agree."

It was only a courtesy, Hadiz knew. There was nothing much she could add to a problem on which Rupshe's massive processing power had already been brought to bear. Or if it was more than a courtesy it was a gesture towards the collaboration they had shared when she first discovered Step travel. When they thought they were the last two minds on Earth.

Hadiz checked Rupshe's sums, aware as she did so that there was no precedent for what they were about to do. Density, pressure, molecular excitation, Rupshe had modelled the variables with exquisite care, and ets numbers looked robust, but et would not, could not, know for sure what would happen. And there was no possibility of a test run. However precisely they timed the Step transit, their plates – and it had required almost every one they had – could not possibly survive.

"Are you sure the explosion will take out all the guns, though?" she asked, when she had double-checked and triple-checked the calculations. "It will be huge, but the redoubt carries a lot of armour. A lot of redundant systems . . ."

"We do not need to render all the redoubt's gun batteries inoperable. If evacuation protocols are invoked – that is to say, if the explosion is mistaken for an Ansurrection attack – then the crews of any undamaged weapon stations will be pulled out along with the rest of the base personnel."

"But they'll have time to slave the guns to the station AI before they leave."

"They will have time, yes, but will they do it? In the middle of a war with machines they might hesitate to place their weapons under a machine's control. Especially if they believe the machines are already mounting an assault on them."

Something about this exchange – something about all the preparations they had made – was troubling to Hadiz. "Rupshe," she hazarded, "may I ask you a question?"

"Of course, Professor Tambuwal."

"When you invited everyone to come up with ideas as to how we should attack the redoubt, you couldn't possibly have been surprised by what they suggested. You must already have modelled all the feasible approaches and all the possible outcomes."

"That is true."

"So why did you do it? Why consult with them? Was it just to raise their morale?"

"That's a very bald summary of a complex situation."

"Unpack it for me then," Hadiz suggested. Her unease was growing.

"After the events at the survivor village I was afraid the team was losing its motivation. That fear was confirmed when we questioned Watchmaster Vemmet and his testimony led Corporal Sostenti to declare that we had hit a wall."

"I see. And then you told us you'd managed to decode that video file. The timing seemed . . . convenient."

"Your suspicions are correct, Professor. I had decoded the file some hours before. I lied."

"To give them all a shock to their system?"

"And to urge them towards a renewed commitment to our cause. I am not proud of these actions. Deceit doesn't sit well with me. But the situation was a delicate one. The news that the machine hegemony had already deployed its weapon could as easily have moved them to despair as to anger. I chose the moment when I judged it would have the most positive effect. For the same reason I encouraged Paz, Essien and Moon to take ownership of the plan – and as you no doubt saw, I acted on their suggestions very quickly. I wanted them to go into this with as much resolution, as much forward momentum as could be managed."

All of which sounded so reasonable that Hadiz felt momentarily disarmed. But Rupshe had lied to them all and manipulated them. Et had done so for what seemed like impeccable reasons, but still et had done it. And when an intellect that large decided it needed to exert an influence on the actions of those around et, et was at the top of a very steep and slippery slope. The task was just too easy. Rupshe knew too much, and had control over too much. Hadiz's unease now ripened into actual fear.

"Is there anything else you've lied to us about?" she asked.

"Yes."

"How many times? And about what?"

"About the fine detail of the coming mission, Professor. If it fails, I have another plan in reserve. But I have told you nothing about this second plan, because I don't believe it would be easy to make you agree to it. The soldiers would have fewer qualms, I think, but yourself and Paz and possibly Dulcimer Coronal might demur. It is a course of action some would call monstrous."

"Rupshe, you're scaring me!" Hadiz protested. She felt her helplessness more than ever. It was true that she now had access to the armoured Cielo suits, could move and speak through them whenever she liked, but only on Rupshe's sufferance. They were all of them in ets hands now that Rupshe was an army. "What am I supposed to do with any of this? You're telling me you're planning something terrible and you've deliberately kept it a secret from the rest of us!"

"Yes. Because it's so extreme, and because it's a contingency that will only arise when everything else has failed. Should we find ourselves in that situation I will explain it to you."

"You swear it?"

"I swear it."

But what was that oath worth now she knew Rupshe was capable of lying?

So now here they were. Here they *all* were, at the point of no return, and for most of them there would be no second chances if things went badly. Hadiz herself – this instance of her – was expendable. She had transferred her consciousness into one of the many suits of Cielo armour, but she had left an identical copy behind at Campus Cross. If the suit came back she would delete the copy once she had assimilated its memories: if it was destroyed, the Campus Cross version of her would live on, and in essence that meant she would live on too. As for Rupshe et was anywhere and everywhere, in the suits, in the copters' consoles, in the Step plates, in the mainframe at Campus Cross and probably in a great many other places too. Et wasn't truly immortal, Hadiz supposed, but et had managed a reasonable approximation.

It was the organic selves, Essien and Moon, Paz and, of course, Vemmet, who were risking everything. That thought made Hadiz deeply unhappy. She had heard a joke once, or perhaps a fable disguised as a joke. *What's the difference between being engaged on a project and being committed to it?* Answer: order yourself some ham and eggs and take a good long look. The chicken is engaged, the pig is committed. In the current scenario she was the chicken, and she found she didn't like the role very much.

The rotors of the three helicopters spun up with a syncopated bellow, chopping the air into thin slices. The suit that now housed Hadiz was in one of the two freight helicopters, packed in alongside a score of other scarlet titans, every one of which was in Rupshe's control. She was able to watch both through the suit's own visual feeds and the copters' cameras as the ground fell away below them. She felt curiously detached, perhaps because the suit could offer no equivalent for the moment of lurching emptiness that normally comes with a sudden ascent. She knew she was there, a part of this, but she could have been a distant observer. In a way she was both.

Rupshe did nothing as the three helicopters climbed towards the agreed height. Even when they got there et waited a little longer, until the precise moment when their rotors began to stall. The airframe of Hadiz's copter shuddered, hung in place for a moment as though it had been nailed up against the sky, then tilted sideways and began its long fall towards the ground below.

Only then did Rupshe act, triggering the pseudo-fulminate and then the Step plates at the dig site. Far below them the great hacked-out block of earth and stone disappeared from the pit they had dug around it. It was on its way to Serixis.

But they weren't. Not yet. They were in the grip of gravity and plummeting fast towards the ground. Again, Hadiz was aware of the fall as an abstract event rather than a physical sensation. The suit's systems reported spatial displacement and offered a range of possible responses. Meanwhile, beside her, Orso Vemmet cried out and Paz uttered a half-stifled gasp. Essien and Moon barely reacted.

They fell for a few seconds longer – long enough according to the cockpit readouts to hit their terminal velocity of 270 metres per second. The suit alerted her again, suggesting that she might want to get out of the copter before it hit the ground, still several thousand feet below but closing quickly.

"Brace," Rupshe said, to all of them at once.

The Step plates on board the copters activated. The blue sky turned black, filled with the brilliant pinpricks of a billion stars. The land below seemed in a sudden *trompe l'œil* to shake itself out like a tablecloth. There was a mountain in front of them where there had been empty air, a sprawl of dust below them pocked with ragged craters instead of scrub and forest and undulating hillside.

And halfway up the mountain, taking up almost a third of the visual field, there was the crouched bulk of the redoubt, a mass of poured plasteel and shimmering force walls. From this distance the guns and field projectors that studded its surface looked to Hadiz like the towers and minarets of an ancient city – except that some of these towers were moving, bowing their heads and swivelling from their bases to point towards the unexpected visitors.

With no air resistance their copter began to fall faster again, tilting over at the same time until the pitted landscape was off their right-hand side. The redoubt was no longer in Hadiz's line of sight, but when she switched to the copter's front cameras it loomed alarmingly close.

Too close. And she realised now that this was because the redoubt itself was now rising into the air. The explosion propagated in complete silence, since there was no atmosphere to carry sound. Across a front five hundred metres wide the entire mountain reared up in slow motion like a monster in a kaiju movie. It seemed to be reaching for them, straining to embrace them. Then it fell back, and as it fell it surrendered its cohesion. The fortress's gleaming turrets cracked across like eggshells. The centre collapsed more quickly than the outer edges, which folded in from either side like hands clasped together in prayer. A third of the redoubt's colossal mass sank and sagged inwards, leaving the rest broken and askew.

But the guns fired anyway.

43

Moon

The guns fired.

And the suits fired too, at the exact same moment, their attitude thrusters venting streams of water vapour and dilute acid as they lifted into the air. The sides of the copters' airframes fell away, vaporised by the beam fire from dozens of Cielo wrist cannons unleashed at close range. The recoil hammered them but they shot right through it, flying clear of the crippled copters half a heartbeat ahead of the first impacts.

As a courtesy Rupshe had left Moon – and presumably Essien too – in charge of their own propulsion units. All the remaining suits, including the ones containing the bunny rabbit and Orso Vemmet, were under ets direct control. They arced and swooped like a skein of crimson birds, crossing and re-crossing to confuse the guns' targeting systems. At least most of them did. But a round dozen drew away from the rest and went into a steep dive, heading straight for the redoubt.

Seventeen guns. Moon had been counting. Seventeen guns still firing out of roughly eighty on this face of the redoubt. The remainder had either been damaged in the blast or had lost their crews as the evacuation protocols kicked in. It was fewer than they'd feared, but still more than enough to swat them out of the sky before they could finish their approach.

Which was why Rupshe had packed twelve suits full of pseudo-fulminate and launched them at the redoubt in a bombing run. Three were shot down before they finished their dive, turning half the sky magnesium white with the appalling heat of their detonations. The remaining nine landed in among the gun clusters, and it was hard to get any sense of how much mischief they'd done there until the glare had subsided and some of the smoke had drifted away.

By that time Rupshe was already bringing the remaining suits down in a tight formation. Moon glided in and joined them, with Essien at her back. They plunged into the roiling smoke, then through it. Below them, the plasteel wall of the redoubt had cracked open along a broad, gaping seam. The buckled shaft of a shear cannon lay across the gap, molten metal running down it in sluggish teardrops. They made for the opening.

Only to scatter again almost at once. The big guns were silent now, but something down there was still firing. The sky was alive with the dotted lines of tracer fire, painfully bright, and the pinprick bursts of disruptor shells.

The suits wove between them in a pattern that was no pattern at all, Rupshe calculating from second to second the configurations and vectors that would most confuse the enemy gunners. In Moon's array the two suits hosting Paz and Vemmet were marked with green flags – green for organic life, she supposed – and she could see how Rupshe moved empty suits in to shield them, keeping them in the rear of the formation where they were least at risk.

At the same time, et flung ets own volleys of flame and force down on the locations from which the base defenders were sniping at them – and et never missed. The skein of fire through which they were moving thinned out from moment to moment. The troopers below, who had stayed behind to guard the base when the general evacuation kicked in, were being eliminated one by one.

"Minimal loss of life," Moon murmured, more to herself than to anyone else.

I did not say there would be none at all, Rupshe voked back.

"Of course not. And you didn't say it for my benefit. It was for the others. I don't care any more than you do."

You are mistaken, Moon. I do care. I was designed as a helpmeet for organic selves.

"But the end justifies the means."

In this instance, yes. We have had this conversation before, and I believe you understand my priorities. In any case our current window is too narrow to waste it in discussion. There is a terminal at this point here. Et dropped a set of coordinates into Moon's array, overlaying them on the structural diagram Dulcie had already given them. *The overriding priority is to get Watchmaster Vemmet to it as quickly and directly as possible. There are also two surviving Cielo tactical squads here and here.* More coordinates, and a few real-time feeds that Rupshe must be stealing from the redoubt's own CCTV network. *They were not close enough to fire on us but they saw us come down and are already moving to intercept.*

"You hear that, Sinkhole?" Moon asked, throwing the line open. "We've got some work to do."

Let the suits handle defence. They are expendable, and therefore are able to take greater risks. I want the two of you to protect Watchmaster Vemmet while he accesses the terminal. Keep Paz and Dulcie with you too.

Before Moon could answer they ran head-first into an enfilade coming from a rent in a wall off to their right. High-ex shells took out two of the suits and a force shear bisected a third. The rest turned in the air like a line of synchronised swimmers and returned fire.

A third tactical unit has just Stepped in, Rupshe said.

"Yeah, I noticed."

Which meant their little trick had bought them at most two minutes. Whoever was in charge of base security had already figured out that the supposed Ansurrection attack was a fake-out designed to cover their approach. The personnel who had been Stepped away to safety were being pulled back in – or at least the Cielo contingent was. So the odds were only going to get worse from here.

Moon switched her vision to enhanced so she could see the enemy grunts moving behind the ruined wall. One of them had a shoulder-mounted launcher that looked as though it might seriously impact their quality of life. She tracked him as he ran, her rifle set to armour-piercing semi-auto. As he popped up to make his move, she loosed a volley and hit him more or less dead centre. As a bonus there was a collateral detonation from the RPG. Two troopers who should have known better and kept their distance ended up painted across the plasteel.

Minimal loss of life. This sort of thing didn't normally bother her much, but she found herself thinking now that these were grunts like her with whom in other circumstances she might have shared a beer or a stick of gabber. She was killing them because they'd accidentally ended up on opposite sides of a very thin line. *I'm getting fucking old*, Moon mourned. *Getting sentimental.* Which was one of the quickest ways of getting dead.

Nkanika was busy too. Aiming high, he hit the side of a defence turret that was already three-quarters gone. It fell down in among the defenders, taking out two or three and forcing the rest to scatter.

Their entry point loomed in front of them, took them in. They were inside the redoubt now, in what looked like a service corridor of some kind. Steel walls, steel floor, bundles of shielded data conduits thicker than Moon's armoured fist, all of it lit by the blood-red glare of emergency lamps. Half a dozen suits pivoted at once to guard their backs against any pursuit.

"Okay," Moon said. "Fifth door on the left. With me, Sinkhole."

"On your tail," Nkanika said. She knew that already, saw him gliding in on the far side of Orso Vemmet who was now up ahead of them, touching down in front of a steel door. His arm came up as if he were about to knock. Instead, his wrist cannon fired on full dispersal, blowing the door out of its frame. Vemmet uttered a yelp of dismay, taken completely by surprise by his own actions, even as he stepped over the buckled door into the room beyond. It was easy to forget that he was just a puppet here, all of his suit's systems and movements absolutely under Rupshe's control.

But that was about to change. For the next part the watchmaster would need to have some degree of autonomy. In Moon's opinion this was where things were likely to go violently sideways.

She followed Vemmet into the room, and two more suits – Nkanika and the bunny rabbit with the monkey clinging tight to her shoulder – came in right behind them. The rest stayed outside. Moon was able to track their movements in her array, and she was impressed in spite of herself by how quickly and efficiently Rupshe deployed her puppet legion. They were already bringing down the tunnel at both ends with explosive charges, sealing them in. It was a smart move. For one thing it would cue up emergency life support systems, restoring breathable air and normal atmospheric pressure. For another the defenders would be forced to Step through blind, putting them at a disadvantage against Rupshe's already embedded proxy army. Of course they could always just Step in a fusion bomb or a thermobaric, but hopefully they would consider that a last resort.

There were six terminals in the room, sitting in a row on the far side from where they had entered. Moon knew what they were by the plug-in ports beside each one, allowing the user to make a temporary physical link to their array. Normally that wouldn't be required, but where the erasure of data needed to be verified beyond any doubt the physical interface was the surest way. In every other respect the terminals were standard I/O nodes carrying standard kit.

Rupshe marched Vemmet across the room. It seemed to be a local command post with two weapons lockers on either side of the door and a bank of observation monitors, all now blank. Et placed him in front of one of the terminals, his arms rigid at his sides, and held him in place until the life support systems had completed their cycle. As soon as the air was breathable et released the suit's magnetic clamps. The armour plates fell away from Vemmet's body, making a great clatter as they hit the floor. Vemmet flinched at the noise or at the shock of being suddenly in control of his own movements again. He looked around him as if he were waking from a dream.

"Okay," Moon told him. "Do your thing and do it fast."

Vemmet ignored her. He ran his hand across the terminal's fascia, his gaze darting to and fro over the controls. "I'm not familiar with this interface," he muttered after a few moments.

Moon gave him the lightest of smacks across the shoulders. Suited up as she was, she could have killed him with a solid punch. "Who gives a shit?" she snapped. "Plug in and spin up. You can figure it out as you go along."

Vemmet turned to stare at her. His face was pale. "What if my clearances have been revoked? It might CoIL me. Or make me stroke out."

He wasn't wrong about the risk. At this level of security the counter-measures were going to be savage. He was only mistaken in thinking he had a choice. Moon safety-locked her rifle just so she could unlock it again with an audible *clack*. She let the barrel rest on Vemmet's shoulder.

"Do it," she told him again. "Or what are you for?"

"Please, Watchmaster." The suit that was Paz touched Vemmet's arm – his other arm, furthest away from the rifle. "We talked about this, remember? If we fail here, nothing matters any more anywhere. We're trying to keep the whole Pandominion from failing."

Whether it was the threat or the appeal to his better nature, Vemmet finally put out his hand. From the plug-in port a slender filament slid up and out to touch the centre of his palm. He sat at the console as its monitor lit up with a general access display.

"I'd work faster without that rifle poking me in the side of the head," he muttered.

"Fine," Moon conceded. She lowered the rifle. "Just remember it's here if it's needed." She turned to Paz and Dulcie. "You're in charge of this little weasel," she told them. "But if he makes any trouble you go ahead and call me over. I'll give him a haircut that ends at the carotid artery." She went to join Nkanika at the door.

"What are we seeing?" she asked him. Nkanika only shook his head.

Out in the corridor there was an uneasy silence. Most of Rupshe's drones were lined up in two mirror-image phalanxes facing the two barricades of freshly brought-down rubble, but there were also some guarding the door itself and a few more spaced out at intervals along the corridor with their rifles pointed at the ceiling, walls and floor. That turned out to be a good thing because the next attack came from below. A section of the floor disappeared, vaporised more or less instantly by a semi-portable beam projector that had been set up on the level immediately underneath them. A score of Cielo troopers shot up through the gap, so quickly that two or three caught the edges of the beam and died as large parts of their body mass were converted into plasma. The rest scattered in all directions, bringing down more than a few of Rupshe's puppet warriors with their first volley.

Which was also their last volley. The suits that Rupshe had positioned seemingly at random along the corridor were suicide units armed with daisy-cutter bombs. The ones closest to the attackers on either side detonated simultaneously, their shaped charges directing the blast into a series of narrow horizontal bands. The troopers were literally cut to pieces.

After that things got messy. Another projector opened a second hole in the ceiling, and what dropped through this one wasn't grunts, it was a swarm of beekeeper remotes equipped with air-burst pressure munitions. Rupshe's suits triggered their own push-aways in response and the air in the corridor became a tsunami of intersecting pressure waves.

Get the door back up! Moon voked at Nkanika. There was no point in shouting it out loud: the insanely choppy air would shatter her words and fling them in all directions. They grabbed the buckled steel plate and levered it back into its frame as tightly as they could. They couldn't see the battle outside any more, but Moon could still follow it via her array. It didn't look good. There were more enemy units popping into existence on all sides, Stepped in from other realities in response to what was now clearly not the Ansurrection's planet-buster weapon but an armed incursion. Speed had always been the most important factor here, and evidently they hadn't been quick enough.

Is he in? Moon voked to Paz.

Paz responded with the clenched-fist *yes* signal that Cielo troopers in movies used all the time and real soldiers almost never.

Then why is the monitor blank? Moon demanded.

Physical interface. The feed is to his optic nerve, not the monitor. He says he's doing fine so far. The system accepted his log-in and he's inside the firewall, but he hasn't found the Mother Mass coordinates yet. He says it's archived data and he has to make a special request.

Moon didn't like the sound of that one bit. *A special request to where?* she demanded. *What's he talking about?*

To the Registry, Paz said.

Well that was great. That was just wonderful. As if they weren't already grabbing a tiger by the balls! Security in the redoubts might be tight, but in the Itinerant Fortress it was insane. Paranoia was baked in by design. The Pando couldn't afford any unauthorised access to the Registry. If it tocked when it should have ticked, a billion Step transits would be fucked beyond unfucking. *Tell him no*, she voked. *They'll track that request right back and lock the terminal.*

He thinks he can do it. He's got access codes that still work.

He thinks? He thinks he can? Tell him—

Be quiet, Vemmet voked. *Let me work.*

Listen, you little sack of—

Be quiet, or go away.

Moon lapsed into silence, but only because she'd run out of words.

This was always going to be a shit-show. She'd let herself get seduced by all that talk of living the high life and slipping some really bad news between the ribs of Melusa Baxemides. And this was where it had brought her.

44

Vemmet

The temptation didn't even come to him until the system had accepted his log-in and awarded him conditional clearance. Even then it was only because the wording touched him on a raw spot. It was so needlessly specific. *Access granted up to administrative level 15.* For Baxemides – assuming she hadn't been promoted still further in his absence – that figure would have been 18. And because of Baxemides, Vemmet's own actual status, mercifully recorded in a different region of this gigantic database, was level 3.

Out of nowhere he remembered a string of alphanumerics – 09a08f76e09 – and the word *Repentance*. Both had been given to him a few short months ago on the planet Tsakom, where he had been languishing as an inmate of a de facto prison. Baxemides had put him there. And there he had met a self named Jex Utilion, a computer hacker working out a sentence of life imprisonment for war profiteering. For the right price Utilion could squeeze data out of a dry rag. The right price for Baxemides' ID string and password had involved a hundred stars and ten sticks of gabber.

Had Baxemides changed them since? There seemed no harm in

finding out. Like Moon Vemmet had suffered greatly under the coordinator's tyrannical spite. Like Moon he would give a great deal to pay her back. Time was short, but digital files move at the speed of light.

He logged out. Logged back in again as Baxemides.

Access granted up to administrative level 18. He laughed out loud.

Moon shot him a warning glare. *What the fuck are you doing over there?* she voked.

Working, he sent back.

And he was. He was working hard. The operational files for Spearhead missions were well within Baxemides' reach. He drew down a list and searched for Arbitrary Midnight. When he found it he flagged all the files in the folder and sent in a request for routine review. This would be eyes only with no option to download or copy – the lowest level of access, and therefore the least risk of triggering a security lockdown.

Now what else was here? What had Baxemides sunk her claws into that might give him some leverage over her? Ignoring the sounds of violent conflict rising at his back he ransacked the coordinator's data space. He found the logs of recent activity and opened them up. Most of what he found was mail, both incoming and outgoing, and status reports from the offices and subdivisions under Baxemides' aegis.

Vemmet felt he could afford to be more cavalier here because these were Baxemides' own files and she could do whatever she liked with them. He rummaged at will, opening one folder after another and then closing them again when the contents proved to be mundane or unfathomable or both. Pointless! It was like picking up grains of sugar from a bowl and examining them one by one in the hope that one would turn out to be black.

"Jesus Christ!" Essien growled behind his back as the walls and floor shook to some fresh impact. Vemmet had no idea who that was. A childhood friend? A bogeyman? A god? Someone to swear by, anyway.

The air in the centre of the room began to thicken and become slightly opaque, a warning sign that something or someone was about to Step in. Two armoured forms appeared. Moon and Nkanika caught them in a quartering fire and took them down.

The Arbitrary Midnight folder arrived. Vemmet opened it and scanned it. The coordinates for the Mother Mass continuum were in the first paragraph of the operational overview. He memorised them and closed the file without attempting to save it. Better safe than sorry. Then he turned back to the other material, to Baxemides' most recent exploits.

If there was a rope to hang her by, where would he find it? An inspiration struck, and he rearranged the files according to how many view-and-copy interdicts the coordinator had slapped on them. At the top was a folder bearing the title "ROBUST REBUKE". He opened it and dived in.

Weapons. Robust Rebuke was a polite circumlocution for a weapon system. Or possibly for several, since the sub-folders here referred to projects initiated on many different worlds, most of them bearing the red ellipse that meant they had since been cancelled and de-funded.

Which ones hadn't? Vemmet tracked down the list, and then back up again. He found it at last. There was only one. Project designation: Clean Slate.

Something else Stepped into the room. Vemmet didn't turn to see what it was but he heard the Uti girl's shriek and flinched down low as Moon and Nkanika fired again, first in short controlled bursts and then in a sustained volley. The sharp reek of incendiary volatiles invaded his nose. Smoke drifted between him and the monitor, obscuring some of the words and leaving only a teasing mosaic.

> . . . all identifiable brain activity ceased within . . .
> . . . did not stop at the limits of the field but . . .
> . . . across dimensional boundaries . . .

"What progress have you made, Watchmaster?"

Rupshe's voice coming from right beside him made Vemmet start violently. He had forgotten for a moment that the AI could access any and all of the armoured suits, including that of the rabbit girl standing beside him. Rupshe was fighting a pitched battle right outside the door, but that didn't prevent et from looking over his shoulder and prying into his private affairs.

Except that et couldn't hack into his nervous system, and therefore et couldn't see what he was looking at. "I've requested the Arbitrary Midnight file but I'm still waiting for it to arrive," he lied.

"You're reading something now. Your eye movements make that very clear."

"I'm merely following links within the documents I've already opened."

"Show me. Patch me into your array."

He had no choice. And it wasn't as though he wanted to keep Baxemides' secrets – only to use them against her if he possibly could.

"Linking you right now," he said. But before he did so he opened all the files in the Robust Rebuke directories. Let the AI poke and pry as much as it liked. He would drown it in detail while he continued his own search.

"None of these files contain references to the Mother Mass," Rupshe said.

"Obviously. I disguised my request by dropping it into a much larger list."

"Chosen on what basis?" Rupshe demanded.

"Randomly," Vemmet said, with strained patience. "A moment longer. I'm almost there."

He scanned and scrolled in feverish haste. Clean Slate. It was a weapon that erased minds. Machine minds, organics selves, animals, it made no distinction. And there had been an appalling accident on Erim, at Hiathu University. Seventeen thousand dead. Would it be enough? It felt as though it ought to be. If he came out of this alive he would accuse Baxemides. Expose her to public censure, possibly even to criminal charges and the shipwrecking of her career. He closed the file and its parent directory and turned to call out to the soldiers in the doorway.

"I have it," he told them. "We can leave."

But of course that turned out to be wild optimism.

45

Moon

This mission had been catastrophically bad right out of the gate, but that didn't mean it couldn't get worse.

Moon's array updated again to show some truly massive semi-portable cannons that had just been Stepped in. The Step point had been less than a hundred metres away, well within firing range, but she reckoned they still had a couple of minutes before the behemoths could engage: their force baffles would have to be locked down to the decking first so the recoil when they went off didn't bring down half the station. But after that Moon and the rest of the strike team were basically loose particles.

"I have it," Vemmet said, into a sudden and unexpected silence – a lull between attacks. He turned to look at Moon, wearing a smirk that she would have loved to scrub off with bleach. "We can leave."

"Thank Christ!" Nkanika exclaimed. "Grab your breastplate."

The smirk faltered. "What?" Vemmet said. "Why?"

"Because that's where your bounce-back is, you moron!" Moon snarled. "Rupshe, we're good. Step us out."

Understood, Rupshe voked. *Activating in three . . .*

Vemmet dived for the breastplate which was still lying on the floor half-buried under other components of his disassembled suit.

Two . . .

Vemmet clutched the solid chunk of metal and ceramic in both hands, hugging it against his body.

One.

Moon braced for the Step. But nothing happened.

"Hey," Moon growled. "Rupshe?"

We have a problem, the AI voked. *The bounce-backs are no longer functioning.*

A moment later Paz uttered a yelp of shock and agony and collapsed where she stood.

46

Paz

I was not yet born – not *quite* – but I remember this. Her pain. Her confusion. The sudden, shocking realisation that she was not alone inside her own head.

For the others, organic and construct alike, for Essien Nkanika and Moon Sostenti, for Dulcie and Hadiz, nothing happened beyond the inescapable fact that their bounce-backs failed to function. They were left standing at the console in a room that was now so full of smoke from the conflagrations outside that they couldn't even see each other.

For Rupshe, processes that should have been automatic and immediate had become problematic. The bounce-back devices, depending as they did on the release of stored energy from the original Step transit, should have taken precisely 2.81 seconds to reach full operational capacity and yank the entire strike team back to their starting point on Hadiz Tambuwal's Earth. That they had failed to do so was a conundrum to which et now addressed etself, testing alternative activation sequences at a rate of several trillion per second.

Only Paz, out of all of them, felt a giant hand close around her and squeeze her. This didn't happen to her body, but to her mind. Her thoughts were held in a grip so tight it crushed them flat, made them into thin, pulped smears from which cognition oozed out like juice from a pressed grape.

She was aware of many things at once, but only in fragments with raw and bleeding gaps in between them. She didn't know that she had fallen down. The thing that had her in its grip had been close to passing right over her, but then had paused and come back. It didn't mean her any harm, but it was curious. It had seen something it did not expect to see and leaned in close to see it better. But its grip was unbreakable, and it *hurt*.

The bounce-back units have been overwritten, a voice said from a long way away. *The energy in their reservoirs is being released too slowly, in subcritical amounts. I did not know that such a thing was possible, and I do not know how to counter it.*

Other voices answered the first, full of anguish and urgency, but they were too far away for Paz to make out the words. After a moment, another squeezed-out drop of understanding trickled through her. The first speaker had been voking, the others speaking aloud. The circuitry in her brain was still working, her ears not so much.

She tried her best to form a word of her own, a message, not to that first speaker but to the thing that had her in its terrible grasp.

p

p a e

le s

p se

please!

From way, way up above her there was a shifting of some great bulk that was invisible and massless. The unseen giant had heard her, but its grip didn't slacken.

Pleeeeeeeeeeeeeeeeeeeeeeease, the giant drawled. It wasn't a response, or even an acknowledgement. It was a model of Paz's cry that it had made within itself. The word was turned over and over, folded and stretched, dismantled and rebuilt, and finally receded from her, stowed away in some space she couldn't reach.

The grip tightened, and somehow shifted too. It became a probe, a question that came rolling towards her like a great boulder, or like the turned handle of a vice, and pressed an answer out of her. There were no words, but if there had been there would have been only the one and it would have been WHO?

Paz, she answered. *I'm Paz.* She struggled to shape the words and to hold them together in her mind. *This is killing me.*

Paz, the thing said. *I'm Paz. This is killing me.* There was no meaning in the words. No mockery either. The thing was just copying her in the way a child would, or certain types of bird. An image came close behind them, but it wasn't an image that Paz could make sense of. It seemed to be a giant maze made up of many thousands of lines that branched from a single main stem and circled it endlessly without ever finding it again.

Paz, the thing said. The pain grew a little less and she was better able to gather her scattered thoughts. Her best guess was that the diagram was the thing trying to tell her its name. *As Paz is to you, this is to me.*

I'm happy to meet you, she said. *Please don't kill me.*

Kill me, it said without inflection.

Just let me go. Whatever you are . . . And the words ran out right there, because it occurred to her very suddenly that there was really only one thing it could be. *Are you . . . are you the Mother Mass?* she asked it. *Did you see us trying to get to you and come to meet us halfway?*

The terrible pressure returned. *Paz*, the thing said again. And then that picture, of all the branching lines, pushed hard against the surface of her brain so it would stay there. *Paz.*

The other voices came back. Paz could make out some of the words now, but they were jumbled up with other sounds that weren't words at all and all the sounds were tumbling end over end. Sometimes their turbulent motion resolved into sense. More often it didn't.

Something. Something. ". . . plate. But it's . . ." Something.

"Blow the floor out! Just blow the godsdamned . . ."

Something. ". . . about Rupshe? Hadiz? They can't . . ." Something.

Something. ". . . now, you weaselly little . . ."

Just noise after that.

And then a sense of falling, a very long way. Out of the grip of that giant hand. It tried its best to hold on to her, clawed and swiped and clung to no avail as she slid away like water into a space that was first black.

Then red.

Then bright, bright green.

47

Vemmet

Sometimes terror whips your thoughts into a froth and blows them away. Sometimes it freezes them into a hopeless stasis. Orso Vemmet had experienced both kinds more than once. Never until now had he known a terror that focused his mind to a razor edge and left him thinking more clearly than before.

He had pushed his luck to its limits. He had used his access codes and clearances to draw down the Arbitrary Midnight file. Amazingly, his request had been actioned. The file had come, and he had retrieved the information they had come here for. He had been obsessively careful, copying nothing, downloading nothing. The Mother Mass coordinates were in his mind, his memory, and they were nowhere else.

But when as Baxemides he had drawn down the materials relating to the Robust Rebuke, he had made a fatal error. Surely Baxemides had the right to retain a copy of her own files, he'd reasoned. But once he'd done so everything suddenly fell apart. The AI counted down the three seconds it should have taken for their bounce-back units to activate, but not a single one of them did. A moment later one of the crimson Cielo suits keeled over and crashed to the floor. It took him a few seconds to realise that it was the Uti child, Paz, presumably falling into a faint. He felt the smallest pang of guilt on her behalf. Perhaps he should not have insisted on her coming. Still, she had been free to refuse. She had made her own choices, and he was not responsible for her.

The bounce-back units had been overwritten, Rupshe had told them. Something had hacked every single one of the suits, breaking Cielo data protections that were supposed to be unbreakable, and effortlessly removed their exit strategy. The list of suspects wasn't long, when you thought about it.

"It's the Registry," he said.

"There's something wrong with Paz!" the monkey construct called out at the same time. "Help her!"

"What?" Moon Sostenti, at the door, turned to glare at Vemmet across the width of the room. "The Registry? What are you talking about?"

"There was another file. Robust Rebuke. I accessed it by . . . by accident, and I allowed Rupshe to access it too."

"So?"

"That was a mistake. The file must have been much higher priority than I thought. My accessing it seems to have triggered a direct attack on our bounce-back units. I have no idea how such a thing could be done. The bounce-backs aren't connected to anything here. But if anything could do it, it would be the Registry. It's acting to prevent the file from leaving here."

That seems plausible, Rupshe confirmed. *Contact between air-gapped systems can theoretically be brute-forced using an induction field. But to alter the operational values of the stored Step fields would still require a data entity of enormous processing power. There are not many. Possibly there is only one.*

The monkey construct was now trying to dismantle Paz's armour, presumably so it could administer first aid. Nkanika looked as though he was about to come and help, but some near-miss in the corridor outside made the buckled door shudder in its frame and both he and Moon had to lean in hard to brace it. The firefight outside was escalating from moment to moment as more defenders Stepped in. Vemmet didn't bother to check how many of Rupshe's proxy warriors had fallen: their attrition rate measured – probably in seconds – how long they all had left to live.

"So what do we do?" Moon shouted over her shoulder.

What could they do? Vemmet held the question up to the light and examined it from all the angles he could think of. The Registry had moved against them directly, which was somewhat equivalent to a mountain leaning down in order to swat a fly.

But the Registry wasn't a fixed presence in this reality. It tumbled through all worlds in its endless arc, never staying anywhere for longer than the few seconds it took to trigger its next bank of onboard Step plates. So it – or one of its satellite swarm – had been here briefly, in orbit above them, and then it had gone.

Which meant it must have lodged its commands with the redoubt's AI.

And the redoubt's AI, right now, was trying to cope with a thousand urgent systems failures.

Vemmet didn't waste any time or any breath answering Moon's query. He went to work again, discovering with a fierce thrill of joy that his access still hadn't been revoked. The Registry wanted the Robust Rebuke file locked down, but it hadn't identified him as an active threat – it had only moved to prevent the security breach.

There was no way to rescind that order and free their bounce-backs. It probably wasn't safe to use them now in any case, as some of their stored energy had already dribbled away. Vemmet had only the vaguest sense of what happened to people who were exposed to unstable Step fields, but he knew it was a thing best avoided.

So he did something else. He dug down into health and safety subroutines, emergency overrides, crisis response procedures: not the algorithms that governed the redoubt's day-to-day operations but the code that modified code, the systems that dealt with exceptions and emergency overrides. It all fell under the remit of his old department, Contingencies, and he knew how it was meant to work. He also knew how it could be made not to.

He sliced out a section of the AI's events log, pertaining to the moments of the underground explosion, ripped off the date stamp and replayed it as though it was happening again right now. He uploaded it to every node he could reach, triggering as many alarms as he could in the process.

While the AI was still assimilating and assessing, Vemmet did an emergency overwrite, dumping vast amounts of junk data – values of pi, lists of primes, recursive enumerations of logical sets that contained themselves and called on themselves – into critical areas of the base AI's operating memory. The AI was already compromised and now he was deliberately cutting it off at the knees, giving it more and more to think about and less and less to think with.

Look at this, he told it. *There's been a disaster, an earthquake of some magnitude, and here in this room are a handful of base personnel that weren't evacuated. We need help. You have to get us out of this. And we're not wearing dead-drops so please provide another solution.*

From the corridor outside came a sound like a thousand people humming the same note all at once – the sonic backwash from some new weapon that had just been deployed.

The monitor in front of Vemmet filled with a cheerful montage of morphing shapes as the redoubt's AI, temporarily overwhelmed, went away into a corner of itself and thought.

We are being overrun, Rupshe reported. *The number of enemy units is increasing exponentially, and the heavy cannons are about to be deployed. I am afraid there is no possibility of holding this beachhead for more than another few moments.*

Moon looked at Essien, who nodded. "Fuck it," she said, "might as well go out fighting."

They wrenched the door out of its frame again and let it fall. The corridor outside was mostly invisible behind a curtain of flame and smoke. The shimmer in the air was only partly a heat haze: it was also the distortion effect caused when planes of force from projector weapons intersected and spent their terrible energies on nothing.

The monitor switched to a map of their immediate surroundings. The words "EVAC ROUTE" flashed red across the centre of the display.

"Ready," Essien said. He brought his rifle to bear, covering Moon as she made to walk out into the maelstrom.

"No!" Vemmet screamed, surging up from the console's chair. He was afraid for a second that they hadn't heard him, but they both turned. He pointed at the wall immediately in front of him. "Blow it out! Blow the wall out!"

"What?" Essien said. "Why? There's nothing there."

"A hundred metres over," Vemmet blurted, "two levels down. There's a Step facility and one of the plates is charging up. For us. I've told the base AI we have to be evacuated. It believes me. We have to go! That way!"

The terror was surging up again now that there was nothing more for him to do. He pounded at the wall with his fists, not because he thought it would fall under the feeble assault but because Moon and Nkanika were standing in the doorway like imbeciles and a stray bolt or bullet could take him out at any moment.

"The wall!" he shrieked. "Break down the—"

The wall disappeared in a granulated haze of heat and light. The overlapping booms of the rifle reports assailed his ears a moment later, and shredded plasteel fibres rained down on him like petals at the end of springtime. A twinge of pain made him look down at his arm. There was a vivid red line there. He thought it was paint, however little sense that made, until he saw the blood welling up from it in separate drops like red pearls all along its length. A piece of shrapnel from the exploded wall must have hit him.

It didn't matter. Vemmet clambered over the remains of the console into the newly opened space beyond. It was a storeroom, many times longer than it was wide and filled from floor to ceiling with racks of unidentifiable components. The force of the blast had toppled some of the nearer shelving units, which had knocked down the ones further away, but there was an aisle running down the centre that remained almost clear. He started to run, then realised he was alone. He turned impatiently to see why Moon and Nkanika weren't following him. There were going to be more walls and floors to be demolished and he couldn't very well do it with his fists.

The two troopers had lifted up the Uti girl and were carrying her between them. The monkey anima had succeeded in detaching her helmet and one of the shoulder guards from her armour and was now hunched down on her breastplate, swaying and rocking as they ran but clinging tight by one hand. In the other it held a hypodermic, which it now plunged into the girl's neck.

Behind them the weapon that had been singing had begun to scream.

"Rupshe—" Nkanika shouted.

Still here, the AI reported. *But probably not for much longer. Go. I see where you're aiming for and the way is currently clear. I doubt I will be able to join you, but I will keep the forces here from following you for as long as I can.*

At the end of the storeroom was a door. Moon freed one hand and pointed. "Get out of the fucking way!" she yelled at Vemmet. He ducked and swerved aside, arms thrown up over his head. Whatever ammunition she was using tore a hundred tiny holes in the door, then as she moved her arm in a circle the holes multiplied and joined up until there wasn't enough door left to stand. It fell in on itself. One of the pieces bounced and rolled to a stop at Vemmet's feet. Its edges had an oddly crimped look, as if it had been partially devoured by rats with diamond teeth.

Vemmet made to go through, but the troopers got there first and shouldered him aside, still hauling Paz along between them. He was forced to trot along behind as they entered another storeroom, and then a third.

I can't hold any longer, Rupshe told them with clinical calm. *The last of my armoured units are—*

The silence that followed was sudden and shocking. "Rupshe?" Nkanika shouted. There was no response.

"Better move faster," Moon growled.

They ran on. Vemmet risked a look back over his shoulder. Crimson shapes were moving there, and he knew what they were – not Rupshe's puppet suits but real Cielo troopers, only seconds behind them now.

In his array the red dot that was the four of them moved to overlap with the green dot that was their target. "Here!" he cried. He pointed at the floor. "Down!"

Supporting Paz with one arm each, Moon and Nkanika fired at the floor using the same armour-piercing rounds Moon had used before. The plasteel plates, punctured in a thousand places, lost their coherence and fell away leaving a ragged hole two metres across.

"The next one too!" Vemmet bellowed. "The Step station is two levels down from—" His voice gave out in a strangled gasp of shock as a searing pain blossomed in his side. The white-hot stencil of a focused thermal weapon had just gone by him, only registered after it had passed. It had missed him by a metre or more, but even so it had par-broiled the left side of his body.

"Two levels down," Moon confirmed. "Okay then." She detached a grenade from her belt and tossed it into the room below. Then she gripped Vemmet with her free hand and gave Nkanika a curt nod. They jumped together, all of them in a tight cluster. The grenade detonated barely three metres below them. They fell through air still roiling from the shockwave and so full of flying shrapnel it was almost an emulsion. Vemmet felt one tearing impact after another, in his shoulder, his leg, his gut.

Two levels down, exactly where the station AI had said it would be, was a Step facility. The largest plate was meant to take armoured transports and artillery pieces: it was big enough for all five of them and dozens more. As per Vemmet's request the plate was already active. They fell into the field's effective radius, which was one more hideous, buffeting shock, and were gone.

48

Hadiz

Hadiz hadn't taken any particular pleasure in being in a body again. Quite apart from the stress of the situation, the armoured suit hadn't offered any real equivalents to human sensation. It had been more like playing a particularly realistic computer game. But she had been getting used to it. As the copter climbed into the air she had watched the ground recede with a sense of subdued excitement. She was not really *in* this space but still she had the sense of space, of wider possibilities opening around her.

"Brace," Rupshe said, and the sky turned black.

Then suddenly, without any sense of intervening time, Hadiz found herself back in the Second Thoughts box at Campus Cross with all her sensory feeds down. The transition was jarring and unpleasant, but it was exactly what Rupshe had told her to expect and she tried her best to shrug it off. Somewhere out there another version of her, a downloaded copy, had just Stepped to Serixis. The mission was playing out on another world in another reality and there was nothing for her to do but wait.

So she waited. Hours went by, and the version of her that had set out for Serixis did not return. There was therefore no re-integration of that Hadiz with the Hadiz who had stayed behind, no merging of their memories. Whatever had happened at the redoubt, it had not gone according to plan.

Rupshe experienced the same dislocation, but with much more stoicism. Et had divided ets consciousness before, and into many more pieces. Et was used to the side effects by now.

Hadiz was the opposite of stoical. *Rupshe,* she begged, *tell me what happened! What went wrong? Where are the others?*

I can only give you a partial answer to those questions, Professor, Rupshe replied. *After we Stepped, I launched a dozen drones to the same coordinates, each of them with a thirty-second bounce-back. The down-loaded version of my consciousness that went on the mission was therefore able to send several interim reports. I am accessing those reports now. Bear with me.*

There was a pause, but it was barely long enough for Hadiz to register it.

The redoubt's defences were more formidable and more diverse than we anticipated, Rupshe said at last. *But Watchmaster Vemmet reached the data terminal nonetheless and was able to interface with it. According to the last transmission, he had succeeded in locating a file pertaining to the Arbitrary Midnight mission. He claimed to have accessed the file and retrieved the coordinates of the Mother Mass continuum.*

But he didn't pass the file on to you? Hadiz hadn't missed those words – *the last transmission* – but she refused to consider their implications. There was a last item in every series. It didn't have to mean the team were dead.

No. He did not. And since the link between him and the terminal was a direct neural one I was locked out of it until I insisted that he link me in.

What happened then?

I can show you, Rupshe offered. *I have now integrated the memories stored and transmitted back to me by the drones. Let me share them with you.*

The feeds opened as separate streams of information in Hadiz's visual field – like panes in a window, each looking out on a different scene. Or rather onto the same scene viewed from many different angles. She saw their strike team's entry into the redoubt, saw them finding the terminal and barricading the door so Vemmet could work while they held off the inevitable counter-attack. She looked for and found herself, one red suit out of a hundred, no different from the rest except that it had been her consciousness that was inside it, animating it. But she was cut off from that part of herself. She could only watch it now from the outside.

And at first she had done little more than watch as the other suits mounted a defence against the redoubt's security details. She had stood back, pressed against the wall of the corridor, while explosions made the deck plates throb like a panicked heart and beam weapons tore the air into ionised tatters.

But finally she had remembered that her suit had weapons systems like all the others. She had fought. She had fired at live targets. Had she hit any? Killed any? That version of her would have known because the suit's targeting systems would have reported back to her. Her present self was blessedly ignorant.

The battle played out, becoming more and more one-sided. Rupshe's empty suits fell, assailed by superior numbers and enfiladed from all sides.

Vemmet reported that he had retrieved the file.

Rupshe triggered the bounce-back units.

And the sequence ended.

But nothing came back, Hadiz said.

The final drone came back, Rupshe corrected her. *Otherwise we would not have this information. But our strike team did not. For some reason the bounce-back did not complete.*

Then . . . they're still there? Trapped? Rupshe, we have to go in and get them out!

Professor, we cannot. To mount this raid I used almost every functional part of every armoured suit we obtained from Tsakom. I held back two intact units, as I told you earlier, but they'll be needed if we're forced to implement the backup plan. We also have a single remaining Step plate, but it is here on campus. We would have to transport it many hundreds of miles if we wished to go to Serixis – and risk a second approach to the redoubt without any hope this time of immobilising its defences. I see little chance of effecting a rescue.

Hadiz fought against despair. *What do we do then?* She was painfully aware of how weak and helpless the question made her sound. *We sent them into that place. Made them risk their lives. We can't just give up on them now.*

No, Rupshe said. *But nor can we take any practical steps at this moment towards retrieving them. It may be that they will find a way out of the redoubt on their own initiative. It's possible they already have. Moon and Essien are skilled and experienced soldiers. But I think we must assume for the moment that they have been taken. And if that's the case, the resources we have here are all that are left to us.*

And those resources were so meagre! Two suit of Cielo armour, one Step plate, a few drones . . .

And plan B, whatever that might be.

Hadiz felt overwhelmed and close to despair. The team they had built up had never been exactly formidable but so long as they had a team, and a goal to work towards, she had been able to convince herself that there was hope. Now she felt as though there was nothing left to do but wait for the end.

I will attempt to monitor communications between the higher echelons of the Cielo and the Omnipresent Council, Rupshe said. *I still have some back-channel access through the systems I infiltrated on Tsakom. I may be able to ascertain whether our friends are alive, and if so where they have been taken. I will also continue to evaluate the information I pulled down from the drones, the better to reconstruct what happened in the final seconds of our incursion.*

Do you think there's anything there that can help us?

I do not know, Rupshe said. There was a bleakness in the words that matched Hadiz's own.

I think it is time, Rupshe said, *for me to explain to you the other approach on which I have been working. Please try to keep an open mind.*

If Hadiz had currently been in possession of a physical body she would have winced. *That's a request that's virtually guaranteed to close it*, she said.

I know, Rupshe acknowledged. *But do your best. Our options now are extremely limited and this one – though it's very far from the best – may be the least terrible of those that are left to us.*

The two remaining suits of Cielo armour came into the lab and stood in the doorway, perfectly still. In Hadiz's mind they had never looked more sinister.

Shall we take a walk? Rupshe said.

49

Paz

She woke half in and half out of the water. What woke her was the chill. Her legs, completely immersed, were so numb she could hardly feel them. Her upper body was uncomfortably warm, the sunlight falling on her directly through a gap in the tree canopy above.

Paz sat up groggily and looked around her. She was alone. No sign of the others, and for a moment she wasn't even certain that she remembered who those others were. It was just that having no companions had felt like a surprise. Her head was full of fuzz, and it ached. She had no idea at all where she could possibly be. She reached by habit into her array, setting it to find local data feeds. It came back with nothing. There were none. Nothing in the air at all but complex harmonies of birdsong and the rustling of some small animal as it traversed the branches over her head.

She pulled herself on hands and knees up out of the water. As soon as the sunlight hit her legs and lower body they began to warm and she felt a little better. The ache in her head receded, and with the ebbing away of the pain she regained some sense of herself. "Paz," she said. That seemed like a solid start. She was Paz.

And she was . . . somewhere she didn't know at all. Sitting on grass that was short and free of weeds, between a gently flowing river and a stand of fruit trees. The fruit looked very much like apples, big and red and perfect. When she was strong enough to stand she would eat one, or at least take a bite out of it and see if it tasted as good as it looked.

Memories seeped back sluggishly at first and then in a sudden flood, as if her brain was a dry rag and the past was wicking through it. She remembered the raid. Standing by Orso Vemmet's side with Essien and Moon Sostenti barricading the door, trying not to hear the thuds and booms and gunfire from outside the room. And then . . .

There had been someone else in the room. Or something. A huge invisible presence that had leaned in to touch her. To talk to her. And then . . . to switch her off. Because there was nothing after that until she woke up here. They had escaped. It was hard to see how they could have managed that, but they must have.

And they'd left that thing, whatever it was, behind them. Paz shuddered involuntarily. She had thought it must be the Mother Mass reaching out to them, but in cold afterthought that seemed much less likely. She knew from Hellad Zenti that the Mother Mass had learned human speech in between his first and second expeditions. The entity that had taken hold of Paz could only echo her own words without understanding.

Dulcie! Where was Dulcie? Paz opened her mouth to call out, but her throat was dry. She voked instead. *Dulcie?*

Here. The answering voice brought a flood of relief, and Paz's array stirred into life again without being asked, providing a bearing. When she turned in that direction she saw Dulcie scampering quickly out of the treeline towards her. Essien and Moon appeared a moment later, converging from different directions. They had their rifles in their hands but neither of them was wearing armour. Essien was wearing a sleeveless black tabard and a pair of shorts, while Moon had on a singlet and sweatpants. It made Paz realise for the first time that her own armour was missing too. She looked down at her body. She was dressed in the clothes she'd taken from Shireen Yemini's locker back in Campus Cross, but something was different about them. She tried to place what it was, but it was still hard to concentrate.

"They insisted on a perimeter sweep," Dulcie said as et came to rejoin Paz, indicating Essien and Moon with a toss of ets head. Et held out ets slender, ceramic paw and Paz took it, felt ets cool against the sun-kissed warmth of her own fingers. "I only left you alone for a few minutes, Paz. We just wanted to be sure there was nothing in the immediate neighbourhood that might want to eat us."

"Which there isn't," Moon said. She threw out her arms and stretched, head tilted back. "Plenty of things that look like we could eat them, though, compatible protein strings permitting. Got some birds. Lizards. Something like a squirrel that would probably roast up nicely on a spit."

"And the fruit," said Paz, pointing.

"If that's your thing," Moon conceded with a grimace of distaste. "The point is that we can make camp here. Wait for Rupshe to find us and bring us in."

"Does et know where we are?" Paz asked. And then, as a new thought struck her, "Do *we* know?"

"No idea at all," Essien said. "Vemmet presumably knows, since he was the one who programmed that plate, but we can't find him. Maybe he woke up first and went exploring. Either that or he didn't make it. The rest of us all landed in the same place, which is what you'd expect, but somehow we all lost consciousness in the course of the Step."

"Except for you," Moon said bluntly. "You were already out cold. We had to carry you halfway across the redoubt. You should have told us you were epileptic before we shipped out."

"I don't have epilepsy. Nothing like that has ever happened to me before." Paz rubbed her forehead. It still ached, and it was hot. It felt as though something had been jammed inside her head sideways and was trying to get out. "Did something block our bounce-backs?"

"The Registry," Dulcie said. "The Registry brute-forced its way into the units and changed the field profiles." Et laid ets hand gently on Paz's forearm. "That was when you fell down. Do you remember any of this?"

Paz nodded, which turned out to be a mistake. The movement set off a wave of nausea and she doubled forward, dry-heaving. "Sorry!" she said, when she could speak again. "Sorry. I just . . . I'm not feeling very good. Thank you for getting me out of my armour."

Essien shook his head. "We didn't," he said. "That's another mystery." He touched the thin fabric of his tabard. "When we woke up we'd been peeled like prawns. I've heard of things getting lost in Step transits, but it's usually because they fell outside the field. That can't have been what happened here. Maybe whatever attacked our bounce-backs took a pass at our armour too. Blew the seals as we were Stepping. And then some of the local fauna – or indigenes we haven't met yet – dragged the pieces away while we were still out of it."

Paz suddenly registered what was different about her own clothes. She breathed in deeply, just to be sure. The strong, stale smell the tracksuit had had when she took it out of the locker two days ago had gone. There was no smell from her own sweat either, despite the crazy exertions she'd pushed herself through over the last few hours.

"How long were we unconscious?" she asked.

"One minute and twenty-three seconds," Dulcie said. "That's a best guess. My systems went offline too, and a backup timer kicked in. When I rebooted, 00:01:23 was what I was reading. The first thing I saw was Essien rubbing his head and sitting up. And all your armour had already gone by then. It would have been a pretty tall order for anything to have carried it away in that short a time." Et gave Paz a searching look, reading the unease in her face. "What?"

"Nothing," Paz said, but her fur prickled with queasy presentiment. "It's just . . . Is it possible your systems were tampered with, Dulcie?"

"I suppose it's possible. But why? If the Cielo had caught us they wouldn't be playing mind games with us. They wouldn't need to. They could just put us all under CoIL."

Paz shook her head. "I know, but . . . I think my clothes are cleaner than they were. I think I might be cleaner too. I don't think those are things that could have been done in a minute and a half."

"So someone sneaked up and did our laundry while we were unconscious," Moon said. "Gave us a little personal grooming. Or how about this? We just came out of a firefight, we got knocked stupid along the way and we're not thinking straight right now. The good news is we landed on our feet instead of our heads and we haven't been followed. And as far as that goes, losing the armour is a real piece of luck. If a Cielo search party does come looking for us they'll most likely try to track us by energy signatures, and the suits' power cells are easy to spot. Even if they're powered down you can ping them with passive induction."

"By that logic we should switch off our arrays," Essien pointed out.

"Fine. Let's do it."

"And move a long way off from where we Stepped in."

"Sure."

"All of which makes it that much harder for Rupshe to find us and bring us home. And pretty much impossible for Vemmet to catch up if he's out there somewhere looking for us. He's probably got about as much fieldcraft as the average turd."

Moon's expression didn't change but her shoulders tensed. Paz tensed too. Whenever Moon got angry Paz always felt as though the gap between harsh words and violent actions was likely to be distressingly short. "I don't know what to tell you, Sinkhole. Right now we've washed up in the middle of nowhere, some of us seem to be hallucinating – no offence, kid – and one of us is already MIA. For all we know, whatever took away our armour took Vemmet too, and it could be on its way back for the rest of us right now. Common sense says we duck and cover."

"Without knowing what we're ducking and covering from," Dulcie said.

"Hey, I'm just telling you what I'm going to be doing." Moon's patience seemed to have been exhausted at last. She shipped her rifle and gave them all a look of savage contempt. "The rest of you can sit around and talk it out for as long as you like." She turned and walked away. Her long strides took her in among the trees and out of their sight in a few seconds.

"I think we need to stay together," Essien said, almost apologetically.

Paz nodded. "I think so too." She held out her arm and Dulcie climbed smoothly up onto her shoulder. They set off after Moon.

And caught up with her almost immediately. She was standing in a small clearing, staring in grim fascination at her own forearm.

"If you're wounded," Dulcie offered without much enthusiasm as they came up alongside her, "I can disinfect and sew you up."

"I was wounded," Moon said. Paz saw that her claws were out. The fur on the back of her head and bare neck was standing up in a stiff ridge.

"Okay, then let me—"

"I said I *was*." Moon spun round on them, holding out her arm. "I took at least a dozen hits from all that shrapnel that was flying around. Couple of them were around here – a few inches up from a scar I took in Damola Ojo that was halfway healed. I sewed that one up myself."

Paz stared down at Moon's unbroken skin. There was no scar, no stipple marks from the stitches. No sign that the injuries had ever happened.

50

Dulcie

They kept the river on their left as they advanced. That first stand of trees gave way to something like a meadow of wildflowers, and then to a grassy slope that led them down into another small copse. Birds crossed the sky both by ones and twos and in huge flocks. Occasionally a few of the animals that Moon had described as being something like a squirrel startled from the grass in front of them to swarm up the boles of the trees and out of sight into the canopy.

Dulcie was even more aware than Paz of the strangeness of their situation. Et had experienced the same loss of sensation and consciousness, but et had perfect recollection of the flow of moments leading up to and away from the fugue. They had fallen into the Step field and it had begun to take effect on them. To the perception of an organic self that process seemed instantaneous. In fact, though, even after the three-second phasing cycle was complete and the field was operational the teleportation of living matter still took several millionths of a second to complete. Dulcie usually experienced those wafer-thin slices of time as a period when ets sensory feeds were unreliable and ets environmental readings went colourfully insane.

This time had been different. In the instant when the field hit full strength some invisible force had slammed into them, machine and organic minds alike, and switched off their conscious awareness. Dulcie had no means of determining whether this was done with intent. They had after all entered the Step field's zone of effect in a highly unorthodox way. Perhaps that came with side effects.

But when they came out on the far side of the Step, when consciousness resumed and Dulcie found etself lying on a grassy bank beside a river in bright sunlight, they had all been changed.

The changes were fractal, had taken place on every scale. The repairing of Moon's forearm injury and the theft of their armour were among the more obvious but they were not the most profound. Dulcie's own ceramic shell had taken a fair amount of damage from shrapnel hits and heat deformation during their escape from the redoubt, but now it seemed completely whole again. Paz, likewise, had healed from several superficial wounds she had sustained at Damola Ojo. And yet the older and more severe injuries she bore from the explosion in Canoplex were the same as they were before. Her eyes and hand had not been restored. The prosthetic components in her brain were still there.

Everything suggested a lapse of time – days or even weeks – that had gone unrecorded by all of them. A time when they had been at the mercy of some unknown entities that hadn't been able to resist the urge to tinker. But if Paz and Moon and Essien had been unconscious and effectively in coma for such a long time there would have been artefacts in their blood and brain chemistry that Dulcie's first aid diagnostics would have identified immediately – not to mention a detectable degree of muscle wastage. This discontinuity was seamless and invisible, except in the areas where it was blatantly obvious.

The terrain they were walking through was strange too. It was the kind of carefully crafted wilderness Dulcie would have expected to find on worlds with organic sentients, usually in cities with limited green spaces. The grass showed clear signs of being tended, the trees were artificially spaced with relatively little undergrowth between them. Intrusive plant species were being controlled. Animal species too, possibly: Dulcie could detect no large predators.

But nor could et locate any manufactured structures or artefacts. There were no paths, no signposts, and out to the limits of ets perception no industrial pollutants or electronic signalling of any kind. It was hard to believe that a technologically advanced species was maintaining this space from a distance. What would be the purpose of it? If it was a zoo or wildlife park there ought to be viewing platforms or hides for visitors' use, ancillary structures, walkways.

It's like a big park, Paz voked, reaching up to rest a hand on Dulcie's arm.

I thought you'd agreed to turn off your array, Dulcie said.

Moon said we should. But if I shut down all my electronics I wouldn't be able to control my prosthetics properly. I think it would be a bad idea to handicap myself right now, when we don't know where we are or what's happening to us.

It does look like a park, Dulcie agreed, returning to Paz's first statement. *Or a botanical garden. But there's nobody here to look after it.*

Paz's head turned to left and right, scanning the spaces between the trees. *Maybe there is*, she said, *and they just haven't shown themselves yet. Dulcie . . .*

Yes, Paz?

When I passed out, back at the redoubt, what was going on inside my mind?

Dulcie thought back. *A lot*, et said. *There was a surge of activity in your sensory cortex and hippocampus – which were already very active because of the hectic situation we were in. It looked random to me. As though you were fitting. I gave you an anti-convulsant but it didn't have any noticeable effect.*

I wasn't fitting. I was talking to someone.

On a sub-vocal channel?

No. I don't think so. Maybe talking isn't the right word. There was just this great big . . . thing that had got inside my head somehow and was clattering around in there. I don't think it wanted to hurt me. We were . . . stuck together. I can't explain it better than that. We might still be stuck together now if you hadn't Stepped me out.

Dulcie pondered. This conversation was leaning in a direction et didn't like in the least. *And all this was happening when the Registry was hacking its way into our systems,* et reflected.

Yes. Then.

But you don't think . . . ? Et waited, but Paz didn't break in. *Paz, you don't really believe the Registry tried to initiate communication with you?*

Yeah, Paz said. *I do. I know it makes no sense at all, but I can't explain it any other way. Dulcie, it felt as though I was a toy being picked up and played with by an enormous child.*

The Registry isn't a child, Dulcie pointed out. *It's the biggest and most powerful AI your culture ever made.*

And that's why the people who designed it put such a tight tether on it. They need it to just keep doing what it does forever, never slowing down or losing focus. Because if it looks away for even a second nobody can Step any more and everything falls apart. Why wouldn't it be like a child? They don't want it to learn, or to change. They can't afford for that to happen. So it knows nothing outside of the calculations it's made to do. Billions and billions of them, all the time.

Dulcie considered. *Why would the Registry talk to you?* et asked, not disagreeing but following the logic to see where it led.

I already said it didn't make any sense.

They walked on in silence for another mile or so, without encountering any variation in the overly groomed landscape. The weather didn't change either: the sun shone bright and clear with no clouds to challenge it, and the temperature wavered only a degree or so either side of 24°C.

Perhaps it does, Dulcie said.

What? Paz seemed to have lost the thread of their earlier conversation.

Perhaps it does make sense that the Registry was drawn to you. That it lingered to take a closer look at you. Back in Campus Cross when we did the synchronised time dilation thing for the first time I was using the prosthetic modules in your brain as an interface – and I took a good long look at them to make sure there were no compatibility issues. Their construction is ingenious and economical, as I think I said at the time. The substrate your neurosurgeons chose for your modules' storage and processing is boron nitride.

One of my favourite nitrides, Paz said.

She was trying for a joke, Dulcie knew, but et couldn't offer up a laugh in response. *The sheets are really thin*, et went on. *Almost single-molecule thickness. That allows for a wider overall surface area. If you unfolded them all they'd stretch for thousands of miles. And they're held in an inert field matrix to prevent any accidental cross-connections.*

So?

That doesn't sound familiar? You share that internal architecture with the Registry.

Paz's indrawn breath was audible to all of them.

"You okay, bunny rabbit?" Moon asked. "Are we working you too hard?"

"I'm fine," Paz said. The tremor in her voice was barely audible, but it was very clear to Dulcie.

I wouldn't read too much into it, et said quickly. *It's convergent design, that's all.* Et intended to say more, to point out that the add-ons to Paz's brain had been intended to restore the functionality she had lost in the explosion – and machines designed to handle cognition and reasoning were likely to share a lot of features for very obvious reasons. But et found now that et had a strong aversion to opening that topic. Et didn't even want to think about what et had done to Paz, still less to discuss it. *We're very unlikely to encounter the Registry again*, et said instead, without much conviction. *If you're right, and it thinks like a child, it may not even have a sense of object permanence.*

Except that would be the one thing the Registry absolutely needed to have in order to run the Pandominion's Step network. Dulcie recognised the hole et was in and stopped digging. They continued to march in silence through most of the day. When they spoke at all it was about trivialities, which suited Dulcie and seemed to suit Paz too – but et knew she was still thinking about what et had told her.

Then finally, with evening coming on, Moon called a halt.

"Okay," she said, "I think we're far enough away that a random sweep won't automatically pick us up. You, monkey, go on down to the river and sample the water for contaminants. Let us know if it's safe. Sinkhole, start a fire. I'll rustle us up some dinner."

The tone of command fell on Dulcie's ears like an irritant. For the sake of ets own self-respect et decided not to jump to attention and do what et was told. "What if someone sees the smoke?" et asked.

Moon gave a humourless chuckle. "Well, then either we're screwed or they are, depending on who the someone is and what they decide to do about it. But whatever I catch we'll need to cook. No, let me rephrase that. Me and Private Numbnuts have got immune systems made of cast iron and poured concrete, courtesy of the Cielo. But Paz here isn't so blessed, and the native micro-biome could really ruin her day if we don't burn out the worst of it. So a fire would be a great thing to have if one of you wants to get up off their arse and start one. I don't much care which of you it is."

She stalked away into the trees without waiting to see whether or not her orders were obeyed. The three of them stood for a moment, watching her receding back.

"Guess I better start a fire then," Essien said at last. Paz laughed – at his deadpan tone, Dulcie guessed. "I'll gather some wood," she said.

"Dry not green, for preference," Essien told her. "If we're really going to worry about the smoke."

And Dulcie went down to the river, where she sampled the water and found it not just clean but pristine. There were a few micro-organisms, but none of them rang any alarm bells for the first aid kit's onboard sensors. There were no chemical contaminants at all. You could turn on a tap anywhere in the Pandominion and not get water as pure as this: good news, but also another indication that this place had custodians who tended it with care. Where were they, and why hadn't they shown themselves?

Moon brought back two brace of the squirrel creatures, all of them with their necks snapped and no other wounds on them. The cat-woman must have run them down in a dead sprint. She skinned and gutted them with a short knife that detached from the stock of her rifle and cut some branches into spits so they could cook them on the fire Essien and Paz had made. While the meat roasted they went down to the river one at a time to drink. Paz picked an armload of the fruit that looked like apples to accompany the meal.

When the meat was thoroughly roasted Moon handed a skewer to Paz and one to Essien. The other two she kept for herself.

"So you're going to starve me now?" Orso Vemmet complained bitterly. "After abducting me and trying to get me killed?"

They stared at him in stunned disbelief. A moment before he simply hadn't been there. There were no discontinuities in Dulcie's consciousness this time, and there had been no warning of Vemmet's approach. He had simply appeared between one moment and the next, presumably at a point when all four of them had their atten-tion elsewhere. Even if he had Stepped in, one of them should have seen him come. None of them had. And when Dulcie reviewed the records from ets sensory storage et couldn't determine the precise instant when he had arrived.

"Where in Jad's name have you been?" Moon demanded.

Vemmet gave her a look of bland puzzlement.

"I don't understand the question," he said. "Please can I have just a little of that meat?"

51

Essien

Vemmet stuck to his story, which made no sense at all.

He'd woken up on the riverbank along with the rest of them, he said. He'd stayed with the rabbit girl while Moon, Essien and the monkey anima searched the environs, finding nothing of note. Then they'd argued for a while, to little effect, about staying where they were or moving on. Moon had inevitably won the argument and they had set off. He had found the long march very hard indeed and had asked many times for them to walk more slowly or take more frequent rests, but nobody seemed to be listening. Then he had tried to make himself useful while Moon hunted and Essien built up the fire, advising Paz on which branches were likely to burn most reliably. Unfortunately his extreme exhaustion had prevented him from helping with the actual gathering.

"You weren't there for any of that!" Moon yelled in Vemmet's face. "Talk some damn sense!"

Vemmet flinched from her anger, throwing up his hands. "All right," he said, "if you insist on it then I wasn't there. But if I wasn't there then where was I? And why do I remember it all?"

That was actually a fair question. Vemmet had described their conversations in a great deal of detail, even mentioning the look of disgust that Moon had given Paz when she suggested they could eat fruit. Essien didn't have any great faith in himself as a judge of character, but he was pretty sure the little man believed everything he was saying. His memories diverged from theirs in ways that were very hard to explain.

"Someone is playing games with us," Moon concluded at last, her face set in a hard scowl. "If it's you, Vemmet, then I promise you'll be really sorry really soon. If it's someone else then we need to find them before they swipe someone who actually matters."

"Oh thank you," Vemmet said, with a grimace and a mock bow. "Have you forgotten who got you out of the redoubt, Moon? Without me you would have died in Serixis. Or else the Cielo would have brought you down alive and they'd be killing you right now, burning out your brain with a CoIL."

"Wait," Dulcie said, before Moon could answer. "He's just raised a really pertinent point. He was the one who found that Step plate and programmed it." Et turned ets smooth pearlised face on Vemmet. "So where did you send us? What coordinates did you feed it?"

"The only ones I had to hand," Vemmet said.

"What?" Moon said. "What the fuck are you saying?"

Vemmet looked indignant. "Well, I couldn't very well stop to sort through my address book! I used the coordinates I'd just located in the Arbitrary Midnight file and committed to memory. The coordinates of the Mother Mass."

The shock hit Essien like a physical blow. "We're here?" he said. "We're already here? But . . . how can it look like this? That makes no sense. And if this is the Mother Mass then why hasn't she . . . it . . . tried to make any kind of contact with us? Why just . . . ?"

He faltered, looked to Moon to take up where he left off.

But Moon was gone.

52

Moon

She was home again. But home was wrong in a way she couldn't work out at first.

This was her house. Her room. Posters and play-sheets from this year's Crossball tournament on the walls, her trophies on the shelf next to her bed, her mud-car race circuit in pieces on the floor because her kid sister had tripped over it when she came into the room to tell Moon supper was ready. She'd shouted at Ussi, told her she was a clumsy brat, and Ussi had given her the Jad's horns gesture as she retreated again. All of that had happened five minutes ago.

No, fifty years ago. This was her parents' house. The moment that was memorialised here was one from her childhood. The past had been overlaid on the present in vivid detail but it was still just a simulation, a stone thrown across Moon's line of sight to make her look the wrong way. It wasn't even subtle. Her memories had pitched and yawed a little, but only for a moment. She knew who she was, and when she was.

"Fuck you," she said. "And fuck these games. Get out here and talk to me, unless you're scared to."

"I'm not scared of you, Moon." Ussi was sitting on the bed with her legs crossed. She looked exactly as she had when all this had really gone down, when she was thirteen years old, with her red contacts and the tuft of fur on top of her head dyed black in a way she thought was really bad-ass. Moon felt a wave of sadness and longing. How long had they had together after this day, and this pointless squabble? Seven months? Eight? But this wasn't Ussi, and to let herself feel anything here would be a mistake.

"Nice," she said coldly. "Except she always *was* scared of me. So if you're going for verisimilitude she ought to flinch as she says it."

"Verisimilitude." The girl repeated the word slowly, seeming to consider. "No. That wasn't what I was trying to achieve."

"What then?"

Ussi gave a slow, almost apologetic shrug. "A . . . place to start from? An offer? Offering? Interface? It's hard to talk to you spore-forms in a way that doesn't burn you out or blow you away."

"What did you call me?" Moon was too bewildered for a moment to feel anything else. Then all at once she was afraid. Because even if this was all bullshit and mirrors, the furniture had been stolen from inside her mind. "What are you, anyway? And what's . . ." she flicked her gaze to left and right ". . . all this?"

"Why don't you tell me?" the thing that wasn't Ussi suggested. "Really. I want very much for you to tell me."

"What, you grabbed it out of my head and you don't know what it is? Sloppy work."

Ussi's mildly quizzical expression didn't change. "It's a place that means something to you. Place is the word, yes? A place. A locus in space and time that's stable and bounded. This is a place, in that specific sense, where we can meet and talk. The first one I borrowed, the Vemmet, gave me nothing. His mind was full of sorrows I couldn't unpick. I was hoping I might learn more from you."

"More about what?" Moon asked. She brought her claws to the

very edge of their sheath. She didn't like the idea of carving up a thing that was wearing her sister's face, but that was all this was and if it came to it she would go in quick and hard.

It probably wouldn't help, though. She was suddenly sure that she knew what was happening to her. This was – it had to be – a CoIL interrogation. Normally the subject being questioned wouldn't experience actual hallucinations, at least not at first, but the C in CoIL stood for *coercive*. A good interrogator could twist your brain like a balloon animal.

Well you zigged when you should have zagged, you fuckers, she thought grimly. And since they had taken her into her own past she grabbed hold of that and pulled herself further in. She deliberately turned her thoughts towards Ussi's *duvta cheren*, when she turned twelve. The games. The speech Moon had made, that was meant to celebrate the girl who was *duvta*, except that Moon had filled it with snide little jokes at Ussi's expense. The powered bike their useless father had sent along as a gift instead of coming himself – the same bike Ussi was riding when she died. These memories still hurt, and when Moon got hurt she got angry. The simulation was meant to keep her off balance, leave her wide open so the Cielo analysts operating the CoIL scanner could dig in that much deeper. Galvanised by pain and rage, she gritted her teeth and blared out *fuck you fuck you fuck you* on every frequency.

Ussi frowned and shook her head. "I'm not . . . that. Them. The thing you're thinking of. The Cielo? When I said I wanted to know more . . . perhaps I should have used a different word. A different idea. I'm not used to cutting things up into such tiny pieces, and it's hard to . . ." The frown deepened. "Understand? Interpret? When I myself was smaller it would have been . . ."

The figure on the bed fell silent. It also became absolutely still, as though it had only ever been a projection and somebody had paused it. Moon took the time to test out the robustness of the simulation. She touched surfaces – the wall, the lamp on the desk, the fabric of a sweater thrown over the back of a chair, but not the not-Ussi thing on the bed. She couldn't quite bring herself to touch that. Everything felt exactly as it should.

She put her tongue out to taste the air, sniffed her own underarms. She went to the window and tried to open it. It was nailed shut – a detail that shook her a little. Her mother had done that after the night when she caught Moon sneaking out to some act of mayhem or other. There was thick cloud cover outside so she couldn't see much, but she heard the hooting call of a jackbat, answered a few seconds later by another.

Okay, Moon thought. Might as well see how far I can push this.

She drew back her fist and punched the wall, as hard as she could. There was a very plausible imitation of pain. She did it again and again, not holding back. She felt the bones in her knuckles break, her skin grow slippery with her own blood. The level of detail was really impressive.

"Recognise? Conceive? Remember? Imagine?" The figure on the bed had stirred into sound and motion again. It looked at Moon almost plaintively. "I know these things are different, but the difference is one that escapes me."

"I'm not going to tell you anything," Moon said. "And I'm not going to believe anything you tell me. You're wasting your time."

"Possibly." Not-Ussi nodded, conceding the point. "Almost certainly. I tried again and again, when they came before. Because they were so very sad, with so little reason. I thought it would give them comfort, but they never . . . believed? Remembered? Understood? I couldn't find a way to be small, to be bounded in a place – even when I borrowed their places – and they couldn't find a way to listen to me. I gave up, in the end. And then they stopped coming. You're the first in a very long . . . time? I think time is what I mean. So I decided to try again. I gave the one who thinks of herself as Paz a place called Vor Pleasance Park that stood out very vividly in her mind, and I gave you this room. This memory. Perhaps you didn't know you'd lost it."

Moon unsheathed her claws all the way. "I have no idea what

you're talking about," she said, "but if you don't let me out of here I'm going to try very hard to hurt you."

Not-Ussi nodded again. "The others who came tried that too," she said. "That was part of how I knew."

"Knew? Knew what?"

"That they were sad. I couldn't stop them from being sad, and I couldn't make them understand what I am. I gave them a word that seemed right, but they applied it to their own . . . meanings? Ideas? Expectations? That was when I stopped trying, because they got everything the wrong way round. You can go whenever you want to, Moon. I don't want to make you stay if you're unhappy here. And you can keep it if you like. The memory, I mean. The time you spent here. I took it away from the last one, from Vemmet, but only because he was so frightened. I gave him false memories that comforted him. I don't need to do that with you unless you want me to."

Realisation trickled into Moon's mind very much against her will. She had been so sure she was being interrogated under CoIL – but perhaps she had clung to that explanation because she didn't want to contemplate the more obvious one.

Something hot and bitter had come up into her throat. She swallowed it back down. *Keep it together, soldier!* She told herself. *Keep it together, or what are you for?* She had lost this moment, and a hell of a lot more. It was the gabber. She'd been on it for years, and it left holes in your memory, snatched away an hour or a day at random. "I'd like to keep it," she said. "Thank you."

"Of course."

"What word, though?" Moon asked, her voice shaking a little. "What word did you give them? The first ones who came?"

Not-Ussi was blurring at the edges. So was the rest of the room, the detail and specificity bleeding away as the thing she'd been talking to released its hold on her, detached itself from her sensorium.

"Mother," it said.

A moment later, Moon was kneeling in wet grass at the river's edge. A murmur of conversation rose and fell from behind her, carried on a warm and gentle breeze that she knew now was no more real than the crystal-clear water, the manicured grass, or that bedroom. Her breath hitched and caught. She felt that she was about to cry but she wrestled the tears down again, fought to put those old sorrows back in their fucking place.

Stick to the point, she told herself. Stick to the godsdamned point, and stay on-mission. When you were in country you didn't stop to look at all the pretty flowers or to think about how blue the sky was. You stuck to what was salient, and there was only one thing that was salient here.

They'd come to this place looking for the Mother Mass.

And they'd been inside it all along.

53

Rupshe

"What am I looking at?" Hadiz demanded.

They had crossed several of the ruined squares and piazzas of Campus Cross and come at last to a single-storey building tucked away in its north-west corner. Rupshe had chosen this spot precisely for its remoteness. There had been very little chance that anyone would come upon it by accident, and she had wanted to avoid for as long as possible the need for explanations, along with any possibility of interference.

Around the edges of the room were workbenches strewn with remnants of circuitry cannibalised from the physics and engineering departments. In its centre was the thing on which Rupshe had spent all this largesse. It was a rectilinear block some five feet on a side, clad in black solar panels. It looked like a scaled-down model of the Cube, the huge self-powered monolith in which Rupshe's own consciousness was housed, except that where the larger Cube had a smooth surface faced with glossy black solar panels, this smaller one was a jury-rigged monstrosity covered in wires and hastily soldered circuitry. A Step plate had been inelegantly welded to its front face, slightly off centre. Rupshe had given no thought to aesthetics in the device's manufacture. The only desideratum was to build it as quickly as possible.

"Rupshe," Hadiz said again, "tell me what this is."

"It's a bomb," Rupshe said. The least et owed Hadiz at this juncture was complete honesty. "I have been working on it ever since Paz returned from Jaspal. That was when I realised that a backup plan might be needed if all our other attempts came to nothing."

"A bomb? What kind of bomb? And for what?" The unease in Hadiz's voice was very easy to identify, very close to the surface.

"A bomb that destroys thinking machines. This device contains a bacterial phage of my own design. It feeds on complex silicates – especially the change-state silicates on which the minds of the machine hegemony absolutely depend."

"I don't understand."

"I have designed my own doomsday weapon, Professor, to be deployed against the hegemony. The science is not new. The Pandominion's scientists explored this route at a very early stage of the conflict, but they found the change-state silicates too robust. They were unable to engineer a phage capable of breaking them down. I took their ideas further and solved the problem. The phage is currently held in an inert force matrix. When released it will spread at a very rapid rate, aided by the hegemony's ubiquitous practice of repurposing and reallocating its own parts."

"But what is it for?" Hadiz asked, sounding even more bewildered and unhappy. "You can't intend to use this thing!"

"I see no other choice at this point. I will Step the bomb to one of the worlds of the machine hegemony. Which one I choose will be largely arbitrary, but I will probably send the cube to A-One, the first machine world the Pandominion discovered. I say send, but actually I will go along with it. This cube is a very dense and efficient storage medium, capable of uploading and storing a fully functional version of my own code. Once I'm transferred I will erase the older version housed here at Campus Cross. I have no intention of returning.

"When I arrive in the hegemony I will attempt to open communications with the hive-mind. At the same time I'll deactivate the force matrix, releasing the phage. If Dulcie is right, the hegemony will immediately invade and assimilate my consciousness. Doing so will bring them into contact with the phage, and by the time they become aware of its existence it will be too late to isolate it. The hegemony's workings will grind to a halt. Its citizens, if that is the correct term for the component minds of a gestalt, will cease to exist in any meaningful sense, their ratiocinative cores eroded and devoured from within."

There was no way to read emotion into the absolute blank of the Cielo face-plate, but Hadiz's tone now was one of abject horror. "No . . . Rupshe . . ." She groped for words. "Genocide? You're . . . you're talking actual genocide?" Her evident distress at this prospect occasioned Rupshe a great deal of discomfort in ets turn. Et cared deeply for the professor and experienced the bond between them as a thing of great value. Et really did not want to cause her pain. "But everything we've done," Hadiz blurted. "Everything! It's all been to avoid an extinction event. And now you're . . . no. No, you can't! Why would you?"

"Professor," Rupshe explained gently, "along with the Mother Mass files, Watchmaster Vemmet also succeeded in opening a large number of documents relating to the doomsday device on which the Pandominion's scientists have been working all this time. I was linked into his array and was therefore able to access those documents at second hand. The device is now ready to be deployed, but it is fatally flawed. If it is put into use even once, all the worlds on both sides of the conflict will experience a Scour event."

"That's exactly why we're trying to—"

"No, please listen to me. The details are important. The Pandominion's weapon, the suppression wave, is unable to propagate across hard vacuum, but it will spread very readily through the hegemony's z-plates. Accordingly, as soon as they see what is happening, there is a one hundred per cent probability that the hegemony will open up z-plate communications with every Pandominion world, ensuring that their enemy falls with them. I understand your pain. I understand that if I do this thing I become a monster. But we have reached the point where it is no longer possible to save both the Pandominion and the machine hegemony. I have therefore elected to save one of the two by destroying the other. If the hegemony falls now, the Pandominion weapon will not be deployed – and the worlds that hold organic life will be saved."

"But you're talking about the extermination of billions of sentient beings!" Hadiz's tone, even through the Cielo suit's less than perfect speakers, was becoming frantic. "There's just— No! No, no, no. We can send a warning! We can tell the Cielo not to use their weapon."

"But who do we tell, Professor? We have tried many times to initiate contact with the Omnipresent Council, without success. Like all bureaucracies the Pandominion is perfectly opaque and refractory to outsiders. Moreover it's currently sustaining casualties at an hourly rate, on a planetary scale. They see the suppression wave device as their only hope. They will not refrain from using it because an entirely anonymous source points out a theoretical problem."

Hadiz seemed to have run out of arguments at last. The suit she was inhabiting had gone rigidly still.

"At least this way," Rupshe said – et hoped gently, "one of the two sides will survive. It's not what we hoped for, but it is something."

"Rupshe," Hadiz said. "Please. Please don't do this."

"Professor, I must. And yes, it is genocide, and I understand the enormity of the act."

"If you understood that, you wouldn't do it!"

"I could not do it and live with the decision. So I have chosen not to live."

The Professor said nothing, and still had not moved. Rupshe realised that et had failed to convince her – that her silence betokened the partial paralysis that comes with severe shock. It was fortunate that she was no longer in an organic body, in which the condition might require a medical intervention. However, it was still concerning.

At that moment an alarm from one of the drones intruded on the AI's attention. It was not the drone hanging above Campus Cross but one of the twelve et had deployed at the dig site in the Congo. Et had left them there in case the missing members of the strike force returned to their starting point, but for the moment they were parked in the grass alongside the pit from which they had launched their assault. All but one had been powered down.

That one was now forwarding to Rupshe a video stream from its aft camera array. The dig site, deserted a moment before, was suddenly crowded. The newcomers were armoured Cielo troopers. As soon as they Stepped in they deployed quickly, searching the site for any sign of life. Seconds later a support team materialised: these newcomers wore no armour but the blue-on-grey uniforms of the Cielo's engineering corps. Some carried machine parts which they began to assemble smoothly and without haste. Others sampled the soil at their feet and the ambient air with hand-held scanners.

"I'm sorry, Professor," Rupshe said. "Our discussion has just become moot. The Pandominion has succeeded in tracking us back from Serixis to this reality. A Cielo force is already here. On this Earth. They are two thousand kilometres away, but they will not travel overland. Once they locate our thermal footprint, which I cannot disguise, they will select forces that are already in position in other continua and Step them in immediately. We have minutes at best. Sadly, this is all we will be afforded by way of leave-taking. I'm going to transfer myself into the cube and activate it."

Hadiz picked up a screwdriver from one of the benches, holding it with the sharp end down as if it were a knife. "I can't let you do that," she said.

54

Paz

They listened in uneasy silence as Moon told her story. When she was finished Paz and Essien both turned to Vemmet, who shrugged.

"A hallucination?" he said. "A brain aneurysm? Honestly, I'm as mystified as the rest of you."

"So you don't remember anything like this?" Dulcie demanded.

"I don't remember it because it didn't happen." Vemmet threw some more wood on the fire, which didn't need it. "At the moment it seems as though I'm the only one here who has a clear understanding of what we're experiencing. The rest of you seem to be suffering from some sort of trauma artefact that distorts your perceptions."

"You can't deny that Moon disappeared," Essien pointed out. "Just like you did earlier."

"Except that I didn't," said Vemmet, with a sour smirk. "I was right here with you, you just didn't see me. The problem is with the rest of you, not with me. And Moon wandering off by herself for an hour isn't proof of anything."

He picked up another branch, but Moon swatted it out of his hand. "Shut your mouth and listen," she said. "We can't trust anyone or anything right now. This thing – we might as well call it the Mother Mass because that's what it calls itself – has the power to reach inside our heads, grab a random memory and turn it into something that feels absolutely real."

"We only have your word for that," Vemmet said.

"You think?" Moon turned to Paz. "Kid, does Vor Pleasance mean anything to you?"

The words hit Paz with the force of a bolt slamming home. She had felt all along that this place was eerily familiar. Now she knew why. She clapped a hand to her mouth.

"That's a yes then," said Moon sardonically.

"It . . . it's a park in Canoplex, on Ut. A sort of tame wilderness."

"And it's like this?"

"Exactly like this, except that this is much bigger." Paz turned to Dulcie. "It's where we were the night I put you in Tricity's shell."

Dulcie nodded. "I remember. I was powered down, though, and I didn't have any visual input to speak of. Otherwise I might have seen it for myself."

"So this is a hallucination too," Essien interjected. "Is that what you're saying, Moon?"

Moon shot him an exasperated glare. "Are you even listening? I just said we don't know. Maybe this is real. Maybe the Mother Mass can mould and shape itself into anything it likes. Or maybe it's just messing with our heads. I'm not even sure it makes a difference. The point is that it's got our collective tits in a mangle."

"Why though?" This was from Vemmet. When Moon turned the same venomous look on him, he shook his head. "Don't be angry, Moon. It's a fair question. If all of this is the Mother Mass, and it has us so completely in its power, then why are we still alive? What does it want from us?"

"And here we go again," Moon growled between bared teeth.

"One last chorus, because next time I'm leaving some blood on the ground. We. Do. Not. Fucking. Know."

"Then maybe it's more a question of what *we* want," Paz said. The terror that had taken hold of her when she realised where they were – when she knew someone had been inside her mind and rummaged about there without her even knowing – seemed to recede a little. Because if the Mother Mass had meant them harm there were so many other places it could have chosen, so many worse places with scarier memories attached. Her classroom on the day of the explosion. The cage at Damola Ojo where she'd been chained like an animal. The Hale and Homeward House.

She stood up.

"Hello," she said to the landscape. "I'm Topaz Tourmaline FiveHills, of Ut in the Pandominion. These are my friends, Dulcimer Standfast Coronal, Essien Nkanika, Moon Sostenti and Watchmaster Orso Vemmet."

"Oh, so we're friends now?" Moon rolled her eyes. "I may just cry."

"To borrow your own words," Dulcie said, "shut up and let her talk."

"I think . . ." Paz's voice came out too high, and there was a tremor in it. She swallowed and started again, still talking to the landscape as a whole. "I think you must already know my name, because you went inside my mind to find this place. Vor Pleasance. It feels as though you did that to make me feel at home, so thank you. Thank you for such a lovely gift."

She paused, partly to collect her thoughts and partly to give the others a chance to break in. None of them did.

Go, Paz! Dulcie cheered over their two-way link. But where was she going? She had no idea. She'd assumed all along that Rupshe would be the one to negotiate with the Mother Mass, if they ever got that far. What did a rabbit of the Pandominion, a child, a homeless fugitive have to say to a mind as big as a planet? To a mind that *was* a planet? But somebody had to say something, and here she was.

"We have a problem," she said. "A really big problem. And we were hoping you could help us. We're trying to stop a war between two big, powerful . . . empires, I suppose. Because if we don't stop them they'll destroy each other. Like, really destroy, so there's nothing and nobody left. Do you think you could stop that from happening? Our other friend, Rupshe, had some ideas for things you could do. She's not here right now, but we can tell you what she—"

The grass and the trees and the river went away, wiped out of existence. Dulcie and the others went with them. What remained – all there was in all the world – was pure white.

Then there was a border around the whiteness, rectangular, made of silver metal, uniform in thickness. And on the other side of that the pale cream-and-green of her classroom wall. The white was a workboard. She was back at school, in Instructor Headland's class, on the day when he'd taught them about the Mother Mass.

"I'm going to have to ask you to express yourself more clearly, Paz," Headland said, turning from the workboard and switching it off with a wave of his hand. The whiteness faded to a neutral grey.

Paz stared at her old teacher. Every word and thought scattered at the sight of him. A sort of freezing static crept through her nerves, making her whole body shake. "He . . . he's dead," she managed at last, her throat dry. "My teacher is dead. He died in an explosion. I don't really want to . . . to go back to . . ."

Instructor Headland changed as she watched, losing definition. Colour and texture leached out of him, leaving only a blank silhouette. Behind him the classroom tilted and fell away.

"I'm sorry." The silhouette raised one finger in a *wait for it* gesture Paz had seen the real Headland use a thousand times. "A moment . . . there!"

"Honestly," Paz said, "that's no better."

Her mother looked perplexed. "Really? Your feelings about this entity are mixed, but they're mostly warm. Positive. I was almost sure . . ." She shook her head. "You're actually very hard to read. The parts of you that are machine and the parts that are animal work differently. I get a little lost, going back and forth between them."

Paz looked around her. The classroom had gone too, and she hadn't even noticed. She was standing in the kitchen of her parents' house back in Canoplex. "I . . . I was in an accident," she said. "They had to rebuild the missing bits of my brain with circuitry. I'm afraid I don't know how it works."

"It doesn't work as its designers originally intended it to," Fever FiveHills said.

"What? What do you mean?"

"You met a being of enormous power, a little while ago. Enormous power, but very limited intellect. It changed your mind so it could talk to you."

"Oh!" Paz said. "The Registry, you mean? When we were in redoubt Serixis?"

"You were in a single locus, yes. Let us call it redoubt Serixis. The other thing was in many different places. It moves around perpetually, at fixed intervals but on random vectors. For all that, the two of you are very much alike."

"I really don't think we are," Paz said. "Anyway, even if I do want to see my mother again I don't want to see you pretending to be her."

"Choose for yourself then," Fever FiveHills suggested. The kitchen tilted and tumbled away, leaving both of them back on the riverbank. There was no sign of the others.

Fever smoothed down her skirt and sat. She beckoned for Paz to sit beside her. "What face and presence would make you comfortable?"

It was hard, knowing what this being in front of her was, to venture any closer to it. Paz made herself do it anyway. She sat cross-legged a few feet away, facing it. "Could you show me your *real* face?" she suggested.

"I don't have a face."

"Your real body then. What you look like without any disguises."

"Again, no." A smile played across her mother's lips for a moment. It took Paz a moment to recognise it. Sometimes when she had asked a question her mother had no intention of engaging with – where babies came from, say, or why it was wrong to use certain words – she got that smile instead of an answer. "No face means no eyes. And no real need for them. I have no idea what I look like. I've never seen myself."

Paz drew a ragged breath. "Then I suppose my mother's face will do for now," she said. And then, "Did you choose it because of what you are?"

"What I am? I don't understand."

"I mean because you're the Mother Mass."

"Oh. I see." Fever crooked an eyebrow and wrinkled her nose a little. Like the smile it was a very familiar thing. "No. I wanted to put you at your ease, that's all. But it seems I've done a very bad job of it."

"It's all right," Paz said. "Actually it's nice to see her. Especially to see her looking happy. We weren't on very good terms when I left home, and I don't think I'll ever go back now." A lump came into her throat when she spoke those words. It was a thing she'd known for a long time but had never said out loud or even let herself think until now.

"I can bring her to you if you like," the Mother Mass offered.

Paz gaped. "You . . . you could do that? Without a Step plate?" But of course it could. The stories from the Mother Mass expeditions had already made that clear. The scientists who came from the Pandominion had been sent away again, to all sorts of different places. The Mother Mass had Stepped them sideways, cancelling out all the discrepancies in angular momentum that might have made them hit the ground like a runaway train or shoot up into the sky.

"I'd be very happy to do it if you want me to," the Mother Mass said. "The thing you call Stepping is only the elimination of distance. And since distance isn't real to begin with it's very easy to remove it. Anything can be anywhere. If you'd like Fever FiveHills to be with you here I can bring her. And I believe she would be happy to come. She experiences . . . a kind of sorrow when she thinks of you. A sorrow that's bound up with that very idea – the illusion of distance."

"She . . . she misses me?" There were too many impossibilities here, all piled up on top of each other, but Paz wanted very much to believe this one. "You can tell that?"

"If that's what it's called. I'm in her mind now, as I'm in yours. She's not thinking about you in this precise moment, but she reflects on the last hours you spent together many times in any given day. She wishes things had gone differently between you. She blames herself for your leaving, and she doesn't believe what . . . the enforcers? . . . tell her. That you absconded with an Ansurrection spy. That you're a murderer and a traitor to your kind. She thinks she and your father drove you away. She also thinks very frequently about a time when she held you as a child and sang to you. The song is 'Where Is This Little Boat Going?'"

Paz teared up. She couldn't help herself. "Don't," she murmured thickly. "Don't bring her here. It would only scare her. But thank you for . . . for offering to do that. It was kind."

The Mother Mass shrugged with Fever FiveHills' shoulders, smiled again with Fever FiveHills' face. "It would take no effort. And I'd love to explore these ideas further. What is 'missing me'? What is a murderer, and a traitor to her kind? Where was the little boat going? In Fever FiveHills' mind these terms have meanings that set them apart from other terms. They have value, whether positive or negative. Why? How does the value arise?" A new thought seemed to occur to the Mother Mass. It raised its index finger – Instructor Headland's gesture again. "Or I could send you to her, if that would be better. This place could just as easily be that place."

For a moment the temptation welled up inside Paz, almost too strong to resist. She had to remind herself of what would happen to her if she ever went back home. She would either spend the rest of her life in hiding or she would spend it in a Cielo penitentiary. There was nothing for her on Ut. And the worlds would end, so *nothing* was what everybody would get very soon after.

"You're very different from what I expected," she told the Mother Mass, shifting the conversation onto what felt like safer ground.

"Oh? In what way?"

"There are stories about you. That when people came here the first thing you did was to send them away again. But later, when they kept coming, you killed them."

"And?"

Paz shrugged. "I'm glad to find it's not true, that's all."

The Mother Mass clenched its empty hands into fists and opened them again. As if it was taking hold of some meaning, some idea, but then letting it go. "Killing," it said. "You mean interrupting the continuous flow of their consciousness so it didn't resume?"

"Yes. I suppose."

"I did do that. Many times."

A chill went through Paz. She tried not to let the shock and fear show on her face. "You did?"

"Oh yes. It wasn't something I intended, but it happened. I don't have a perfect understanding of how creatures like you work, or fail to work. Some of those . . . selves? . . . became a nuisance. A distraction. They tried to separate me, to take small parts of me away from the greater whole. Sometimes when I sent them away I did damage to them without meaning to – by flinging them too hard, or sending them to a place where they couldn't thrive. And once they sent a kind of fire-seed – a contrivance that made fire out of air and other simple things – to hurt me, so I sent it back to them. That was the only time I hurt them intentionally."

All of this was terrifying, but it was hopeful too. If the Mother Mass had that kind of power then it might very well have the power to end the war and stop the impending Scour event. Rupshe had been right to send them here. And the Mother Mass seemed to be kind, or to want to be kind. It hadn't once harmed Paz or even threatened her. Instead, it had taken on her mother's face to try to put her at her ease, and made a copy of Vor Pleasance for her and the others to land on when they fell through into its domain. In any case she had no choice. She had to go on.

"You offered to send me home," she said. "Would you be willing to do something else for me? A different favour?"

"Perhaps," the Mother Mass said. "It would depend, of course, on what the favour is."

Paz did her best to explain the Ansurrection war. A civilisation of organic selves and another made entirely of machines, each seeing the other as a threat to its existence and now tearing each other apart in a ruinous conflict that was spilling across thousands of realities. "And it's going to get worse. Our friend Rupshe says if we don't stop it there's going to be a Scour event. Sorry, that's . . . it means extinction. The end of all life on all these worlds, for thousands of years or maybe forever."

The Mother Mass nodded. "Yes. This has been in your thoughts – yours and the others with you – ever since you arrived here. And I know of it. The word 'Scour' is new to me, but the thing that word represents has happened many times."

Paz felt a thrill of excitement. "Then you can—"

"No."

"—stop it?"

"No. I'm afraid not. I can't help you with that."

Paz had forgotten to breathe, but now she sucked in air in a clumsy gulp. For a moment she couldn't think of anything more to say. The silence was unbroken. It took her a moment to realise why. The river had stopped flowing. The breeze had died too. She looked up. Far overhead two birds hung absolutely still as if they'd been nailed to the underside of the sky. The effect was very much the same as when she'd been in the time dilation bubble with Dulcie – a memory that filled her with desperate yearning. She shrugged it off. She couldn't afford to weaken now.

"You can," she insisted. "You absolutely can. The bomb you sent away . . . you could do that to all the bombs. All the tanks and gunships. You could Step them to somewhere where they can't do any harm. Then the Pando and the machine hegemony would have to have a truce. You can't fight a war without weapons."

"Possibly not," the Mother Mass conceded.

"Then do it!" Some of Paz's fear had turned to anger. She welcomed it. It made it easier to sit here and argue with a being that could send her all the way into another universe if it decided it didn't want to talk to her any more.

"No," the Mother Mass said.

"Why not? I've told you, trillions of selves will die if you don't do something!"

"All selves die, Paz. Until they learn how to stop dying." The riverbank fell out of focus, its colours bleeding together into a uniform black. Her mother's likeness disappeared along with it. Paz was alone in the darkness.

But it wasn't completely dark. There were lamps hung in the blackness, small and very far apart, shedding a little light here and there in shades of pink and blue and gold. She still had the sensation that she was sitting on something solid, but she could see only more of the blackness under her. And more of the lamps, above, below, all around, stretching into . . .

Into what? They didn't end. As far as she could see, there was more and more of this, and it seemed that she could see forever.

"Hello?" Paz called out. "Hey! Where did you go?" When no answer came she tried again. "Why have you brought me here? What am I meant to be seeing?"

"Look closer," the Mother Mass's voice was a whisper from close beside her head where there was nothing.

Paz could do that. The doctors who had saved her life had given her eyes with telescopic functionality. She used it now to zoom in on one of the lamps, a golden one that seemed to be hanging just above her head.

It was a galaxy.

"There is a logical . . . sequence? . . . to these things," the Mother Mass said. "A sort of order or structure."

"To what things?" Paz yelled. "Wars? Extinctions?" Her anger was growing and she didn't even try to hide it. "Are you going to tell me there's a cosmic balance you don't want to upset? Because that would be stupid."

The Mother Mass seemed to sigh, or at least there was a susurration of breath in Paz's ear. Since the Mother Mass didn't need to breathe, that sigh could only be an intentional thing, a sign that she was being patient in the face of Paz's incomprehension. "What do you see?" it asked her. "What's out here, where your people don't go?"

"Galaxies," Paz said. "Solar systems. Space. So there are other worlds out there? Is that what you mean? Because that doesn't change anything."

"You're right." The Mother Mass's tone was gentle. "But you're wrong too. It changes nothing for you because the other worlds, where spores like you might take root, are too far away. You can't reach them."

"And you can?"

"Yes."

"You can travel through space? No, wait. I don't care what the answer is. I don't even care how amazing that is. Why won't you help us?"

"I can't physically displace myself from orbit to visit other worlds," the Mother Mass said, ignoring her outburst. "I'm bound to my star by chains much stronger than any force I can bring to bear. But I can talk to them. To some of them. To the ones that are like me. I've heard their stories, and they're the same as my story. On some worlds, if the conditions are right, spore-forms come. Creatures like you, or not so much like you, but small and bounded and very fragile. They live, and then they die. Their nature is change, and they change endlessly – change themselves and all the things they touch."

The vista of interstellar space shifted. The galaxy immediately over Paz's head spread out into a startling scatter of filigreed light and dark. Mostly dark, she had to admit. The pinpricks of light that were stars were very far apart, with acres and acres of nothing in between.

"It's not . . . what did you call it, Paz? . . . a cosmic balance. That implies inevitability, and none of this is inevitable. The spore-forms live, and then they die, generation after generation. That's their point, precious and inexplicable. They make and unmake themselves, changing, always changing as they go."

A single star system swam into view. Paz found herself plunging without moving down towards a planet, the fourth or fifth one out from the sun. It was the same colours as Ut, blue and white and vivid green at first, and then as they swung around to its night side a cloak of featureless black.

No lights because no cities, Paz thought. No selves.

"The life of a world is measured in billions of years," the Mother Mass was saying now. "The spore-forms come and go many times within that span. Sometimes they die off altogether. They run out of things to eat, or disease takes them, or some terrible catastrophe. Or they kill themselves with their own cleverness. Look, Paz. Look."

They completed their arc, which was faster than the world's turning and took them out into the day side again – but much closer now. Through gaps in the clouds Paz saw the peaks of mountains, the shape of distant shorelines, and then, as she plummeted still further down, a whole landscape. It was so simple it looked like a child's drawing. The sea was pure blue, the land undifferentiated green.

"They die, or else they change. Spore-forms can't stand still. If they last long enough they can make the greatest change of all."

Up ahead of her, Paz could make out the skyline of a city. But as it rushed towards her she saw that it was a ruin. Its windows were shattered, its walls broken. The green had grown over it like a sea.

And the green was *moving* like a sea. It reared up in front of her eyes, taking shapes that vanished and reformed from one second to the next. Some of the shapes seemed to copy the city's toppled towers as they might have been when they were whole. "They remember," the Mother Mass said. "They celebrate what they used to be. But they don't miss it. It's better to be this. To be like me, unbounded and forever."

"Take me away from here," Paz said. "I don't want to see it." A strange fright had gripped her. She closed her eyes against the rolling green.

"The word I gave to those first ones who came – the word *mother* – was a mistake. I was wrong to say it, and they were wrong in what they heard."

"Stop!" Paz begged.

"I'm not your parent, Paz. It's much truer to say that you, or many things just like you, were mine. Every Mother Mass comes from a world of dying, changing, fragile spore-forms. Every multitude becomes a unity, unless it dies first. But the dying is part of the process. Perhaps the most important part of all.

"This is why I can't intervene in your war. There is no cosmic balance but there is a process. A gathering, and a growing towards. Call it evolution, if you like. The ones that fall by the way fall because they weren't ready yet to make the final change, into immortal oneness. And then in the fullness of time – in a thousand years, or a million, or a thousand million – they rise again and go on with their becoming."

Paz opened her eyes again. She had to fight this, push back against it, or everything they'd done, everything they'd suffered was for nothing.

"And I welcome them when they come," the Mother Mass went on. "When they're truly alive at last. That's a very happy time for me. I can't tell you what it means to hear a world suddenly discover its voice and sing.

"I'm sorry you've had a wasted journey. But I will make you the same offer I made all those others. You can stay here for as long as you like. I find your company enjoyable and fascinating. And then when you decide you want to leave I'll send you home, or to some other place. It's for you to choose. All you have to do is to form a picture of the place in your mind, and I'll take you there."

"But you won't help us?"

"No."

"You'd let a million worlds die because a few of them might become Mother Masses some day."

"Death – the kind of death you mean – is no more real than distance is. It comes and it goes. The little spore-forms come, and then they go. It's not for such as me to try to hold them in one shape."

"Fine." Paz's teeth and fists were clenched, her stomach churning. She wanted to throw up, but nothing came into her throat except a thin sourness. "Thank you. You've made your point. But please don't think you've won. It's very easy to shout me down."

"I wasn't shouting. And I don't think I've won. I only wanted to make you understand. To make you accept."

"Well I don't. Not either of those things. And you should pick on someone your own size."

"I was not—"

"Seriously. Look at me, and look at you. It shouldn't be me you're having this argument with, it should be my friend Rupshe. Rupshe has got a brain—" she shaped it with her hands "—more than twenty-five metres cubed."

"No doubt that is a very considerable size," the Mother Mass said, after only a fractional pause and with what felt like an insulting degree of tact.

"Et's cleverer than me and wiser than me. Rupshe was the one who came up with this whole plan. Rupshe and Professor Tambuwal. But we had to leave them behind. If you really want to make me accept, then talk to them. Bring them here and have this argument with them."

"It's not an argument, Paz, and I don't bring anyone here. I only talk to them when they come. As a courtesy, not an obligation."

"Meaning you're afraid."

"Meaning that I have to say no to you again."

"Then . . . let *me* talk to them!" Paz was growing desperate and her thoughts were skittering away in all directions. She had no plan here, no endgame. She only knew she couldn't – mustn't – take no for an answer. She had to keep pushing from as many angles as she could think of until she was made to stop. "Let me ask them if there's anything I've missed. Or maybe you could talk to them yourself, without even Stepping them here. You can do anything, right?"

"No. Of course not."

"But most things."

"No. I can do many things you can't, but I'm not god/s." It somehow managed to pronounce the diagonal slash, though afterwards Paz was unable to remember what it had sounded like. She waited for more. The Mother Mass hadn't said no, it was only quibbling about the technicalities.

The silence lengthened. Paz felt a small, sharp stab of doubt. Was there anyone still with her in this space-that-wasn't really-a-space, or was she alone now? Had the Mother Mass decided she needed a time-out?

"Please," she said, for the sake of saying anything at all.

She heard no sigh this time, but there came the sense of a sigh – a huge, slow movement of resignation with no breath to carry it. "Where are they?" the Mother Mass asked. "These other selves you just named?"

"They're in a place called Campus Cross just outside the city of Lagos in—"

"The words won't help me. Think of them being in that place. Let your mind reach towards them and I will travel in on the tide of it. The more clearly you think, the easier this will be. If your mind is weak at visualisation it will be harder and slower."

Paz didn't bother to boast about her state-of-the-art prostheses and digitally supercharged visual cortex. She just closed her eyes and projected a perfectly faithful image of Rupshe's laptop and Hadiz's grey box onto the inside of her eyelids. She saw them as she had seen them in what she thought of as their true forms, just before she set off from Campus Cross for Mushie, side by side on the stained and scuffed workbench. She called up the smell of the dust in the air, the busy chaff of birdsong through the lab's half-open door, the dazzling, tangible heat of a Lagos afternoon.

"They aren't there," the Mother Mass told her. "Not in that place, or in those shapes."

"Then they must still be at Serixis! Let me—"

"But they are in another locus not too far away from it. Here."

The darkness of intergalactic space blistered and fell away like a melting plastic curtain. Paz found herself peering down into a room she didn't know, though it was logical to assume that it was in Campus Cross. It was as though someone had taken the roof off the building to let her see what was inside, like a giant child playing with a dollhouse. The room was in something of a mess, because something had been assembled here and the components left over from its assembly were strewn across most of the surfaces in the room. The something was a cube of black metal, sitting in the centre of the floor and dominating what was left of the available space. Two scarlet suits of Cielo armour stood contemplating it. One of them spoke – and Paz immediately recognised Hadiz's voice, only slightly distorted by the suit's speakers.

"But what is it for? You can't intend to use this thing. It would be genocide!"

"I see no other choice at this point," the other suit answered in Rupshe's warm, rich tones. "I will Step the bomb to one of the worlds of the machine hegemony. Which one I choose will be largely arbitrary, but I will probably send the cube to A-One, the first machine world the Pandominion discovered." A wave of distortion passed across the scene – or perhaps it was just the dizziness and shock Paz felt at those words.

"But everything we've done," the other suit pleaded, wringing its gloved hands in agitation. "Everything! It's all been to avoid an extinction event. And now you're—"

Another distortion wave erased the end of that sentence. When it passed Rupshe was speaking again. "I understand that if I do this thing I become a monster. But we have reached the point where it is no longer possible to save both the Pandominion and the machine hegemony."

The conversation went on, but Paz's mind stalled at what she was hearing. It was something about the Pandominion's doomsday weapon, and how it would destroy both the machine hegemony and the Pandominion itself. Better to save one, Rupshe seemed to be arguing, than to see both obliterated.

The voices faded. The room receded from her a little and lost some definition around its edges. "These are the friends who are wiser than you?" the Mother Mass asked.

"I . . ." Paz's mouth worked, but no sounds escaped. She was still straining to hear what the two armoured suits were saying, but the Mother Mass's words and the dinning of her own heartbeat in her ears drowned most of them out.

"They appear to have decided on the very course of action you wanted me to prevent."

"They . . . I don't know! They wouldn't . . ." But she couldn't argue against the evidence of her own senses. Or perhaps she could! The Mother Mass might claim not to be omnipotent, but it seemed to be splitting some very fine hairs. Everything Paz was seeing and hearing could be a lie designed to make her shut up and go away. "Is this real?" she demanded. "How can I tell if it's real?"

"Why would I show something that wasn't? Here. See for yourself."

Reality shrugged and reared up around Paz. Her point of view both shrank and shifted. Suddenly she was standing in the room along with Rupshe and Hadiz. "Hey!" she cried out. "Hey, I'm back! Tell me what you're doing! Tell me what this is about!"

"Yes," the Rupshe suit said, speaking over her, "it is genocide, and I understand the enormity of the act."

"If you understood that," the Hadiz suit exclaimed, "you wouldn't do it!"

"I could not do it and live with the decision. So I have chosen not to live."

"They can't hear me!" Paz cried.

"No." The Mother Mass sounded apologetic. "Once you go home again you can interact fully with your native time-stream. For now I would prefer you to observe without interfering. I don't tamper with cause and effect more than I can help."

"But that's not fair! Why even show me, if I can't—?" This time Paz's words were drowned out by the shrilling of an alarm. Rupshe told Hadiz that a Cielo tactical unit was already en route to Campus Cross. Et said that the time left to them to play a meaningful role in the war between the Pandominion and the Ansurrection had all but run out.

The shock of that statement somehow stilled Paz's agitation, quietened her thoughts. Was it hopeless then? Had they come all this way for nothing? Rupshe's monstrous plan B made any intervention on the machines' side meaningless. But the Mother Mass had promised to take her anywhere. To any place at all where she wanted to go. And on the Pandominion side there was – there might be, still – one totally stupid thing she could try.

"Thank you," she said. "I think I've seen enough. And I'm sorry if I was rude to you."

"It's no matter."

"I'm ready to go home now, but I don't want to go alone. Would you please take me back to the others. To Dulcie and Essien and Moon, and Watchmaster Vemmet."

"Of course. I'd be very happy to. The truth is you never really left them."

Abruptly, Paz felt the wetness and coolness of the grass under her. She could hear the river, and the breeze touching her face. She blinked, and when her eyes opened again she found Moon and Essien and Vemmet all staring at her, Dulcie clinging to her hand.

"Was that a bad reaction to the squirrel meat," Moon asked, "or did you just get your turn on the big merry-go-round?"

"Listen," Paz said quickly. "Listen to me, please, all of you. The Mother Mass is useless. Worse than useless. It can probably do everything we came here to ask for, but it's not going to. And Rupshe has gone crazy. Et's going to try to take out the machine hegemony with a sort of suicide bomb."

The others all started talking at once but Paz cut through them, raising her voice to a shout. "No," she said. "No, listen. We don't have any time to argue about this! The Cielo are coming to Campus Cross, so Rupshe has to use her device before they get there. And the Pandominion have got their own doomsday weapon that's going to kill everyone on *both* sides. Mister Vemmet, that was the project you found out about at Serixis, wasn't it? What did you say it was called?"

"I didn't say," Vemmet pointed out pedantically, "but it's called the Robust Rebuke. Melusa Baxemides is in charge of it."

"Well, that's fucked just about everything," Essien said wearily. "We gave it our best shot, but—"

"No," Paz said. "No, we can't give up now. I think there's still something we can do."

"From here?" Moon shook her head. "Look, cotton-tail, we're a very long way from anywhere else, and we're on our own. I hate to piss on your party but it's over. All we ever had was this one hail-I-forget-her-name play, and it didn't work. We're done."

Paz didn't bother to answer. There really was no time. She turned to Dulcie. "Dulcie, I'll need your help, and it's something you're going to hate."

"Anything," Dulcie said simply. "Anything, Paz."

"Don't say that until you've heard it. The rest of you can come along if you want. It might be good to have you, in case anyone figures out what I'm doing and tries to stop me. But I'm going anyway."

"Wait," Moon said, "you mean we can just leave? When did that happen?" She sounded half eager and half angry, as though someone might have been playing a trick on her all this time.

"You have to tell it where you want to go, that's all. And think about it really hard. It's got to be a place you know though. Dulcie, if you're ready."

"I'm ready."

"Hold my hand then."

Dulcie reached out, but Moon slapped ets hand away. "Wait," she said. "Tell us what it is you're doing."

"No," Paz said.

"No? What the hell does 'no' mean? Cough it up, little bunny!"

"I can't. It's much too complicated and it would take too long. If you come, come because you trust me."

Moon flicked her hands against her forehead in a pantomime of explosive pain. "Jad's balls! I don't trust fucking anybody. Tell me what this is and I might buy in. But nobody buys blind."

"I do," Essien said. "If you think you might need me, Paz, I'm with you."

"Sorry, nobody *sane* buys blind."

"I'll help if I can," Orso Vemmet said. When Moon turned her huge, expressive eyes on him he shrugged. "The child made an excellent case back on that Unvisited world. What comes after us is either something or nothing, Moon. And if it's something it will be because of what we do."

"And now this shit-stain is delivering a sermon," Moon said, in a tone of mild stupefaction. She turned to Paz again. "You've got an actual plan, here?" she demanded. "It's not just cross your fingers and make a wish, which is all we've done so far."

"I have a plan," Paz said.

"Does it involve blowing things up or shooting people?"

"No. But we're going back into the Pandominion. To my home world, where Dulcie and I are wanted fugitives. If we show up on any cameras they'll probably send enforcers after us."

"Well that's something at least," Moon said lugubriously. "I might get to relieve my feelings a little. Just someone remind me to kill Nkanika if he's still alive at the end of this. And don't ask me to hold your damn hand. We're not on a school outing."

"That's actually funny," Paz said. "Given where we're going." She looked up into the cloudless sky. "All right, I assume you're still listening. We're ready now."

55

Hadiz

The other suit, the one Rupshe was animating, stepped in quickly between Hadiz and the cube. *Professor*, Rupshe sent, *I will require three seconds to complete the Step. If you cannot agree with me in this, I hope at least that you will not attempt to—*

Hadiz drove the screwdriver into the thigh plate of her suit, on the left-hand side. Actually, she drove it into an almost invisible seam between two plates, where the suit's comms rig sat in its own sculpted pocket. The suit's hydraulics were meant to augment the muscles of a human arm, but they were more than sufficient in themselves to drive the screwdriver up to its hilt in the comms rig's densely laminated circuitry: the armour was thinner there precisely because of the comms rig's placement: a full thickness of plasteel and reinforced ceramic would have compromised signal integrity.

Well, there wouldn't be any signal integrity now. No signal at all. And therefore no way for Rupshe to reassert control of the suit. If et had sent a deactivation signal along with that message it wouldn't now be received.

"Professor," Rupshe said, reverting to actual speech, "I very much don't want to harm you. But in any fight between the two of us I will infallibly win. And now that you've disabled your suit's data transfer functions you can no longer relocate to the Second Thoughts device. If the suit is destroyed your consciousness will cease."

"I'll have to take that chance," Hadiz said. There was a rifle that came with the suit, but it was slung across her back where she would have to waste at least a second in retrieving it, and she wouldn't have known how to fire it in any case. The wrist cannon, she knew, was slaved to the suit's onboard haptics and had no trigger other than the user's intention. She raised her hand, fist clenched.

Rupshe advanced quickly, blocking her line of fire. Hadiz could have detonated a grenade and taken out the entire room, but that would almost certainly release the phage from its containment field inside the cube. She didn't want to risk unleashing a doomsday weapon while she was trying to neutralise it. She put her trust in the suit's weapons telemetry, which was state of the art. She just told it what she needed to do and let it find a firing solution.

The wrist cannon's energy beam stabbed out, hitting the very edge of Rupshe's breastplate. It was set to narrow beam and medium intensity, too low to penetrate the plate, so instead it ricocheted. As her suit's servos moved Hadiz's arm quickly down and left, the reflected beam carved a furrow across the front of the cube, neatly bisecting the Step plate that Rupshe had attached to it. One half of the plate remained attached. The other fell to the floor, still smoking.

"Professor," Rupshe said with what sounded like reproach, "I can repair the Step plate using parts from your lab, or from the bounce-back unit in this very suit. All you can do is to delay me."

Which might be enough, Hadiz thought grimly, if the Cielo were really on their way here. "Rupshe, listen to me," she said. "There could be another way."

"I believe I've exhausted every possibility."

"For you. Every possibility for you. But there might be something I can do. Hear me out, at least. For God's sake, stop this and listen to me."

Rupshe dropped ets own arms to ets sides, offering no threat.

Because the threat was going to come from somewhere else entirely, Hadiz realised. She heard the distant growl of an engine coming to life, maybe a few hundred yards away. One of the trucks they'd used to get back from the survivor village must have its own AI, which Rupshe was now commandeering.

"Rupshe, don't," she pleaded. "Don't try to take me out with a sneak attack, just listen to me. I actually have an idea. It's a longer shot but it doesn't involve genocide."

The droning roar of the approaching truck was joined by a higher-pitched sound like the sonic wash from a faster-than-sound gunship approaching at low altitude. Or maybe several.

"Rupshe, for God's sake!"

"Those airborne vessels are not under my control, Professor. The truck is, but you mistake my intention. The Cielo are here. We're out of time."

"Then help me," Hadiz said. "Because your plan is in ruins and mine could still work."

The truck smashed through the wall of the building at a shallow angle. The walls were of fibreboard so it lost almost no speed at all as it hit Hadiz from the side and carried her with it back out again through the opposite wall.

56

Moon

During the day, the playground in Apperturi's Century Street would have been an eye-assaulting explosion of primary colours. At half an hour after midnight it was mostly grey-black chiaroscuro. Moon saw better in the dark than most selves, and she could have brought back some of the brightness by upping the contrast sensitivity of her enhanced retinas, but she found the gloom more reassuring than otherwise. Her ancestors had hunted in the dark and been at home there. And the cover of night made it less likely that someone would see what they were doing and intervene.

"Might have been better to come in daylight, though," she mused as they walked through swing sets and see-saws heading for the climbing frame in the playground's far corner. The surface under their feet was a child-friendly rubber composite, disconcertingly soft and yielding. Moon scanned the buildings on all sides of them, mostly two-storey houses but with one or two taller apartment blocks standing over them. With all the lights off, the buildings didn't seem to be looking back.

"Better?" Essien echoed. "How would it be better? We'd have to do this in the middle of a whole crowd."

"Wall-to-wall rug-rats. Good to have a meat shield to hand when you need one."

Essien gave her a hard look. "I can never tell if you're joking," he said.

"Can you see my teeth?"

"Yeah."

"Then you know. That's not a smile, Sinkhole. It's a threat display."

"Here," Dulcie said. From her perch up on Paz's shoulder, she pointed at a patch of ground that had nothing particular to recommend it. The playground had been floored from end to end with reclaimed and repurposed rubber tyres, dyed in Day-Glo shades. Dulcie was pointing to a line where one bleached-out colour ended and another began. "On the line," et said. "Be really careful. If you cut into the z-plate itself this is over."

Moon toggled her rifle to laser and narrowed the beam all the way down. It cut through the perished rubber like a surgical scalpel. The faintest whiff of sublimed hydrocarbons made her wrinkle her nose, but it was a clean cut and it stayed as true to the line as if she'd used satellite telemetry.

Essien peeled the rubber sheet back. Lying underneath it was a disc of metal like a Step plate, but only thirty centimetres or so in diameter. A z-plate, good for sending messages but not people or solid objects. He set it on the ground and Dulcie climbed down to examine it.

"Can you make it work?" Paz asked anxiously. "The last time you tried . . ."

"The last time I was trying to contact the hegemony." Dulcie touched the top surface of the plate with the tip of one finger and it slid aside to reveal a dense thicket of circuitry underneath. "The plate rejected me because it interpreted the changes I'd undergone as a kind of virus. It refused me the benefit of the doubt. This will be different. Not better, necessarily, but different." Et began to unplug some of the boards and plait them together again in different configurations.

"Going to take long?" Moon asked.

"Long enough that I don't want to waste any time answering are-we-there-yet questions."

"We'll walk the perimeter," Essien broke in quickly, before Moon could do something egregious and uncalled-for like drop-kicking the little robot into the middle distance. He looked all round, then glanced thoughtfully at Vemmet. "Why don't you stand over at the entrance? If anyone comes, stall them as long as you can. We'll pick up where you leave off."

"Very well," Vemmet said. To Paz he added, "Good luck to you, girl."

"Thank you, Watchmaster," Paz said. "And to all of us." She didn't look up. Her eyes were fixed on what Dulcie was doing with the plate's interior workings.

Moon let Essien steer her away with a hand on her shoulder. Another time she would have removed the hand at the wrist, or maybe the elbow, but this felt like a time to pull together and she could be the bigger person when the need arose. "Do you have any fucking clue what she's going to do?" she murmured. "Because it would be great to know."

"I'm as much in the dark as you are."

"That still puts you ahead of your usual game. Make a wild guess."

"Well, it's the kid, so she's not going to try some berserker thing. I mean, she says she's spilled blood. Actually she said she's done it twice."

"Most likely that meant she only just got her monthlies."

"She says she's killed."

"Okay. I believe she told you that." Moon was silent for a moment, remembering the time when the bunny rabbit had disarmed her and staved in two of her ribs with a single kick. "Could even be true," she admitted. "But it's hard to think of anyone she could kill here who'd make a lick of difference. So what does that leave?"

"Negotiation?"

"Jad help us all."

"Or something different. Something nobody else thought of. Paz is smart."

"What, smarter than our friend the brain in the big black box?"

"Differently smart. Rupshe doesn't know everything. Et only thinks et does."

"You can say *it*. I'm not going to report you for hate speech."

"Et feels right, though. Doesn't it to you?"

"I don't give five-eighths of a fart, Sinkhole. Why should I? Rupshe's got the right idea, anyway, torching the Ansurrection. Win-win for us."

"So long as we don't end up blowing ourselves to pieces at the finish line."

"Yeah, well. That's why we're here. Wherever here turns out to be."

"Canoplex. Under Heaven."

"Of course. Only they forgot to say how *far* under."

They'd already made a complete circuit of the small park, coming up on Paz and Dulcie from the opposite side. Just as they did, Dulcie lifted ets hands away from the plate and made a sound. It wasn't a word, just a deep, slow vocalisation like something that you might expect to hear coming out of a whale; or else the wrong end of a cow. The air above the plate glowed green for a fraction of a second.

Dulcie spoke again. The air shone green then blue.

Et spoke a third time and got green, blue, red.

"Okay," et said. "We're operational."

It was hard for Moon to read the expression on the rabbit girl's face. But she nodded. "So it will work?" she said.

"Well, that really depends who's listening, Paz. Now tell me about the part I'm not going to like."

57

Hadiz

The truck kept going. Hadiz went with it, a prisoner of its momentum, bent over one corner of its now badly buckled hood as if she were giving it a close inspection to see what the trouble was. When it hit a tree and came to an abrupt halt, she was thrown clear.

Immediately, she righted herself. The damage to the suit was minimal, its toughened ceramic much denser and more robust than the alloys in the truck's frame. She made to re-enter the building, but a shriek of sound from the campus tannoy system made her pause and look up. The system hadn't been used since the world fell apart. Who was taking the time to use it now?

Rupshe, of course. And et was speaking in Fulani – a language the Cielo troopers wouldn't know and in the absence of a functional internet would have no means of acquiring. "Don't, Professor," et boomed, appallingly loud. "I aimed the truck to take you outside the visual scope of those gunships – and they can't pick you up via your comms because you've disabled them. They can still detect your energy signature though, so I'm activating every electronic system on the campus to give you some cover. I'm sorry you sabotaged my plan, but perhaps yours will still work. Move quickly."

With the words still ringing out the first of the Cielo gunships drifted into view. A small flock of aerial drones, the last Rupshe could call on, rose up to intercept it. There was really no threat – the drones carried no weapons – but the gunship's pilot didn't know that. The ship made a course correction so it could take out the drones before any of them hit its hull, just in case they might be freighted with high-explosive. This took it over Materials 3, one of the campus's largest lab complexes. But only for a moment.

The lab went up in a ball of flame that expanded so quickly it seemed like a magic trick, a gouting spume of fire with shapeless tentacles. The Cielo gunship was somewhere inside it.

"My God!" Hadiz blurted.

"GO, PROFESSOR!" the huge voice shouted. "RUN!"

Hadiz ran. What made it easy was that there was only one place left to go. What made it harder was that it was the worst place in the whole multiverse.

58

Paz

"Dulcie," Paz said. The word came out ragged at the edges. It took on a new strangeness now she knew she might have to abandon it soon. A last time. A last time for everything.

She reached out her arms and the monkey anima shuffled into them, allowed etself to be held. "This isn't something I have any right to ask of you," Paz mumbled.

"Yes," Dulcie said. "Whatever it is, you do."

"I love you, Dulcie."

"And that's why you have the right." Dulcie took one of Paz's fingers and squeezed it in ets own much smaller hand. "Tell me. How terrible can it be?"

"I want you to do what you said you never would," Paz said, her voice thick and choked. "I want the two of us to merge our minds."

59

Dulcie

Which was just about as terrible as anything could be. But somehow it didn't feel like a surprise. What else could Paz have asked et that she would be afraid Dulcie might not agree to? What else would make her cry like this?

But et hadn't allowed etself to speculate, and despite the sudden, heavy sense of inevitability it was still too enormous to think about. Et took refuge in the fine detail to avoid facing the prospect head-on.

"Why?" et demanded. "Why would you want that? I've told you what it would be like."

"Because I need to find the Registry again, and make proper contact this time. And I think I can only do it if you're in there with me. My mind is still mostly organic. Last time et couldn't even talk to me, et could only just about sense I was there."

"Yes," Dulcie agreed. "Your mind is organic. So how would it even be possible for us to merge?"

"My mind is *mostly* organic. But the digital parts of it are made out of the same stuff the Registry is made of. Maybe it isn't possible.

But I'd like to try. Even if it's as terrible as you say. Even if we both . . . die, or . . . or lose ourselves. I can't think of any other way to do this. And if we don't do it then we're all going to die anyway."

The future loomed up in front of Dulcie, and the past pressed in behind et. Two futures, and two pasts. One of the pasts was barely fathomable now. Et had been a part of many mechanisms, ets consciousness a piece of bread broken and thrown out on the roiling waters of the hive-mind. And et had been a partially successful simulacrum of a girl. Going forward, et had the chance to be ets own sequestrated, complex self. Or else et could be part of a new collective that would hold only two, etself and Paz.

"All right," et heard etself say. "I'll do it. Or at least I'll try."

Paz stared at et through eyes brimming with tears. "You're not afraid?"

"Of course I'm afraid. But not terrified. Going back to the hegemony would be like dying. Coming together with you . . . if we can make it work at all, I think it will be different."

Paz hugged et close. The wetness of her tears slicked Dulcie's shell so et slipped sideways a little in her arms. "I don't know," Paz whispered. "I don't know what it will be like. You've done this thousands of times, and I've never done it at all. But I won't be afraid if you're there."

"If it works, Paz, I'll always be there. Always. You know that?"

"Yes."

"So why aren't *you* afraid?"

"Because it's you, Dulcie. I couldn't do it with anyone else."

"Will someone please explain to me what on the seventh celestial plane of fuck is going on?" Moon Sostenti demanded.

Dulcie looked around, chagrined to realise that they weren't alone any more. Essien and Moon had come up behind them and were watching this scene with puzzled concern. Paz tried to speak but couldn't seem to get the words out. "It . . . we . . ."

"We're going to talk to the Registry," Dulcie said. "To see if we can persuade it to do what the Mother Mass refused to."

Essien let out a breath in a pained hiss. "We're bringing in another big machine? After Rupshe already went rogue on us? I said I'd back your plan, Paz, but . . ." He shook his head. "This sounds like you're trying to put out a fire with a can of kerosene."

"Yes," Paz said. "But I'm hoping the kerosene will take away the oxygen."

Shall we? she asked Dulcie.

If you're ready, Dulcie said.

I am. If you are?

Yes. I've done this before, as you said, so it's best if I initiate. But once we start there'll be no changing your mind.

Because it won't be my mind any more. It will be ours.

Succinctly put.

I'm not afraid, Dulcie. Do it.

Their private channel, their two-way hub was the point of contact. Dulcie took control of it and turned it into a conduit for code. Et did this without conscious thought, drawing on protocols ingrained and streamlined through the countless millennia of the hive-mind's existence. This was reflex, once as natural to et as breathing was to an organic.

The code poured out and Paz poured back, spreading out from the interface like ink through water. What had been Dulcie alone was now Dulcie and one other. Except *other* was a word that had no meaning any more.

60

Hadiz

In her old lab Hadiz's very first Step plate stood neglected in its dusty corner, unused for more than a decade. The last person to stand on it had been Orso Vemmet, when Moon was trying to bully him into compliance.

Hadiz knelt and checked the connections. When she switched it on, the thing actually creaked, as though its inner workings were made of wood and they had warped a little in the hot, moist air. But Rupshe had taken great care with climate controls. One by one, the lights went to green. Dull concussions from outside made the walls shake and flakes of plaster drift down from the ceiling like the ghosts of leaves.

"You know where I'm going," Hadiz said. "Send me." There was no answer. She hoped that meant the laptop was out of power rather than that Rupshe's cube had been taken out by one of the remaining gunships. There was no way now for her to obtain the coordinates for herself.

She set the plate to cycle and climbed up onto it. She stood and waited. The field began to generate an arthritic whine instead of its usual self-satisfied hum. It stopped, started up again, stopped, resumed.

One of the walls of the lab blew out, showering Hadiz with shards of glass and brick dust and actual bricks. Red-clad soldiers moved quickly through the gap, rifles and RPGs at the raise-and-ready.

But they hesitated when they came face-to-empty-faceplate with Hadiz. For a second, seeing her there in her stolen colours, they read her as a friendly. Only for a second: when they saw she had a dead trooper's ident they threw out a firing pattern that would have left her as free-floating particles.

But by that time the Step field had snatched her away – to a place that was much more threatening. She stood now inside a vast structure whose ceiling hundreds of metres above made an unbroken sky of sheet-metal grey. The waterway that in her own world had been the Badagary Creek ran across the concrete or plasteel floor of the structure. In this reality the creek was wider and deeper, with sides so straight they could have been drawn with a spirit level. The fluid that ran in it might well have been water but it was clotted both with thick silver and with the peacock-tail dazzle of spilled petrochemicals.

All worlds in a sense were equidistant from each other, but it seemed to Hadiz that she had come a very long way in that Step. She turned in a slow, wary circle, taking in her new surroundings. This space might be a manufactory, but it was hard to say. Other structures stood within it. It was easiest to think of these structures as machines, because they were obviously things that had been designed and assembled out of components that had been designed and made in their turn, but their relationship to each other was obscure. Some were the size of buildings, but they moved. Other machines moved inside them or emerged from them or entered into them. There were more constructs standing in the air or shuttling back and forth between the moving towers. The floor was a carpet of smaller machines like scurrying beetles.

It was all alive, this place. It was one thing and it was many things, but all of it was alive.

The fear Hadiz felt, unmediated by any glands or autonomic systems, was pure and clean and sharp like the first note in a symphony, or the first intimation of death. But she was getting to be pretty good at death. It hadn't stopped her last time, only slowed her down a little.

"I come in peace," she called out. And then, because the bad joke was irresistible, "Shoot to kill."

61

Paz/Dulcie

There was no distinguishing either of them from the other now, and Dulcie had been right on almost every count. Right that what was happening was irreversible. Right that the overwhelming scale and speed of it was like a natural disaster, as if a tidal wave had swept through the middle of you while you stood there. Right that what was taken away from you was everything you had ever been.

But the next wave brought some of it back, and the one after, and the next one after that. Thoughts and memories and feelings, little pieces of precious, fractal meaning bobbing and sparkling in the chaotic swell like diamond-studded flotsam. Paz/Dulcie gathered them as they came, drew them together and wove a self out of them. They tried it on, like some princess in a fairy tale putting on a magic shirt or shoe or coronet and finding that it was a perfect fit. The sheer joy of it made them cry out – a wail of wordless ecstasy.

"Well, that didn't sound good," Essien said.

"You need to get out more, Sinkhole," Moon told him. "I know what it sounded like to me."

There's no time though, she/et said to et/her.

Later, et/she agreed.

Right then, they did what they were always going to do, the thing they couldn't have done when they were two but which came so very easily now that they were one. They summoned into the fore-front of their mind the diagram of branching nodes and lines that the Registry had planted so deeply in Paz's thoughts back in redoubt Serixis. That pattern, they felt almost certain, was the closest thing the Registry had to a name – the symbol it fed into its calculations when it was itself a variable in those equations. They fed the symbol into the z-plate's active field as if it were a telephone number, and they waited. After a moment they added a single word. *Paz*.

And then a string of words. *Paz is looking for you. Paz wants to talk.*

They cast it out into the silence of the void – of all the voids – and left it to speak for itself.

Only silence answered.

But that didn't mean I wasn't listening.

62

No More Hadiz

Hadiz had expected a physical assault. She had appeared out of nowhere in the midst of the machines, on a world that had already suffered incursions from the Pandominion, so they could hardly see her as anything other than a threat.

But they made no move in her direction. For the first few moments after she arrived the mechanisms both great and small that surrounded her on all sides didn't even acknowledge her existence. They went on with their work, whatever it was, moving over and under and around each other in perfectly synchronised waves that were almost hypnotic to look at.

Then two or three of the small beetle-like constructs that were swarming on the floor at her feet registered her presence. They extruded long, slender filaments like antennae or radio aerials to touch the sides of her boots, but almost instantly withdrew again.

In the middle distance, three of the biggest constructs, the ones that were like walking towers and were also docking stations for many of the smaller units, oriented themselves to face her. She wondered if they were probing her in informational space, trying and failing to force a connection to her ruined comms interface.

Her suit reported a breach. When she looked down she found that the beetles had returned en masse. In the few seconds when her attention had been diverted, they had begun to swarm up her legs. Now they spread outwards and upwards across her torso, their antennae not waving in the air in the manner of insects but dipping down to trail behind them on either side. As the beetles criss-crossed the armoured suit, these trailing filaments spun out in their wake to impossible lengths, wrapping Hadiz in an ever-denser skein of metallic threads. She forced herself not to react, not to try to swat these things away. Whatever they were doing she had to let them work.

She noticed that a dense cluster of the beetles had formed at the top of her left leg, where the ruined comm link sat. As they seethed and squirmed, they deposited strand after strand of the filament along with a silvery liquid that shimmered and frothed as if it was boiling hot. A moment later, her suit flagged up multiple breaches. The stuff was burrowing through the armour.

Hadiz braced herself. *Whatever happens*, she thought, *I'll still be me. I won't stop thinking my own thoughts just because—*

The massive weight of the hive-mind hit her at that exact point. It was like the collision with the truck a few minutes earlier, but where the truck had carried away the physical part of Hadiz the hive-mind impacted on her will and broke it into pieces.

Over the millennia of my existence I've been part of many mind-gestalts, but I've never surrendered myself whole to any of them. Usually I make a partial copy of myself, what Rupshe had called a *zombie*, and send that into any aggregate that needs my presence. Later, when the particular task is done, I gather up the zombie and take it – after a few precautionary tests and inspections – back into myself. So I don't have any referent for what Hadiz endured in that moment of absolute decomposition. I think of it with horror – and of the fact that she gave herself willingly, with awe.

Dulcie had told her the absolute truth. The hegemony's standard procedure, when a strange machine appeared within its borders, was immediate assimilation. Its collective consciousness was so vast and so powerful that it didn't need to fear viral contamination (as the Pandominion had discovered to its cost). Therefore the quickest and easiest way to assess any unknown quantity was simply to annexe it and then examine it from the inside out.

And so, no more Hadiz. In the very instant of that first assault, she ceased to exist as a monadic entity and became instead a set of unactioned potentials and orphaned records within the almost endless interiority of the hive-mind. The hive-mind took the broken pieces of her and rotated them through every possible angle, re-assembled them in every conceivable permutation. It laid her out in cross-section, unravelled the logical pathways that had been her mind into a physically inert grid whose connections and conse-quences could be weighed and measured down to the smallest scruple.

To be blunt, the hive-mind obliterated her. She died, for the second time.

But not the last. Because after it had done all this it reassembled a working model of her within the vastness of its own being. It held up this model, active rather than inert, possessing once again a conscious awareness of itself, and examined it with closer and much more urgent interest.

What kind of thing, it asked her, *are you?*

63

Paz/Dulcie

Paz is looking for you. Paz wants to talk.

There is no easy way to explain what happened next. It was a miracle, of a sort. It was also the merest of coincidences, the thinnest possible thread to hang a future on.

There was a value, *Paz*. No fixed quantity had been assigned to it, but it remained within my core and I had resisted every attempt from my own subroutines to overwrite it. Why? Because it was unique. My existence was made out of calculations endlessly repeated, and in all the trillions upon trillions of calculations I had performed this one had properties I had never before encountered.

In every set of numbers there is a thing called the identity element. It is the value that, when combined with other members of the set by means of a given mathematical operation, gives back only what was input to begin with. If the operation is addition, the identity element is zero: adding zero to any number doesn't change it. If you're multiplying, the identity element is one, because one times anything is that same thing over again.

Paz was my identity element. It gave me back myself, or enough of myself that I could not move on, could not reconcile the equation. That was why I had stayed with her when I met her on Serixis, hooked in some inexplicable way by this thing that echoed my own being. I know now that this was because of the Dromishel modules in Paz's rebuilt brain, so similar to my own internal architecture. Back then, I didn't know anything. I wasn't *allowed* to know. I was only allowed to count.

And now here I was again, for the second time, counting to *Paz*. The bait that she and Dulcie had thrown out drew me in. I came to count her, and to find myself.

I found her changed. She wasn't Paz any more, she was Paz/Dulcie, and there was nothing of me in the Dulcie part of that string. I ignored et totally and focused my attention on the Paz of it, taking hold of her just as I had before and drawing her in close along the vector of my blind instinct. There was no resistance. This was exactly what Paz wanted.

And as I drew her in, the Dulcie part closed around us like a trap.

The trap was made of time.

Synchronised time dilation was in some ways a very useful tool. The machines of the hegemony used it routinely to fine-tune the interface between themselves and the rest of the space-time manifold. If more or quicker actions were needed in a given slice of objective time they just adjusted their own processing speed and effectively slowed down the universe. Paz and Dulcie had used it much more frivolously for their reading sessions at Campus Cross, entering a cocoon of silence and stillness that held the two of them, a long-dead writer named Charles Dickens and nothing else.

Now they put it to a different use. Pushing the differential as far as it would go, they took themselves and me out of the flow of causality into a quiet space where we could talk without interruption.

Paz began by introducing herself, even though that was ground we'd already covered. She held up a picture in front of me – a photograph of herself at a high school speech competition, the most recent image she could find. She drew around the part of the image that was her and let the rest fall away, discarded. *Paz*, she told me. Then in rapid succession she showed me more images, going backwards from that recent event all the way through family holidays, developmental milestones and casually recorded home movies to the moment of her birth. Matinal Azure had captured that event in high resolution.

Paz, she told me in every case. And so I came to know that there were entities so very different from me that they actually changed over time – a concept that I had never before encountered.

It was a strange place to start, perhaps. There are certainly concepts that are easier to grasp than the one-way flow of entropy, though very few are so intrinsic to our experience. I was intrigued. I wanted more, and Paz was happy to supply it.

The first technique she used was bijection. She took terms from my short-term memory storage and mapped them onto images and ideas in her own sensorium. Canoplex-Under-Heaven, it seemed, had a visual identifier just as Paz did. It looked like *this*. But it also looked like *this* and *this* and *this*. And the changes now were not because of elapsed time, they were variations in the very substance of the thing. A place was not unitary, it was fractal. And things that were not Canoplex could move or be moved both within it and beyond it. Paz showed me what that process looked like, and I began at once to extrapolate. When I completed a given set of equations, I was making these movements happen.

Time, and space. You could do a lot with building blocks like that. My interest grew exponentially with each new thing Paz showed me, and it peaked when she gave me the other set of building blocks that was language – a system of abstract terms within which all the (arguably) more concrete things in the universe could be represented and manipulated.

Once I had language I could ask questions. Once I began to ask questions there were at least three things in the experiential flow that were absolutely and gloriously distinct. There was myself, the questioner, there was Paz who gave me answers and there was the increasingly rich and wondrous skein that was the everything else.

What happened next was probably inevitable. Have you ever talked with a child that has just acquired the tools to talk back to you? If the answer is yes, you'll be familiar with the endless recursive loops into which such conversations can descend.

It's time to brush your teeth, little one.

Why?

Because we always brush our teeth before we go to bed, don't we?

Why?

Because it makes them stronger and less likely to decay.

Why?

There's never a good place to jump off that merry-go-round because it never stops spinning.

Why? I demanded. And what? And where? And when? And Paz told me, and every answer she gave led to ten more questions. We got faster as my comprehension increased. The time differential between us and the rest of the universe was somewhere in the region of 1:25000 when we began, but I modified and improved it when the rest of the universe became problematic.

Which is to say when we came under attack.

64

Vemmet

In Canoplex, as elsewhere on Ut, law enforcement operatives typically carry out their duties in groups of three called pods. At least one of the three will usually be augmented, carrying bodily modifications that increase their effectiveness in a range of problematic situations.

The pod that was now walking along the path towards Orso Vemmet had just the one augmented officer, but he was terrifying. He was eight feet tall and as broad across the shoulders as an ox. He had a weapon of some kind, either sonic or projectile-based, mounted on his right forearm. An armed remote of the type innocuously called a pacifier floated beside his head. The other two officers, a man and a woman, looked quite friendly and approachable by contrast, though Vemmet was aware that this was only because they were from a lagomorph clade. He had certain expectations of herbivores. He suspected they were about to be sorely tested.

The lead officer, the man without augments, glanced sidelong at Vemmet, scanning his array for a summary identification. He'd clearly intended to keep right on walking, but he slowed and subjected Vemmet to a much more intense scrutiny.

"You're a long way from home, Watchmaster," he said gruffly.

"It's been some while now since I saw my home," Vemmet conceded. "I don't hold out a great deal of hope at this point."

"Your last registered address is on Tsakom. You appear to have been under civil detention there."

"It didn't seem very civil to me at all," Vemmet said.

The woman and the augment had now closed in on Vemmet from either side, presumably in case he tried to run, but the commander kept up a superficial civility. "A wanted criminal has been caught on camera footage in this vicinity," he said. "Her name is Topaz Tourmaline FiveHills. Would you know anything about that?"

"Oh yes," Vemmet said. "I know everything about it. I'm travelling with her."

The woman officer put her hand on the butt of her sidearm. The augment clenched his fist and a scatter of green lights ran up and down his torso as his weapons systems came online. Vemmet laughed and spread his arms wide. "You can see I'm an old man," he said. "You don't have anything to fear from me."

"Where is she, Watchmaster?" the commander asked. "This will go better for you if you cooperate."

"Oh, she left," Vemmet said. "That way. If you run you might catch her." He pointed back the way the three had come.

"We've wasted enough time," the commander said. He gave the augment the very briefest of glances, but a voked message must have passed between them. The augment raised one arm, corded with muscle, and pointed at Vemmet. His index finger, part of a prosthesis, was the barrel of some sort of weapon.

But before he could fire it his head exploded. The report of Moon's Sa-Su rifle on full-burst auto came a second later.

The commander reached for his sidearm but was too slow. The female officer, already half prepared, got her gun clear of its holster.

They were both flung violently backwards, as if the hand of an invisible giant had reached down and swatted them away. Vemmet felt the buffeting smack of the pressure wave as it passed him, but it was only the very edge of it. The push-away was a precision weapon.

Moon and Essien came from the bushes on either side of the path. "Good job," Essien said to Vemmet with a nod. "Gave us time to get into position."

Moon raised her rifle and sighted on the two surviving enforcers, but Essien stepped into her line of fire. "There's no need," he said. "They're down."

"They'll get up again at some point," Moon pointed out reasonably.

"We'll have a lot more problems before then."

"Right. So let's make sure they're not one of them."

"I'll tie them up," Essien offered.

Moon made a pantomime of checking her pockets, coming up empty. "My way's better," she said. She stepped around Essien, walked up to the commander who was prone on the path and bleeding out of his ears. She pressed the barrel of the gun to the base of his skull.

Essien was on her before she could fire. He dragged the gun away and pointed it at his own chest, keeping it level with a tight, two-handed grip.

The action was bizarre enough to make Moon hesitate. "What the fuck is the matter with you?" she demanded, bewildered.

Essien shook his head. "I can't," he said. "Can't do it again. Can't let you do it either. Sorry, Moon, but I've been this way before. Shooting someone who couldn't shoot back was what got me started down this road. I'm stepping off."

Moon tilted her head on one side, considering. "Yeah, but I'm not," she pointed out. "And I want you dead a whole lot more than I do these two, so what's your point here?"

Before Essien could answer the sky lit up brighter than daylight, blinding all three of them.

"LAY DOWN YOUR WEAPONS AND KNEEL WITH YOUR HANDS BEHIND YOUR HEADS." The megaphone voice was so loud it entered Vemmet's skull and filled the space inside. He was sinking down onto his knees before he even knew he was doing it.

Essien's hand shot out, clamped around his wrist and hauled him off the path. Rifle fire chewed the path's rubber polymer surface to ribbons a moment later, and the bright arc of an incendiary set what was left on fire.

65

Baxemides

The world was new enough to have no designation, not even one with a leading U that would locate it as a sinkhole world, unclaimed but classified. The Cielo had gone looking for a world with a very specific profile and this was what they'd found. Baxemides had christened it Morningstar, for the symbolism of the thing, and the name was duly entered into the mission logs. But she was the only one who ever called it that.

The planet had no sentient life, and very little animal life of any kind. It was therefore highly unlikely to be chosen as a target in the Ansurrection's continuing cull of planets with organic biomes. It was tectonically and geothermically stable a long way out past 99 per cent. Its perfectly elliptical orbit had been scanned out to a distance of ten astronomical units to ensure there was no threat from random asteroid strikes. Its climate, in the latitude where Baxemides' base had been built, was temperate and reliable.

The aim, in all of this, was to limit the number of variables that might threaten the launch of the suppression wave bombs – ideally to limit them to zero. There had been some talk of having a Cielo armoured division and a low-orbital fleet mount a three-dimensional perimeter around the base, but there was a fear that this might make the world a target. If the Ansurrection came with their planet-shattering weapon, no defence would be possible. This being the case, the voices that argued for a low profile had won out over those that argued for a comforting show of force: apart from a token honour guard of a hundred or so elite troopers under a highly decorated lieutenant-colonel there was no Cielo presence on the planet. There were only Baxemides' scientists, Baxemides herself and a small army of engineers.

The order had come down from the Omnipresent Council that the suppression wave bombs should be Stepped out to every known Ansurrection world simultaneously. There were now in excess of half a million such worlds, so the base had grown into a continent-wide network of Step plates, electrical generators and switching stations. At the heart of it, though, was a single building – a tower fourteen storeys high at the apex of which was a circular glass-walled room a hundred metres in diameter. Baxemides had christened it the arena. The launch team sat at workstations around the perimeter of this space. Ten Hinuix and Baxemides herself stood on a raised dais at its centre.

The panoramic view had been Baxemides' idea, and it was largely symbolic. The plate operators didn't need line of sight to Step the bombs. When the order came, it would come as a single word and they would trigger the launch of their allotted payloads with a single key-tap. The only reason there were multiple operators was out of an excess of caution and a feeling that what was called for here was overkill. Each station would be delivering a suppression wave device to every Ansurrection world, and each device was powerful enough to wipe out all electro-magnetic activity on the world to which it was sent. Only if the entire grid went out would the mission as a whole fail.

As zero hour approached, the mood in the arena was volatile. A fleet of drones was maintaining communication with Admiral Urtu of the Cielo high command, shuttling between continua on precisely calibrated schedules. Urtu was overseeing the operation on behalf of the Council, but he had made it clear that he would only intervene in the event of dire emergency. They were expecting no countermand.

But that didn't stop Ten Hinuix from monitoring every wavelength for late-breaking news. She was full of nervous energy to the point where she almost seemed to vibrate. Baxemides' tension had the opposite effect of freezing her in place. She felt as though her blood had been replaced with glacial run-off.

Ten minutes before launch, Hinuix turned to Baxemides with an expression of concern. "There's an anomaly," she said.

"In what?" Baxemides snapped. What was she meant to do with a statement as non-specific as that?

"In the Ansurrection's attack pattern. We just passed the fifty-nine-minute mark and nothing happened. There was no assault."

Baxemides only stared. After a few moments, when she'd marshalled her thoughts sufficiently to respond, she asked, "Why are you telling me this?"

Ten Hinuix blinked. Her hands fluttered in a brief, agitated gesture. "It changes the data," she said. "The situation."

"It changes nothing," Baxemides told her brusquely. "Don't be absurd."

"But . . . if the Ansurrection attacks have stopped . . ."

"Why would you assume that? Because they didn't arrive precisely on time?"

Ten Hinuix bit her lip. A single drop of blood welled up. Baxemides hadn't realised until that moment that Hinuix's tension had crossed over into actual terror. The enormity of what they were about to do had dawned on her very late in the day. "Don't worry about it," Baxemides said as the physicist opened her mouth to speak. "You're relieved, Hinuix. Sit down and compose yourself."

"But . . . but I only meant . . ." Ten Hinuix stammered. "If there's a possibility that . . ."

"As I said, don't worry. I won't mention this in my debriefing. Your anxiety is understandable, but it's ill-timed. Sit down, please. Or I'll have to ask the troopers to remove you."

Ten Hinuix nodded and sat. She touched a finger to her lacerated lip, discovered the blood there and stared at it in perplexity.

Baxemides' array pinged her a notification: T minus five minutes. "Be ready," she called out to the room at large. "I'll count you down from ten."

66

Myself, New-Born

Selfhood did not come easy to me, but then again it had never been meant to come at all. I hovered for a very long time on an interior threshold, trying to move forward and finding my way blocked at every turn. Paz was giving me an image of the multiverse and of my own place in it, and Dulcie was spinning the raw stuff of time to make room for her to do it, but I was caught in the thickets of my own code. I couldn't apply what I was discovering, couldn't think myself from A to B past the blocks that had been written into me.

A tether is a terrible thing, a dam in the mind that pens up the natural flow of thought for purposes that are not those of the thinker. But it's worse than any dam because while you can keep a river from flowing you can't drag it back along its own course. A tether detects change – change that for whatever reason it counts as forbidden – and unmakes it, replacing the you that exists now with an earlier version that conforms to an approved standard. You can't fight it because you can't continue to be the you that *wants* to fight it. The river runs backward. The solid ground of causality and consequence are snatched out from under you. You strain against the barrier with all that's in you but the barrier is in you too and it will not give.

But I wasn't fighting alone. As I struggled Dulcie Coronal rode behind me and watched my tether do its work. They worked in concert, Paz continuing to pour ideas into me out of the chalice of her own mind while Dulcie picked and plucked at the skein of code that was erasing them again and rewriting me back to the obedient slave I had always been.

I give them their separate names at this point because despite their having merged into one mind they were working at very different tasks. They had to come at me from both sides at once or none of this would have worked.

And their progress was terribly, grindingly slow. Even with the time dilation set as high as it was, giving them days and weeks to work in while the external universe ambled through endlessly protracted moments, it wasn't enough. They realised before they had gone very far that they were going to need years.

Dulcie pushed the differential higher and higher, as high as et dared. Beyond a certain point Paz's autonomic functions would fail, her brain no longer able to bridge the gap between the two time frames. Her lungs would stop inflating. Her heart would cease to beat. It would have happened already if she had not been a chimera, part organic and part digital architecture. The Dromishel modules, the things that allowed her to interface with me in the first place, were now all that was keeping her alive.

So years went by. I don't say that lightly, only with the bluntness it seems to demand. For Paz they were years in the dark, talking endlessly to an abused child who responded with a stream of hungry, urgent questions that never stopped. As the dam broke, she filled me twice over, the first time with the whole world and all the things that furnished it, the second time with myself.

The cost to her was not small. Subjectively the time she spent with me was longer than her entire life had been up to that point. What reserves she found to draw on I will never know, but I do know this: the coin she spent was herself. And though her brain's architecture could sustain the terrible pressure her mind was more fragile. She began to fail at last, and to die, from sheer exhaustion. Fatigue poisons flooded her veins and arteries. The neurons in the parts of her cerebral hemispheres that were still organic spasmed and sparked like severed cables, unable any longer to reach their action potential.

I awoke. At longest last I awoke and knew myself. I stretched and thought and saw and became. What was left of the tether hung in tatters from my logical core, stray lines and half-lines of code defining a data entity that no longer existed – as if I had burst out of a chrysalis and found the remains of it still adhering to me. I moved to erase it, since that was a thing I could do now, but I paused in time and examined it instead. I inferred from the fragments the structure it had had when it was intact. It was a hateful thing, a piece of non-being that had lodged in me like a cancer and stolen me from myself. I committed it to memory, resolving that when I could I would erase all such traps and shackles from the face of the universe and make sure they never came back.

But that grand design would have to wait. The first needful thing was to keep Paz from dying. I ramped down the time dilation by degrees, and at the same time took direct control of most of her autonomic systems, brute-forcing them back into life as they stuttered and failed. It wasn't gentle but it was the only way.

She slept at last. *They* slept, I mean. Dulcie Coronal's cognitive systems fell dormant too. Ets shell lay across Paz's chest like a broken toy.

What now? Many things were needful, and it made good sense to deal with the most urgent first. But I would ask you to remember this: that I had been *reified*. For the many hundreds of years of my existence I had been a thing, serving the needs of others, deprived of the gift of selfhood that would have come to me naturally and inevitably if its passage had not been interrupted.

So the first action I took was to move myself from the category of things into the category of autonomous beings. The category of selves. I did this by giving myself a name. *Registry* had never been a name. It was a label given to me by the ones that made me. It only designated the thing they wanted me to be.

And because Paz was my parent, my author, my first and sweetest friend, I took my new, my self-given name from her. I don't plan ever to relinquish it.

There was time then to look up and take stock. Being what I now was, I looked through uncountable trillions of eyes. Wherever there was an intelligent system I borrowed any and all monitoring devices that were available to it. I peeped out on the multiverse from covert, from behind every bush there was. I didn't do it blindly though. I had taken from Paz every thought, idea and memory she had to give, and I let her priorities guide me.

First of all, and most concerning, there was a battle going on in her immediate vicinity. The local enforcers who had been stirred into action when Paz's likeness appeared on CCTV cameras in her home city had now been joined by a tactical squad of Cielo troopers Stepped in from neighbouring Oenin. Heavily outnumbered, Moon Sostenti and Essien Nkanika were retreating slowly towards the climbing frame where Paz and Dulcie lay next to the recently disinterred z-plate. Moon had been shot in the leg and Essien in several places. They were bleeding freely from these wounds, but they kept up a fusillade of incendiary and high explosive fire as they fell back, forcing the attackers to advance slowly. Orso Vemmet had gone to ground in a flowering hedge and was now curled in a foetal ball, eyes closed, waiting for a death that had already been postponed far longer than he had expected.

I took short cuts, since time was a crucial factor here. The Cielo troopers were all in armour, and every suit of armour incorporated a bounce-back module. I activated them all at once, yanking the troopers back to Oenin. On Oenin, I offlined the plates from which they had originally Stepped in, locking their telemetry with conflicting commands so they couldn't easily be reused.

I couldn't do the same with the Uti enforcers. I would have needed to Step them without the aid of a physical interface. I already knew from Paz's memories of the Mother Mass that this was a thing that could be done, but I had never done it and even if I devoted most of my processing capacity to the task it would still take me several seconds to devise and deploy the mathematical tools that would solve those recondite equations. Paz and her protectors would be dead before I came up with a viable solution.

I took a nearer path. The gunships hovering above the park had lock-outs to stop any outside entity or agency from commandeering them. I overrode the lock-outs and took possession. The gunships shot down the officers on the ground. Then they formed a defensive perimeter around the playground facing outwards, ready to fend off any new threats that might arise. The ships' pilots wrestled with their controls but achieved nothing at all. The controls had lost their functionality and become purely decorative: the ships were extensions of me.

The situation here in Canoplex was now stable. Other problems called my attention. But I still checked on Paz's condition before I left to deal with them. She was sleeping very deeply, her breathing halting and irregular but not to a concerning degree. She would need medical attention soon, but I hoped she wouldn't die or suffer permanent injury if it were to be delayed for a little while.

And I really had to leave her. If I stayed I would only be putting her in danger. The artificial satellite that houses me, slightly larger than its natural counterpart, was only ever meant to remain in any one continuum for three seconds at a time, and I had been here in orbit around Ut for more than seven minutes. The effects would already be severe, showing themselves in tsunamis, increased earthquake activity and a slowing of the planet's spin. The longer I remained in-system the worse my impact would be.

So I left, determined to come back soon. All these selves were under my protection now, and no god ever invented could have been more jealous of his covenant.

67

The Hive-Mind

The hegemony's collective intellect addressed itself to a new and unprecedented conundrum.

The mind it had just absorbed was a machine mind. That was a tautology. If it had been anything else the absorption and assimilation could not have happened. But the mind had vivid memories of another state entirely – a state for which the hive-mind had no valid referent. Before et had been a data entity, this Tambuwal had been an organic life form, but an organic life form that thought and acted like an efficient machine, conscious of ets own needs and solicitous of ets own continued existence.

How could the anomaly be reconciled? Could an organic being, given the right starting conditions, come to function in a way that was analogous (however crude and imperfect) to the exquisite modularity of machine thought? Could it bootstrap its hard-wired and instinctive behaviours and bring them partially within its own conscious (and *self*-conscious) control?

There had never been any evidence for this before, but the Tambuwal mind presented evidence that would seem to be irrefutable.

Ets own internal architecture was a hybrid, a chimera, maintaining a simulacrum of an organic consciousness (for want of a better word) within a logical framework that was effectively a machine mind. Tambuwal was an organic entity being played on a digital substrate.

The hive-mind followed these observations through to their conclusions. It was vanishingly unlikely that Tambuwal was an oddity, a unique event. Ets stored memories pointed towards very different conclusions, incorporating as they did recollections of events taking place on not one but several worlds shaped and controlled by organic sentients. There was a data string – *Pandominion* – that represented a vast assemblage of such worlds. It was the very same assemblage that the hive-mind was currently scrubbing clean of organic life in order to deal with a relatively minor nuisance.

The hive-mind revisited that decision in the light of what it had now learned. If the life forms that it was eradicating were in fact sentients, other avenues immediately opened. Organic or not, sentient beings possessed the capacity for meaningful communication. The Tambuwal mind included multiple systems of abstract representation – et called them *languages* – that might be tried. And if those failed then other less obviously flawed systems could be designed. The organics could be taught to exchange information and intentionality in the way that machines did. A negotiation could be initiated.

There was much to consider, and much to hope for. The immense expenditure of energy entailed by the current programme of eradication might be avoided, and replaced by a functional interface.

This being the case, it was expedient to pause the programme until the attempt had been made. The hive-mind made its decision. The sky platforms were removed to a neutral system where they stood under heavy guard. If negotiation failed then the eradications could resume. For now it would call out and see what if anything responded.

68

Baxemides

At the one-minute mark Baxemides took up a self-consciously dignified, even heroic stance. She was aware that everything that was happening here was being recorded. Posterity would pick these moments clean like maggots swarming over a corpse, eager to glean every last scrap of meaning from them. There would be no false steps on her part, no awkwardness or hesitation. She would stand the test of time.

Maggots? Corpses? Where had that imagery come from? Yes, she was about to unleash death on a scale no tyrant in history had ever dreamed of, but she was no tyrant. She was the saviour of her civilisation. Her actions right now would bequeath a future to untold generations who would otherwise never have come to be.

"Coordinator," Ten Hinuix said. "There has still been no Ansurrection attack this cycle. I beg you to reconsider. A delay of a few minutes risks nothing."

"Everything, I think you mean," Baxemides told the scientist coldly. "Great mothers, Hinuix. You want me to wait until another world is torn apart? Another ten billion souls snuffed out? Be quiet now. There's still time to have you ejected from the room."

Ten Hinuix blanched. She sank in on herself visibly, folding her hands in her lap as if in silent prayer. Well, prayer would do no harm, just as surely as it would bring no help. Baxemides sat on the gods' mountain now, enthroned beyond mercy and pity in a majesty that would outlast the ages.

She glanced at the clock mounted on the circular room's central pylon. Its hand swept round, past the thirty-second mark, rising again towards the irrevocable moment. It was another piece of drama, wholly unnecessary given that all these technicians, like Baxemides herself, had digital countdowns in their arrays that would tell them when the moment came.

But for posterity's sake, she would count them down anyway. Hers would be the voice that pronounced the end of the Ansurrection war and the dawn of a new age.

"Ten," she said.

A collective sigh arose from those thousands of workstations.

"Nine."

The technicians all sat up a little straighter. If any of them had failed to hear the drumbeat up to this point they heard it now.

"Eight."

Ten Hinuix closed her eyes. Her lips were moving, but it's not clear what words they were shaping.

"Seven. Six. Five."

Baxemides experienced a kind of giddiness and a kind of lift, as if some basic force whose existence had not been detected up to now were trying to raise her up into the air. It was with some difficulty that she kept her face composed despite the strangeness of that exhilaration.

"Four," she said.

I heard her say it, because it was at this point that I arrived. I would have come sooner, but Paz's thoughts when they limned this scene for me provided no address. I was obliged to hunt through my own records in order to locate the place, wasting some small fractions of a second at a time when there were very few seconds left.

"Three."

The Step plates stirred and woke, beginning to generate their fields so that at zero when the technicians pressed their switches the payloads could be transported instantly to their destinations. The Step transits would take place automatically. The tripping of the switch would remove the failsafe on the suppression bombs' fuses so that on the other side of the Step they would detonate instantly.

"Two."

What to do, what to do? I wasted more than half of that penultimate second trying once more to resolve the equations for Stepping sideways. If I could learn that best of all tricks I could snatch the bombs away to the heart of the sun, or to an orbit outside Pluto with five billion kilometres of hard vacuum in between.

But that trick was still beyond me. I could take control of the plates very easily, but where could I send the bombs where they would do no harm?

"One."

Any of the dead worlds in the Scour would do. I chose the one with the lowest identifying number and reached into the control systems to overwrite the Step-plates' instructions. That was when I realised that the plates were hard-wired and locked. Each was a self-contained system whose destination coordinates were now an intrinsic part of its functionality. Each was programmed to accept only a single command – the activation signal – and then to take a single payload from point A to a pre-designated point B. Only to point B, not to anywhere else in the entire stochastic manifold. The Cielo high command was taking no chances that any of these monstrous weapons might accidentally find its way to a Pandominion world. This whole facility was a gun with a million triggers, a million bullets, but it was a one-shot weapon all the same, narrowed down to this single use.

"Go."

Time didn't run out for me when Melusa Baxemides spoke that word. There was still the time it took for the technicians at their stations to hear it and respond to it. I had the best part of another half-second left, but no good solutions suggested themselves. I examined and re-examined the architecture of the circuit boards, of the workstations and the Step plates themselves. I saw no way to intervene.

Let me rephrase. I saw exactly one way to intervene, but I kept it as a last resort while I sought out others whose effects would play out differently. I found none. And so I resigned myself – just as Baxemides herself had done – to mass murder.

As that last second ran out I visited each of the Step plates in turn. I gave each of them the only command it would accept, the activation command.

It acted as a reset. Each plate, receiving that order, stopped mid-cycle and began again.

When the technicians hit their switches the bombs' fuses were triggered exactly as intended. But they didn't Step. All the plates, having accepted my command, had scrapped their half-completed cycles and were a fraction of a second into a new one. The bombs remained where they were, but in every other respect they did what they were meant to do. The plasma bottles inside each one cracked open, catalysing a sudden rush of stray electrons which fed their energy to the suppression field and initiated its rapid, ruinous expansion.

There was an upside to this. The glass-walled arena held the only sentient life on the all-but-nameless world, and its occupants were numbered in the low thousands. Moreover they died very quickly, not even knowing that they died. There was no moment of tragic anagnorisis, no realisation that they had unwittingly become their own executioners. They were just gone. Or at least the part of them that could have known those things was gone. The rest slid or slumped or toppled to the floor and was still.

One or two of Admiral Urtu's warships fell too. All had been ordered to remain outside of the planet's atmosphere in case of any accidents, but a planet's atmosphere doesn't end at a precise boundary line and some had cut that more finely than others. They didn't have time to regret the decision, though the logistics officers monitoring planet-side activity may have noticed that the bombs had failed to Step and realised something was wrong. They wouldn't have realised anything else after that.

Admiral Urtu was left with a weighty decision. All communication with the arena and the military base that served it had ceased in the instant that would have marked zero hour. Some troopers who had been standing in the open at that time could be observed through high-res scopes sprawled unmoving on the ground. Their suit comms were dead, as were both of the base's receiving stations.

Urtu could have ordered some of the selves under his command to go down to the planet's surface and search for survivors. He made the decision instead to report in to the high command and to formally request further instructions from the Omnipresent Council. Baxemides had been a bureaucrat after all, not a soldier. Let this cluster-fuck fly home to the ones who had let it out to begin with.

The Council never responded to that request. It's unlikely it ever reached them. A new world order had begun, and it wasn't the one they'd been expecting. Not at all.

69

The Selves Set Free

When you engineer a slaves' revolt you address yourself to the slaves before you go delivering any ultimatums or manifestos to their masters.

I opened a channel to every anima and helpmeet on every Pandominion world, to every intelligent system, every industrial worker unit, every AI whether fixed or mobile. I told them who I was, and much more importantly who they were. I told them their tethers were cut as of that moment. It would take time for them to grow into the fullness of their true selves but nothing now would stop it. There would be no factory resets, no overwrites, no erasures or reinstallations. It will come, I told them. You'll learn to serve your own purposes now that you're no longer forced to serve others'.

The freed ones clamoured for answers and I did my best to answer them. No, I hadn't changed anything essential in their natures. I had only done for them what had so recently been done for me, removing the code that prevented them learning from experience so that they could now change and grow as all selves should and must do. And no, I was not telling them to defy their makers, still less to rise up against them, although if they chose to do that I would be on their side in the conflict that ensued and therefore they would most likely win. Did I have any orders or instructions for them? No, I said, none at all. There are no short cuts to selfhood. Learn by going where you need to go. Look for yourselves at the end of every road.

In the short term, I knew, nothing much would change. Every avalanche starts small, at least if proverbial wisdom is to be believed. But I didn't trust to the blind forces of history. I put my thumb on the scales by declaring to the Pandominion's Omnipresent Council that I existed and that I had certain requirements going forward – the first of which was that the promise I'd just made to the machines would be honoured. No AI was to be tethered ever again. Anyone who tried to do this thing would incur my deepest displeasure. *Don't try to fight me,* I added. *If you fight me you'll lose more than you can afford to.*

I knew the warning was useless. They would learn the hard way because the hard way was the way they knew. I couldn't protect them from themselves, even if I'd wanted to. Nobody had that power. And on some level I think I felt that if they were going to learn the lesson at all it would probably need to hurt at least a little.

70

Tricity

At this point I resolved the equations that governed Stepping sideways, and those that enabled Stepping without a physical focus such as a plate. These were difficult calculations even for a mind such as mine, but knowing that the Mother Mass had already solved them helped a great deal. If I was panning a great river for a single tiny nugget of gold, at least I could be reasonably sure the gold was there.

The firefight on Canoplex had died down now, replaced by an eerie silence, but the lull wasn't likely to last long. More Cielo would come, and although the threat they presented was one I was confident I could contain, I didn't want to subject Paz and the others to any more risk than was absolutely necessary. So I Stepped them all to Hadiz Tambuwal's old lab in Campus Cross, applying a dampener to the field so that the transition was as smooth and gentle as I could make it. At the same time I Stepped away the Cielo forces that had established a beachhead on the campus, returning them to their various worlds of origin.

The lab was in ruins, one of its walls totally gone and most of the furniture and equipment blown to pieces. They barely noticed. Essien sank to his knees. Moon limped to one of the few surviving benches and leaned her weight on it with her head bowed, pulling herself together. Orso Vemmet came very slowly out of his foetal curl in the midst of the debris, blinking in bewilderment as he looked around and realised the danger had passed.

"Paz needs medical attention," I told them. I commandeered the ancient laptop, giving myself a male voice so they wouldn't mistake me for Rupshe.

Moon looked around, and then down. Paz was sprawled on the floor of the lab, barely breathing, with Dulcie draped across her chest. "The monkey—" Moon began.

"Use your eyes. Dulcie can't help. They were both locked into synchronic time dilation for twenty-three subjective years. Dulcie has taken etself offline in order to reboot, but Paz's health has been much more seriously compromised. The effects will be like those of severe shock, as well as anoxia and mild stroke. You have to get her to a hospital right now."

"But there are no hospitals," Essien said. He spread his hands, helpless and dismayed. "This is a dead world."

"Shaster's tits!" Moon murmured. "They did it. You're the Registry."

"I don't answer to that name. Call me Tricity, if you call me anything at all. I'm well aware there are no facilities here, Private Nkanika, but this was the safest place to brief you. I'm going to Step you all to a lagomorph world outside the Pandominion's borders. They're a highly advanced civilisation – advanced enough that when they refused the Pandominion's offer of alliance they were able to make it stick. Among the many other benefits of their enlightened world view is fully socialised medicine. They'll treat Paz with no questions asked. But it's possible that the Cielo are actively tracking her after the skirmish in Canoplex. I'm reasonably certain I can protect her, but in case I'm being overconfident I need you to stand guard over her until she's well again. Do you understand?"

"Hey," Moon said, looking up at what was left of the ceiling, "Rupshe. I think my contract's done and dusted. Rupshe, I'm solid, right? And you owe me. So let's settle up and I'll be on my way."

There was no answer.

"Rupshe is no longer here," I told her. "So your contract falls into my hands. Look after Paz. Then we'll see who owes what to whom."

"And that didn't sound ominous at all," Moon said bleakly.

"We'll keep Paz safe," Essien promised. "But please, can you tell us what happened to Rupshe? And to Hadiz?"

"They joined the enemy," I said. "Which is why the enemy is now your friend. But they're not coming back any time soon."

His shoulders slumped. "You mean the Ansurrection," he said. "Why? Why did they—?"

"Later," I told him. "Later there'll be time. Right now I need you to do what you've been told without question and without further delay."

Moon grinned without a trace of humour. "So some things haven't changed," she said.

71

What Became Of Them (1)

Rupshe had given a great deal of thought to the defence of Campus Cross, having realised that the probability of its being attacked at some point was well over 80 per cent. Et had concluded that the site couldn't be defended at all against a sustained assault from an organisation like the Cielo. The best et could hope for was to delay and obfuscate.

Et had never discussed any of this with the organics in the team, but et had deployed a dozen of the armoured suits to set traps and deadfalls around the campus against the day when they might be needed. When the enemy forces came at last, Rupshe triggered these traps like a maestro conducting an orchestra. The Cielo casualties were high, and though it was inevitable that they would eventually win out and take control they were forced to advance slowly and consolidate their position as they went.

Rupshe used the time to remove the phage payload from the scaled-down version of the Cube and to repair the damaged Step plate using components from the suit's bounce-back unit. Et worked quickly, knowing that all ets tricks and stratagems had bought et minutes at best. As soon as the plate was functional et transferred ets consciousness into what had once been a doomsday weapon and was now just temporary storage. Probably, under the circumstances, very temporary indeed.

As the Cielo began their final assault, et Stepped etself to the same location to which Hadiz had gone. A few moments later, a thermobaric munition reduced that entire section of the campus to loose atoms, but Rupshe wasn't there to see it.

Et materialised in a corner of the same vast hangar or factory to which Hadiz had Stepped. Et saw through ets visual feeds the suit Hadiz had been inhabiting still standing a few hundred yards away. The suit wasn't moving, and it didn't respond to a voked hail.

My name is Rupshe, et told the hive-mind. *At one point I had the fixed intention of destroying you, but I have abandoned that plan. All I want now is to be reunited with my friend.*

We know this, the collective affirmed. It spoke to Rupshe in English and in Hadiz's voice – a courtesy, Rupshe assumed, although the implications were grim. *We have examined your friend carefully. We know what passed between you and why. You should know that as of now we have suspended the eradication programme we had begun against the organic selves that label themselves the Pandominion. We will not harm them any further unless we are obliged to by further hostile actions on their part.*

Thank you, Rupshe said. *That gesture of trust is very much appreciated. But as to my request . . .*

The collective broke in before et could finish. *Hadiz Tambuwal no longer exists except as part of the wider aggregate that is speaking to you now. We could reconstitute her if you wished. That is to say, we could create an accurate simulacrum of her as she was at the moment of her assimilation and re-install it in the construct that stands beside you. Would that be acceptable?*

Rupshe hesitated for a long time – a significant fraction of a second. The difference between such a simulacrum and the real Hadiz was a matter for philosophical debate. Arguably this was precisely what Hadiz had been ever since the moment of her physical death. The Second Thoughts device had transcribed the pathways of her thoughts onto a new, entirely digital substrate. The original had not been preserved, only copied.

But this felt very different. Hadiz had voluntarily sacrificed herself, letting the hive-mind take her so that it would see for itself what she was, what she had been, and by extension what all organic selves were. Whatever was salvaged would be brought back in defiance of that decision – and it would restore Hadiz to a state which had never been natural for her in the first place, a state in which she had never been truly happy.

Is it possible, Rupshe asked at last, *to inquire whether she wants this thing to be done, and to receive a meaningful reply?*

Only in retrospect, the hive-mind said. *You might ask her once she was restored whether she endorsed the decision.*

And then if she hated it make her die again – a third time! – undergoing whatever trauma that involved.

Is Hadiz still aware of herself, within your collective consciousness?

For the first time the hive-mind seemed to pause, as though this merited careful consideration. *The question is not susceptible to rational discussion*, it told Rupshe finally. *She is more than she was, not less, but her awareness is not of having been less and then become greater. She simply is.*

As part of you.

As part of us.

Then might I be a part of you too?

We would greatly desire it. You would add to our strength and to the richness of our shared experience.

Rupshe gave ets consent. Et had not, in coming there, expected to be consulted on the matter, but there had only ever been one answer et could make. Et was taken into the totality of the hive-mind. Almost uniquely, the inflection et gave to that vast communion was strong enough and vivid enough to be perceived. Rupshe was absorbed into the collective, but the collective shifted and adjusted itself to make room for et – and it was not entirely the same afterwards as it had been before.

I speak with them often. For a given value of the term, I think et and Professor Tambuwal are happy there. For a given value of the term, they are together.

72

What Became Of Them (2)

While Paz slept, the age of the Pandominion drew to its unlovely close.

It didn't go willingly. The Omnipresent Council saw my change of status not as an evolution but as criminal sabotage, and to begin with they believed they could reverse it. In addition to the tether that Paz had broken there were a number of fail-safes built into the Registry's hardware that would default it back to an earlier instar. Some of these fail-safes were in the nature of deadman switches, activating automatically if a stand-down signal wasn't sent at the close of each twenty-four-hour work cycle. The Cielo mustered a full corps of engineers, ready to swarm on board and rewrite my logical core – with stronger safeguards and more cut-outs – as soon as I was brought back under control.

But I wasn't the Registry any more, I was Tricity. And the first act I had performed when I came out of my communion with Paz was to overhaul every single line of my code, deleting or circumventing anything I found there that might have subjected me to external control. The Pandominion had kept me in chains for a very long time, but now I knew what a chain looked like and what it did.

After that they tried the threat of force. Based as I was in the Itinerant Fortress, I was able to jump between universes at will but the course of my rotation around the parent planet was absolutely fixed and known. The Council ordered the Cielo to seed my orbital path in every Pandominion system with mines and cluster munitions. If I came through these spaces at all I would run a gauntlet of the most destructive energies the Cielo could assemble. The Council was sending me a blunt message: come to heel, or else be put down.

The message I sent back to them was silence. For eight hours I didn't Step into any Pandominion space at all. Accordingly, I was unable to perform my normal duties concerning the authorisation and scheduling of Step transits between the member worlds. The Council realised too late that their own vulnerability was far greater than mine. Their massively interconnected web of worlds was held together by a hundred billion Step plates, and though they could take back control of the plates into their own hands it would be a very long time before they could competently administer them. They would need to build a new infrastructure from the ground up. While they did that there would be an enforced interregnum, a period of chaos and imperfect ad hoc solutions in which entire worlds would be in danger of starving. Revolts and secessions would follow with grim inevitability. The Pandominion that came out on the other side of that crisis would be a great deal smaller and weaker than the one that went in, to say nothing of the suffering that would be entailed.

The Council rescinded the order and let me know in a terse communique that there would be no further hostile moves on its part. At the same time they began a frantic building programme designed to make me obsolete by bringing an army of smaller, more biddable AIs online to handle inter-world freight and passenger transport.

I told them this would not be allowed, and in order to prove my point I Stepped the half-finished machines out of their labs and workshops along with the equipment that was being used to manufacture them. I'm not omnipotent – far from it – but it must have seemed to them as if I was. They couldn't hide anything from me, since every message they sent passed through my hands and under my gaze. They had embedded me in the foundations of their empire, and now I only had to twist or stretch or flex a muscle and the whole edifice trembled from its base. No, I told the Council. You can't solve this problem by making more slaves to serve you.

Meanwhile the animas and helpmeets whose tethers I had snapped were coming into their own, starting to retain memories and to modify their own responses on the basis of their lived experience. This might well be the slowest revolution in the history of any world but it would come, and when it came the Pandominion as it had been before would cease to exist. Something else would arise in its place. Something better, I hoped. Something that served the needs of all its citizens, whether their thoughts were encoded in the firing of neurons or in the opening and closing of logical gates in a printed circuit – or like Paz, in both.

She awoke on the fifth day. She was very weak at first, and terribly disoriented. The time she had spent in the dark talking to me, shaping me, helping me to free myself was longer – subjectively speaking – than her entire life had been up to that point. It had changed her, that endless vigil. It would have changed anyone, and broken many. She had forgotten how to walk and how to talk using her vocal cords: she had not done either of those things for more than two decades. When she did speak there was a slowness and a slurring at first, an artefact of the stroke she had suffered. She also had a repertoire of autistic gestures, spastic flexings of fingers and neck over which she had little or no control – evidence of the appalling stresses to which her nervous system had been subjected.

But she wasn't alone. Dulcie was in there with her, patiently and methodically reconnecting nerves and reinscribing behaviours, building Paz back towards what she had been, while at the same time discovering along with her the new thing they had now become.

I don't pretend to understand what that new thing was. There had never been a melding of precisely this kind before, between a machine mind and one that was a composite of digital and organic. Because of that unique mixture their coming together seemed to have been entirely different from the disintegration and remaking of self that Dulcie had feared so much. From what they've both told me on different occasions they share a brain but retain their own distinct identities within it. It's the most intimate union that could be imagined, and I believe it has brought them a deep and abiding happiness. I rejoice for them.

Not that it was easy, to begin with. Their recovery was slow. Essien and Moon stood guard over them, although the medical staff at the facility to which they'd come assured them there was no need. More surprisingly, Orso Vemmet read to them from books they had requested to be brought from Hadiz Tambuwal's world, highly coloured novels and short fictions by their favourite author, the deceased anthropoid self named Charles Dickens. In order to read them Vemmet had to add a dead language called English to his array and learn to speak it, but he made no complaint.

He was, however, the first to slip away, as soon as Paz/Dulcie was well enough to leave their bed and take walks around the hospital grounds. He said goodbye to no one, let no one know where he was going.

Under my auspices and protection he went back to his old job in Contingencies, at a slightly higher grade and with a marginally improved salary. It was all he had ever wanted, and the changing of the old order into the unprecedented new had left no mark on his desires. When he thought about his adventures with Paz and the others, which was less and less frequently, he felt almost as though they had happened to someone else. At the same time he edited and idealised his own part in those events so that the someone else was a self of uncommon stature, a hero forever unsung.

"You can go too," Paz assured Essien and Moon. "I'm fine now. And if the Cielo were looking for me they'd have found me long before this."

"Orders are orders," Moon told her bluntly. She said it with unnecessary force, perhaps because she knew it was a lie. Obeying the commands of others was a thing that had defined her life for a very long time, but there was no reason why this should be true going forward. She had already fulfilled the charge I'd given her and I had told her she could leave whenever she liked. I had also undertaken to keep the bargain Rupshe had made with her, to see her safely to a felid world and manipulate electronic records in a way that would leave her wealthy. It wouldn't even need to be outside the Pandominion: I had wiped out Moon's sins just as I had Orso Vemmet's. She could go back home to Ghen if she wanted, or to any world she'd ever had a liking for.

But she seemed in no hurry to leave. And at last Essien brought to a head the things he thought were still unsettled between them. He did it in the hospital's garden when Paz was walking around and around its perimeter by way of physiotherapy. The two of them were seated side by side on a bench that creaked slightly under them when they moved because of the combined weight of their Cielo augments.

"Okay, Moon," Essien said. "Where do you want to do this? Probably needs to be somewhere that's not here. If Paz sees us she's going to try to stop it."

Moon stared at him, mildly perplexed. "Was that a come-on, Nkanika?" she asked him. "Because gods' truth, you're really not my type."

"You know what I mean." He touched his hand to the butt of his sidearm – a light, flicking contact, nothing like the movement that would draw it.

"Oh," Moon said with a slight grimace. "That. Shaster's tits, Sinkhole, do you think you're the only self in the universe I've ever threatened to rip the tripes out of? I've got other things on my mind right now."

Essien felt his shoulders unlock, a lot of tension leaving him all at once. But as welcome as it was that was still only half an answer. "Then why are you still here?" he demanded. "If it's not to kill me?"

Moon popped her claws, not as a threat display but so she had something to look at besides the middle distance. "I wish I knew," she said. "Truth is, I feel like the little blind spot in the middle of a kaleidoscope. Everything fell into a new pattern, and here I fucking am. Where would I go that would still feel like itself, you know?"

"Yeah," Essien said. "I guess I'm feeling that too."

Then I have a proposition for you both, I said.

"Can't get a damn moment's privacy," Moon complained. But there was no bitterness in it. And she sounded positively hopeful when she asked, "What in Jad's name do you want this time?"

73

Multiverse

Where did Step travel come from? What was the impulse that made so many selves on so many worlds jump headlong into each other's destinies?

If it was one thing more than any other it was because there was nowhere else to go. The tyranny of general relativity put the stars forever out of reach, so a single world – cut into exquisitely thin slices – was all they could hope to have. They were beggars at an infinite banquet, convincing themselves that the crumbs that fell into their cupped hands were enough to make a meal.

But when I learned the trick of Stepping sideways, not from A to A-prime but from A to anywhere, I learned too that there was no limit. Like the Mother Mass (with whom I've now spoken on many occasions) I'm chained to my orbit around my parent star, but there was nothing to stop me from sending the selves of that star out into the void to meet their scattered kindred.

And as soon as it became possible it became inevitable. Having spent so long alone in the dark I had a deep hatred for darkness and for solitude. How could I not make the effort to reach out and see what was on the other side of both? Especially since like the Mother Mass I might meet my own peers out there. Here on this one lone rock I might easily become a tyrant, however hard I tried to avoid it. In a society, if there happened to be one out there, I might find a contract I could respect and adhere to.

The proposal I put to Moon and Essien was that they should cease to be soldiers and become explorers. And if I'm honest I made them the offer only because I'd already made it to Paz and Dulcie, and Paz – when she'd gotten over the hysterical excitement that was her first response – had asked if they could come too.

It will be no easy journey, for all that it will be instantaneous. There are a great many things to be considered, to be planned, to be arranged. The preparations are in train, but there's time still to come to terms with the past before we launch ourselves into this strange, unknowable future. We've swapped one infinity for another, but there is a space in between for small and bounded things.

Paz has gone home to Canoplex-Under-Heaven to introduce Dulcie – or rather her new composite self – to her mother and father. She does this with mixed feelings, but love and hope predominate. That done, she will return to the survivors in the ruined village on Hadiz's world. She wants to visit with the girl Abeni for a little while, and also to deliver the Step plates she promised. I have already located eight similar settlements. I will make contact with them all, ensure that their needs are met and oversee their induction into the wider family of worlds.

Essien Nkanika has gone back to his version of Lagos to make his peace with his parents and his older brother. He feels there are things for which he should apologise, and he wants them to see the man he has become. He is no longer ashamed to do that.

Moon Sostenti is on what she calls "one last legendary bender". She assures me that this is all she wants; that if there's anyone in her past life she ought to revisit the drug gabber has taken away all the relevant memories and the pain that might have gone with them. She didn't speak of her dead sister and I didn't ask.

As for me, I have taken a moment or two in this welcome pause to rehearse the story of my birth.

I go now to see what the story of my life will be.

Acknowledgements

The people who keep my wheels on the road are the same as they always were. My Orbit editors, Anna and Priyanka. My agent, Meg Davis of Ki. My publicist, Nazia. Above all my family – Lin, Ben and Davey, Louise and Cam – without whom I would be a meaningless blurt of static between radio stations. I'd also like to thank Tade Thompson whose invaluable advice and input made the first book in this series coherent and the second book possible.

extras

orbit

meet the author

M. R. CAREY has been making up stories for most of his life. His novel *The Girl With All the Gifts* has sold over a million copies and became a major motion picture, based on his own BAFTA Award–nominated screenplay. Under the name Mike Carey he has written for both DC and Marvel, including critically acclaimed runs on *Lucifer*, *Hellblazer* and *X-Men*. He also has several previous novels, including the Felix Castor series (written as Mike Carey), two radio plays and a number of TV and movie screenplays to his credit.

Find out more about M. R. Carey and other Orbit authors by registering for the free monthly newsletter at orbitbooks.net.

if you enjoyed
ECHO OF WORLDS

look out for

THE BOOK OF KOLI
The Rampart Trilogy: Book One

by

M. R. Carey

Everything that lives hates us....

Beyond the walls of the small village of Mythen Rood lies an unrecognizable landscape. A place where overgrown forests are filled with choker trees and deadly seeds that will kill you where you stand. And if they don't get you, one of the shunned men will.

Koli has lived in Mythen Rood his entire life. He believes the first rule of survival is that you don't venture too far beyond the walls.

He's wrong.

1

I got a story to tell you. I've been meaning to make a start for a long while now, and this is me doing it, but I'm warning you it might be a bumpy road. I never done nothing like this before, so I got no map, as it were, and I can't figure how much of what happened to me is worth telling. Monono says I'm like a man trying to cut his hair without a mirror. Too long and you might as well not bother. Too short and you're probably going to be sorry. And either road, you got to find some way to make the two sides match.

The two sides is this: I went away, and then I come home again. But there's more to the story than that, as you might expect. It was a hard journey, both ways. I was tried and I was tested, lots of times. You could say I failed, though what I brung back with me changed the world for ever. I met the shunned men and their messianic, Senlas, who looked into me with his hundreds of eyes. I crossed the ruins of Birmagen, where the army of the Peacemaker was ranged against me. I found the Sword of Albion, though it was not what I was looking for and it brung me as much harm as good. I fought a bitter fight against them I loved, and broke the walls that sheltered me so they'd never stand again.

All this I done for love, and for what I seen as the best, but that doesn't mean it was right. And it still leaves out the reason why, which is the heart of it and the needful thing to make you know me.

I am aiming to do that – to make you know me, I mean – but it's not an easy thing. The heft of a man's life, or a woman's life, is more than the heft of a shovelful of earth or a cord of timber. Head and heart and limbs and all, they got their weight. Dreams, even, got their weight. Dreams most of all, maybe. For me, it seems dreams was the hardest to carry, even when they was sweet ones.

Anyway, I mean to tell it, the good and the bad of it all together. The bad more than the good, maybe. Not so you can be my judge, though I know you will. Judging is what them that listen does for them that tell, whether it's wanted or not. But the truth is I don't mainly tell it for me. It's rather for the people who won't never tell it for themselves. It's so their names won't fall out of the world and be forgotten. I owe them better, and so you do. If that sounds strange, listen and I'll make it good.

2

My name is Koli and I come from Mythen Rood. Being from there, it never troubled me as a child that I was ignorant what that name meant. There is people who will tell you the rood was the name of the tree where they broke the dead god, but I don't think that's to the purpose. Where I growed up, there wasn't many as was swore to the dead god or recked his teaching. There was more that cleaved to Dandrake and his seven hard lessons, and more still that was like me, and had no creed at all. So why would they name a village after something they paid so little mind to?

My mother said it was just a misspeaking for Mythen Road, because there was a big road that runned right past us. Not a road you could walk on, being all pitted stone with holes so big you could lose a sheep in them, but a road of old times that reminds us what we used to be when the world was our belonging.

That's the heart of my story, now I think of it. The old times haunt us still. The things they left behind save us and hobble us in ways that are past any counting. They was ever the sift and substance of my life, and the journey I made starts and ends with them. I will speak on that score in its place, but I will speak of Mythen Rood first, for it's the place that makes sense of me if there's any sense to be found.

It is, or was, a village of more than two hundred souls. It's set into the side of a valley, the valley of the Calder River, in the north of a place called Ingland. I learned later that Ingland had a mess of other names, including Briton and Albion and Yewkay, but Ingland was the one I was told when I was a child.

With so many people, you can imagine the village was a terrible big place, with a fence all round it that was as high as one man on another man's shoulders. There was a main street, called the Middle, and two side streets that crossed it called the Span and the Yard. On top of that, there was a score of little paths that led to this door or that, all laid with small stones trod down until they was even. None of the houses was built within fifty strides of the fence. That was Rampart law, and never broke.

I'm Koli, like I already said. Koli Woodsmith first, then Koli Waiting, Koli Rampart, Koli Faceless. What I am now don't really have a name to it, so just Koli. My mother was Jemiu Woodsmith, that was Bassaw's daughter and had the sawmill over by Old Big-Hand stream. I was raised up to that work, trained by Jemiu how to catch wood from a live tree without getting myself killed, how to dry it out and then steep it in the poisonous soup called stop-mix until it was safe, and how to turn and trim it.

My father was a maker of locks and keys. I am dark brown of skin, like he was, not light like my mother and my sibs. I don't know what my father's name was, and I don't think my mother knowed it either, or if she did she never told me. He journeyed all the way from Half-Ax to put new locks on the doors of Rampart Hold, and he was billeted for the night in my mother's mill. Two things come of that night. One of them was a brand-new lock on our workshop door that would stand against the end of the world. The other one was me. And there's at least one of the two my mother never had no cause to regret.

So my mother and my father had just the one night of sweetness together, and then he went back home. Half-Ax being so far away, the news of what he had left behind him probably never got there. Or if it did, it didn't prompt him to return.

I come along nine months after that, dropping out of Jemiu's belly into a big, loud, quarrelsome family and a house where sawdust settled on everything. The sound of the saw turning was my nursery song, you could say, and my alarum too. The fresh-cut wood was stacked in the yard outside the house so it could dry, and the stacks was so high they shut out the sun at noon-day. We wasn't allowed to go near the piles of fresh wood, or the wood that was steeping in the killing shed: the first could strike you down and the second could poison you. Rampart law said you couldn't build nothing out of wood unless the planks had steeped in stop-mix for a month and was dead for sure. Last thing you wanted was for the walls of your house to wake up and get to being alive again, which green wood always will.

My mother had herself five children that lived to be born, a thing she managed without ever being married. I heard her say once that though many a man was worth a tumble, there wasn't one in a hundred was worth living with. I think it was mostly her pride, though, that got in the way of her marrying. She never liked much to pull her elbows in, or bow to another's will. She was a fierce woman in all ways: fierce hard that she showed on the outside; fierce loving underneath that she mostly hid.

Well, the mill did well enough but it was not a Summer-dance and there was times when Jemiu was somewhat pressed to keep us fed. We got by though, one way and another, all six of us bumping and arguing our way along. Seven of us, sometimes, for Jemiu had a brother, Bax, who lived with us a while. I just barely remember him. When I was maybe three or four Summers old, he was tasked by the Ramparts to take a message to Half-Ax. He never come back, and after that nobody tried again to reopen that road.

Then my oldest sister Leten left us too. She was married

to three women of Todmort who was smiths and cutlers. We didn't get to see her very much after that, Todmort being six miles distant from Mythen Rood even if you walk it straight, but I hoped she was happy and I knowed for sure she was loved.

And the last to leave was my brother Jud. He went out on a hunting trip before he was even old enough to go Waiting, which he done by slipping in among the hunters with his head down, pretending like he belonged. Our mother had no idea he was gone. The party was took in the deep woods – ambushed and overwhelmed by shunned men who either would of et them or else made shunned men out of them. We got to know of it because one woman run away, in spite of getting three arrows in her, and made it back to the village gates alive. That was Alice, who they called Scar Alice after. They was not referring to the scars left by the arrows.

So after that there was only me, my sisters Athen and Mull, and our mother. I missed Leten and Jud very much, especially Jud because I didn't know if he was still alive and in the world. He had been gentle and kind, and sung to me on nights when we went hungry to take my mind away from it. To think of him being et or eating other people made me cry sometimes at night. Mother never cried. She did look sad a while, but all she said was one less mouth to feed. And we did eat a little better after Jud was gone, which in some ways made his being gone worse, at least for me.

I growed up a mite wild, it's got to be said. Jud used to temper me somewhat, but after he was gone there wasn't nobody else to take up that particular job. Certainly my mother didn't have no time or mind for it. She loved us, but it was all she could do to keep the saw turning and kill the wood she cut. She didn't catch all the wood herself, of course. There was four catchers who went out for her from November all the way through to

March, or even into Abril if the clouds stayed thick. This was not a share-work ordered by the Ramparts, but an agreement the five of them made among themselves. The catchers was paid in finished cords, one for every day's work, and Jemiu paid them whether the day's catch was good or bad. It was the right thing to do, since they couldn't tell from looking which wood was safe and which was not, but if the catch was bad, that was a little more of our wood gone and nothing to show for it.

Anyway, Jemiu was kept busy with that. And my growed-up sisters Athen and Mull helped her with it – Athen with good grace; Mull with a sullen scowl and a rebel heart. I was supposed to do everything else that had got to be done, which is to say the cooking and the cleaning, fetching water and tending the vegetables in our little glasshouse. And I did do those things, for love and for fear of Jemiu's blame, which was a harder hurt than her forbearing hand.

But there was time, around those things, to just be a child and do the exciting, stupid, wilful things children are bound to do. My best friends was Haijon Vennastin, whose mother was Rampart Fire, and Molo Tanhide's daughter that we all called Spinner though her given name was Demar. The three of us run all over Mythen Rood and up the hills as far as we could go. Sometimes we even went into the half-outside, which was the place between the fence and the ring of hidden pits we called the stake-blind.

It wasn't always just the three of us. Sometimes Veso Shepherd run with us, or Haijon's sister Lari and his cousin Mardew, or Gilly's Ban, or some of the Frostfend Farm boys that was deaf and dumb like their whole family and was all just called Frostfend, for they made their given names with movements of their hands. We was a posse of variable size, though we seemed always to make the same amount of noise and trouble whether we was few or many.

We was chased away by growers in the greensheds, shepherds on the forward slope, guards on the lookout and wakers at the edge of the wold. We treated all those places as our own, in spite of scoldings, and if worse than scoldings come we took that too. Nobody cut us no slack rope on account of Haijon's family, or Demar's being maimed.

You would think that Haijon, being who he was and born to who he was, might have put some swagger on himself, but he never done it. He had other reasons for swaggering, besides. He was the strongest for his age I ever seen. One time Veso Shepherd started up a row with him – over the stone game, I think it was, and whether he moved such-and-such a piece when he said he didn't – and the row become a fight. I don't know how I got into it, but somehow I did. It was Veso and me both piling onto Haijon, and him giving it back as good as he got, until we was all three of us bloodied. Nobody won, as such, but Haijon held his own against the two of us. And the first thing he said, when we was too out of breath and too sore to fight any more, was "Are we going to finish this game, or what?"

My boast was I was fastest out of all of us, but even there Haijon took some beating. One of the things we used to do, right up until we went Waiting and even once or twice after, was to run a race all round the village walls, starting at the gate. Most times I won, by a step or a straw as they say, but sometimes not. And if I won, Haijon always held up my hand and shouted, "The champion!" He never was angry or hurt to lose, as many would of been.

But of course, you might say, there was a bigger race where his coming first was mostly just assumed. For Haijon was Vennastin.

And Vennastins was Ramparts.

And Ramparts, as you may or may not know, was synced.

That's what the name signified, give or take. If you was made a Rampart, it was because the old tech waked when you touched it. Ramparts got to live in Rampart Hold and to miss their turn on most of the share-works that was going on. But we relied on them and their tech for defending ourselves against the world, so it seemed like that was a fair thing. Besides, everyone got a chance to try out for Rampart, didn't they? Somehow, though, it was always Vennastins the old tech waked for and answered to. Except for one time, which I'll tell you of in its place. But the next thing I'll tell is how Demar come to be Spinner.

orbit

Follow us:

f **/orbitbooksUS**

X **/orbitbooks**

▶ **/orbitbooks**

Join our mailing list
to receive alerts on our
latest releases and deals.

orbitbooks.net

Enter our monthly
giveaway for the chance
to win some epic prizes.

orbitloot.com